AMULET

AMULET

KAZU KIBUISHI

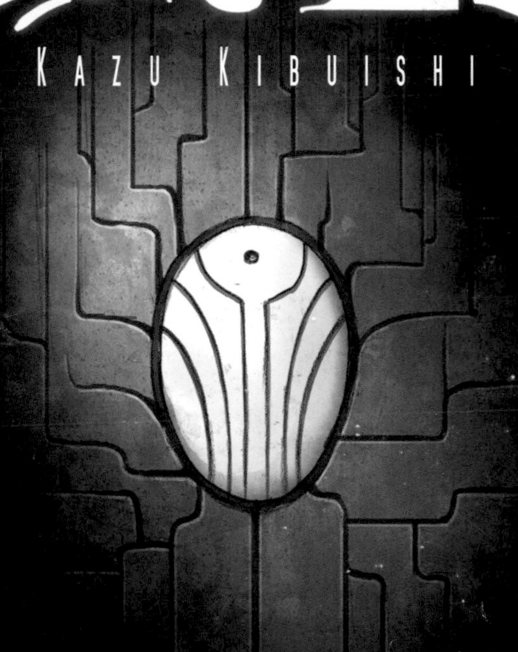

BOOK TWO
THE STONEKEEPER'S CURSE

graphix

AN IMPRINT OF

SCHOLASTIC

ISBN 978-0-439-84682-0 (hardcover)
ISBN 978-0-439-84683-7 (paperback)

10 9 8 7 6 5 4 3 16 17 18 19

Printed in Malaysia 108
First edition, September 2009
Edited by Sheila Keenan
Book design by Kazu Kibuishi and Phil Falco
Creative Director: David Saylor

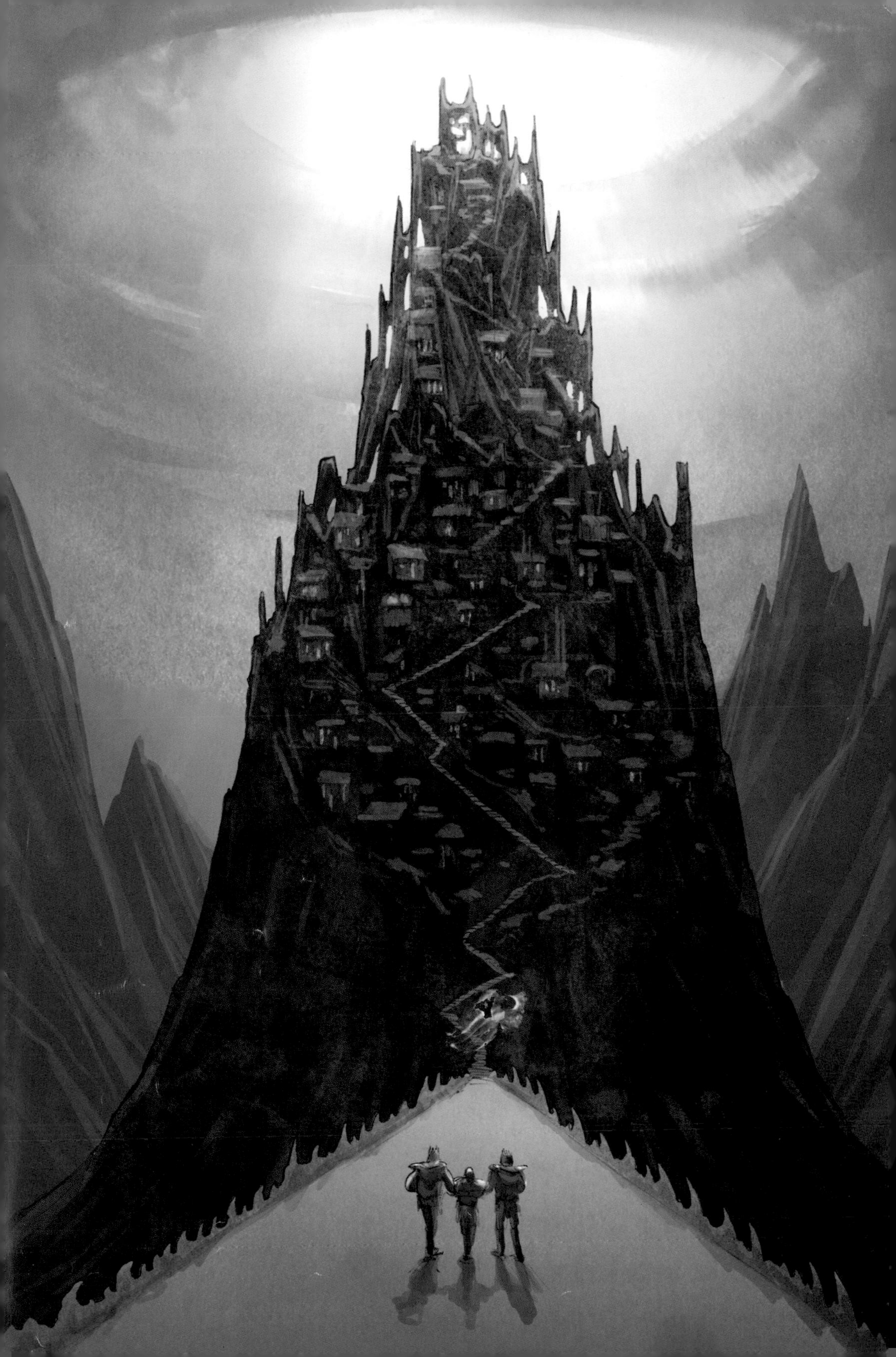

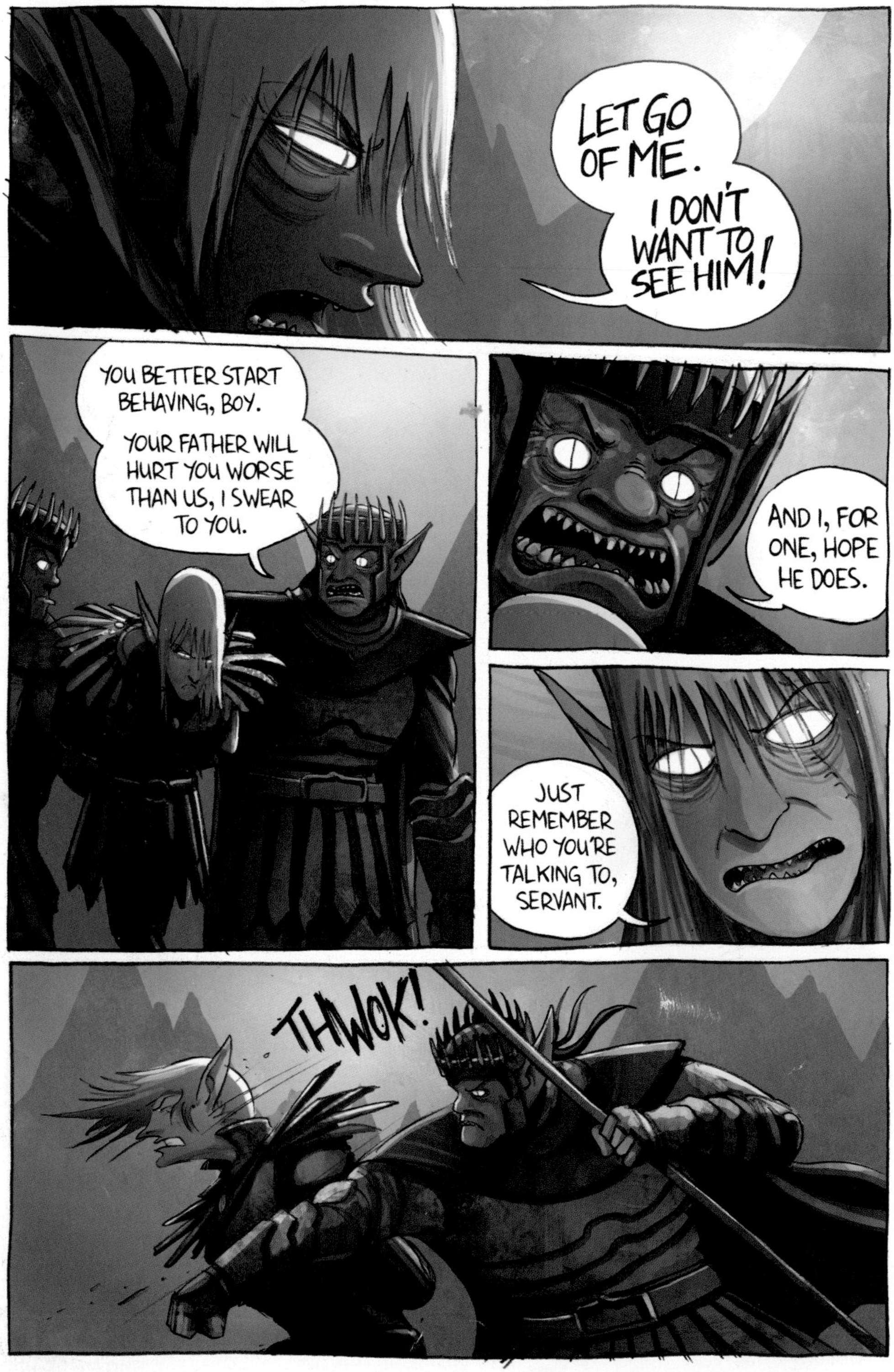
LET GO OF ME.
I DON'T WANT TO SEE HIM!
YOU BETTER START BEHAVING, BOY.
YOUR FATHER WILL HURT YOU WORSE THAN US, I SWEAR TO YOU.
AND I, FOR ONE, HOPE HE DOES.
JUST REMEMBER WHO YOU'RE TALKING TO, SERVANT.
THWOK!

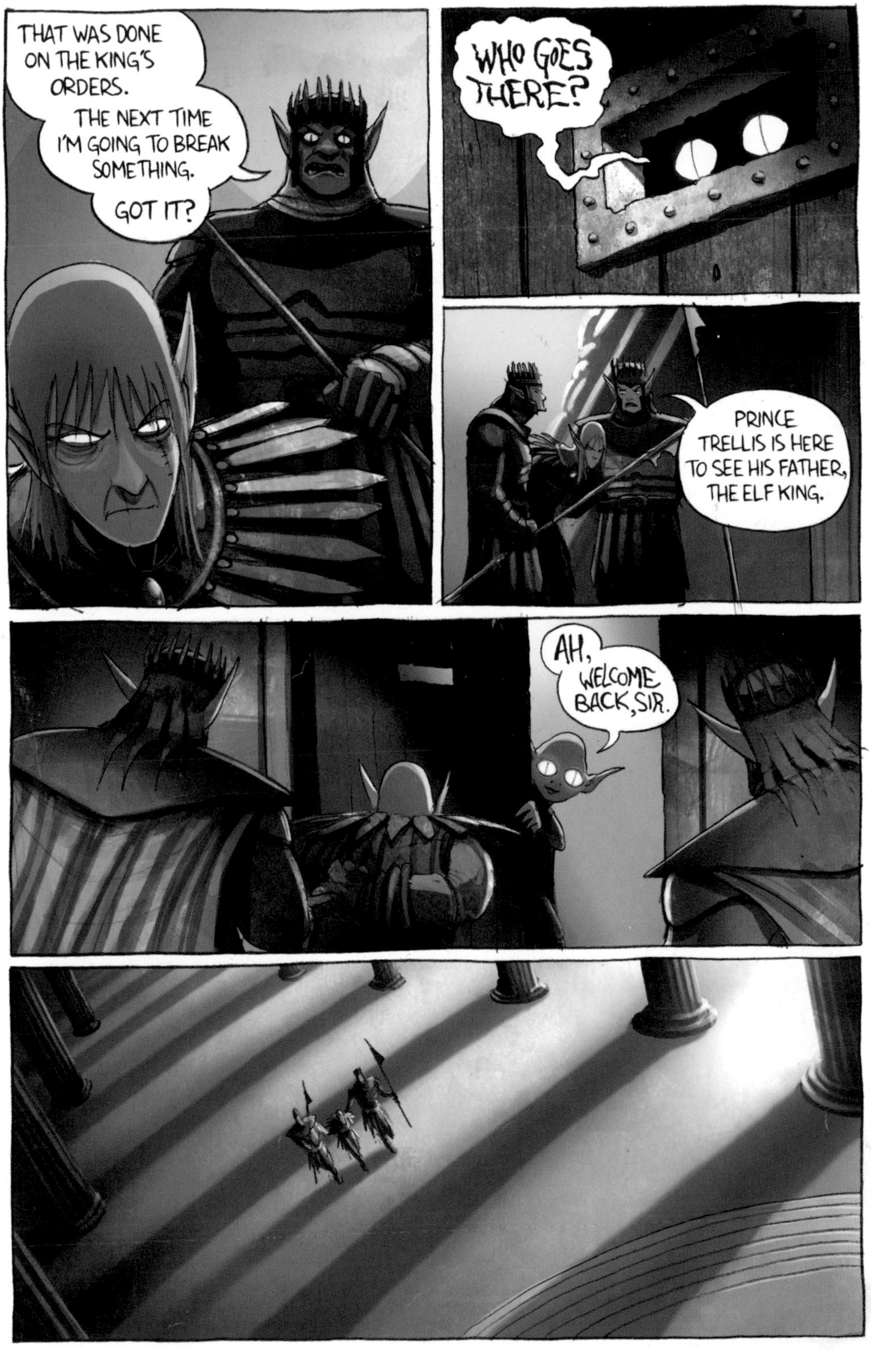
THAT WAS DONE ON THE KING'S ORDERS.
THE NEXT TIME I'M GOING TO BREAK SOMETHING.
GOT IT?
WHO GOES THERE?
PRINCE TRELLIS IS HERE TO SEE HIS FATHER, THE ELF KING.
AH, WELCOME BACK, SIR.

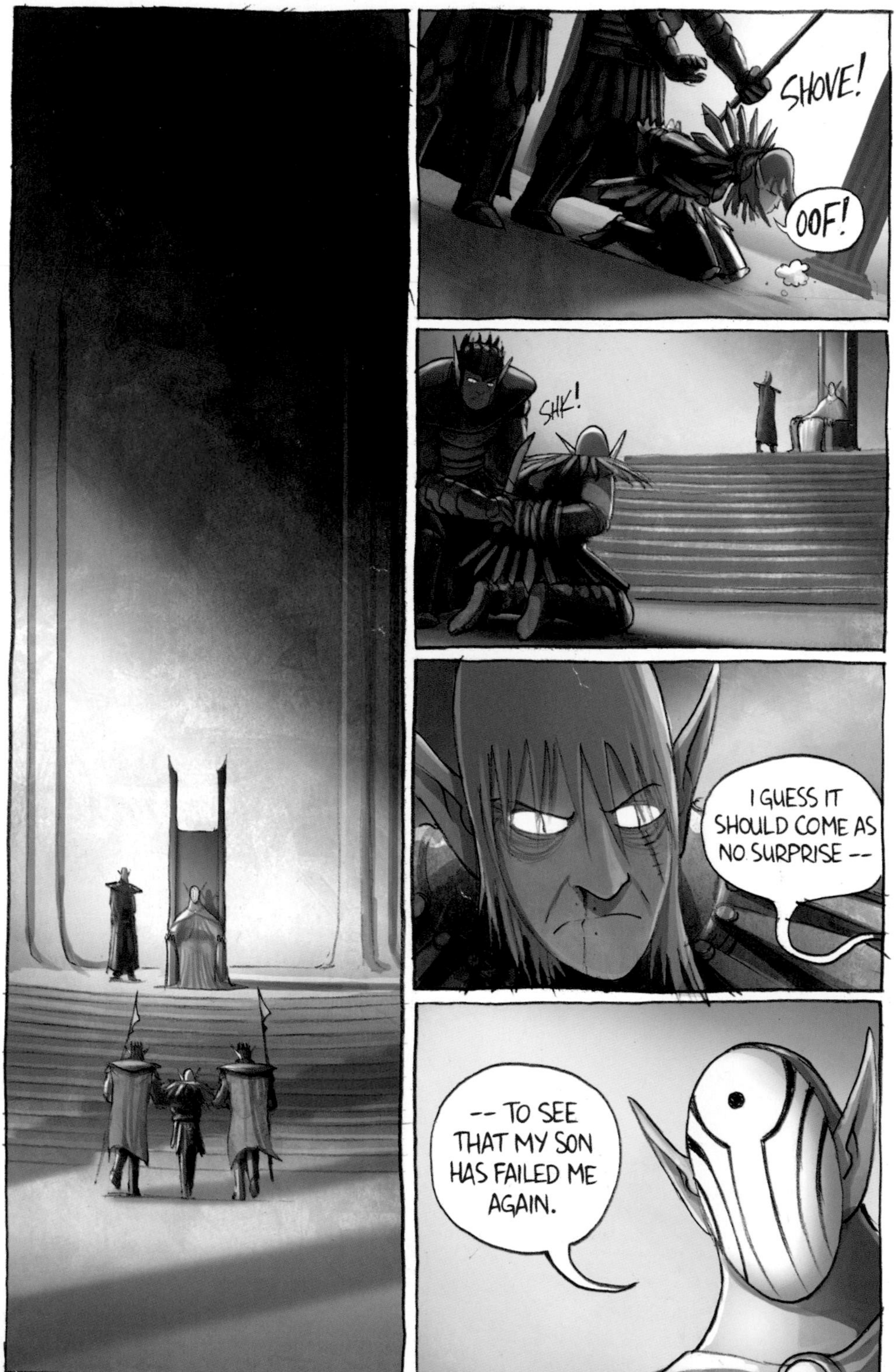
SHOVE!
OOF!
SHK!
I GUESS IT SHOULD COME AS NO SURPRISE --
-- TO SEE THAT MY SON HAS FAILED ME AGAIN.

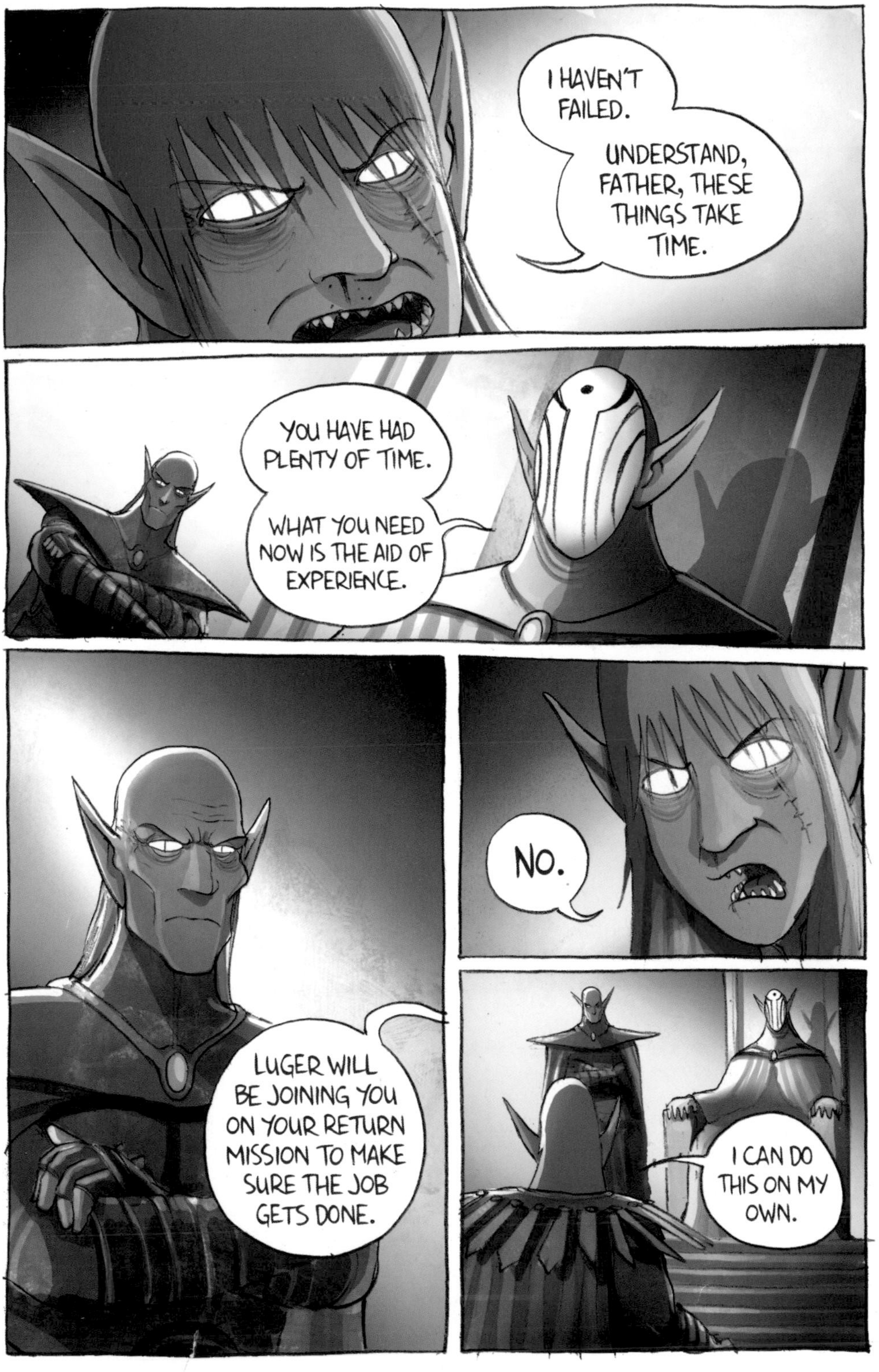
I HAVEN'T FAILED.
UNDERSTAND, FATHER, THESE THINGS TAKE TIME.
YOU HAVE HAD PLENTY OF TIME.
WHAT YOU NEED NOW IS THE AID OF EXPERIENCE.
NO.
LUGER WILL BE JOINING YOU ON YOUR RETURN MISSION TO MAKE SURE THE JOB GETS DONE.
I CAN DO THIS ON MY OWN.

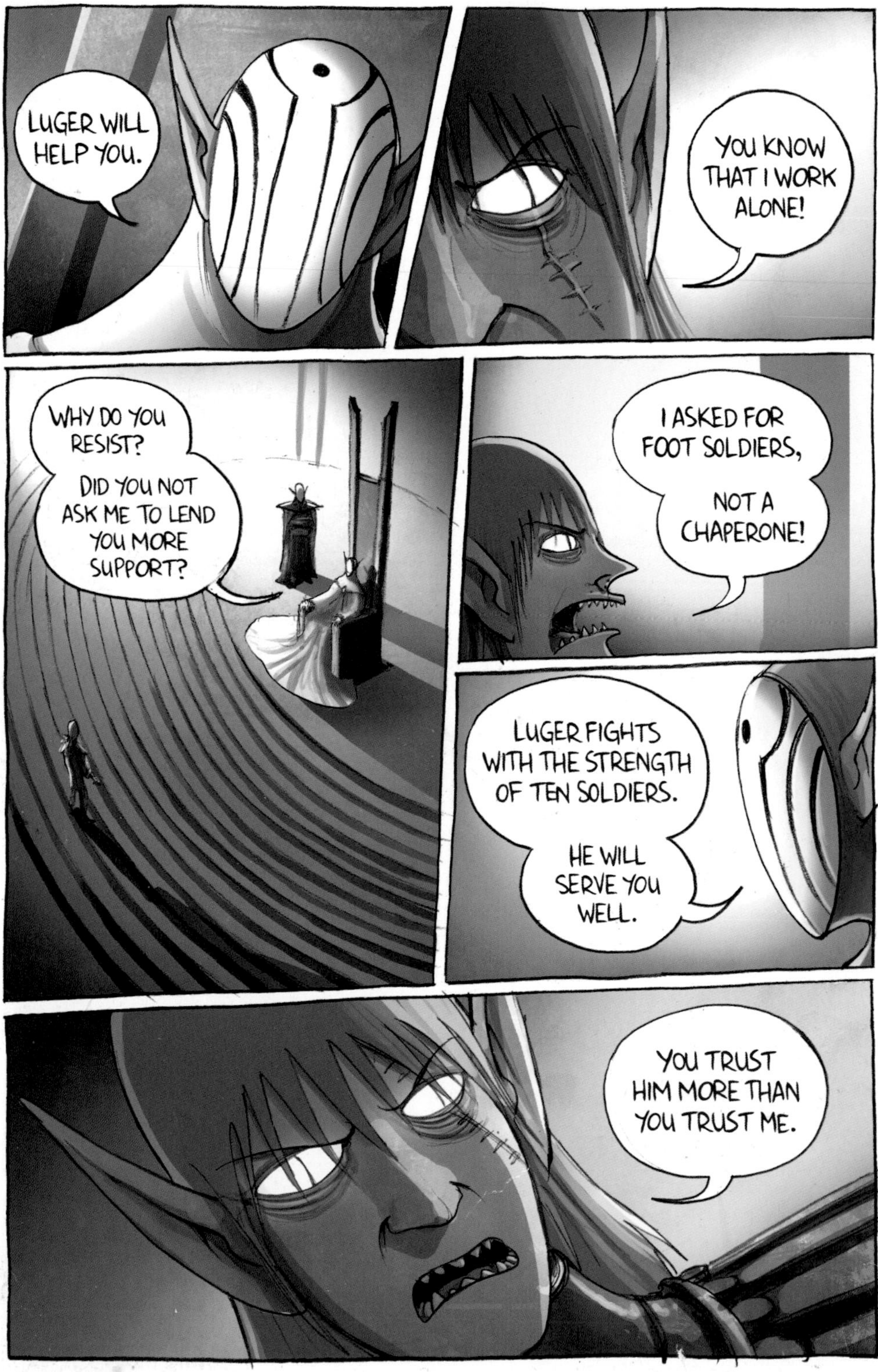
LUGER WILL HELP YOU.
YOU KNOW THAT I WORK ALONE!
WHY DO YOU RESIST?
DID YOU NOT ASK ME TO LEND YOU MORE SUPPORT?
I ASKED FOR FOOT SOLDIERS,
NOT A CHAPERONE!
LUGER FIGHTS WITH THE STRENGTH OF TEN SOLDIERS.
HE WILL SERVE YOU WELL.
YOU TRUST HIM MORE THAN YOU TRUST ME.

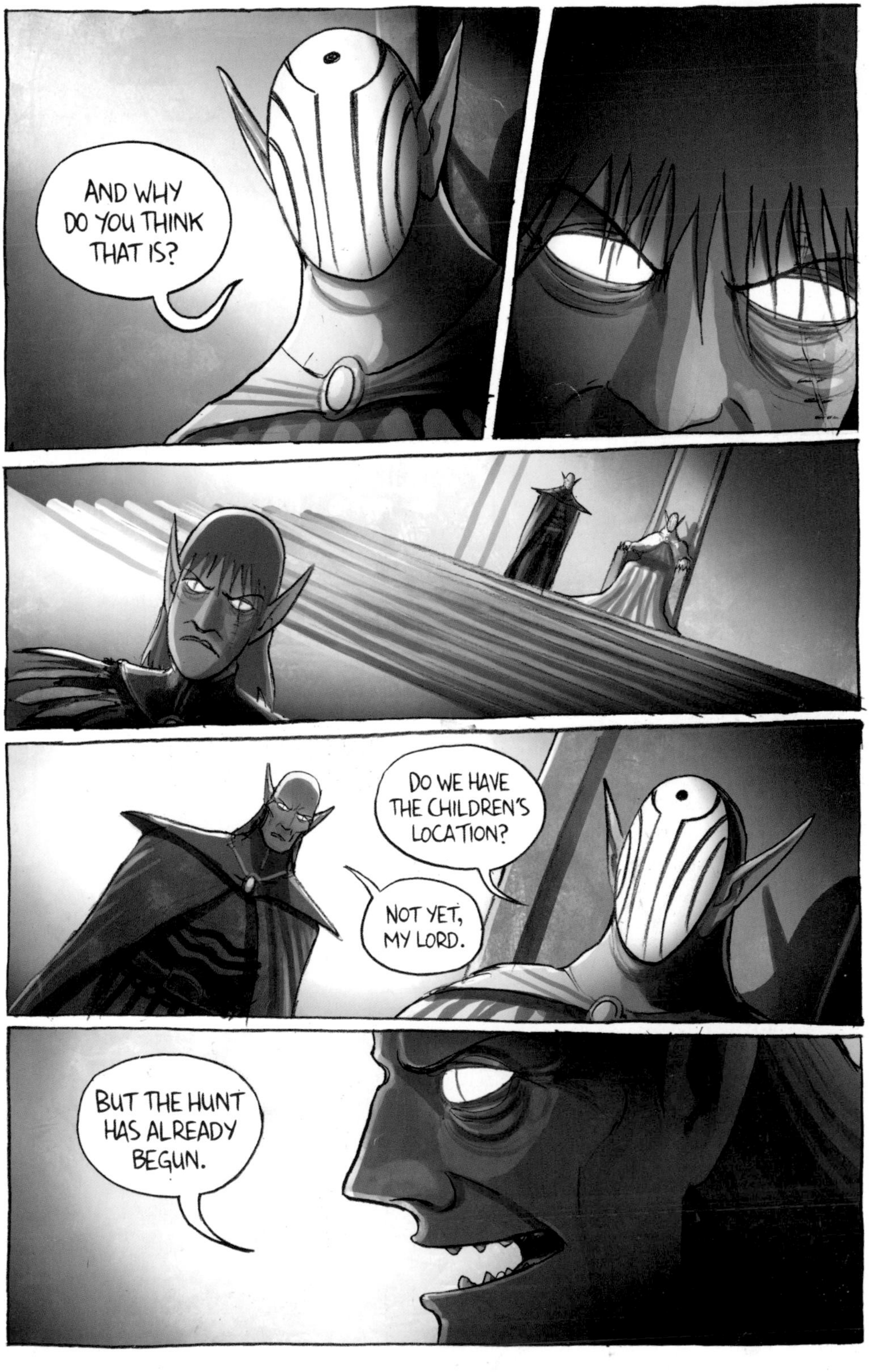
AND WHY DO YOU THINK THAT IS?
DO WE HAVE THE CHILDREN'S LOCATION?
NOT YET, MY LORD.
BUT THE HUNT HAS ALREADY BEGUN.

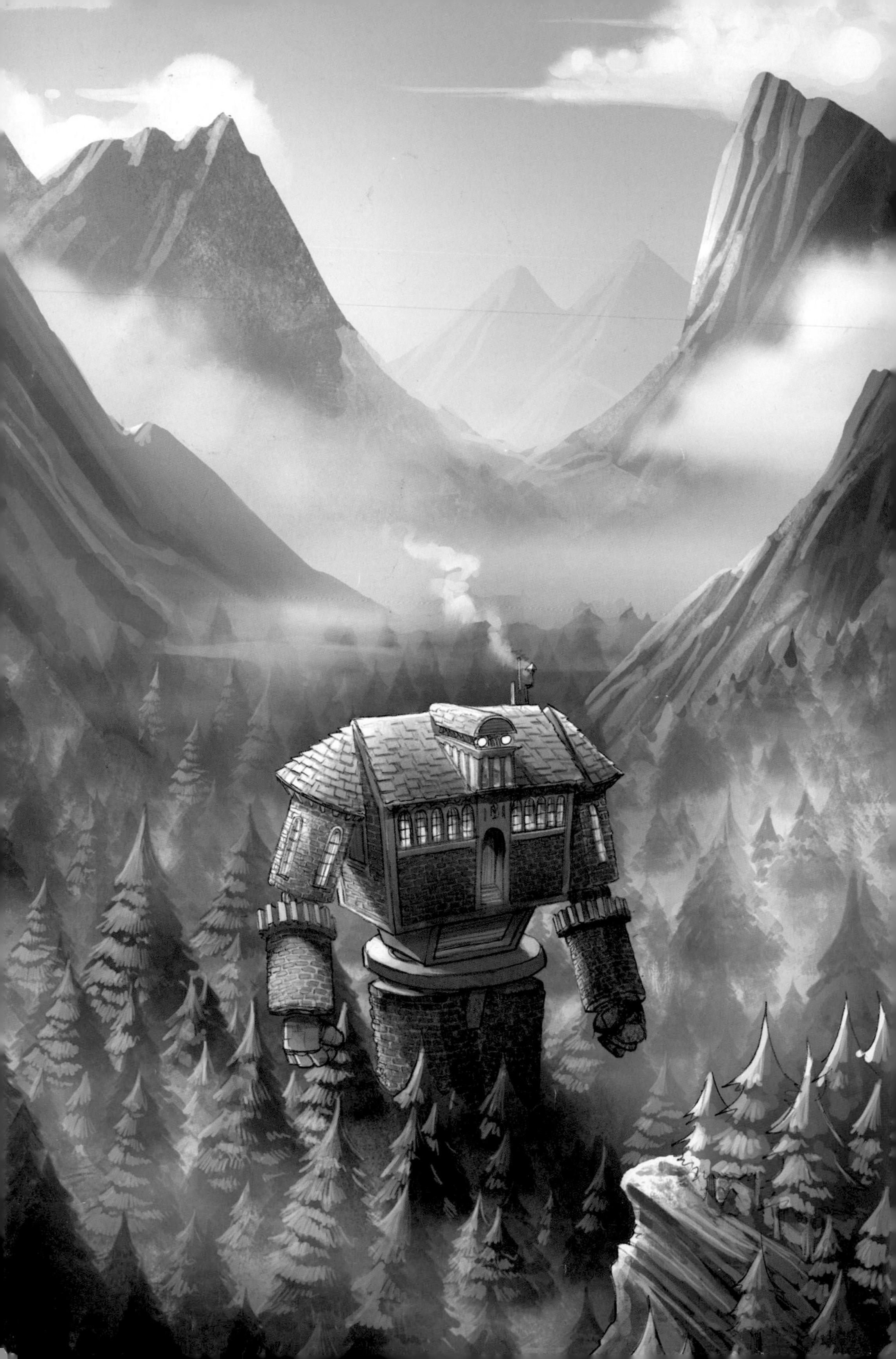

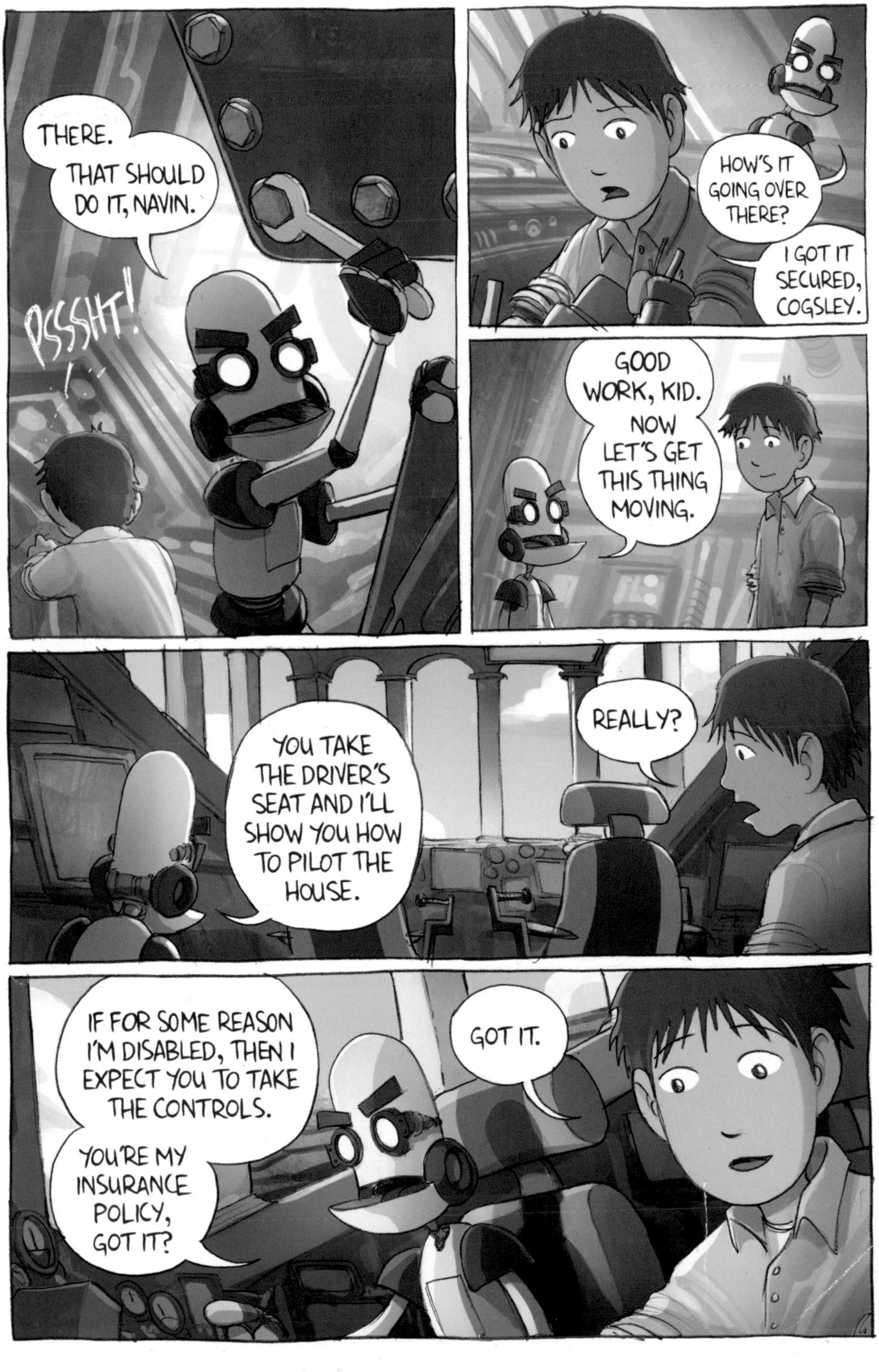
THERE.
THAT SHOULD DO IT, NAVIN.
PSSSHT!
HOW'S IT GOING OVER THERE?
I GOT IT SECURED, COGSLEY.
GOOD WORK, KID.
NOW LET'S GET THIS THING MOVING.
YOU TAKE THE DRIVER'S SEAT AND I'LL SHOW YOU HOW TO PILOT THE HOUSE.
REALLY?
IF FOR SOME REASON I'M DISABLED, THEN I EXPECT YOU TO TAKE THE CONTROLS.
YOU'RE MY INSURANCE POLICY, GOT IT?
GOT IT.

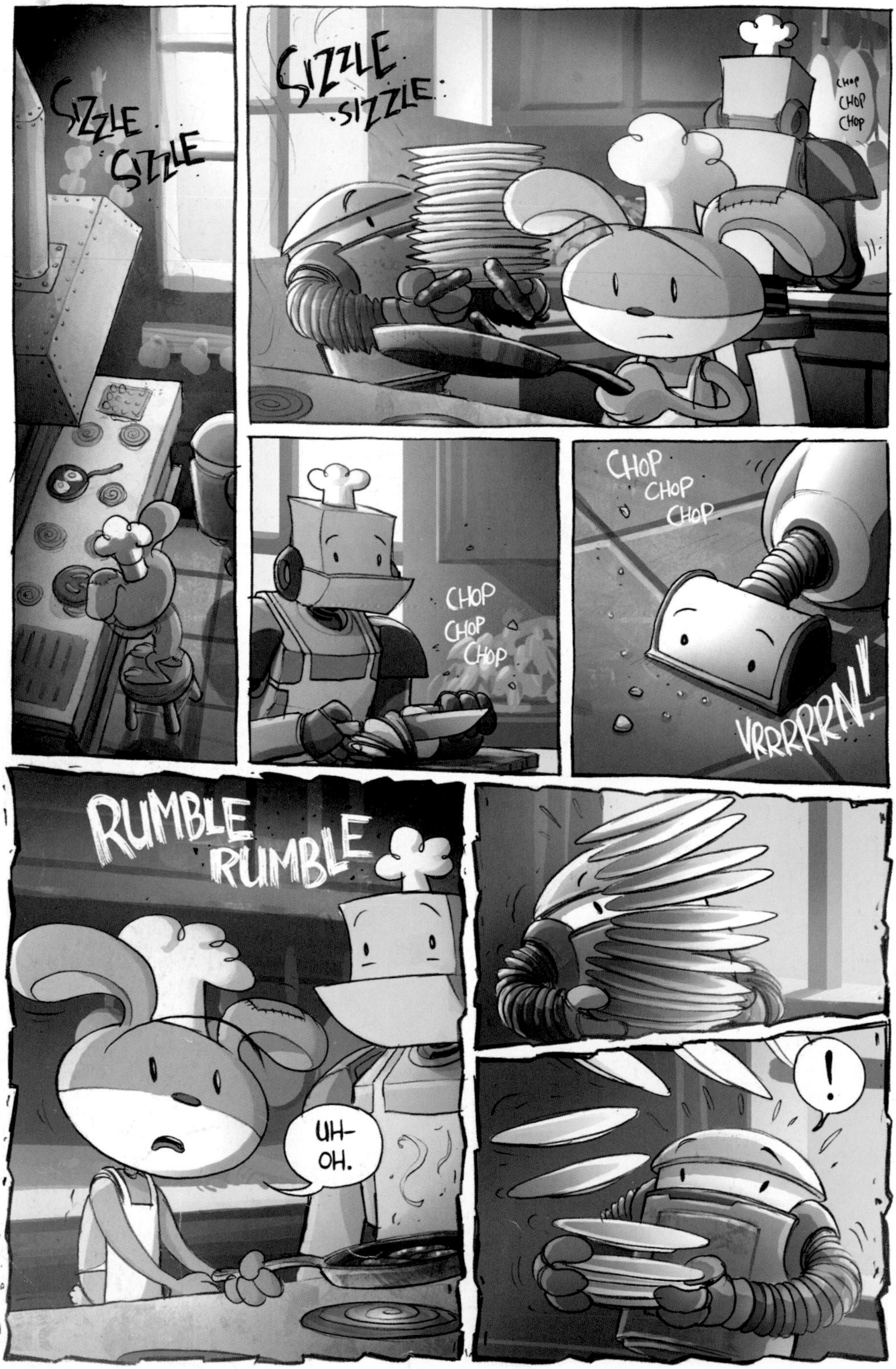
SIZZLE SIZZLE
SIZZLE SIZZLE
CHOP CHOP CHOP
CHOP CHOP CHOP
CHOP CHOP CHOP
VRRRRRN!
RUMBLE RUMBLE
UH-OH.
!

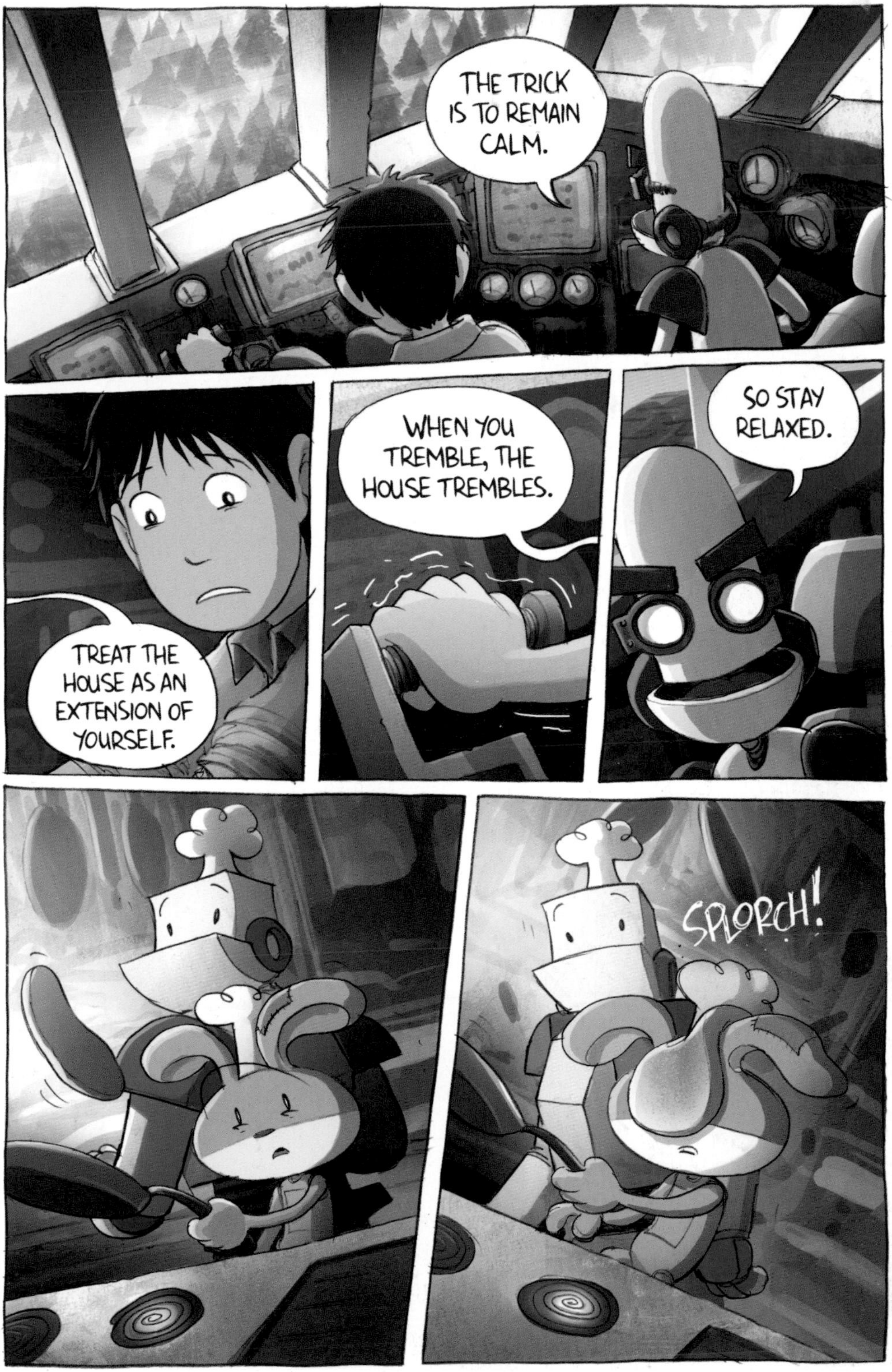
THE TRICK IS TO REMAIN CALM.
TREAT THE HOUSE AS AN EXTENSION OF YOURSELF.
WHEN YOU TREMBLE, THE HOUSE TREMBLES.
SO STAY RELAXED.
SPLORCH!

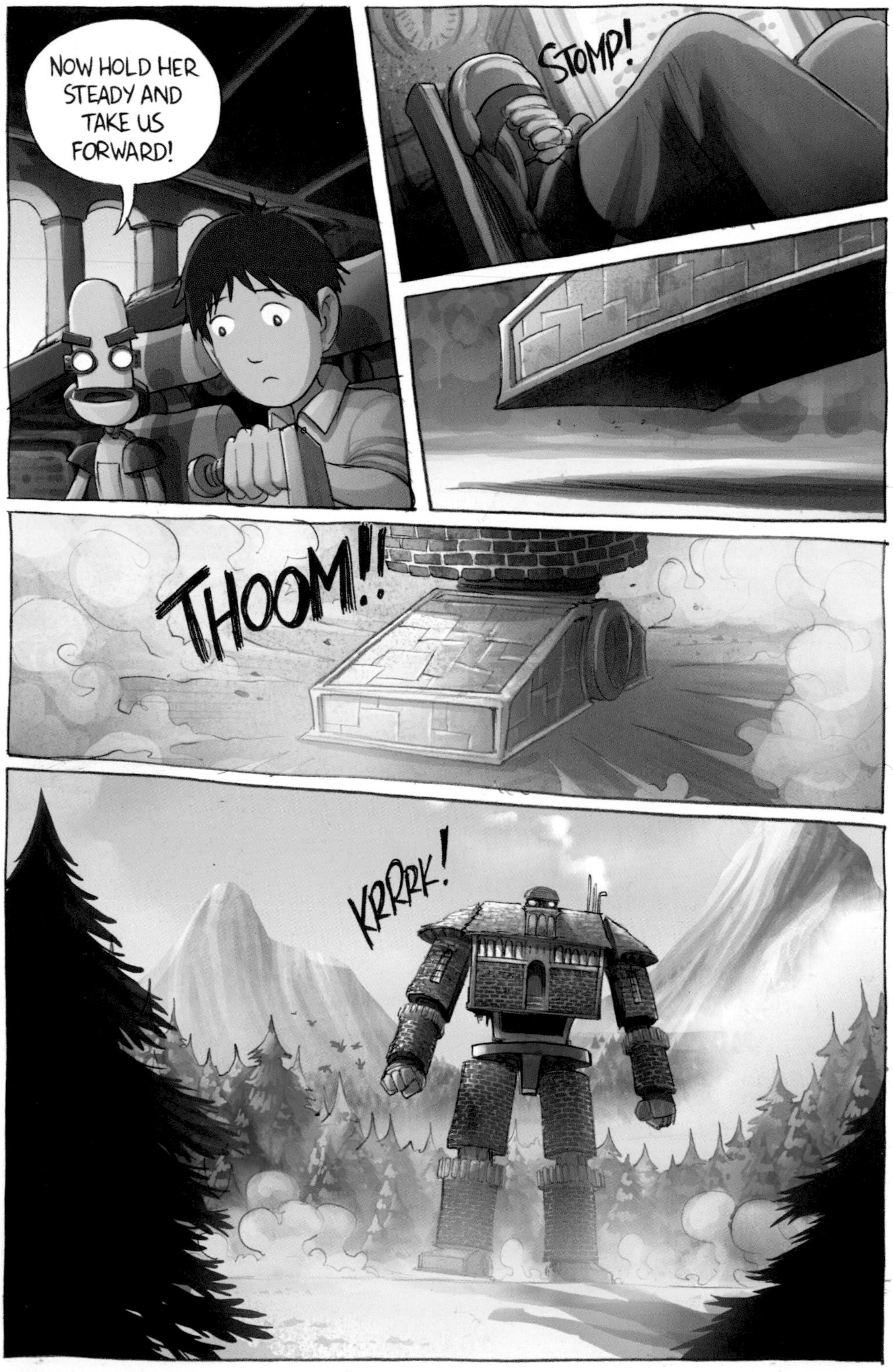
NOW HOLD HER STEADY AND TAKE US FORWARD!
STOMP!
THOOM!!
KRRRK!

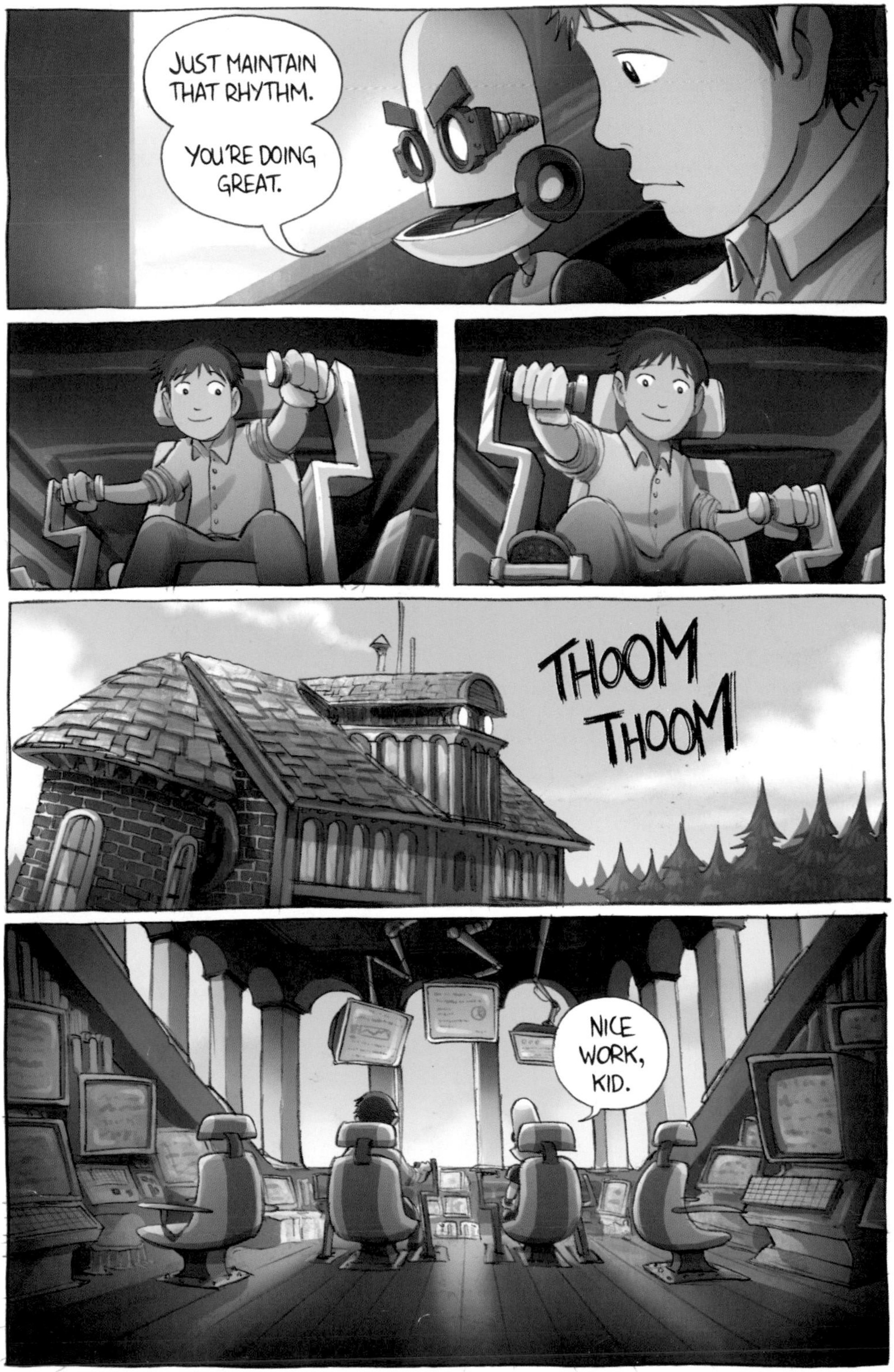
JUST MAINTAIN THAT RHYTHM.
YOU'RE DOING GREAT.
THOOM
THOOM
NICE WORK, KID.

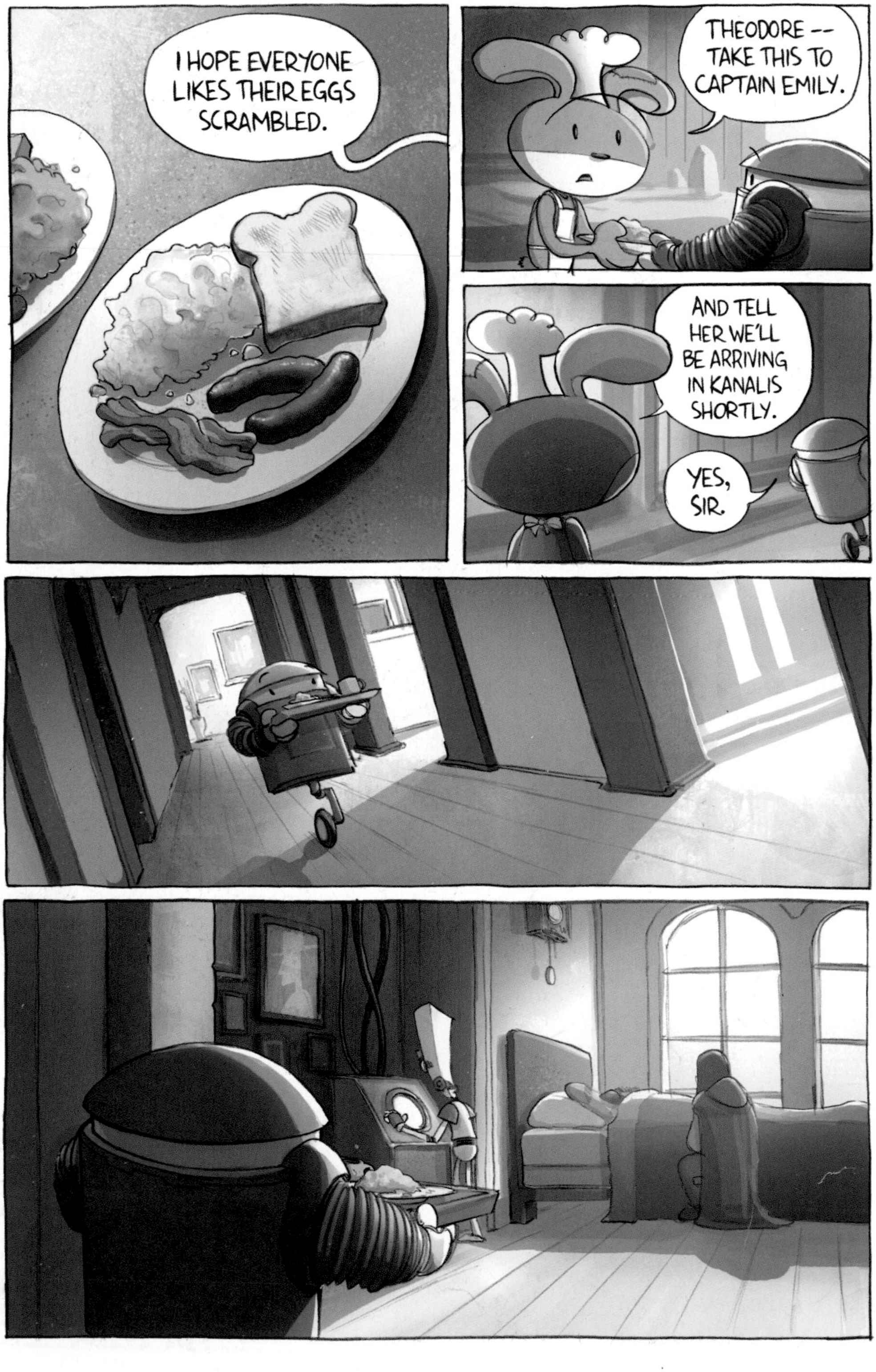
I HOPE EVERYONE LIKES THEIR EGGS SCRAMBLED.
THEODORE -- TAKE THIS TO CAPTAIN EMILY.
AND TELL HER WE'LL BE ARRIVING IN KANALIS SHORTLY.
YES, SIR.

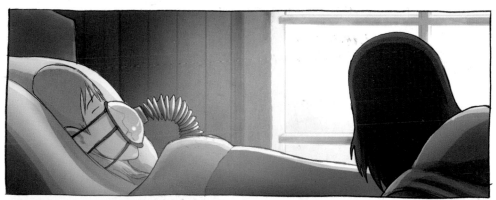

KLAK!

WE WILL BE ARRIVING IN KANALIS SOON.

THANK YOU, THEODORE.

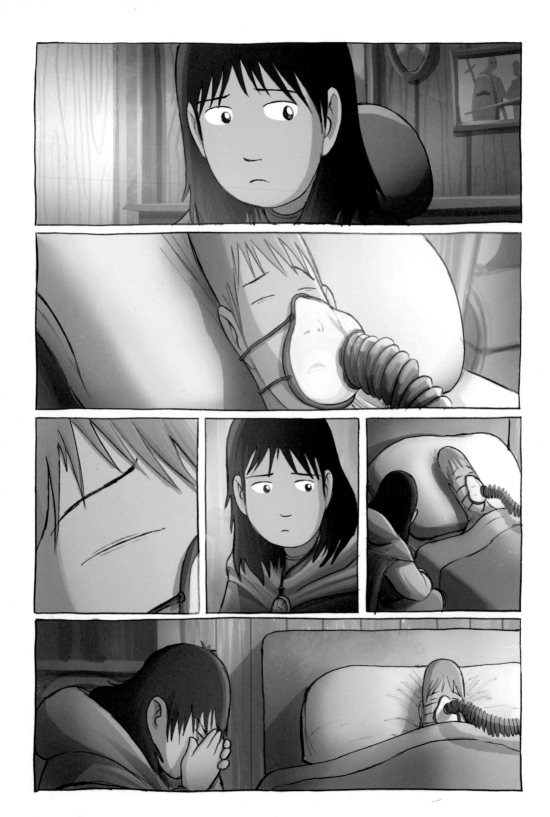

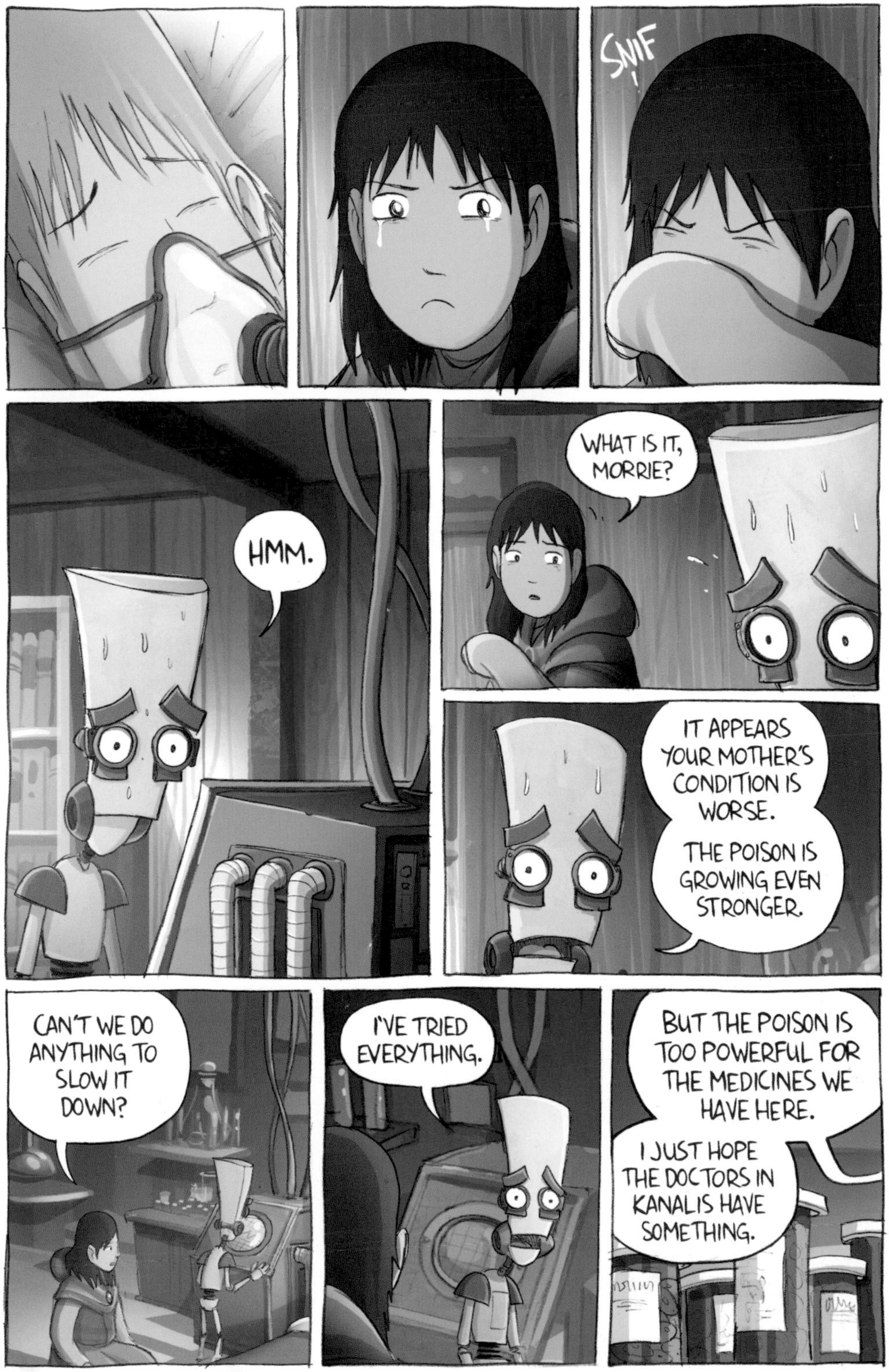
SNIF
HMM.
WHAT IS IT, MORRIE?
IT APPEARS YOUR MOTHER'S CONDITION IS WORSE.
THE POISON IS GROWING EVEN STRONGER.
CAN'T WE DO ANYTHING TO SLOW IT DOWN?
I'VE TRIED EVERYTHING.
BUT THE POISON IS TOO POWERFUL FOR THE MEDICINES WE HAVE HERE.
I JUST HOPE THE DOCTORS IN KANALIS HAVE SOMETHING.

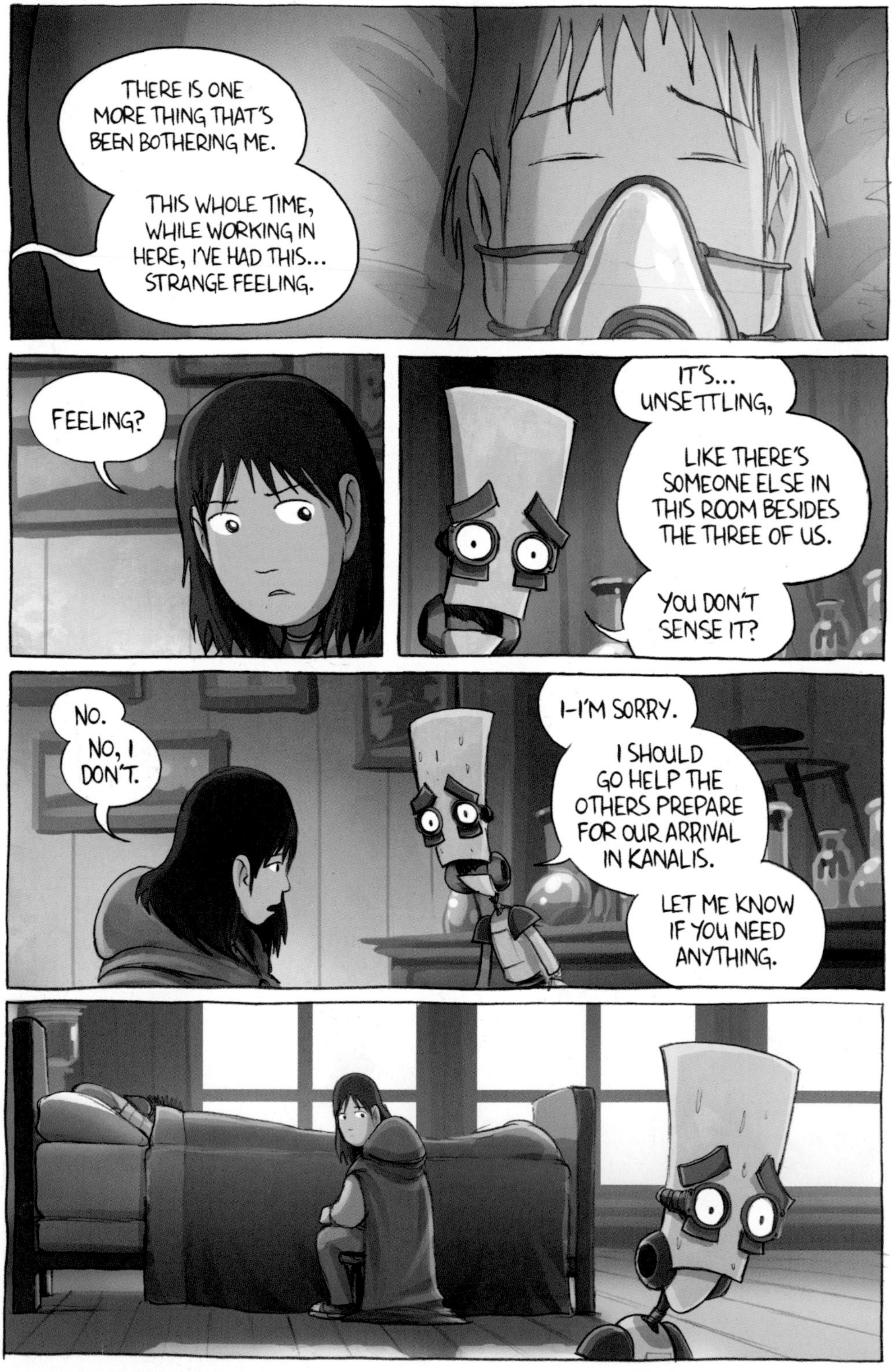
THERE IS ONE MORE THING THAT'S BEEN BOTHERING ME.
THIS WHOLE TIME, WHILE WORKING IN HERE, I'VE HAD THIS... STRANGE FEELING.
FEELING?
IT'S... UNSETTLING,
LIKE THERE'S SOMEONE ELSE IN THIS ROOM BESIDES THE THREE OF US.
YOU DON'T SENSE IT?
NO.
NO, I DON'T.
I-I'M SORRY.
I SHOULD GO HELP THE OTHERS PREPARE FOR OUR ARRIVAL IN KANALIS.
LET ME KNOW IF YOU NEED ANYTHING.

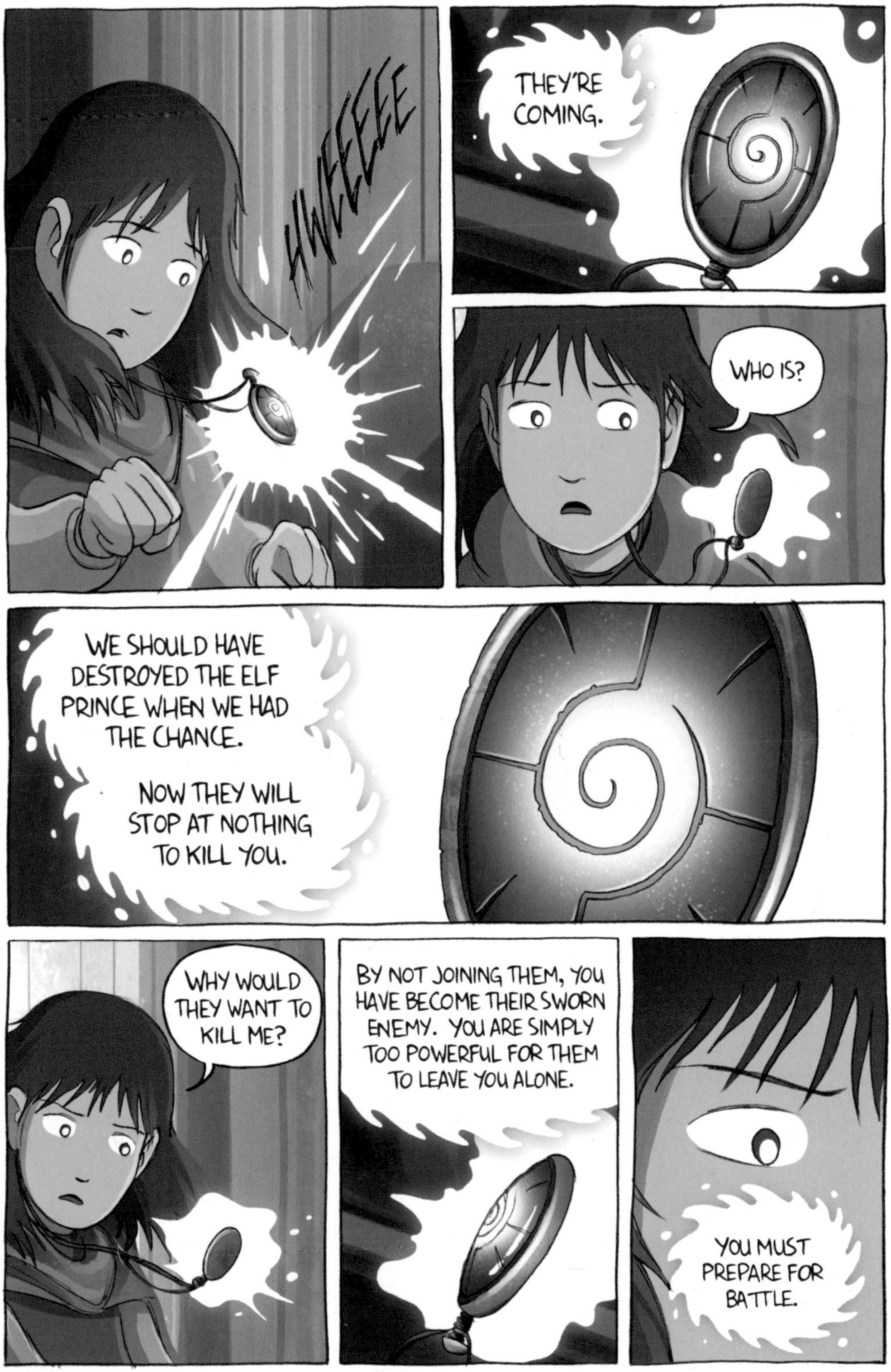
HWEEEEE
THEY'RE COMING.
WHO IS?
WE SHOULD HAVE DESTROYED THE ELF PRINCE WHEN WE HAD THE CHANCE.
NOW THEY WILL STOP AT NOTHING TO KILL YOU.
WHY WOULD THEY WANT TO KILL ME?
BY NOT JOINING THEM, YOU HAVE BECOME THEIR SWORN ENEMY. YOU ARE SIMPLY TOO POWERFUL FOR THEM TO LEAVE YOU ALONE.
YOU MUST PREPARE FOR BATTLE.

BATTLE? WHAT BATTLE?

HWEEEEE...

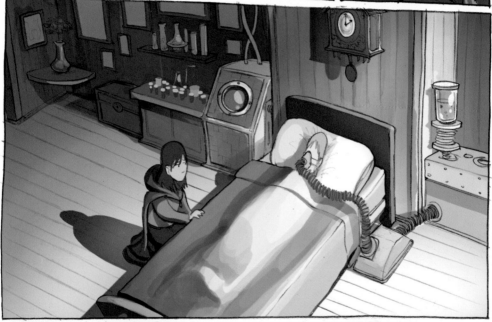

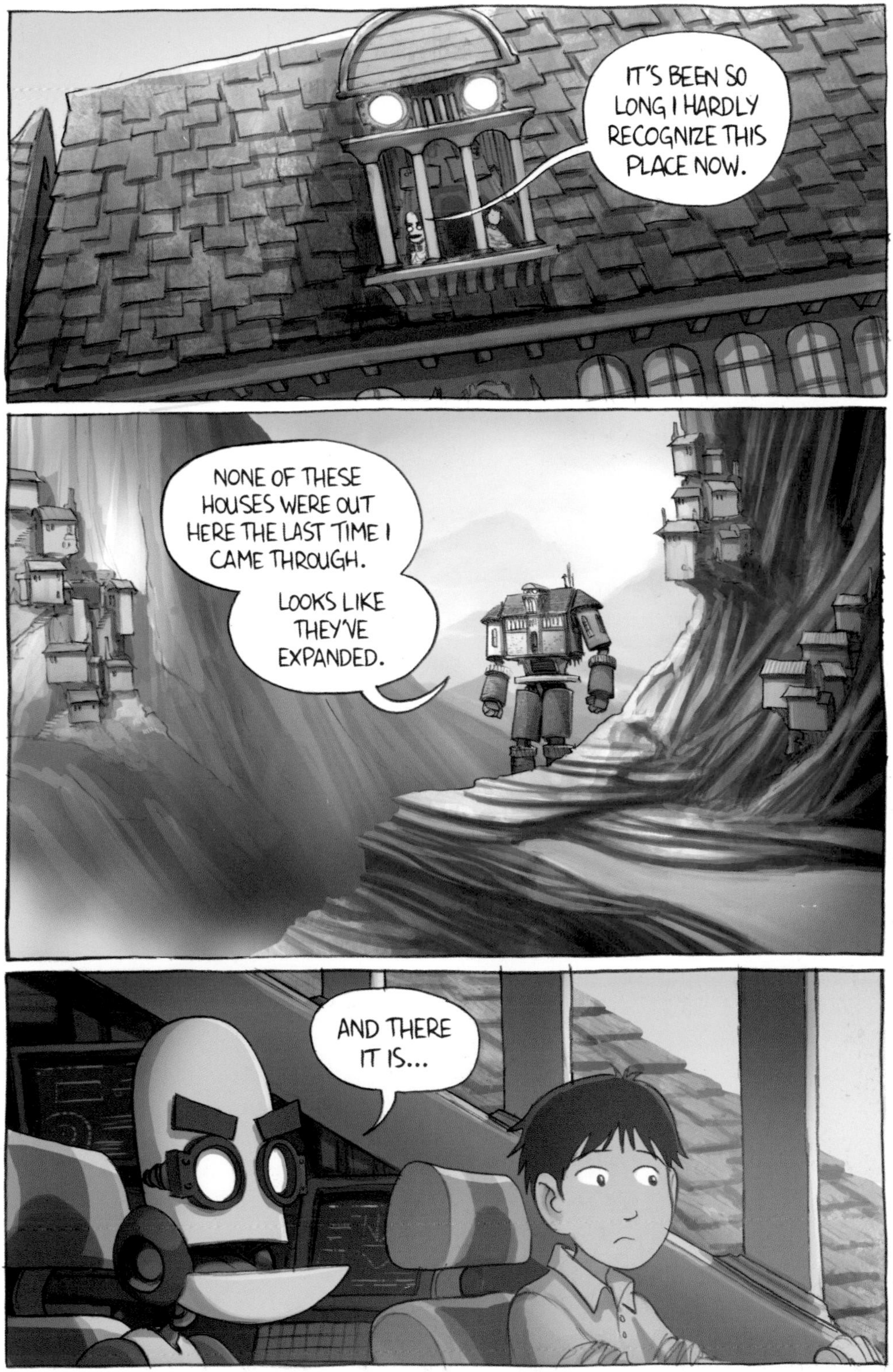
IT'S BEEN SO LONG I HARDLY RECOGNIZE THIS PLACE NOW.
NONE OF THESE HOUSES WERE OUT HERE THE LAST TIME I CAME THROUGH.
LOOKS LIKE THEY'VE EXPANDED.
AND THERE IT IS...

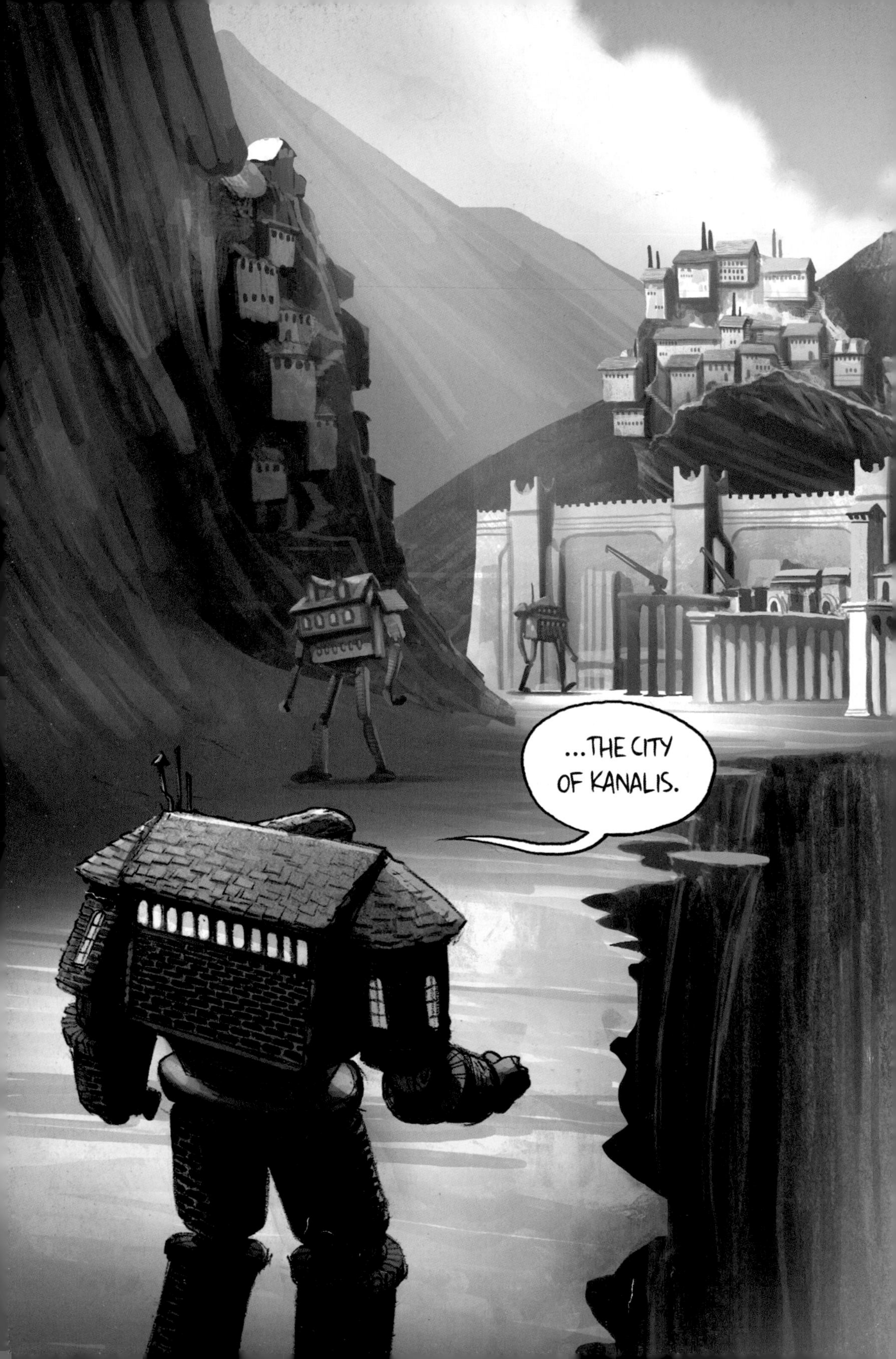
...THE CITY
OF KANALIS.

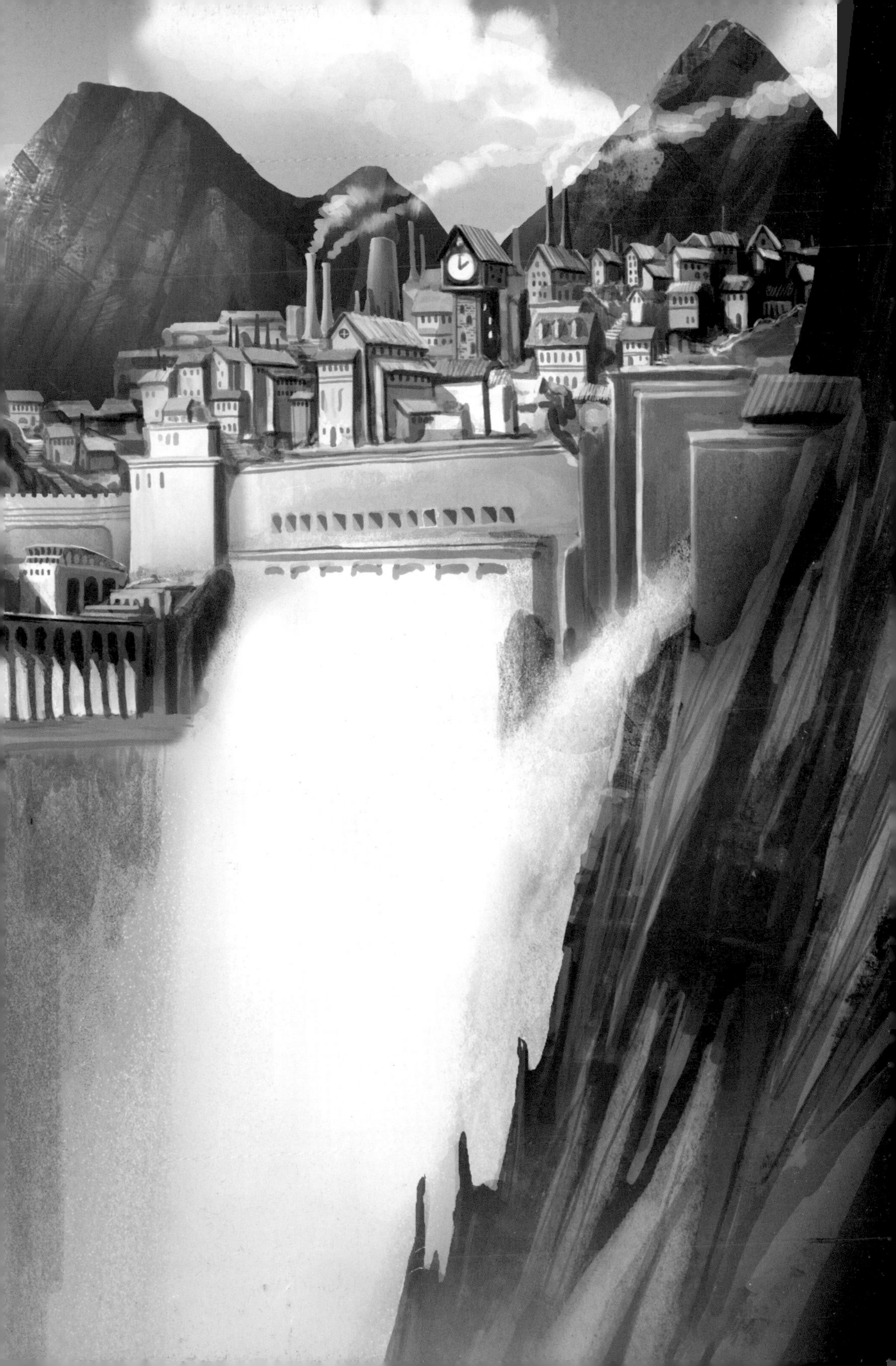

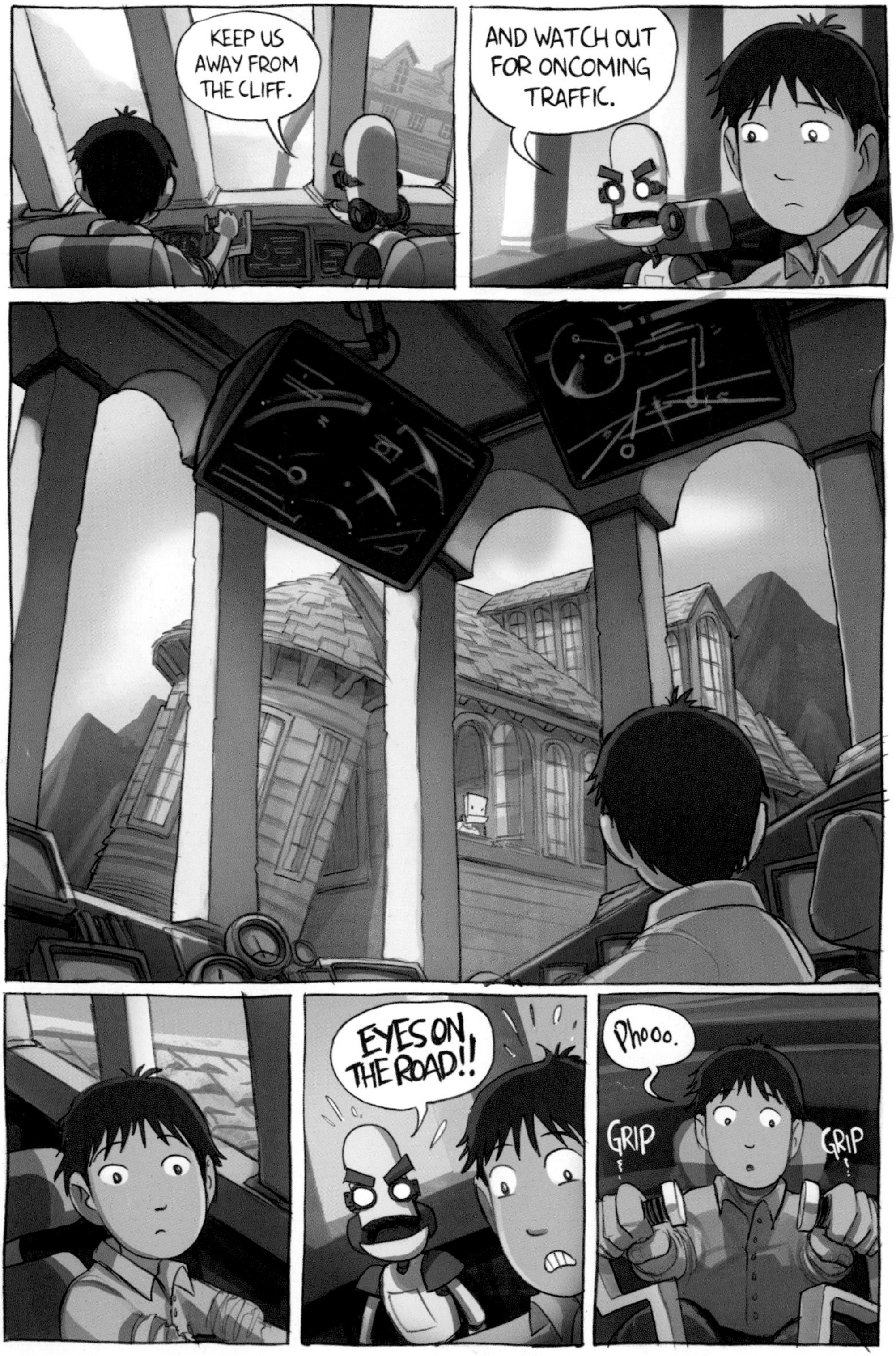
KEEP US AWAY FROM THE CLIFF.
AND WATCH OUT FOR ONCOMING TRAFFIC.
EYES ON THE ROAD!!
Phooo.
GRIP
GRIP

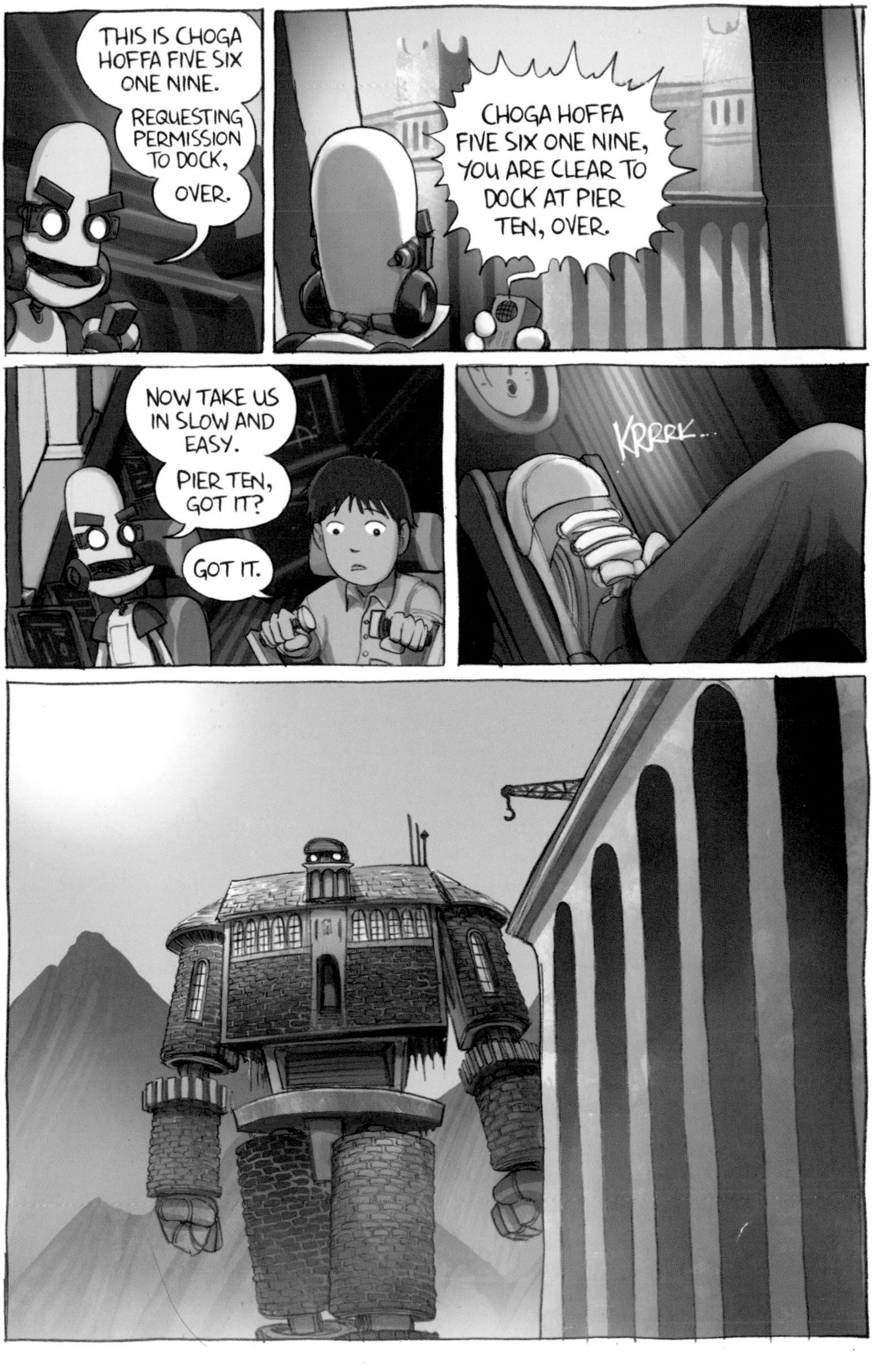
THIS IS CHOGA HOFFA FIVE SIX ONE NINE.
REQUESTING PERMISSION TO DOCK,
OVER.
CHOGA HOFFA FIVE SIX ONE NINE, YOU ARE CLEAR TO DOCK AT PIER TEN, OVER.
NOW TAKE US IN SLOW AND EASY.
PIER TEN, GOT IT?
GOT IT.
KRRRK...

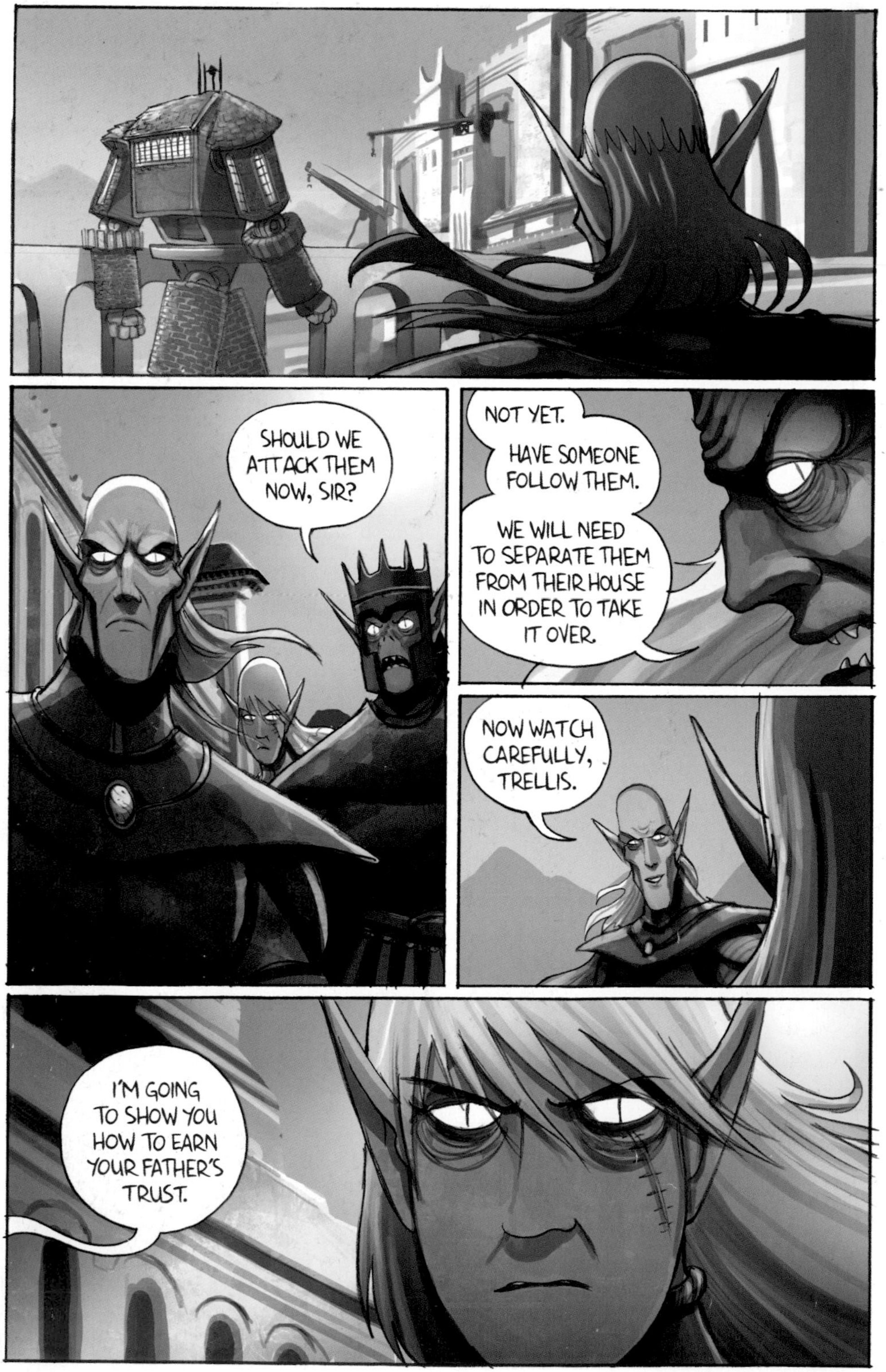

SHOULD WE ATTACK THEM NOW, SIR?
NOT YET.
HAVE SOMEONE FOLLOW THEM.
WE WILL NEED TO SEPARATE THEM FROM THEIR HOUSE IN ORDER TO TAKE IT OVER.
NOW WATCH CAREFULLY, TRELLIS.
I'M GOING TO SHOW YOU HOW TO EARN YOUR FATHER'S TRUST.

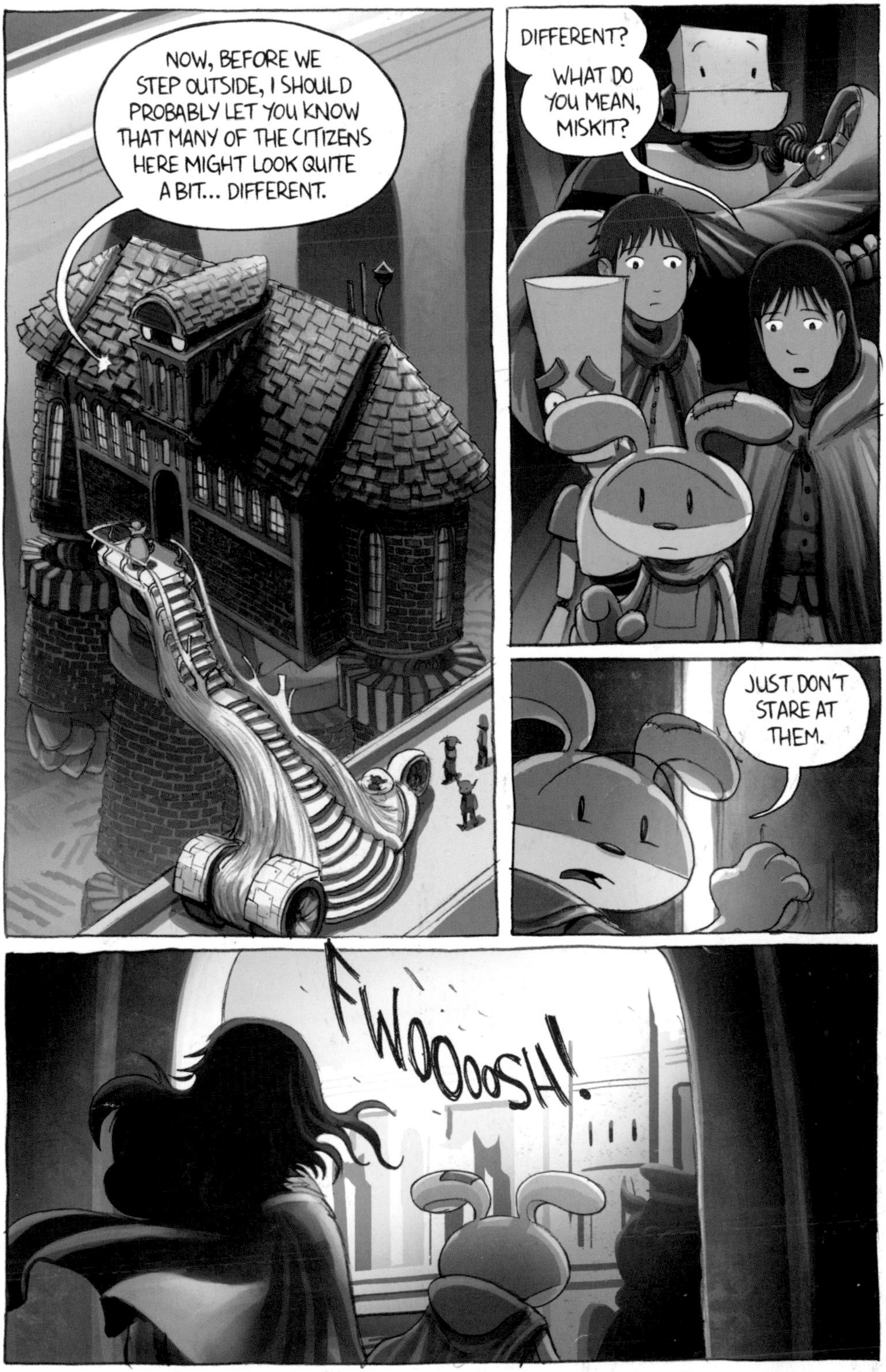
NOW, BEFORE WE STEP OUTSIDE, I SHOULD PROBABLY LET YOU KNOW THAT MANY OF THE CITIZENS HERE MIGHT LOOK QUITE A BIT... DIFFERENT.
DIFFERENT?
WHAT DO YOU MEAN, MISKIT?
JUST DON'T STARE AT THEM.
FWOOOOSH!

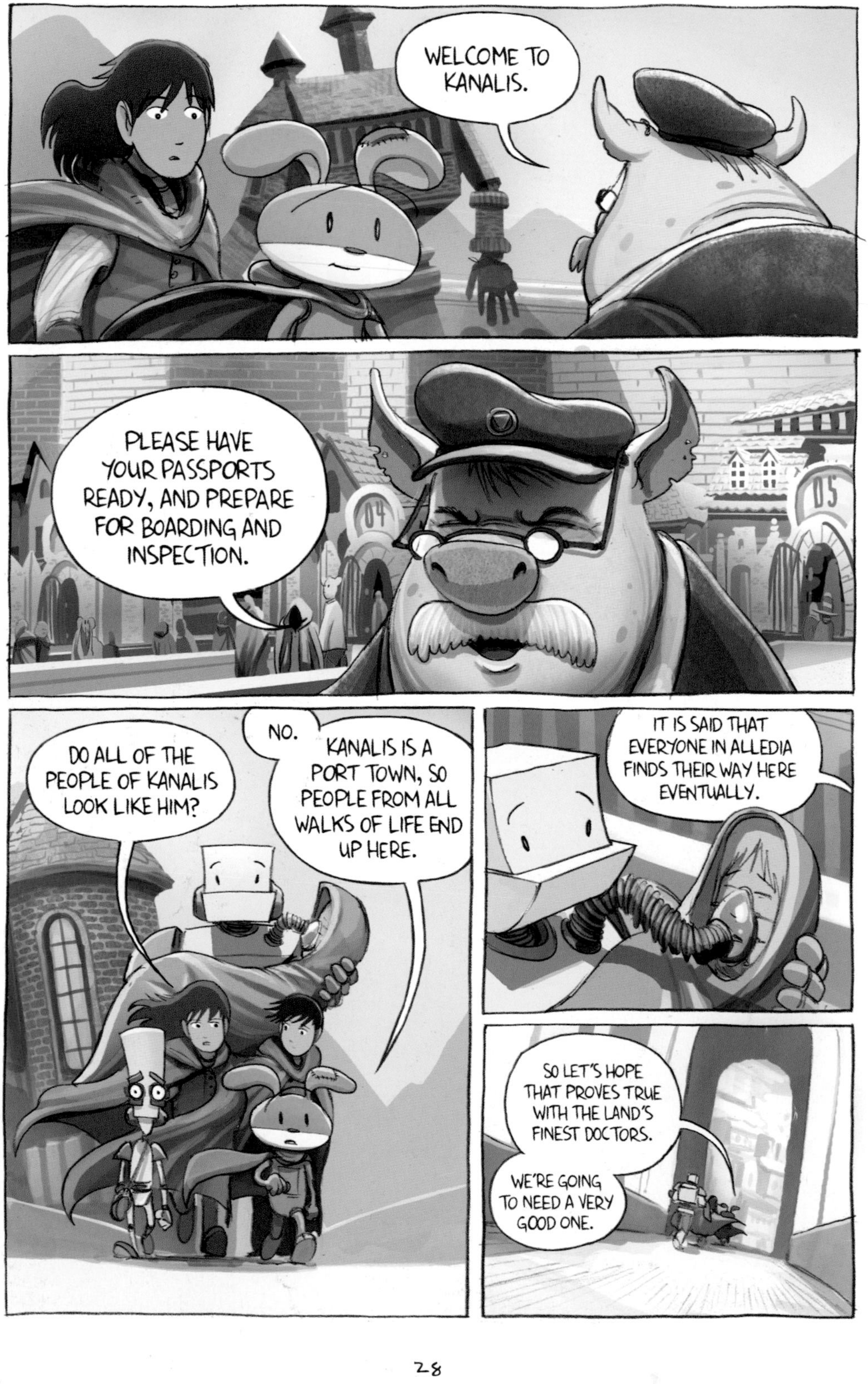
WELCOME TO KANALIS.
PLEASE HAVE YOUR PASSPORTS READY, AND PREPARE FOR BOARDING AND INSPECTION.
DO ALL OF THE PEOPLE OF KANALIS LOOK LIKE HIM?
NO.
KANALIS IS A PORT TOWN, SO PEOPLE FROM ALL WALKS OF LIFE END UP HERE.
IT IS SAID THAT EVERYONE IN ALLEDIA FINDS THEIR WAY HERE EVENTUALLY.
SO LET'S HOPE THAT PROVES TRUE WITH THE LAND'S FINEST DOCTORS.
WE'RE GOING TO NEED A VERY GOOD ONE.

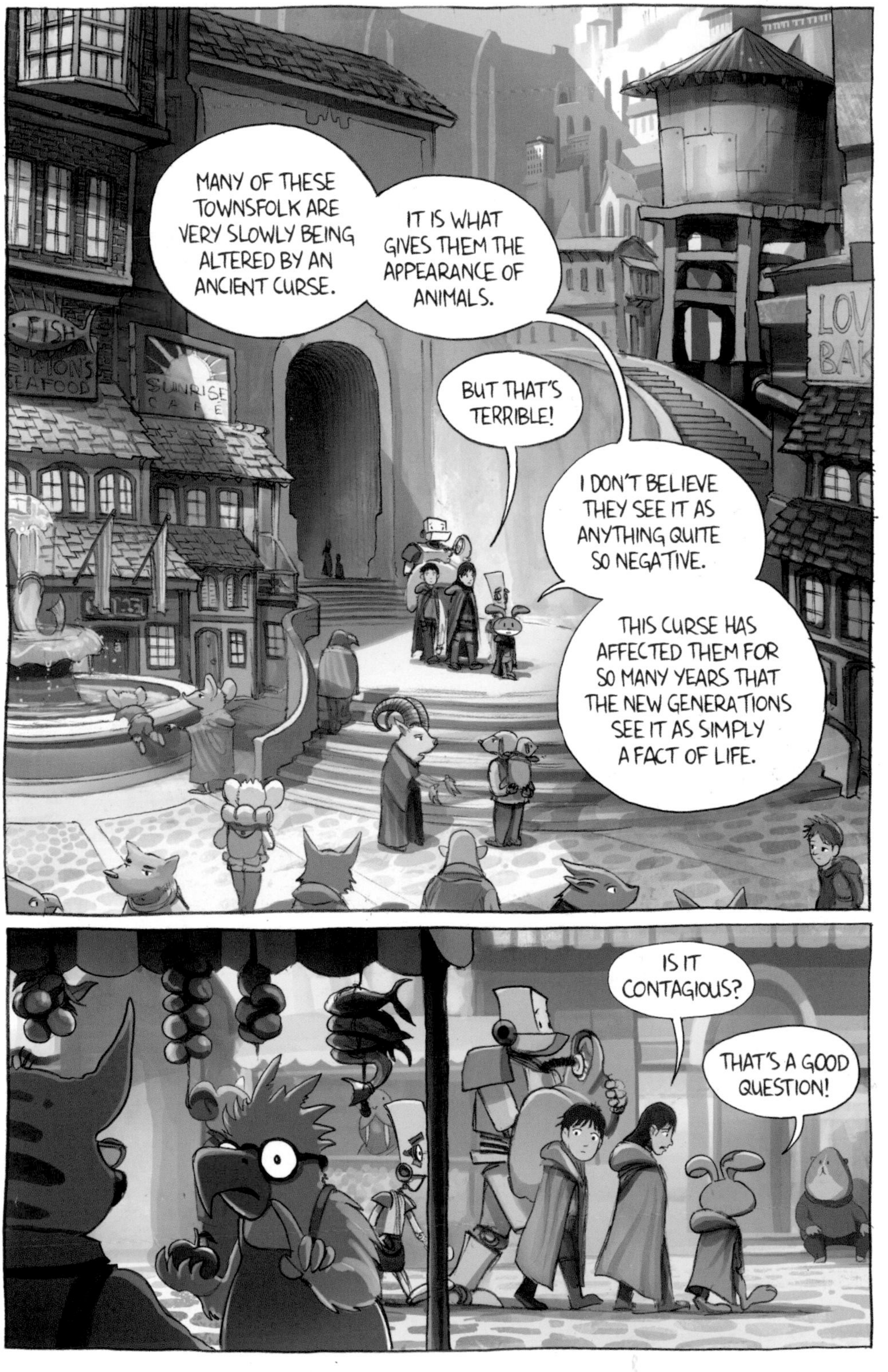
FISH
SUNRISE CAFE
MANY OF THESE TOWNSFOLK ARE VERY SLOWLY BEING ALTERED BY AN ANCIENT CURSE.
IT IS WHAT GIVES THEM THE APPEARANCE OF ANIMALS.
BUT THAT'S TERRIBLE!
I DON'T BELIEVE THEY SEE IT AS ANYTHING QUITE SO NEGATIVE.
THIS CURSE HAS AFFECTED THEM FOR SO MANY YEARS THAT THE NEW GENERATIONS SEE IT AS SIMPLY A FACT OF LIFE.
IS IT CONTAGIOUS?
THAT'S A GOOD QUESTION!

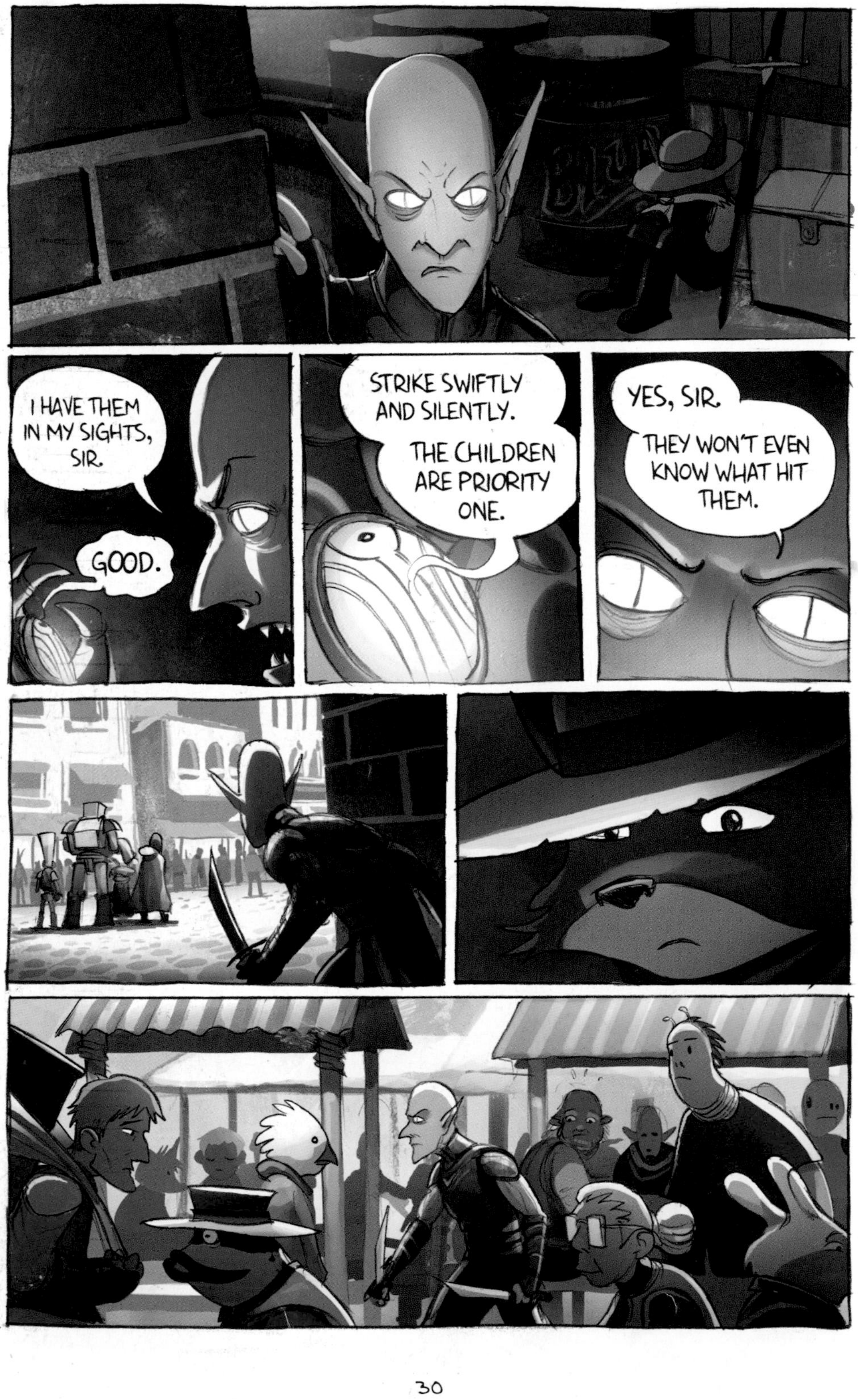
I HAVE THEM IN MY SIGHTS, SIR.
GOOD.
STRIKE SWIFTLY AND SILENTLY.
THE CHILDREN ARE PRIORITY ONE.
YES, SIR.
THEY WON'T EVEN KNOW WHAT HIT THEM.

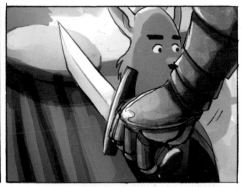

WHAT ARE YOU DOING!? GET OUT OF MY WAY!!

HUH?

I SAID, GET OUT OF MY--

WAY!!

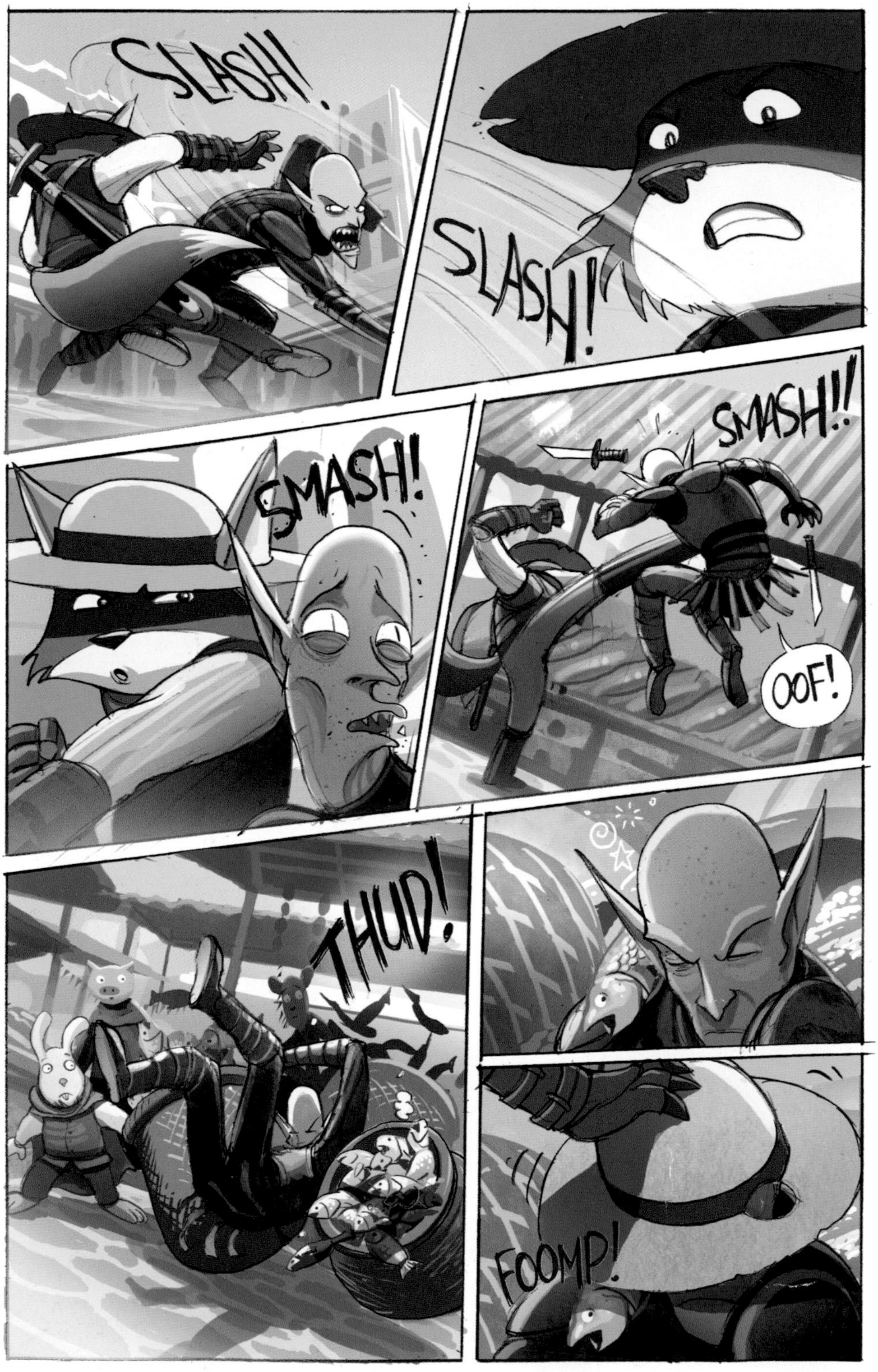
SLASH!
SLASH!
SMASH!
SMASH!!
OOF!
THUD!
FOOMP!

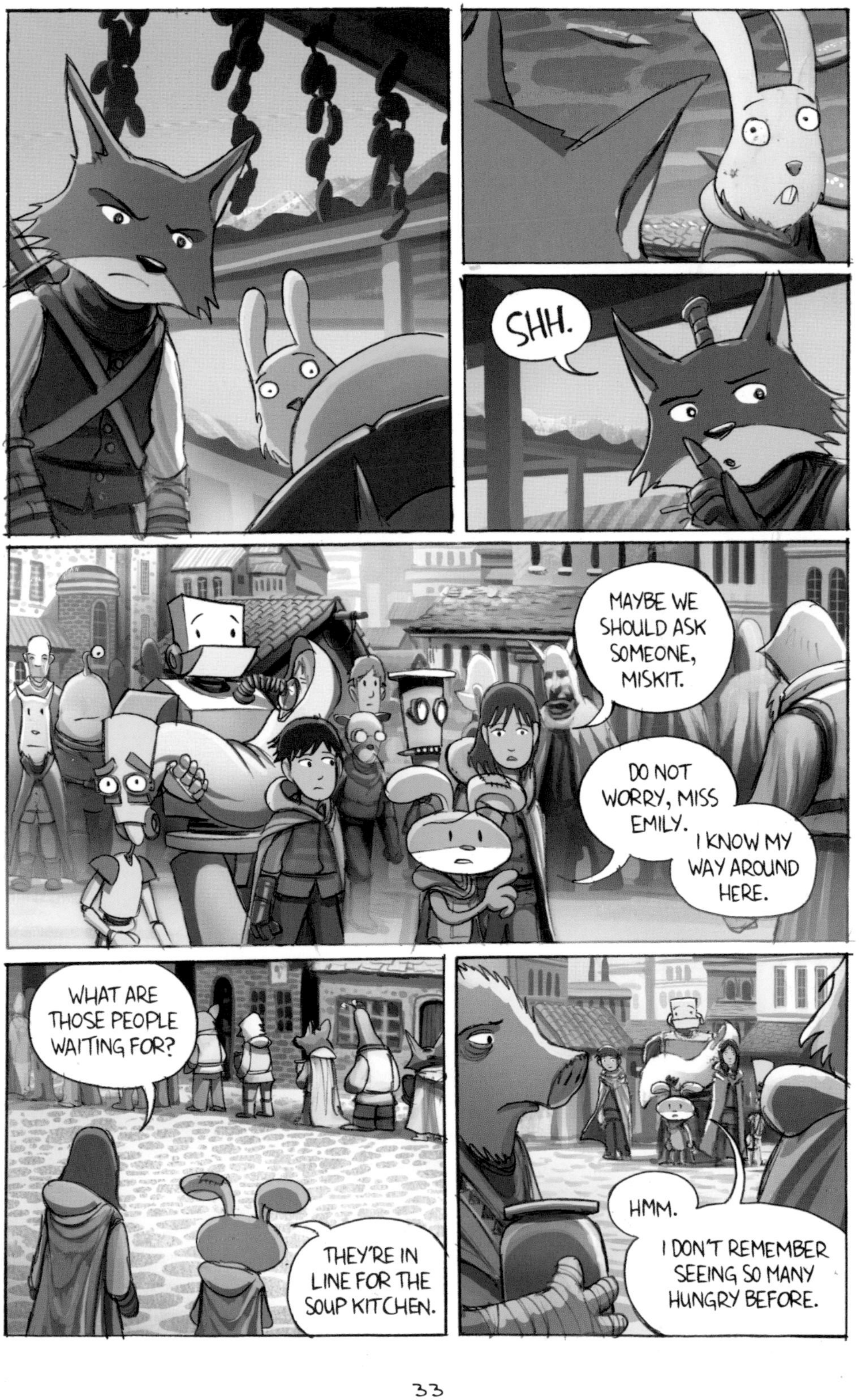
SHH.
MAYBE WE SHOULD ASK SOMEONE, MISKIT.
DO NOT WORRY, MISS EMILY.
I KNOW MY WAY AROUND HERE.
WHAT ARE THOSE PEOPLE WAITING FOR?
THEY'RE IN LINE FOR THE SOUP KITCHEN.
HMM.
I DON'T REMEMBER SEEING SO MANY HUNGRY BEFORE.

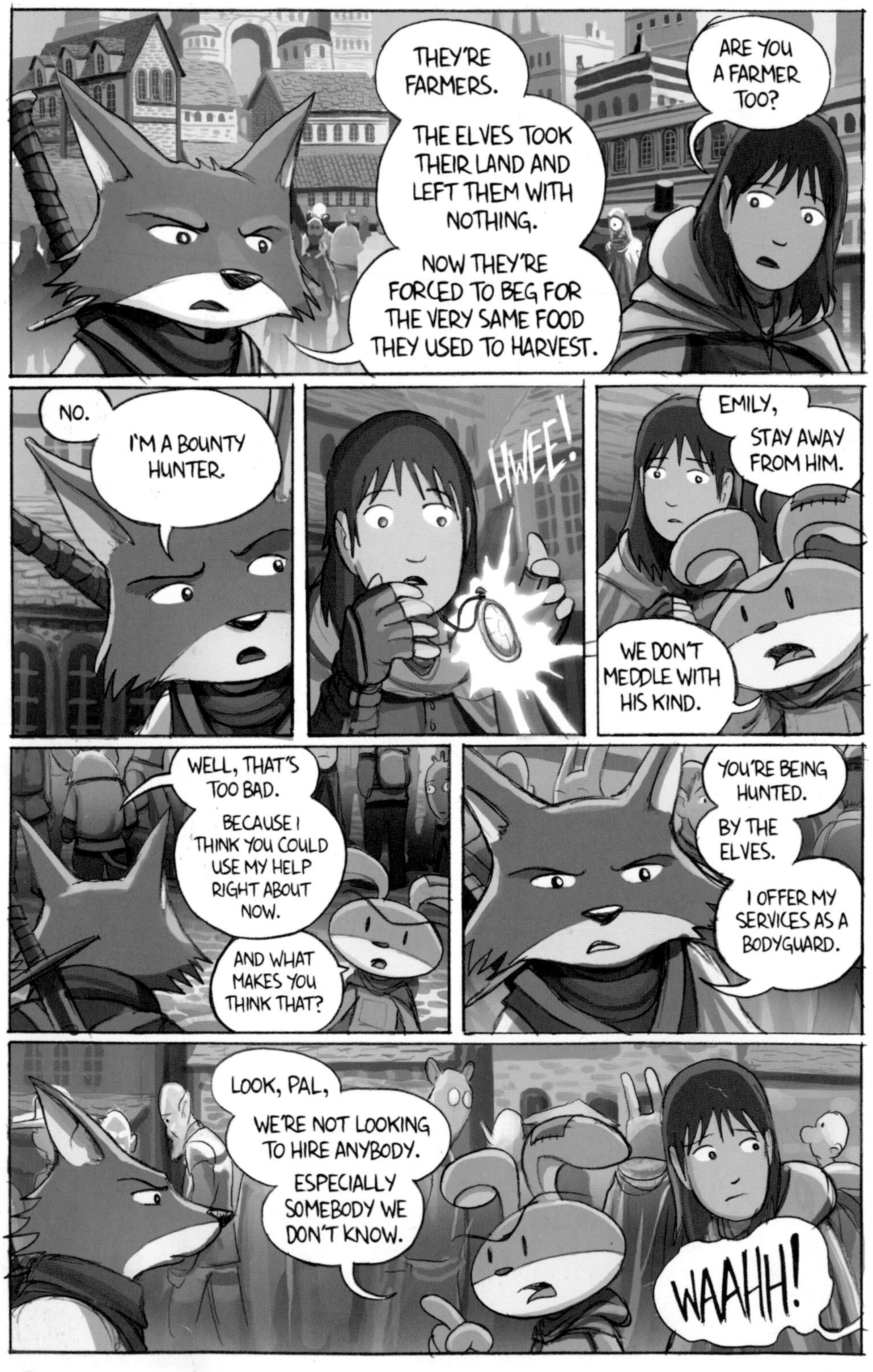
THEY'RE FARMERS.
THE ELVES TOOK THEIR LAND AND LEFT THEM WITH NOTHING.
NOW THEY'RE FORCED TO BEG FOR THE VERY SAME FOOD THEY USED TO HARVEST.
ARE YOU A FARMER TOO?
NO.
I'M A BOUNTY HUNTER.
HWEE!
EMILY,
STAY AWAY FROM HIM.
WE DON'T MEDDLE WITH HIS KIND.
WELL, THAT'S TOO BAD.
BECAUSE I THINK YOU COULD USE MY HELP RIGHT ABOUT NOW.
AND WHAT MAKES YOU THINK THAT?
YOU'RE BEING HUNTED.
BY THE ELVES.
I OFFER MY SERVICES AS A BODYGUARD.
LOOK, PAL,
WE'RE NOT LOOKING TO HIRE ANYBODY.
ESPECIALLY SOMEBODY WE DON'T KNOW.
WAAHH!

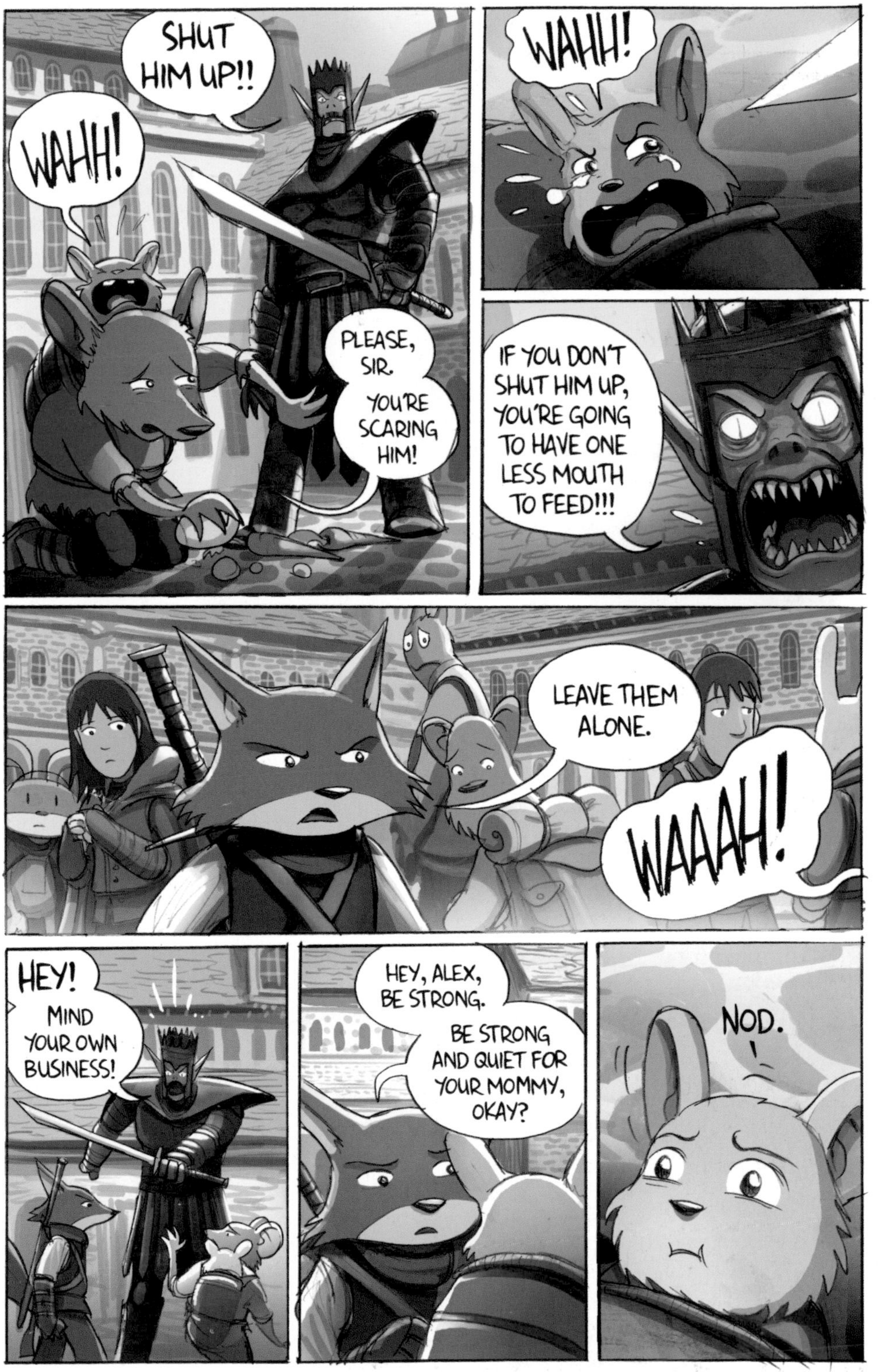
SHUT HIM UP!!
WAHH!
WAHH!
PLEASE, SIR.
YOU'RE SCARING HIM!
IF YOU DON'T SHUT HIM UP, YOU'RE GOING TO HAVE ONE LESS MOUTH TO FEED!!!
LEAVE THEM ALONE.
WAAAH!
HEY!
MIND YOUR OWN BUSINESS!
HEY, ALEX, BE STRONG.
BE STRONG AND QUIET FOR YOUR MOMMY, OKAY?
NOD.

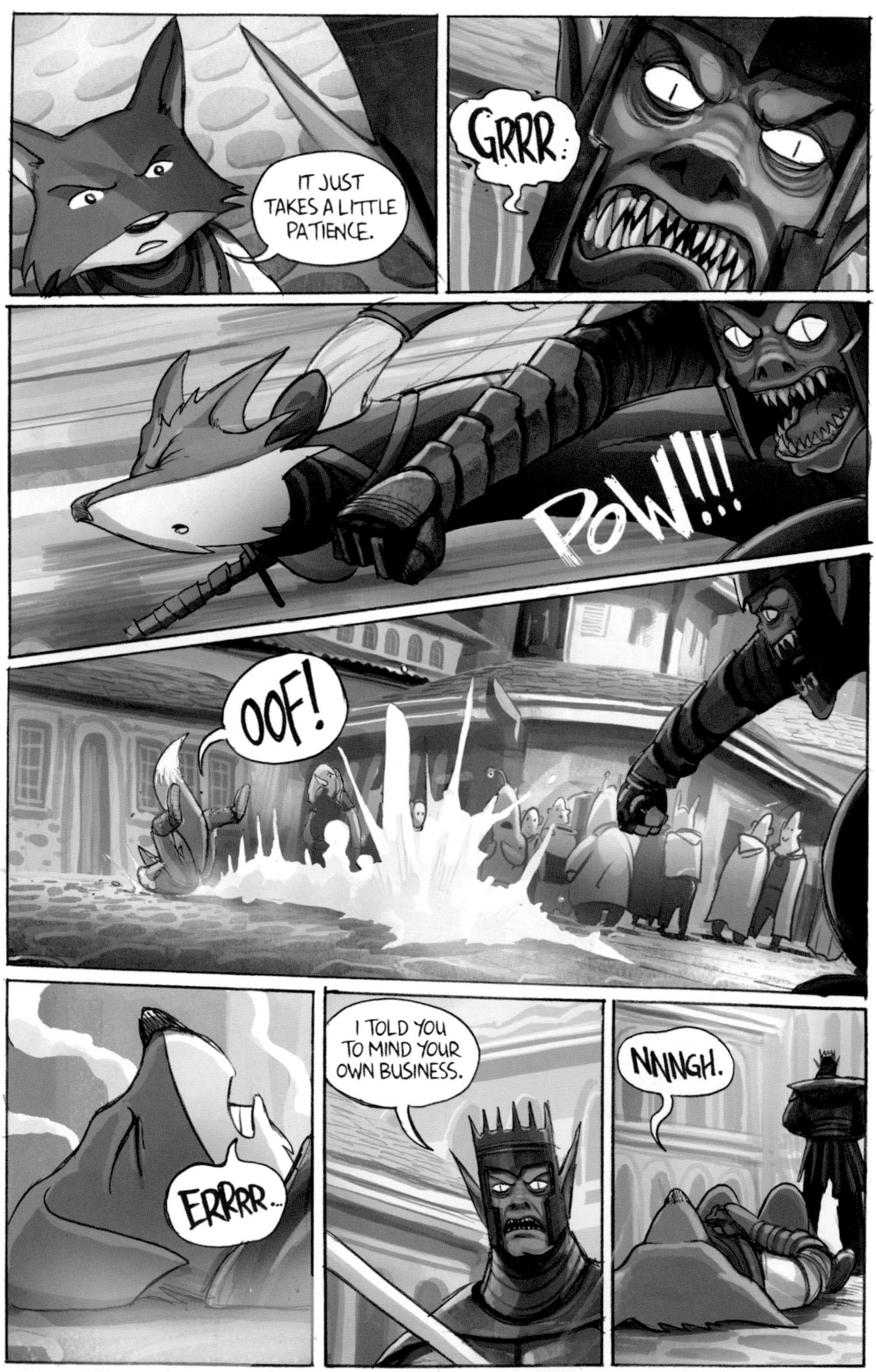
IT JUST TAKES A LITTLE PATIENCE.
GRRR
POW!!!
OOF!
ERRRR...
I TOLD YOU TO MIND YOUR OWN BUSINESS.
NNNGH.

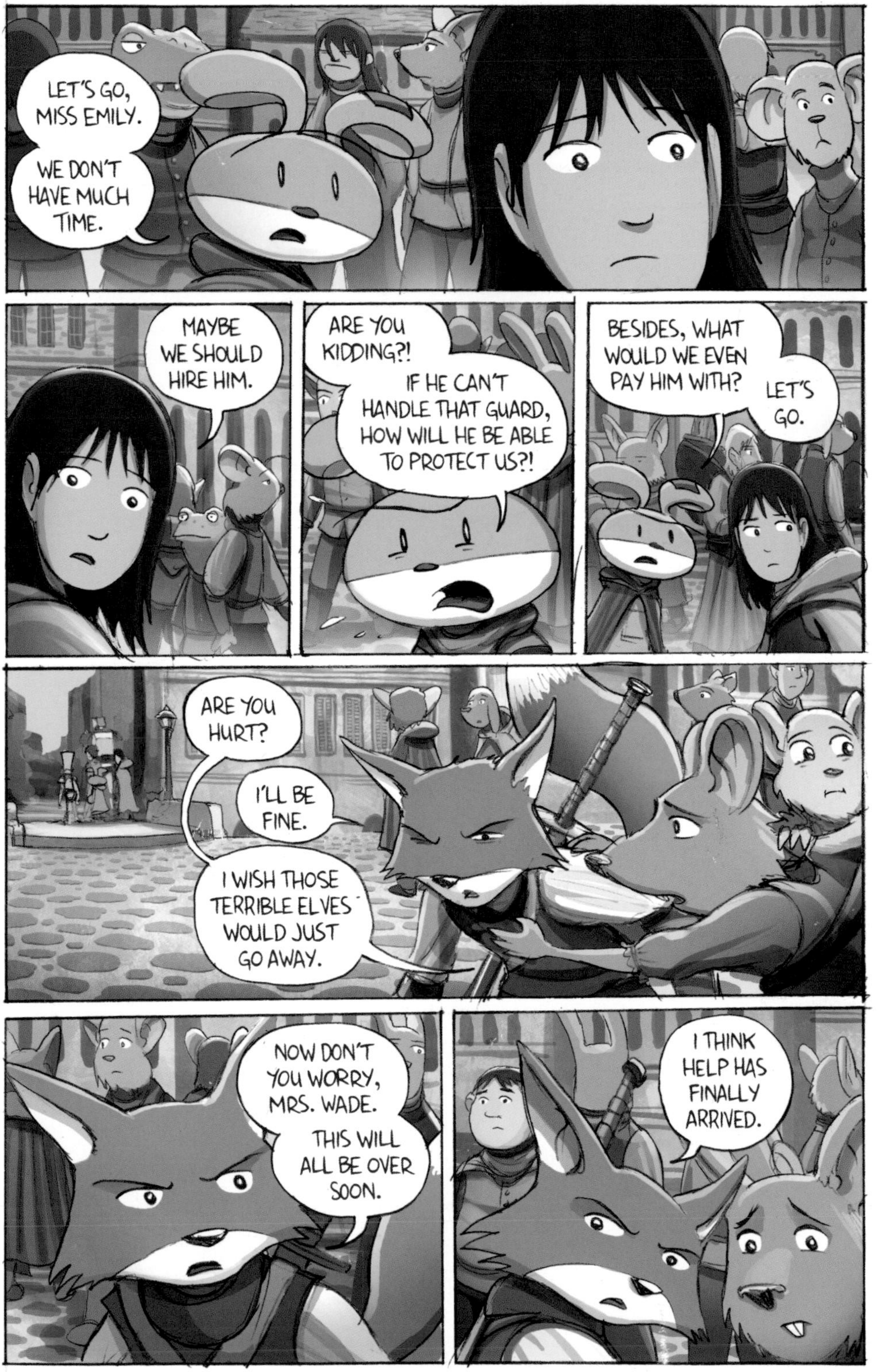
LET'S GO, MISS EMILY.
WE DON'T HAVE MUCH TIME.
MAYBE WE SHOULD HIRE HIM.
ARE YOU KIDDING?!
IF HE CAN'T HANDLE THAT GUARD, HOW WILL HE BE ABLE TO PROTECT US?!
BESIDES, WHAT WOULD WE EVEN PAY HIM WITH?
LET'S GO.
ARE YOU HURT?
I'LL BE FINE.
I WISH THOSE TERRIBLE ELVES WOULD JUST GO AWAY.
NOW DON'T YOU WORRY, MRS. WADE.
THIS WILL ALL BE OVER SOON.
I THINK HELP HAS FINALLY ARRIVED.

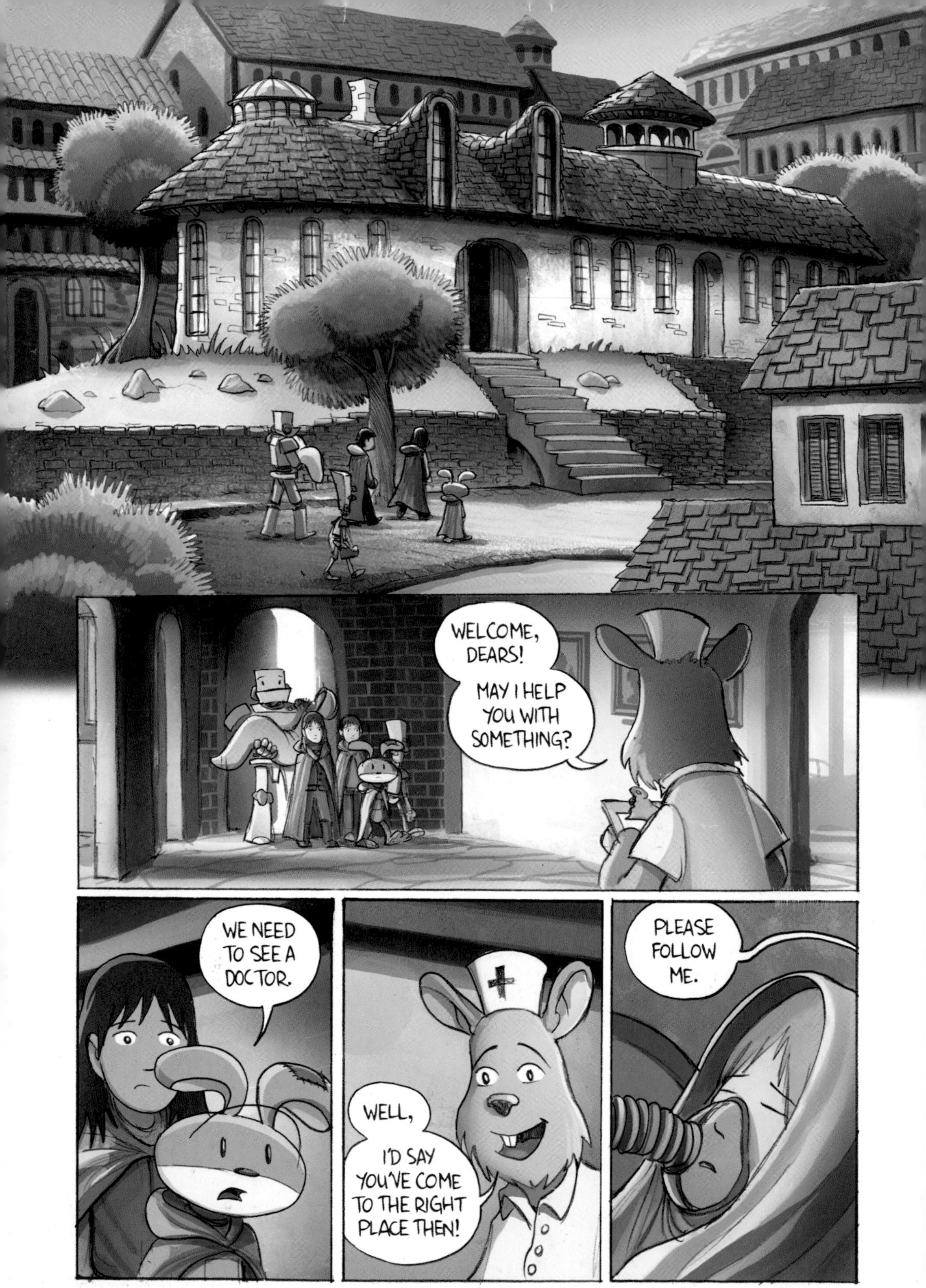
WELCOME, DEARS!
MAY I HELP YOU WITH SOMETHING?
WE NEED TO SEE A DOCTOR.
WELL,
I'D SAY YOU'VE COME TO THE RIGHT PLACE THEN!
PLEASE FOLLOW ME.

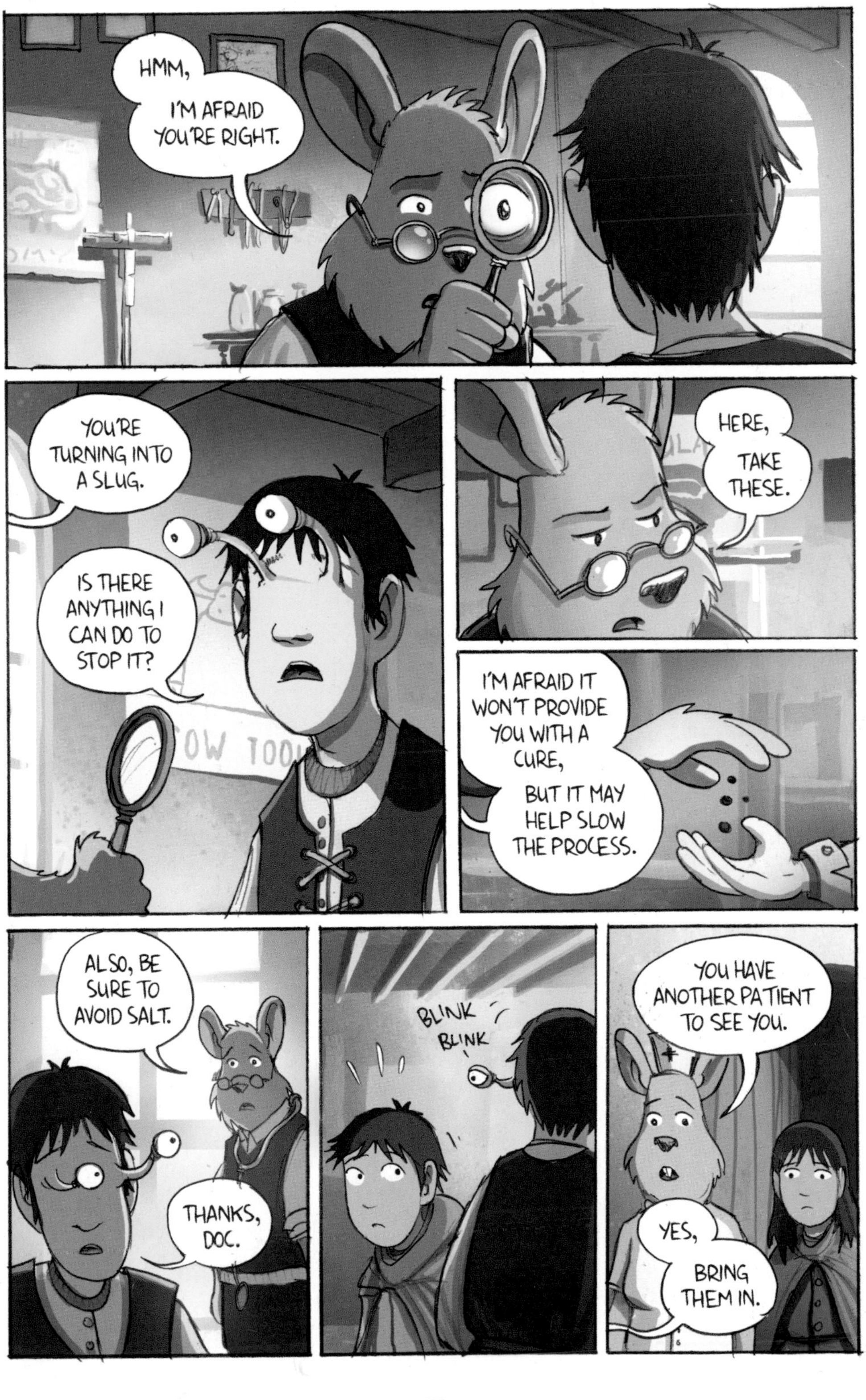
HMM,
I'M AFRAID YOU'RE RIGHT.
YOU'RE TURNING INTO A SLUG.
IS THERE ANYTHING I CAN DO TO STOP IT?
HERE,
TAKE THESE.
I'M AFRAID IT WON'T PROVIDE YOU WITH A CURE,
BUT IT MAY HELP SLOW THE PROCESS.
ALSO, BE SURE TO AVOID SALT.
THANKS, DOC.
BLINK
BLINK
YOU HAVE ANOTHER PATIENT TO SEE YOU.
YES,
BRING THEM IN.

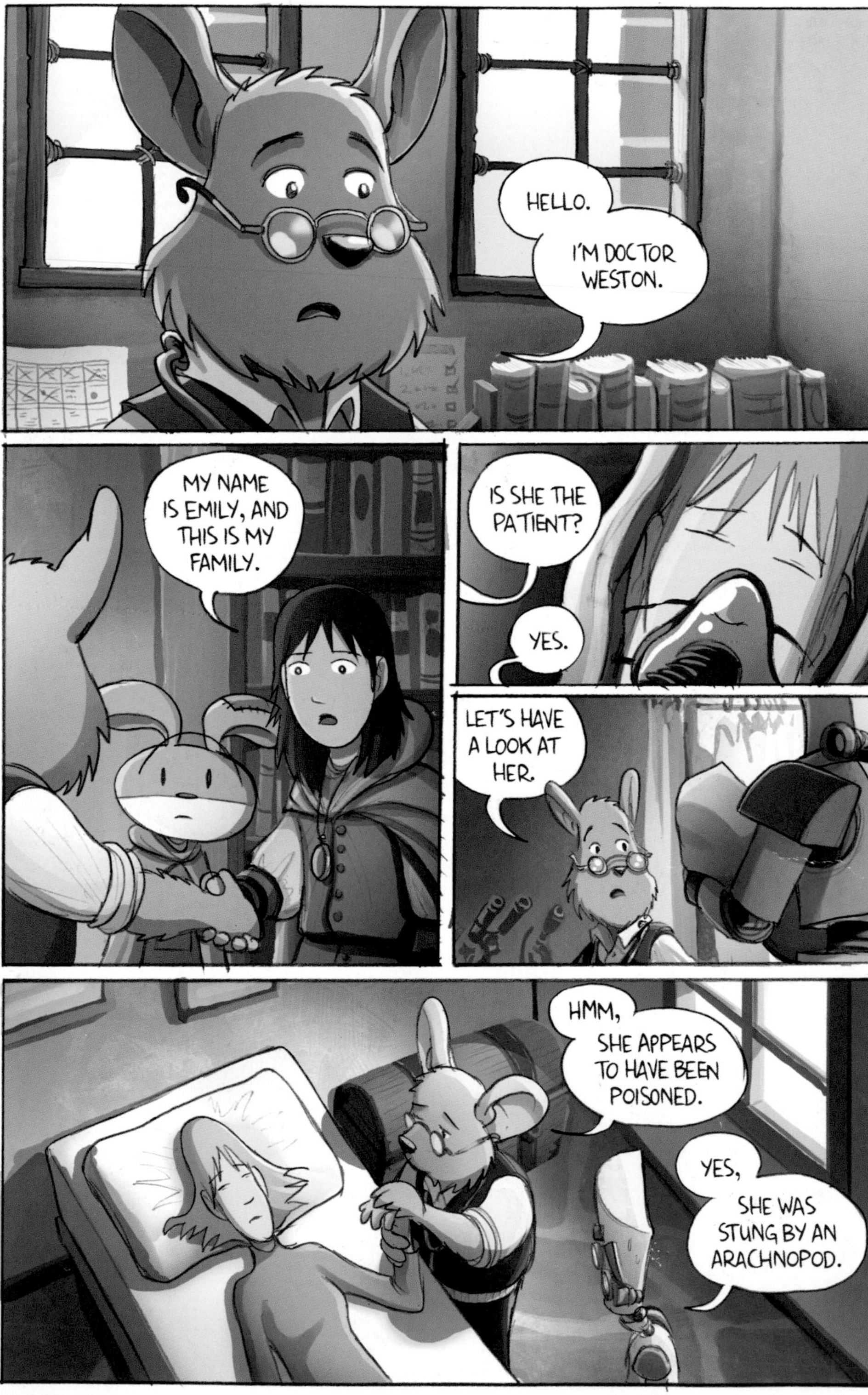
HELLO.
I'M DOCTOR WESTON.
MY NAME IS EMILY, AND THIS IS MY FAMILY.
IS SHE THE PATIENT?
YES.
LET'S HAVE A LOOK AT HER.
HMM,
SHE APPEARS TO HAVE BEEN POISONED.
YES,
SHE WAS STUNG BY AN ARACHNOPOD.

ARACHNOPODS ARE HIGHLY TOXIC.

MOST CASES RESULT IN DEATH.

SHE'S LUCKY TO STILL BE ALIVE!

CAN YOU HELP HER?

ONLY THE FRUIT OF A GADOBA TREE CAN FIGHT THE VENOM AND CURE HER.

DO YOU KNOW WHERE I CAN FIND ONE?

THE LAST REMAINING TREES STAND AT THE PEAK OF DEMON'S HEAD MOUNTAIN...

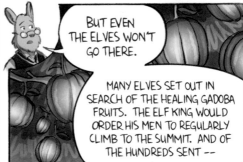

BUT EVEN THE ELVES WON'T GO THERE.

MANY ELVES SET OUT IN SEARCH OF THE HEALING GADOBA FRUITS. THE ELF KING WOULD ORDER HIS MEN TO REGULARLY CLIMB TO THE SUMMIT. AND OF THE HUNDREDS SENT --

-- NONE HAVE RETURNED.

I CAN'T LET YOU GO THERE IN GOOD CONSCIENCE.

IT'S FAR TOO DANGEROUS.

HEY, GUYS?

I DON'T THINK GOING THERE'S A GOOD IDEA.

I'M HERE FOR ONLY ONE REASON, AND THAT'S TO GET MY FAMILY HOME SAFE.

IF THAT MEANS WE HAVE TO CLIMB A MOUNTAIN, THEN THAT'S WHAT WE'RE GOING TO DO.

IS THAT REALLY THE ONLY REASON?

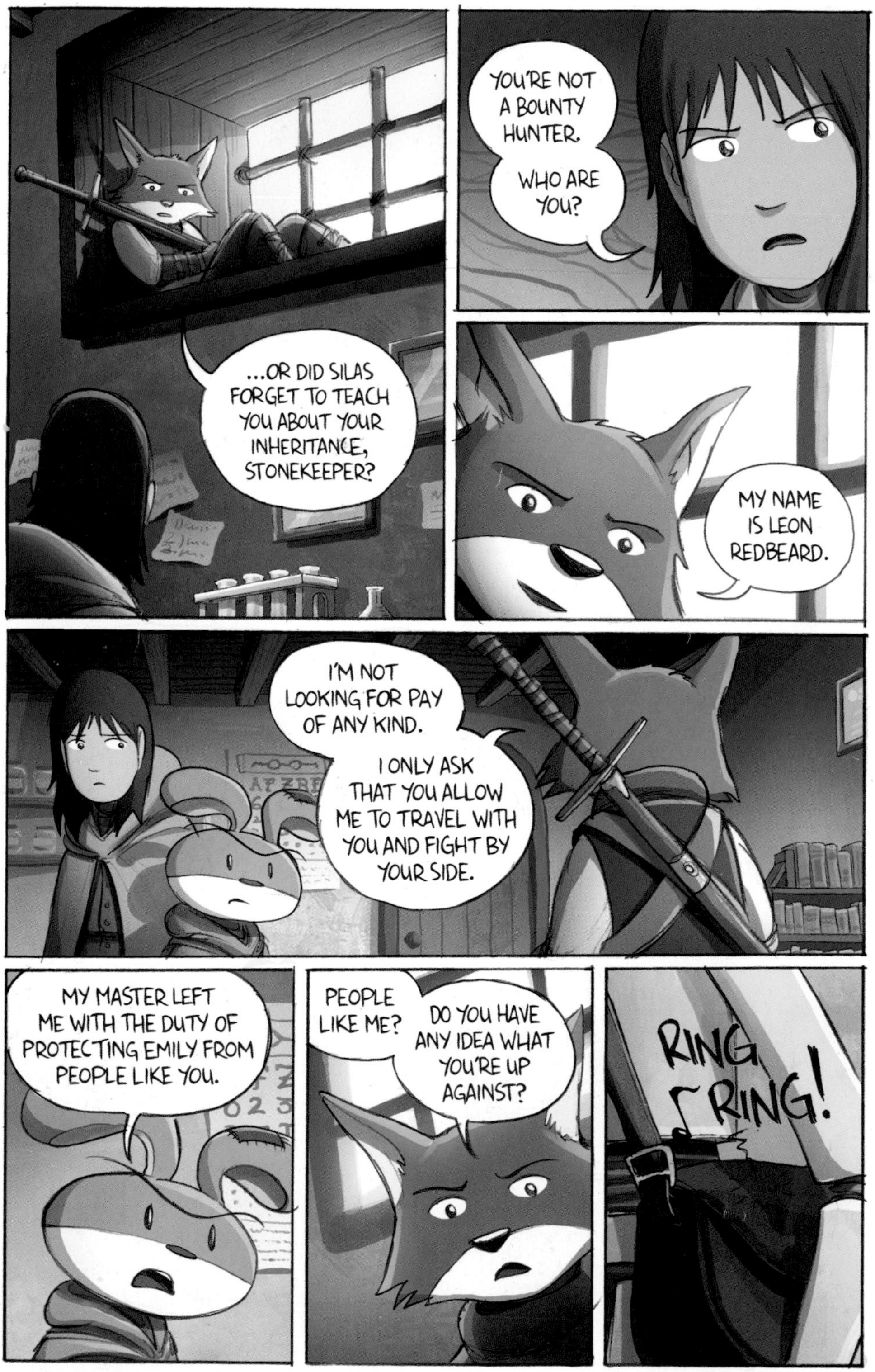
YOU'RE NOT A BOUNTY HUNTER.
WHO ARE YOU?
...OR DID SILAS FORGET TO TEACH YOU ABOUT YOUR INHERITANCE, STONEKEEPER?
MY NAME IS LEON REDBEARD.
I'M NOT LOOKING FOR PAY OF ANY KIND.
I ONLY ASK THAT YOU ALLOW ME TO TRAVEL WITH YOU AND FIGHT BY YOUR SIDE.
MY MASTER LEFT ME WITH THE DUTY OF PROTECTING EMILY FROM PEOPLE LIKE YOU.
PEOPLE LIKE ME?
DO YOU HAVE ANY IDEA WHAT YOU'RE UP AGAINST?
RING RING!

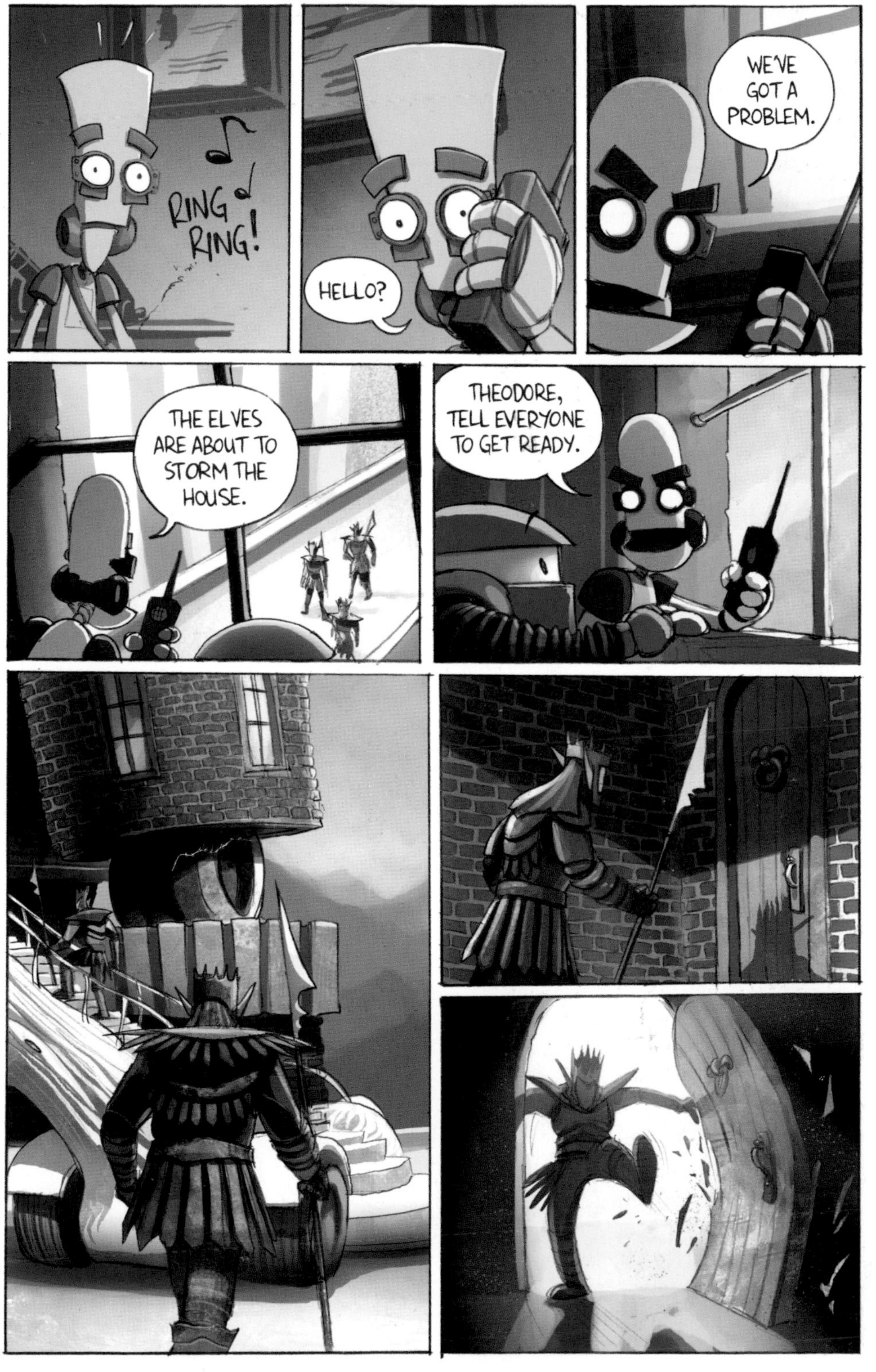
RING RING!
HELLO?
WE'VE GOT A PROBLEM.
THE ELVES ARE ABOUT TO STORM THE HOUSE.
THEODORE, TELL EVERYONE TO GET READY.

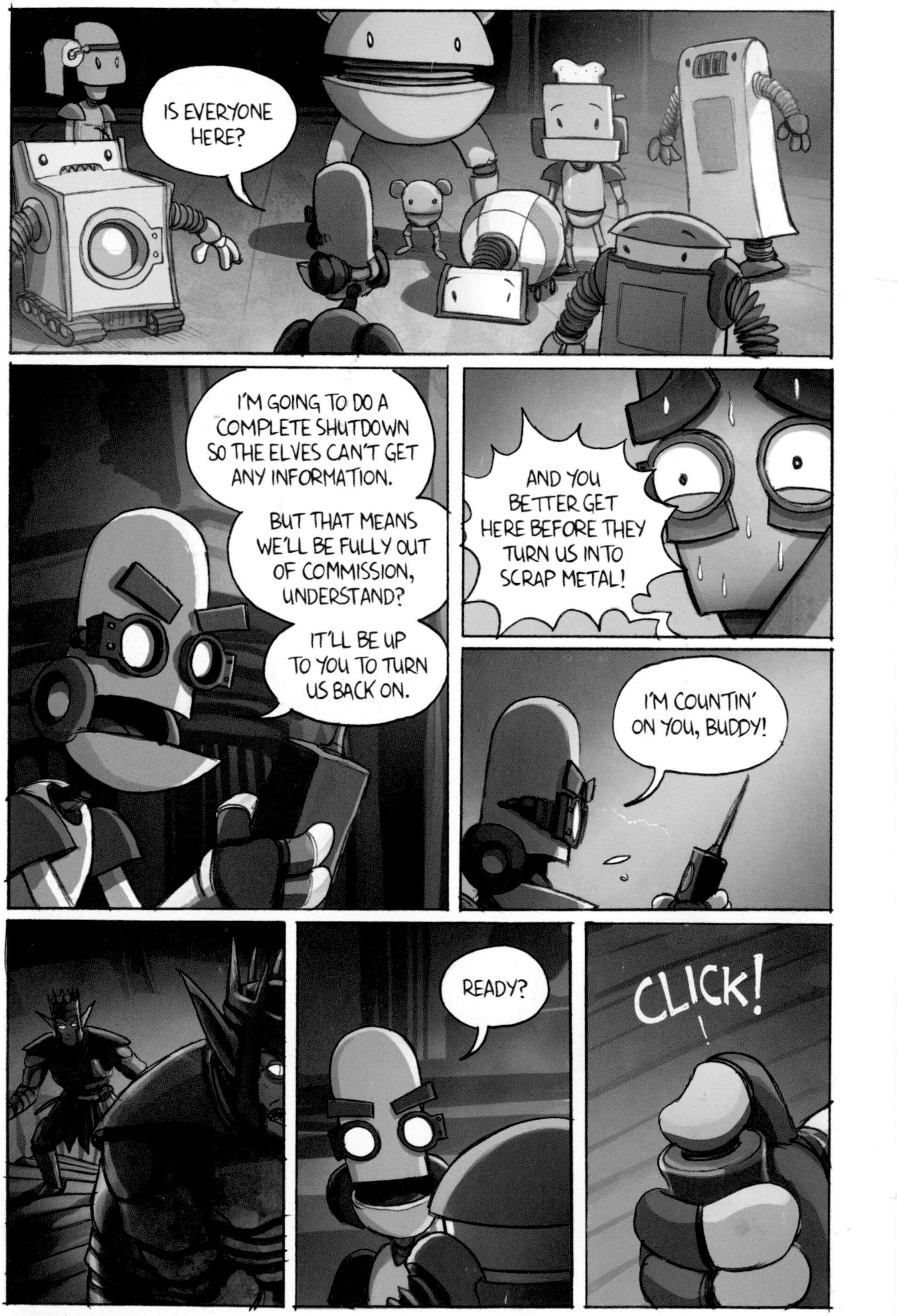

IS EVERYONE HERE?
I'M GOING TO DO A COMPLETE SHUTDOWN SO THE ELVES CAN'T GET ANY INFORMATION.
BUT THAT MEANS WE'LL BE FULLY OUT OF COMMISSION, UNDERSTAND?
IT'LL BE UP TO YOU TO TURN US BACK ON.
AND YOU BETTER GET HERE BEFORE THEY TURN US INTO SCRAP METAL!
I'M COUNTIN' ON YOU, BUDDY!
READY?
CLICK!

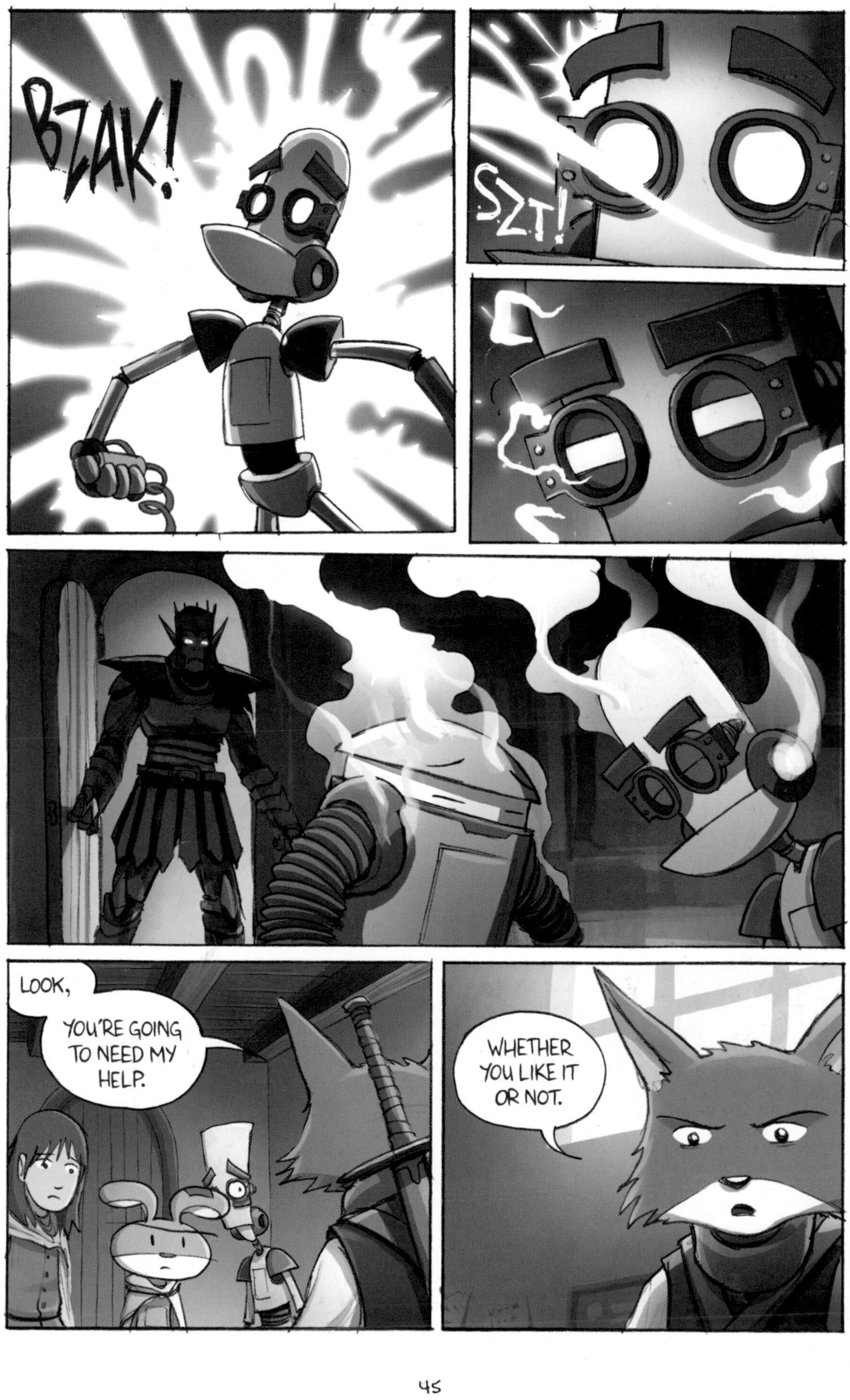
BZAK!
SZT!
LOOK,
YOU'RE GOING TO NEED MY HELP.
WHETHER YOU LIKE IT OR NOT.

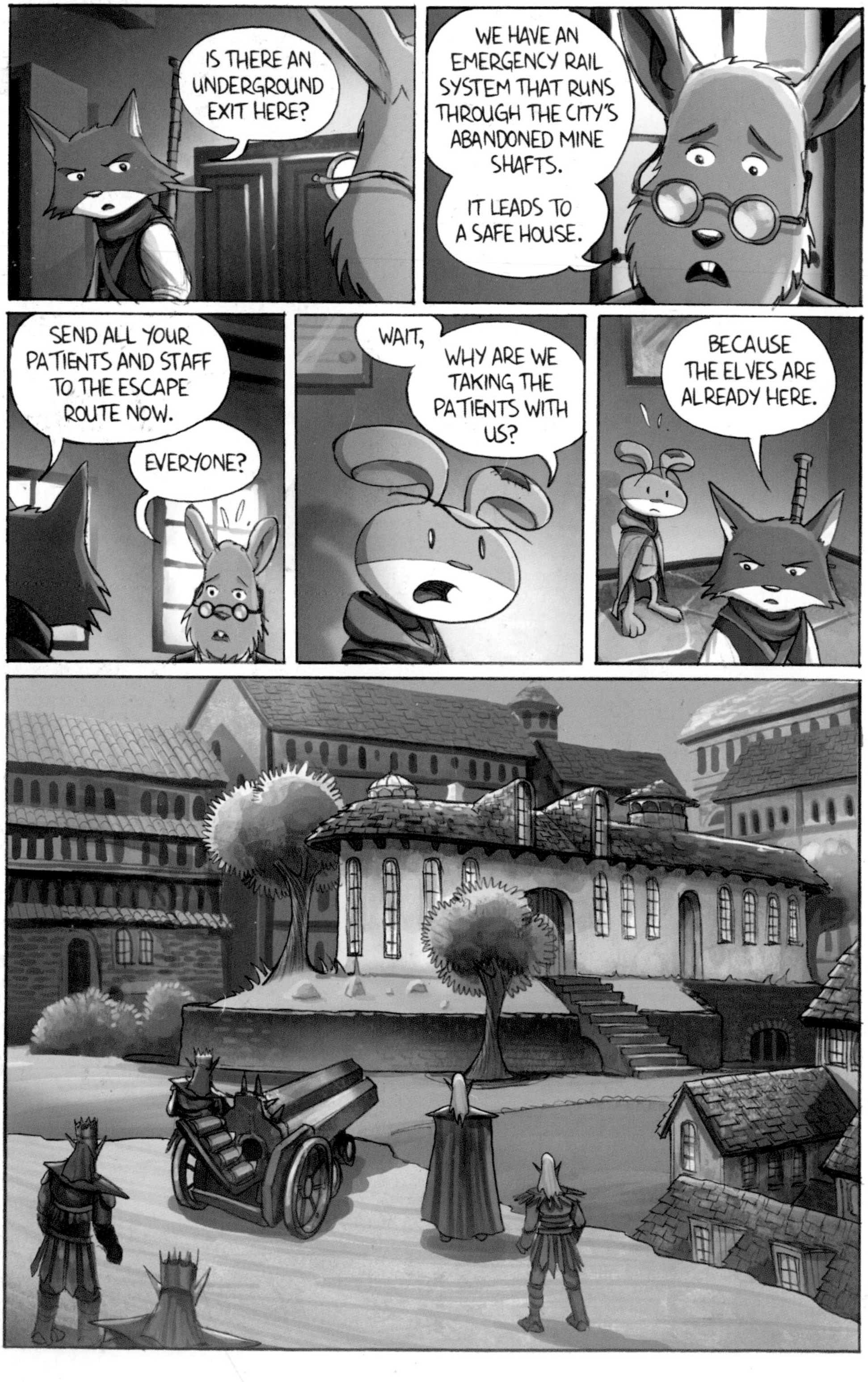
IS THERE AN UNDERGROUND EXIT HERE?
WE HAVE AN EMERGENCY RAIL SYSTEM THAT RUNS THROUGH THE CITY'S ABANDONED MINE SHAFTS.
IT LEADS TO A SAFE HOUSE.
SEND ALL YOUR PATIENTS AND STAFF TO THE ESCAPE ROUTE NOW.
EVERYONE?
WAIT,
WHY ARE WE TAKING THE PATIENTS WITH US?
BECAUSE THE ELVES ARE ALREADY HERE.

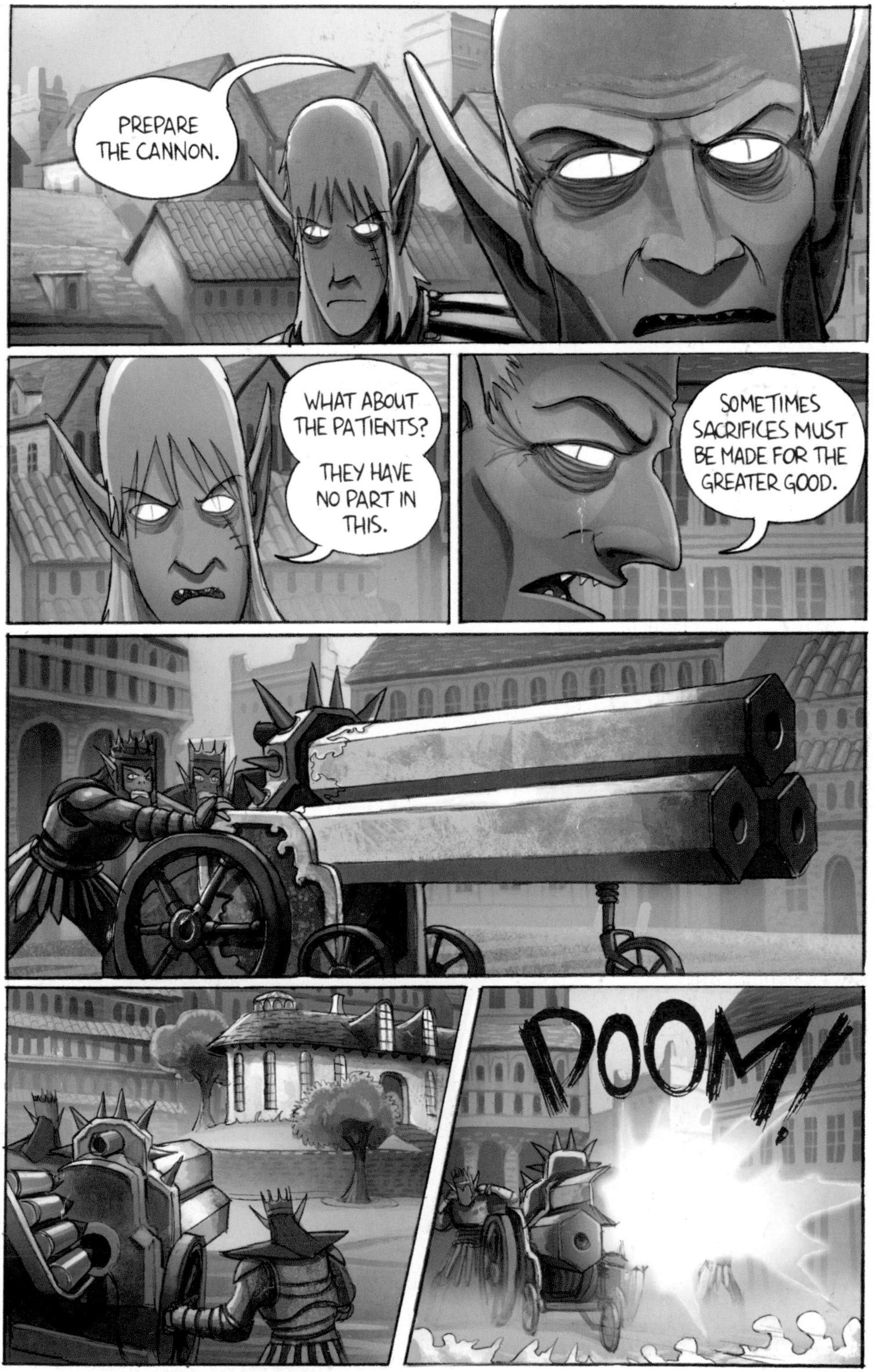
PREPARE THE CANNON.
WHAT ABOUT THE PATIENTS?
THEY HAVE NO PART IN THIS.
SOMETIMES SACRIFICES MUST BE MADE FOR THE GREATER GOOD.
DOOM!

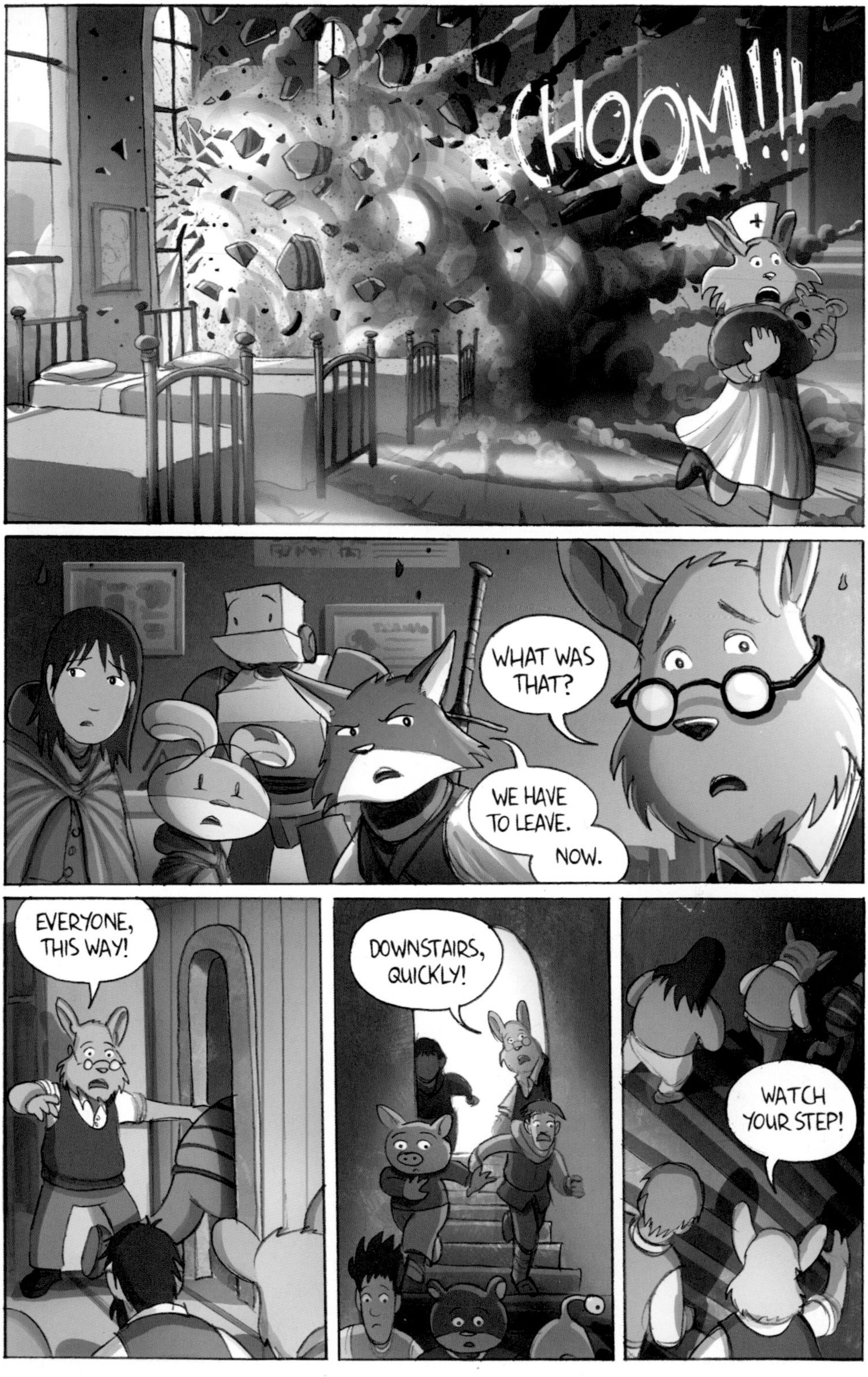
CHOOM!!!
WHAT WAS THAT?
WE HAVE TO LEAVE.
NOW.
EVERYONE, THIS WAY!
DOWNSTAIRS, QUICKLY!
WATCH YOUR STEP!

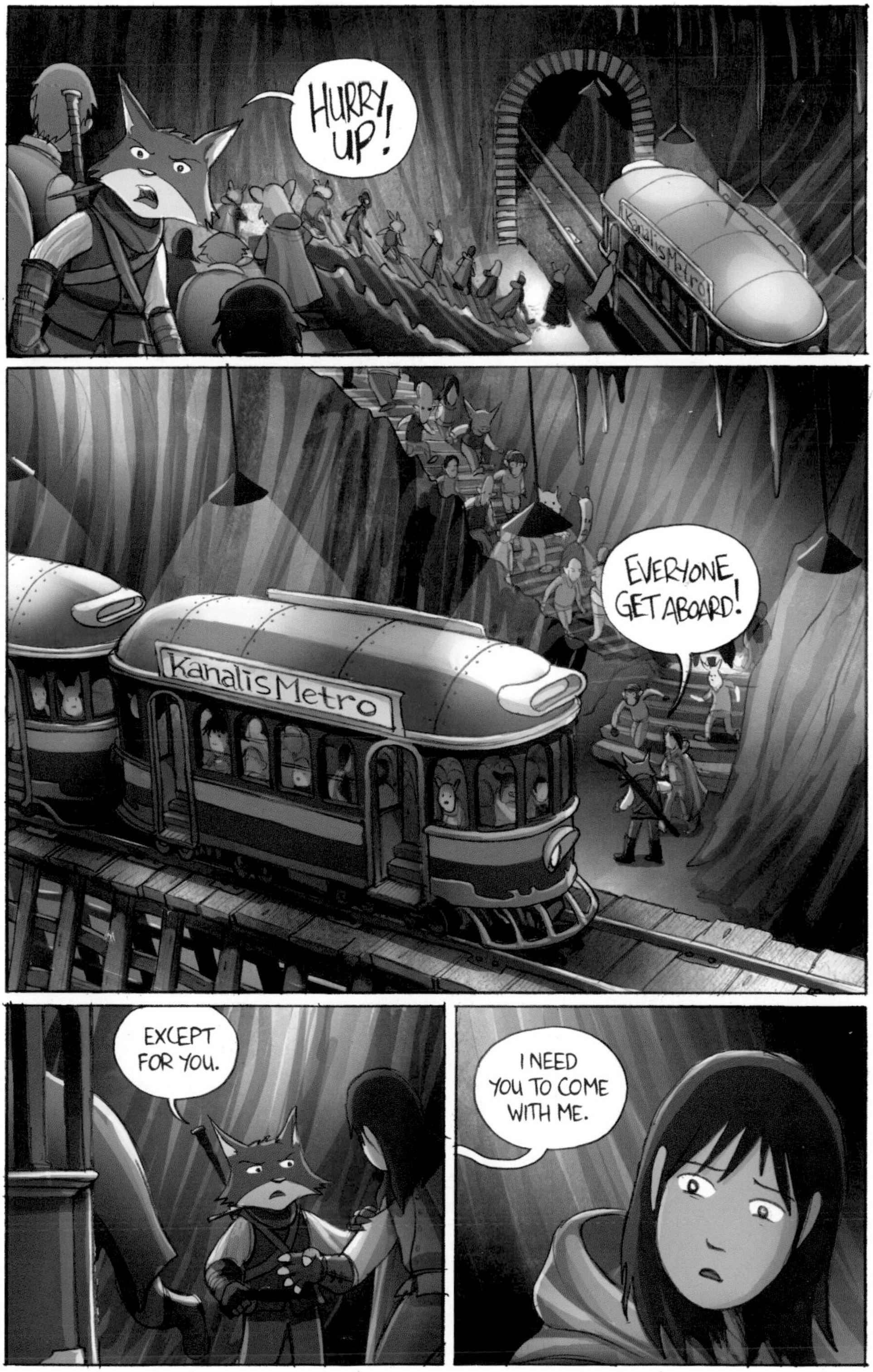
HURRY UP!
KanalisMetro
KanalisMetro
EVERYONE GET ABOARD!
EXCEPT FOR YOU.
I NEED YOU TO COME WITH ME.

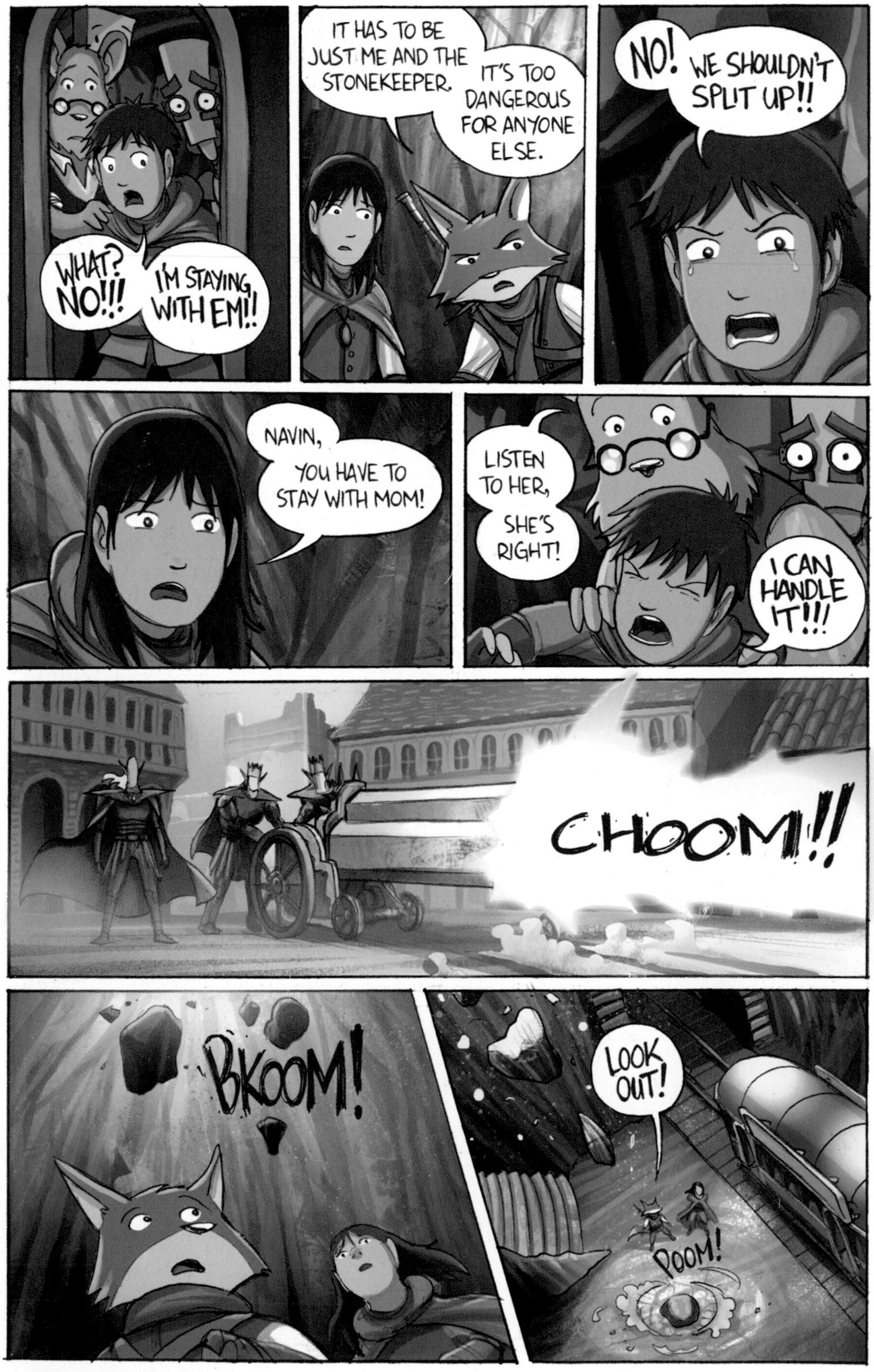
WHAT? NO!!!
I'M STAYING WITH EM!!
IT HAS TO BE JUST ME AND THE STONEKEEPER.
IT'S TOO DANGEROUS FOR ANYONE ELSE.
NO!
WE SHOULDN'T SPLIT UP!!
NAVIN, YOU HAVE TO STAY WITH MOM!
LISTEN TO HER, SHE'S RIGHT!
I CAN HANDLE IT!!!
CHOOM!!
BKOOM!
LOOK OUT!
POOM!

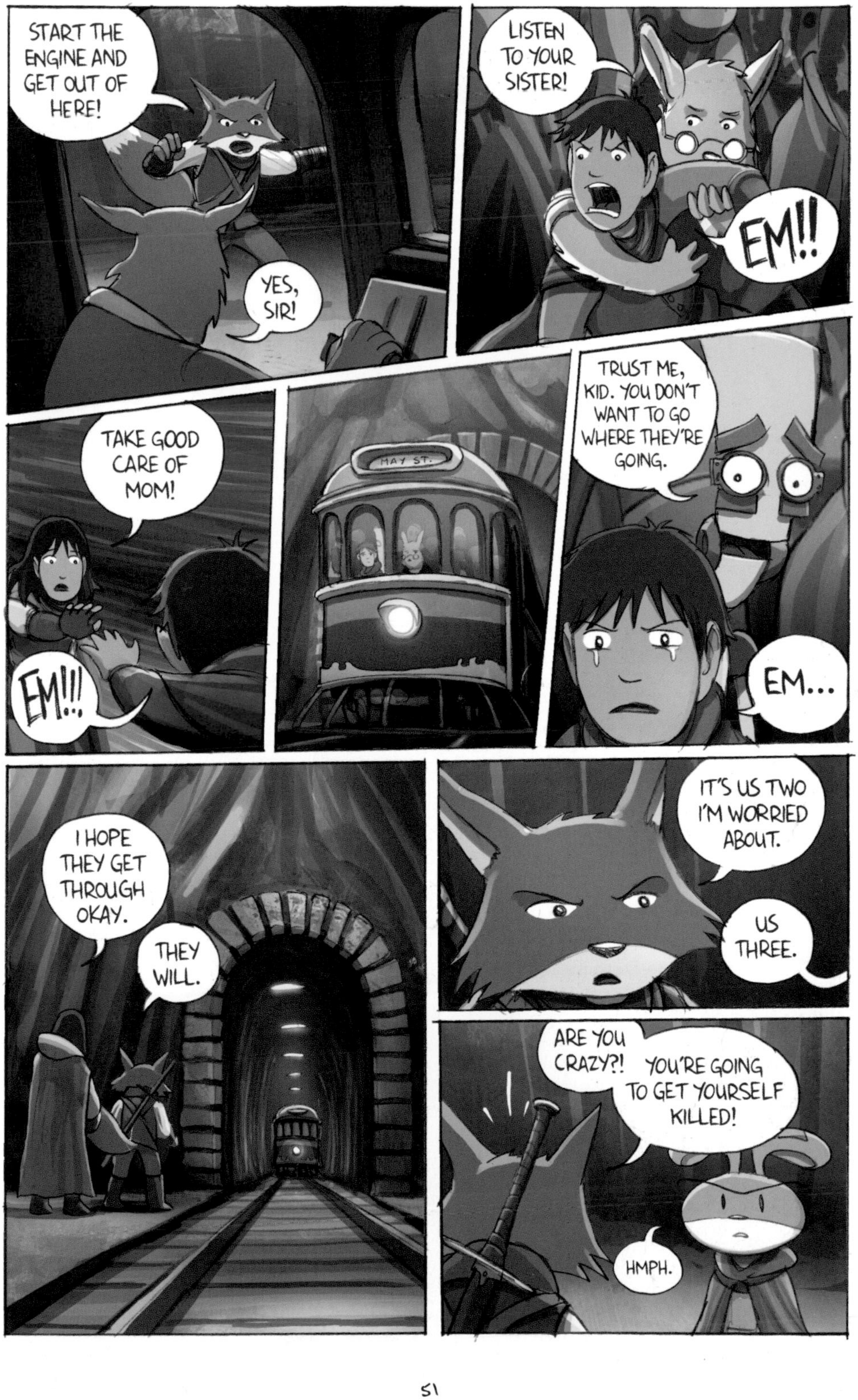
START THE ENGINE AND GET OUT OF HERE!
YES, SIR!
LISTEN TO YOUR SISTER!
EM!!
TAKE GOOD CARE OF MOM!
EM!!!
MAY ST.
TRUST ME, KID. YOU DON'T WANT TO GO WHERE THEY'RE GOING.
EM...
I HOPE THEY GET THROUGH OKAY.
THEY WILL.
IT'S US TWO I'M WORRIED ABOUT.
US THREE.
ARE YOU CRAZY?!
YOU'RE GOING TO GET YOURSELF KILLED!
HMPH.

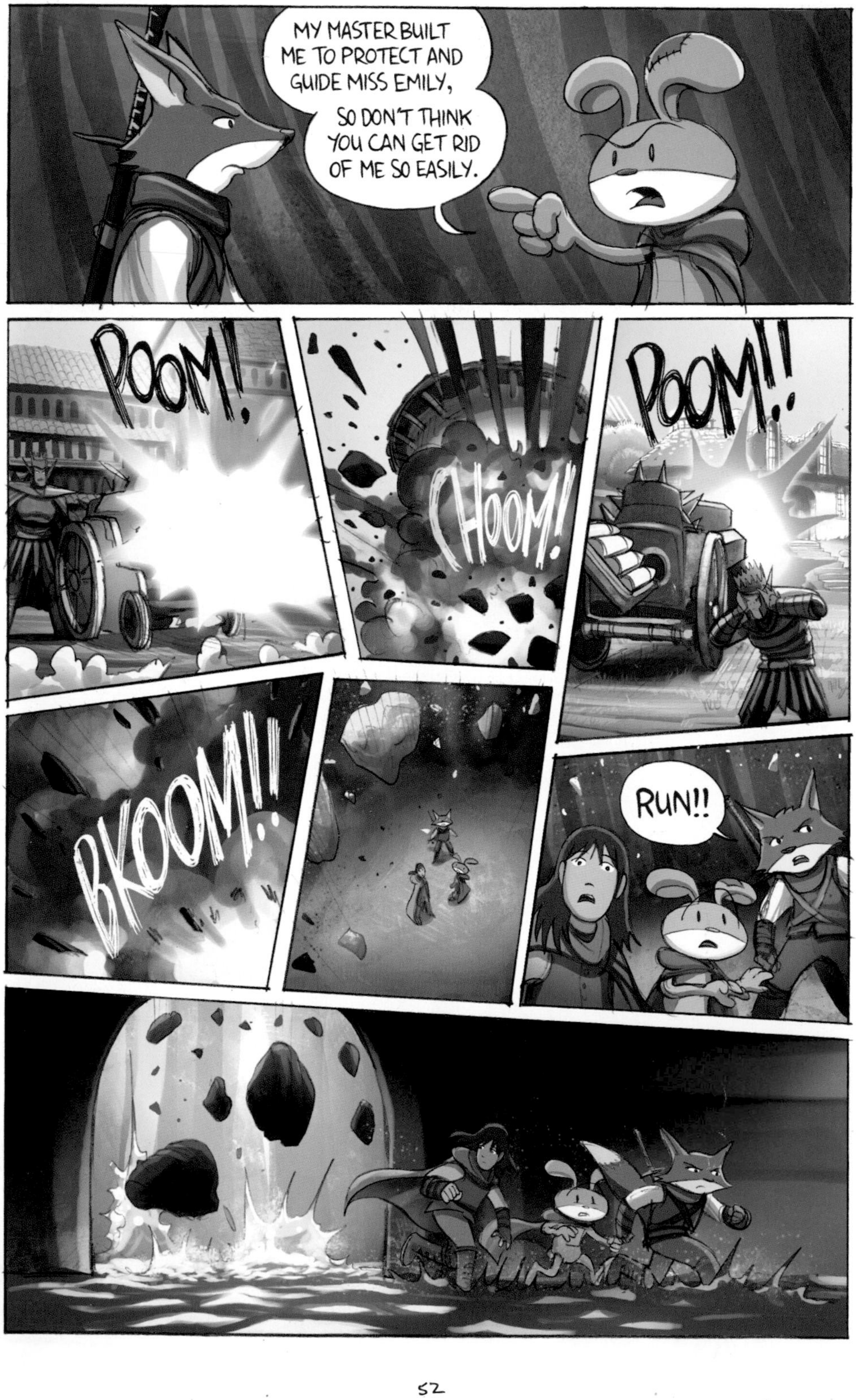
MY MASTER BUILT ME TO PROTECT AND GUIDE MISS EMILY,
SO DON'T THINK YOU CAN GET RID OF ME SO EASILY.
POOM!
CHOOM!
POOM!!
BKOOM!!
RUN!!

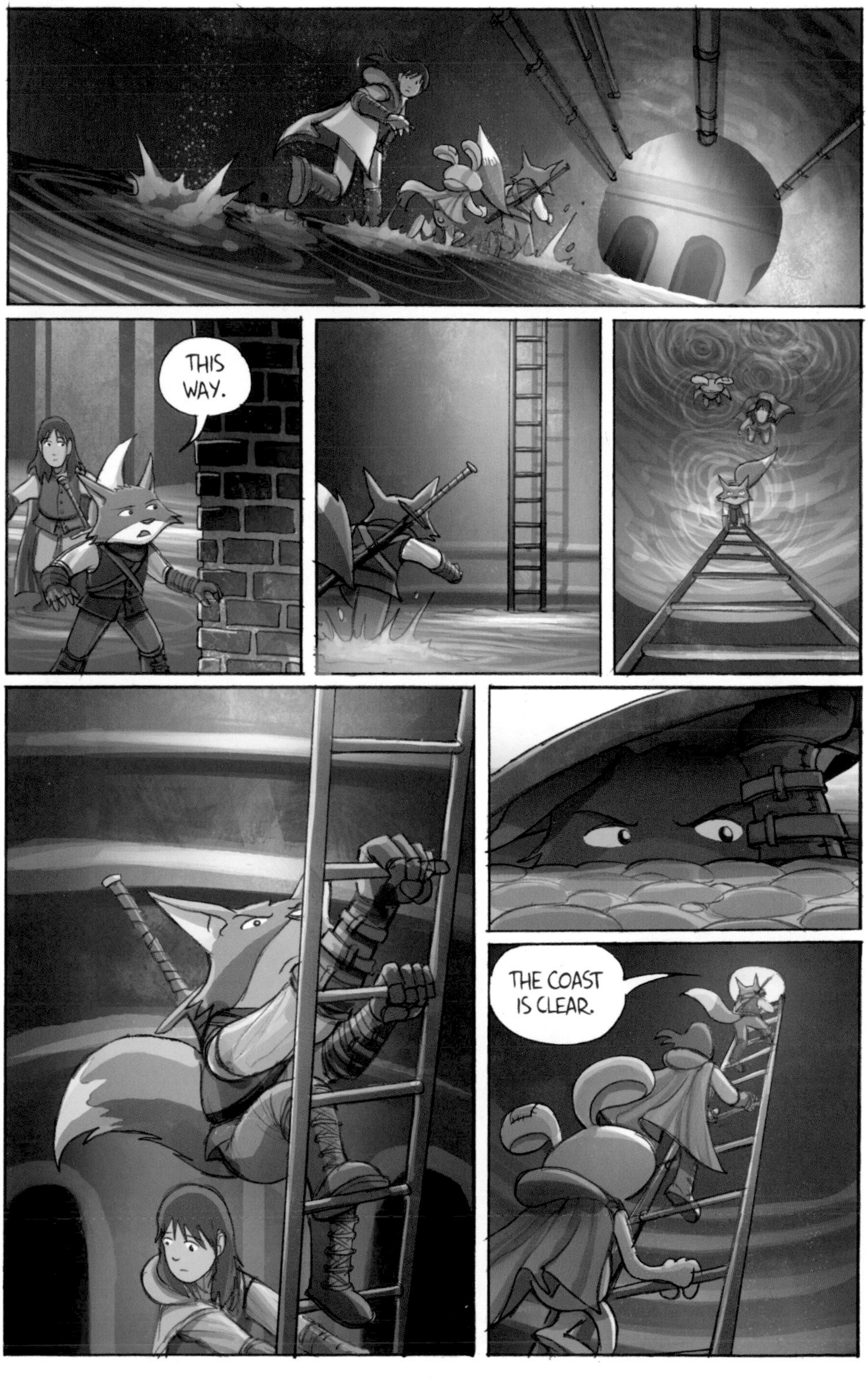
THIS WAY.
THE COAST IS CLEAR.

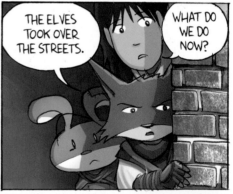

THE ELVES TOOK OVER THE STREETS.

WHAT DO WE DO NOW?

WE TAKE THE HIGH ROAD.

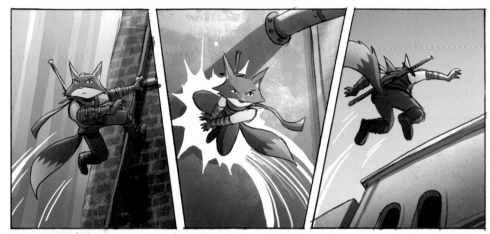

WHAT ARE YOU WAITING FOR?

ARE YOU KIDDING?! WE CAN'T DO THAT!

THIS IS WHY YOU SHOULDN'T HAVE TAGGED ALONG!

YOU CAN'T, BUT SHE CAN.

I DON'T KNOW HOW.

SHE DOESN'T KNOW HOW!!

YES SHE DOES.

NOW STOP FOOLING AROUND DOWN THERE OR YOU'RE GOING TO GET US KILLED!

GET ON MY BACK.

DON'T LET HIM BULLY YOU.

C'MON.

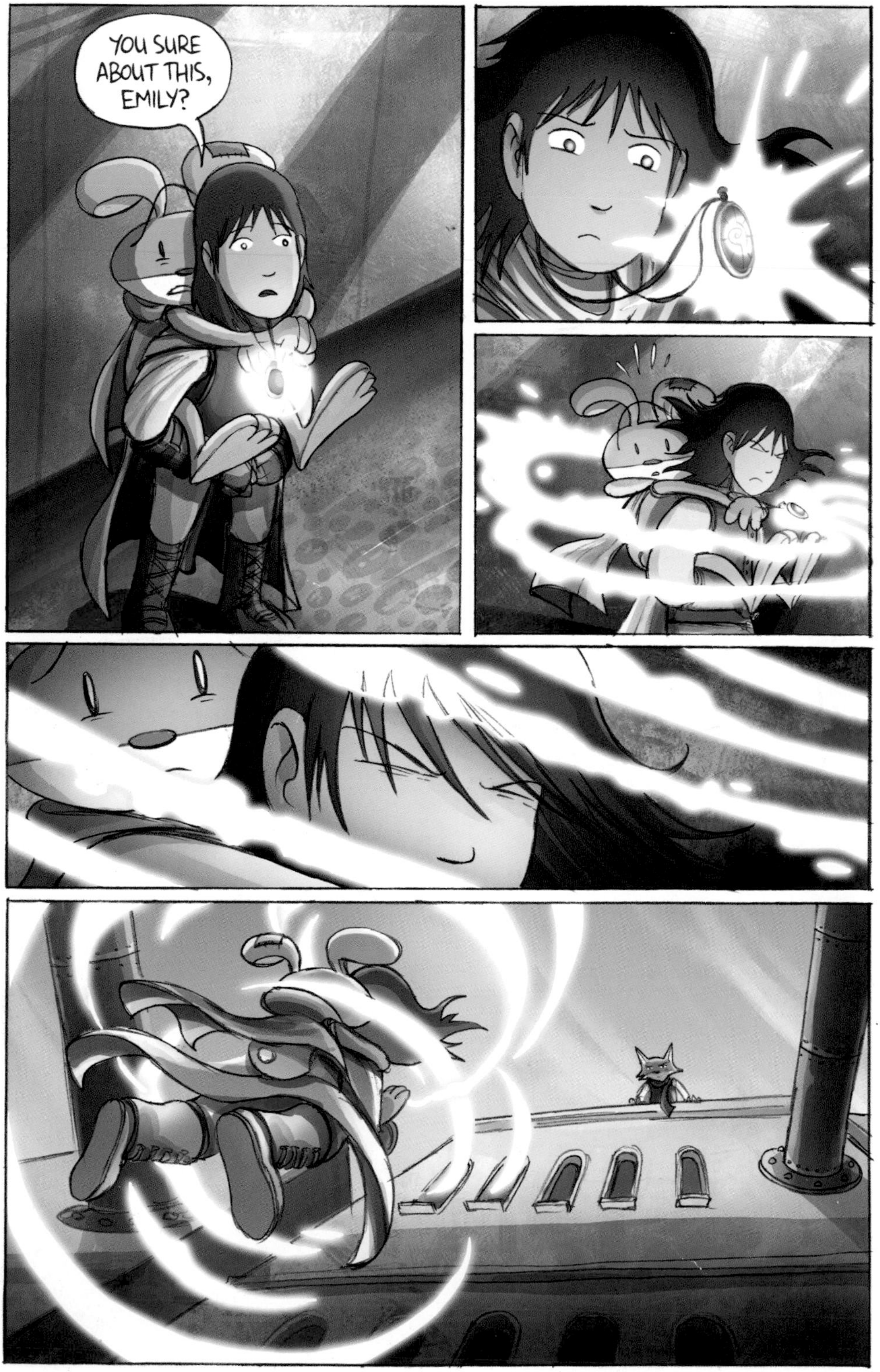
YOU SURE ABOUT THIS, EMILY?

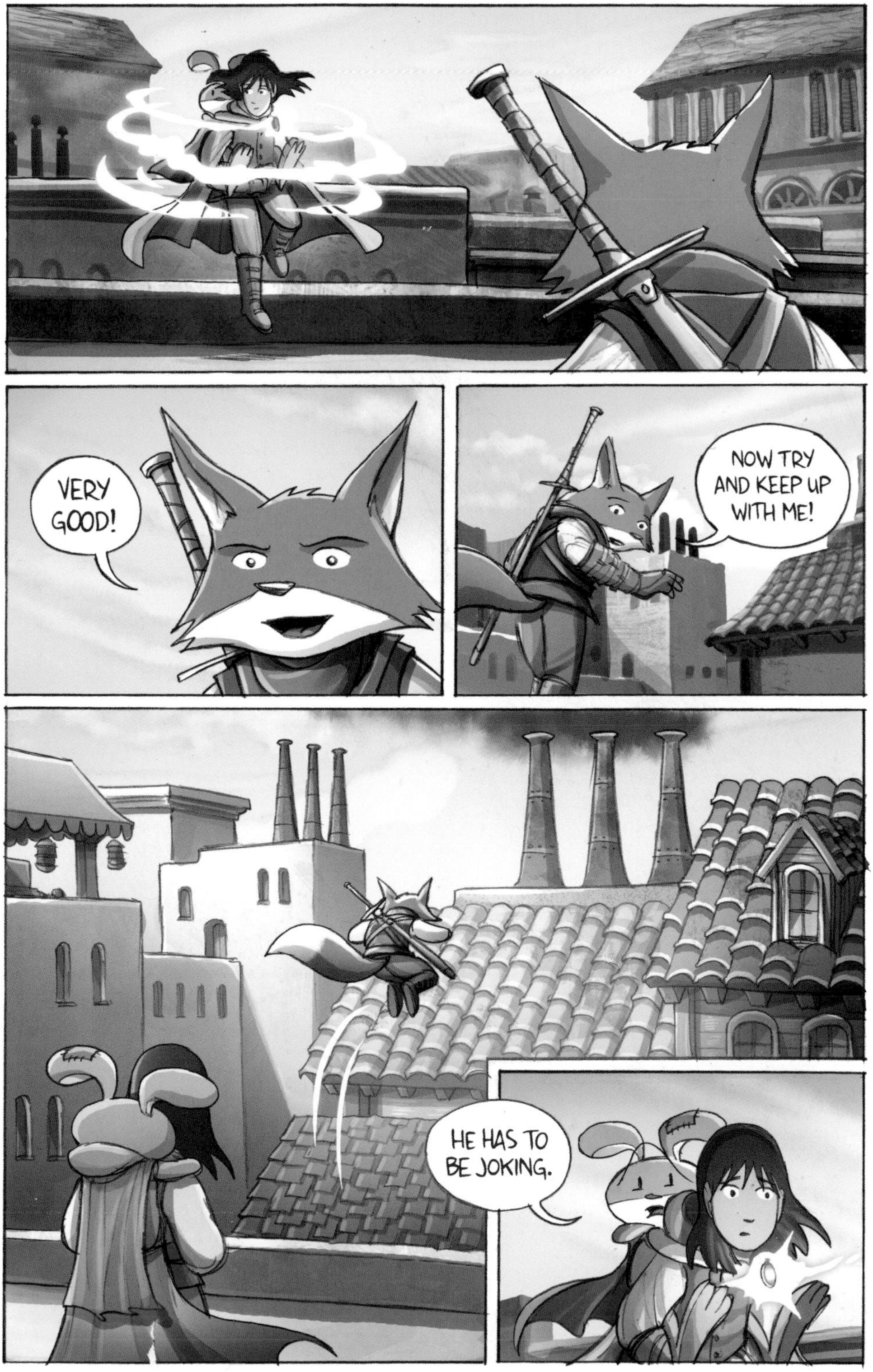
VERY GOOD!
NOW TRY AND KEEP UP WITH ME!
HE HAS TO BE JOKING.

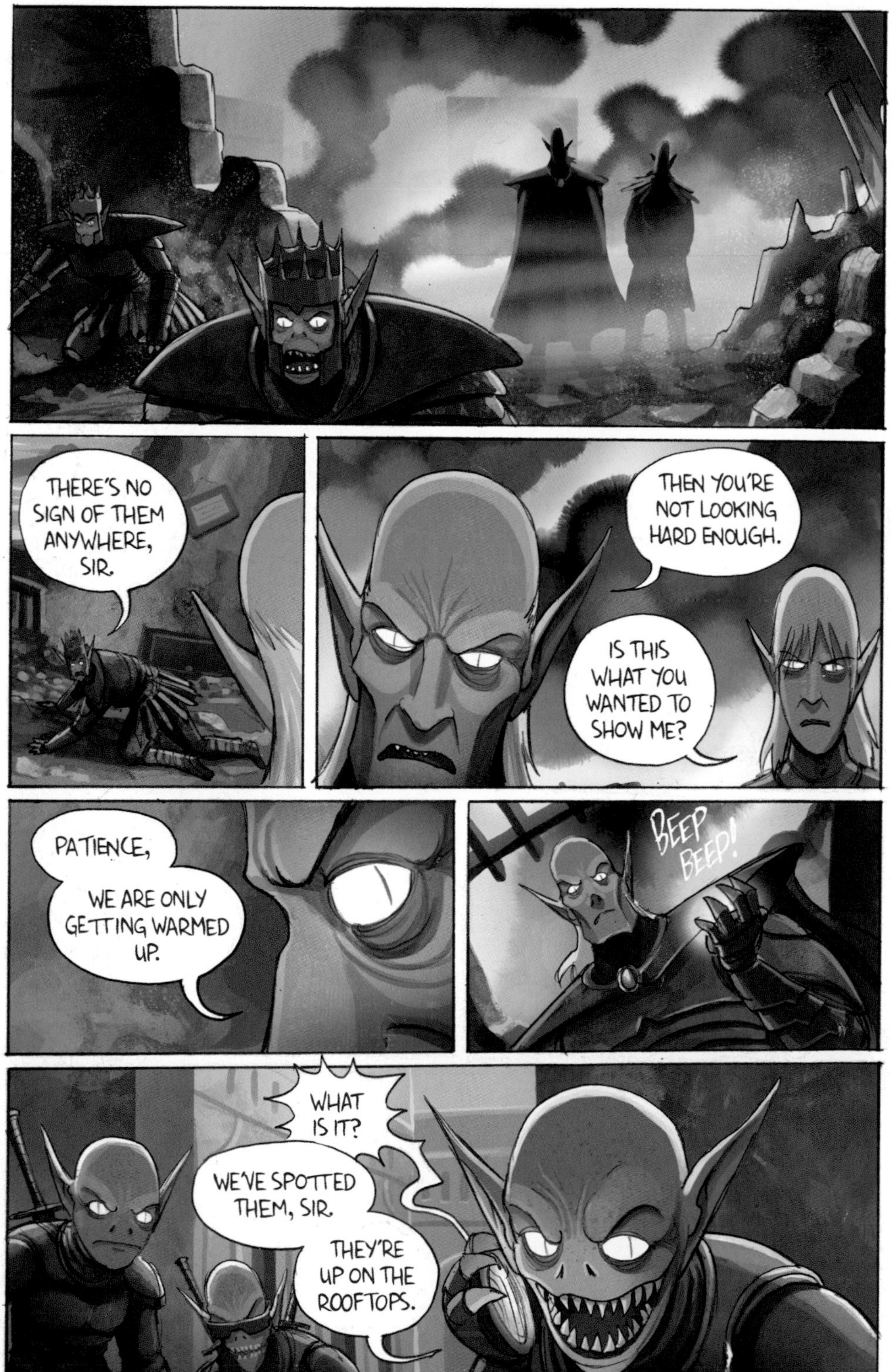
THERE'S NO SIGN OF THEM ANYWHERE, SIR.
THEN YOU'RE NOT LOOKING HARD ENOUGH.
IS THIS WHAT YOU WANTED TO SHOW ME?
PATIENCE,
WE ARE ONLY GETTING WARMED UP.
BEEP BEEP!
WHAT IS IT?
WE'VE SPOTTED THEM, SIR.
THEY'RE UP ON THE ROOFTOPS.

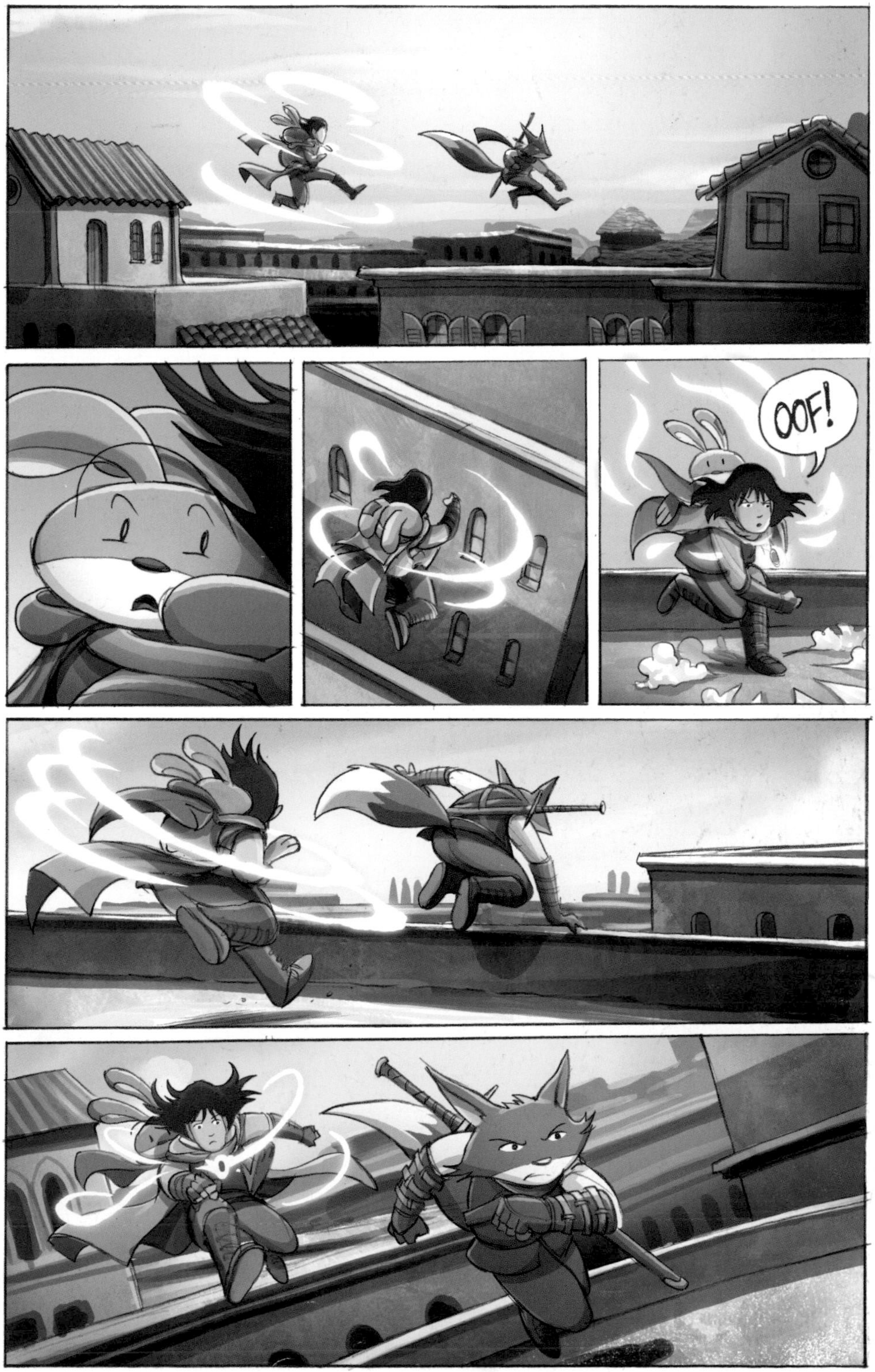
OOF!

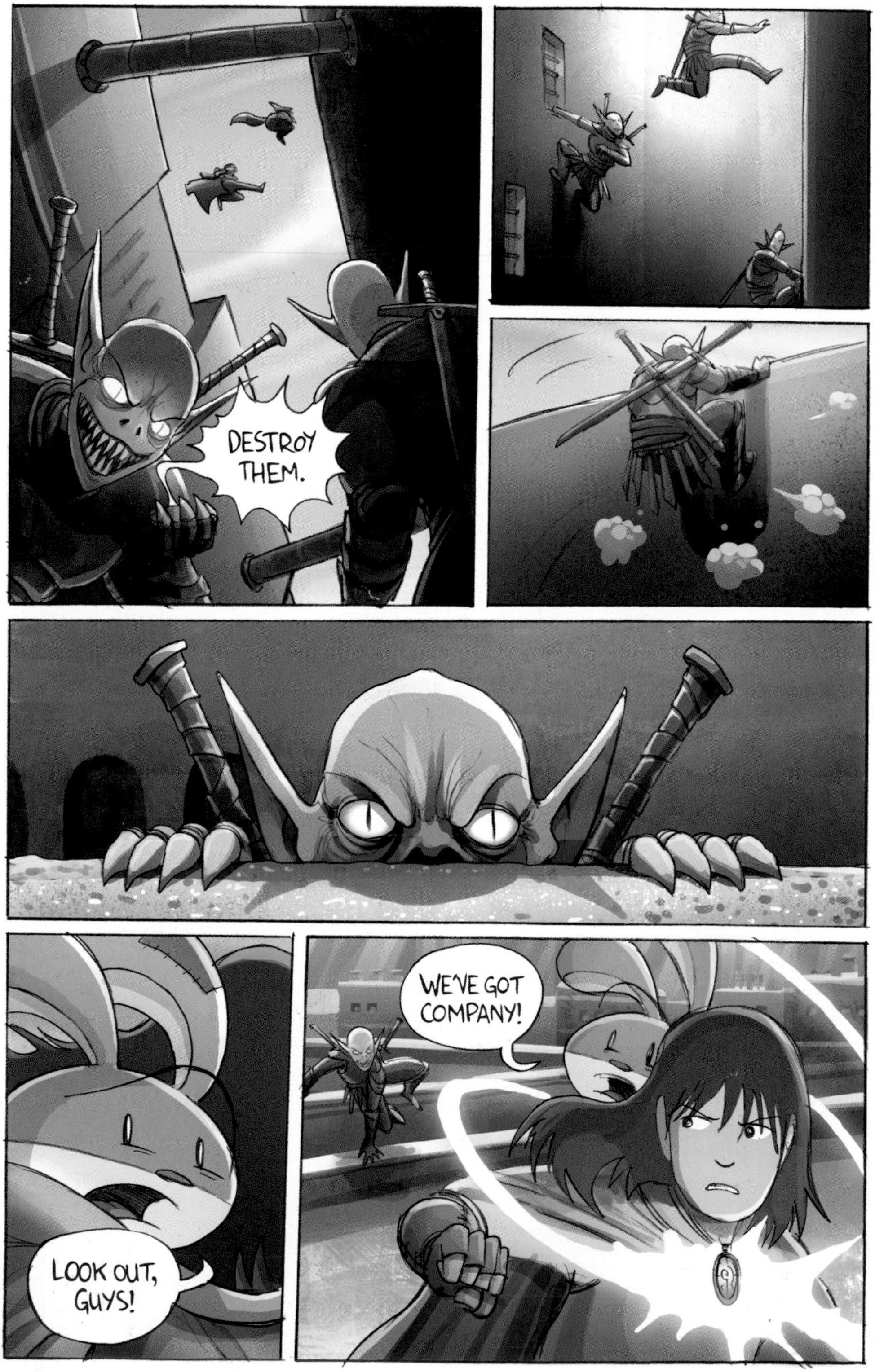
DESTROY THEM.
LOOK OUT, GUYS!
WE'VE GOT COMPANY!

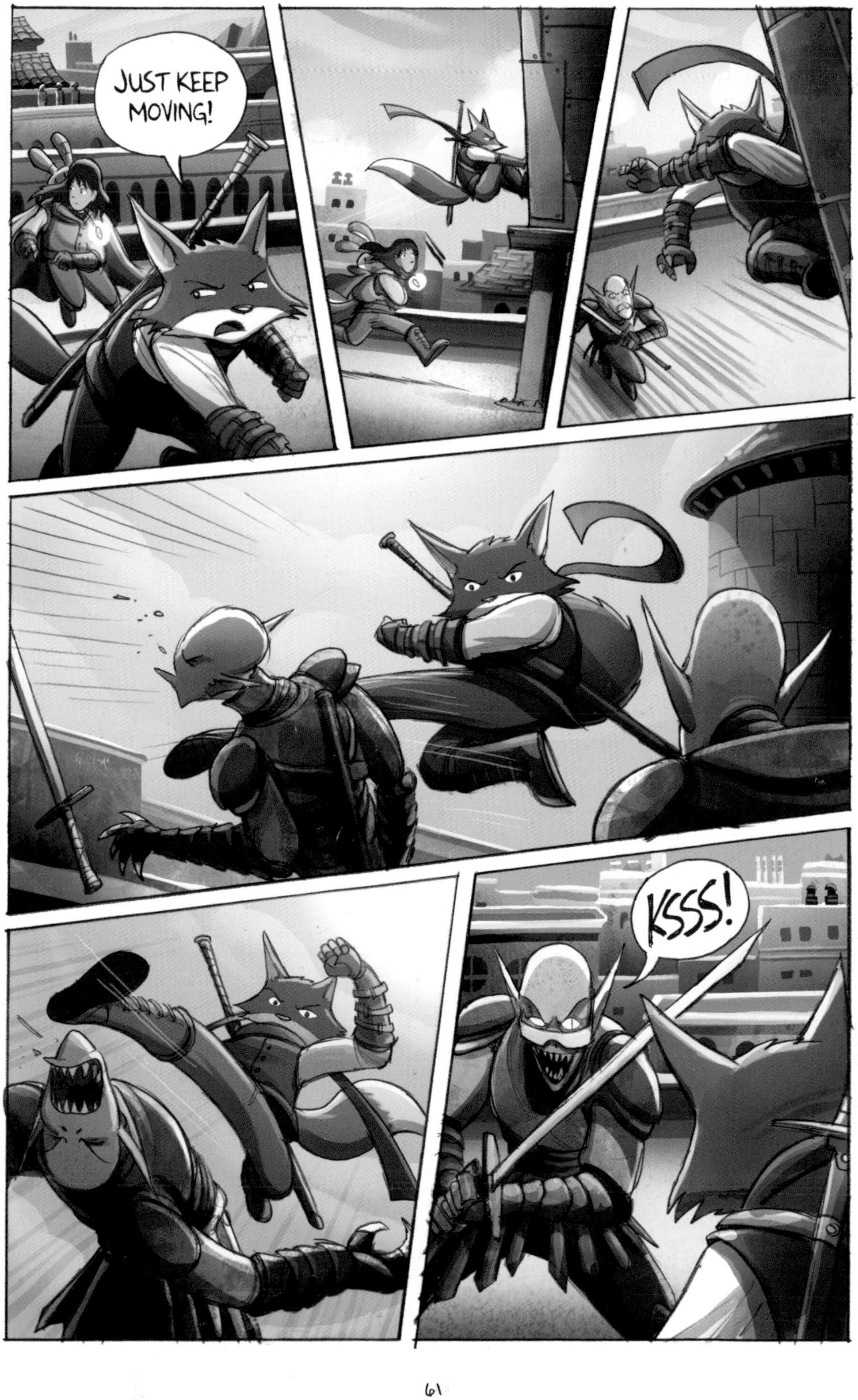
JUST KEEP MOVING!
KSSS!

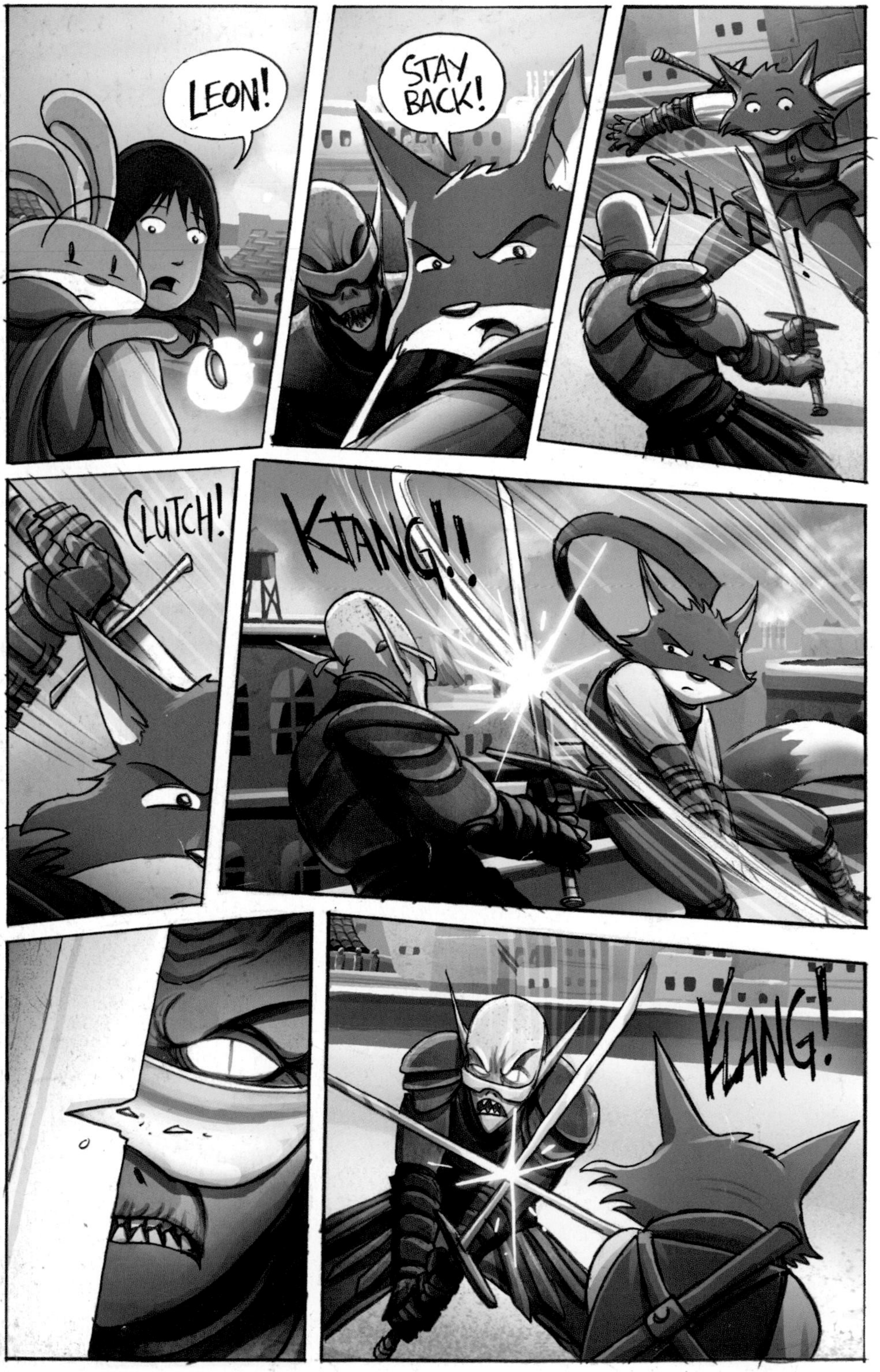
LEON!
STAY BACK!
SLICE!
CLUTCH!
KLANG!!
KLANG!

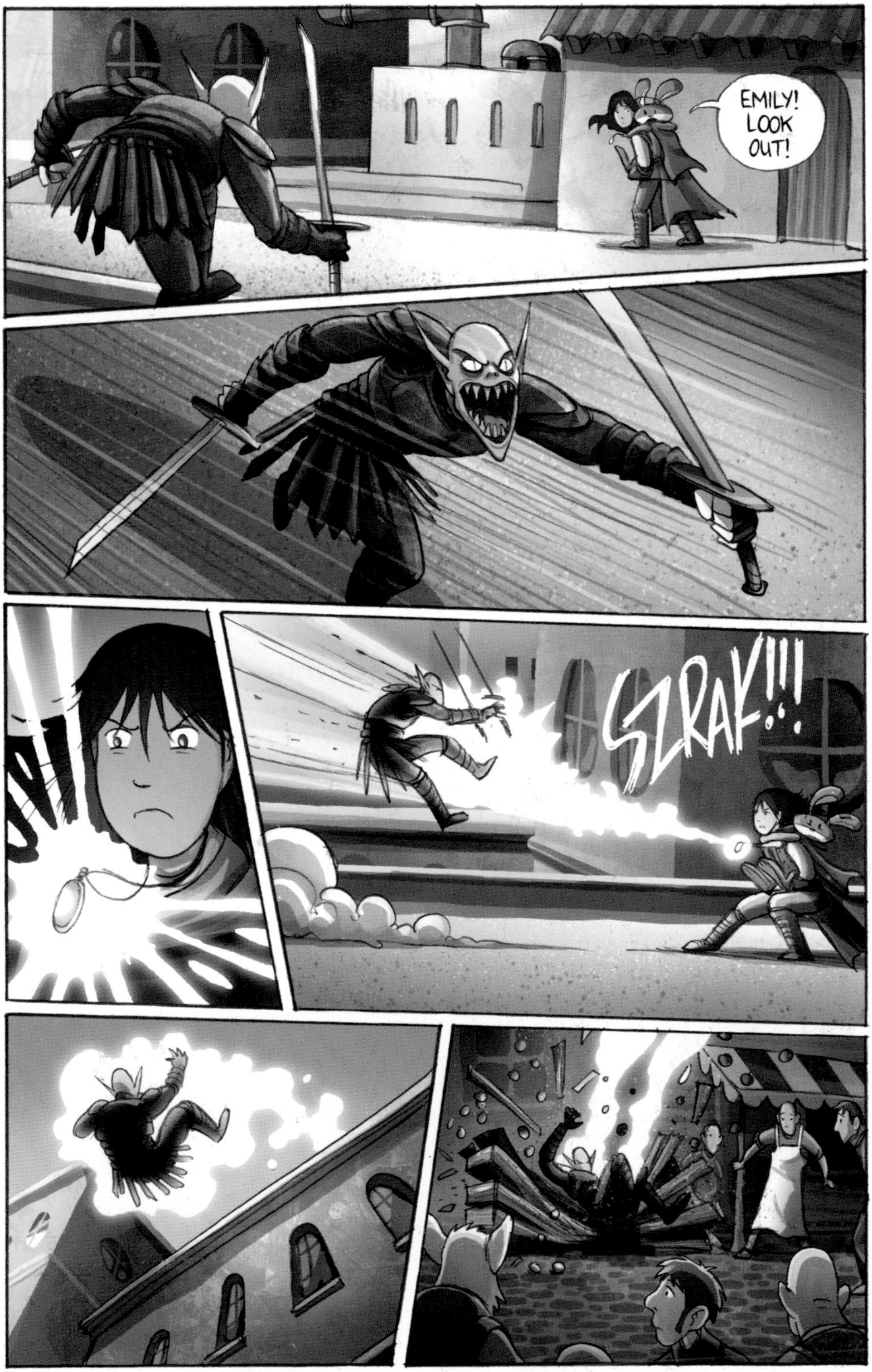
EMILY! LOOK OUT!
SZRAK!!!

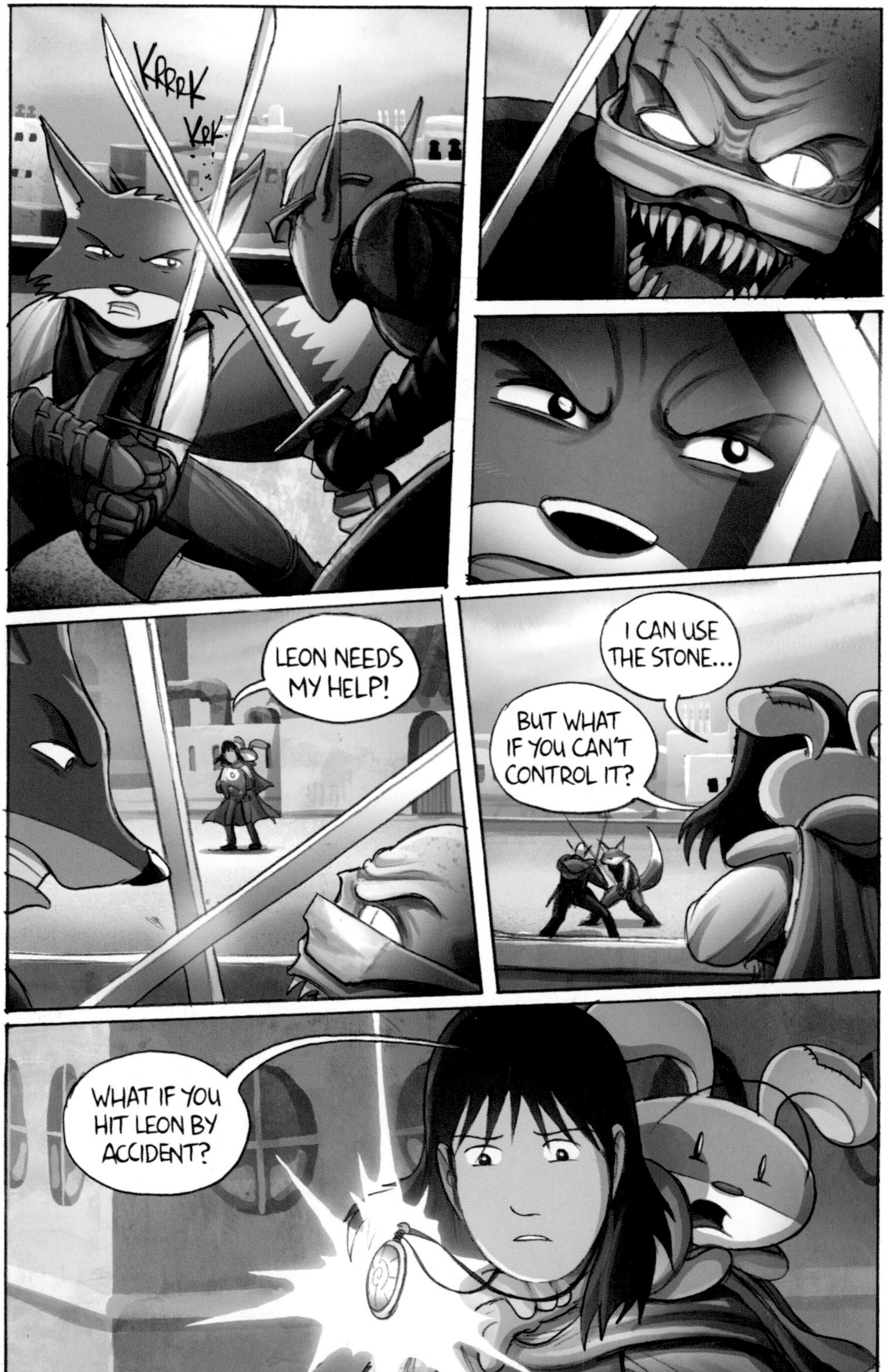
KRRRK
KRK
LEON NEEDS MY HELP!
I CAN USE THE STONE...
BUT WHAT IF YOU CAN'T CONTROL IT?
WHAT IF YOU HIT LEON BY ACCIDENT?

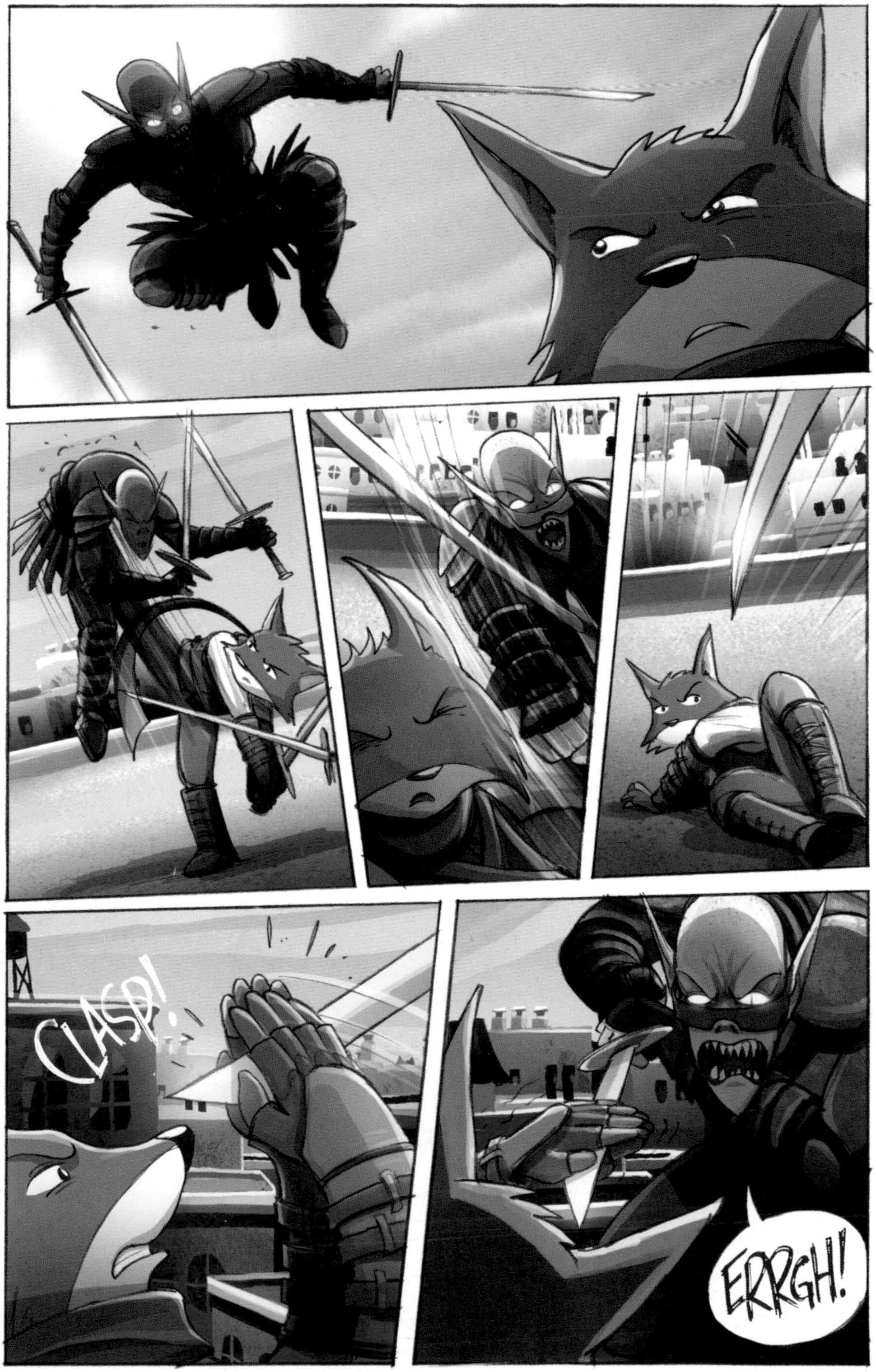
CLASP!
!
ERRGH!

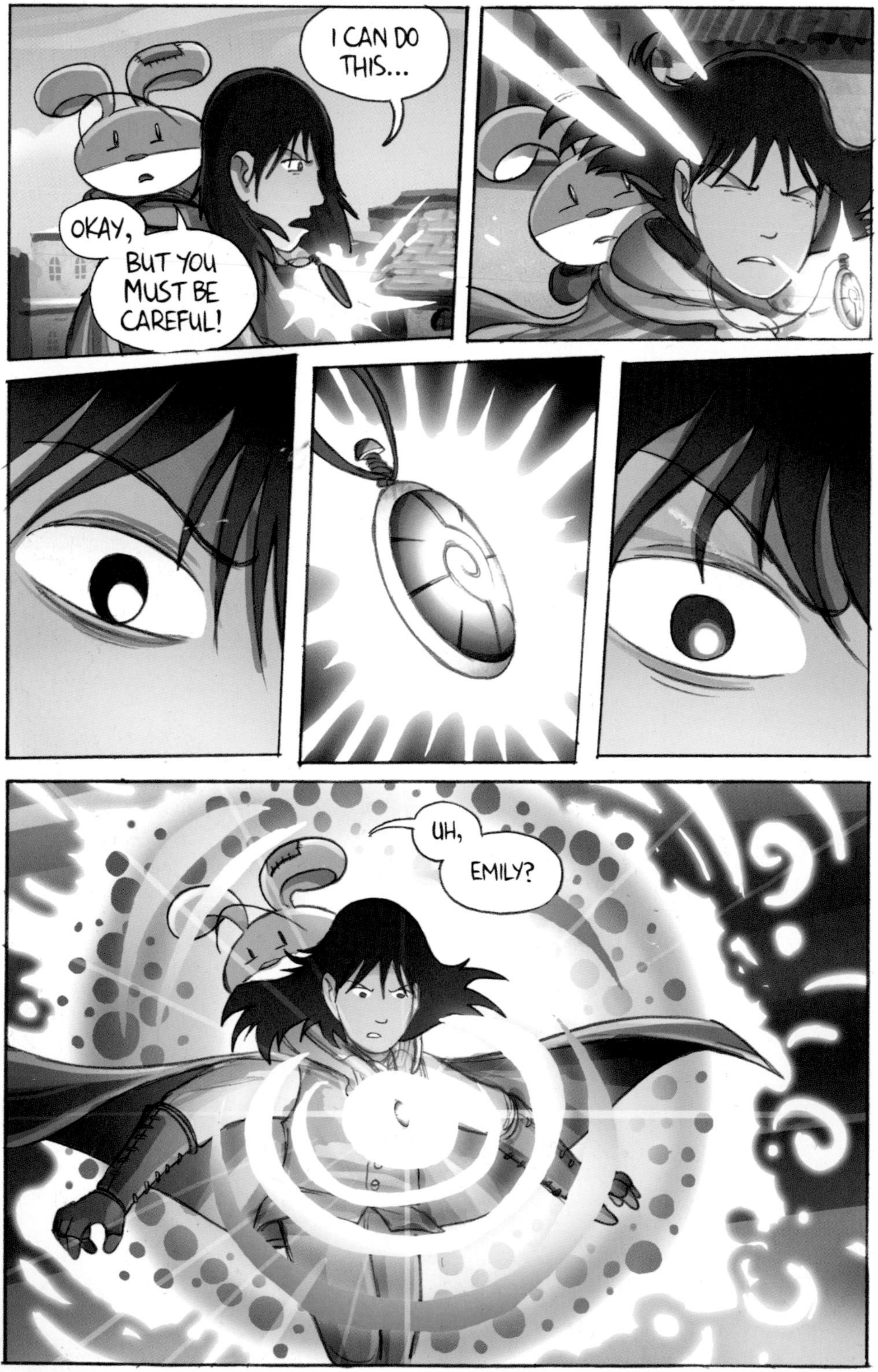
I CAN DO THIS...
OKAY, BUT YOU MUST BE CAREFUL!
UH, EMILY?

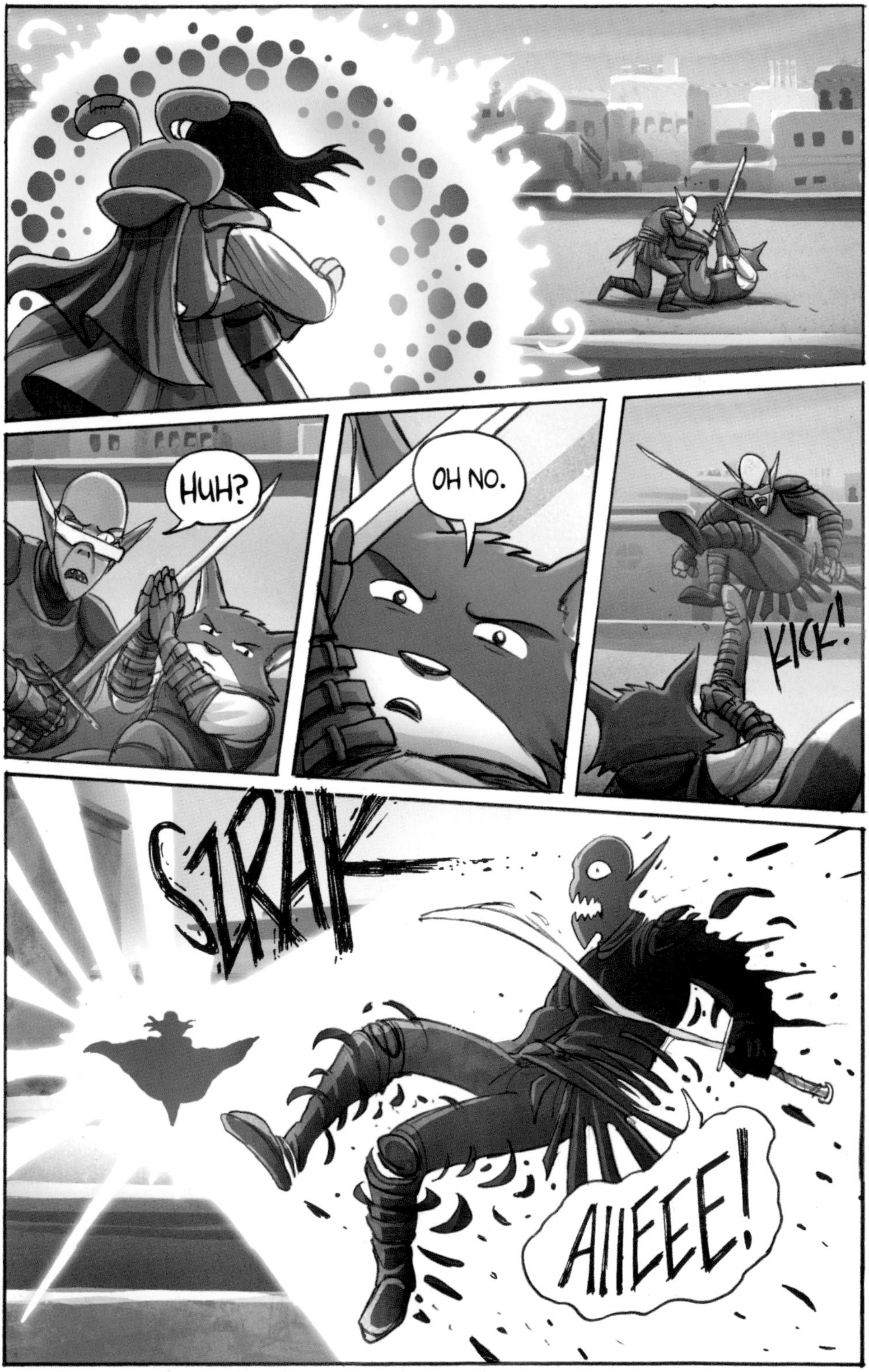
HUH?
OH NO.
KICK!
STRAK
AIIEEE!

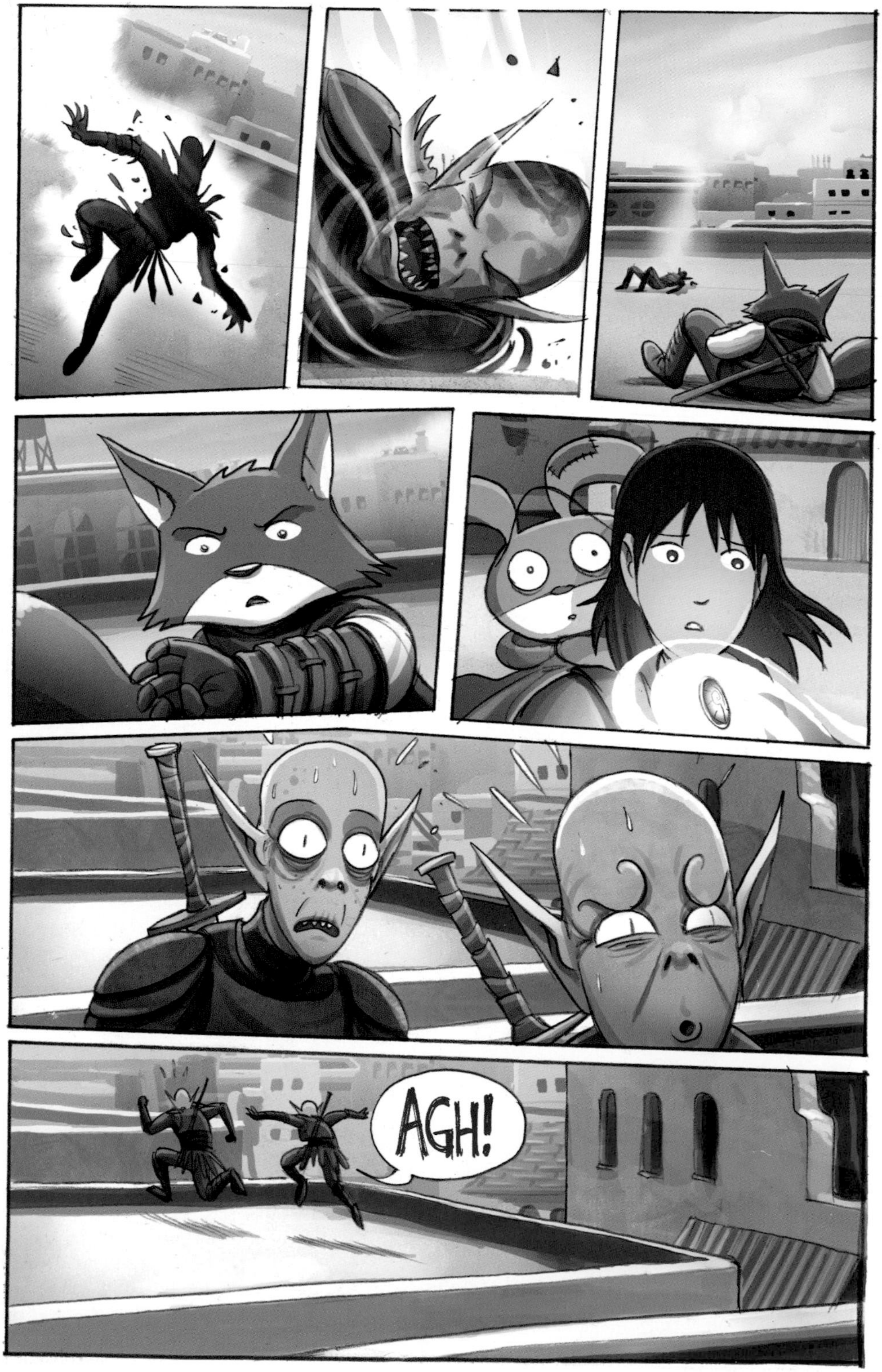
AGH!

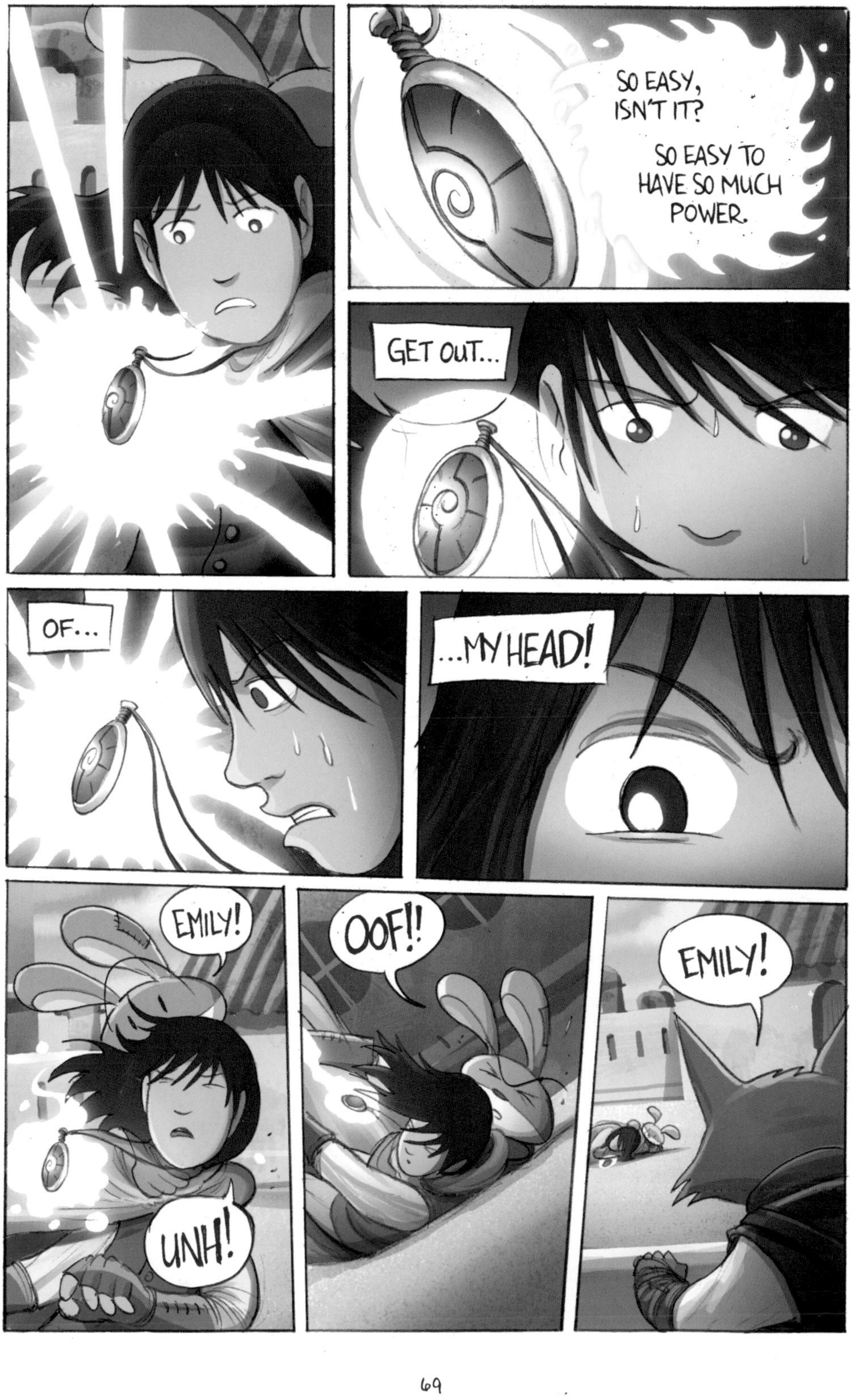
SO EASY, ISN'T IT?
SO EASY TO HAVE SO MUCH POWER.
GET OUT...
OF...
...MY HEAD!
EMILY!
UNH!
OOF!!
EMILY!

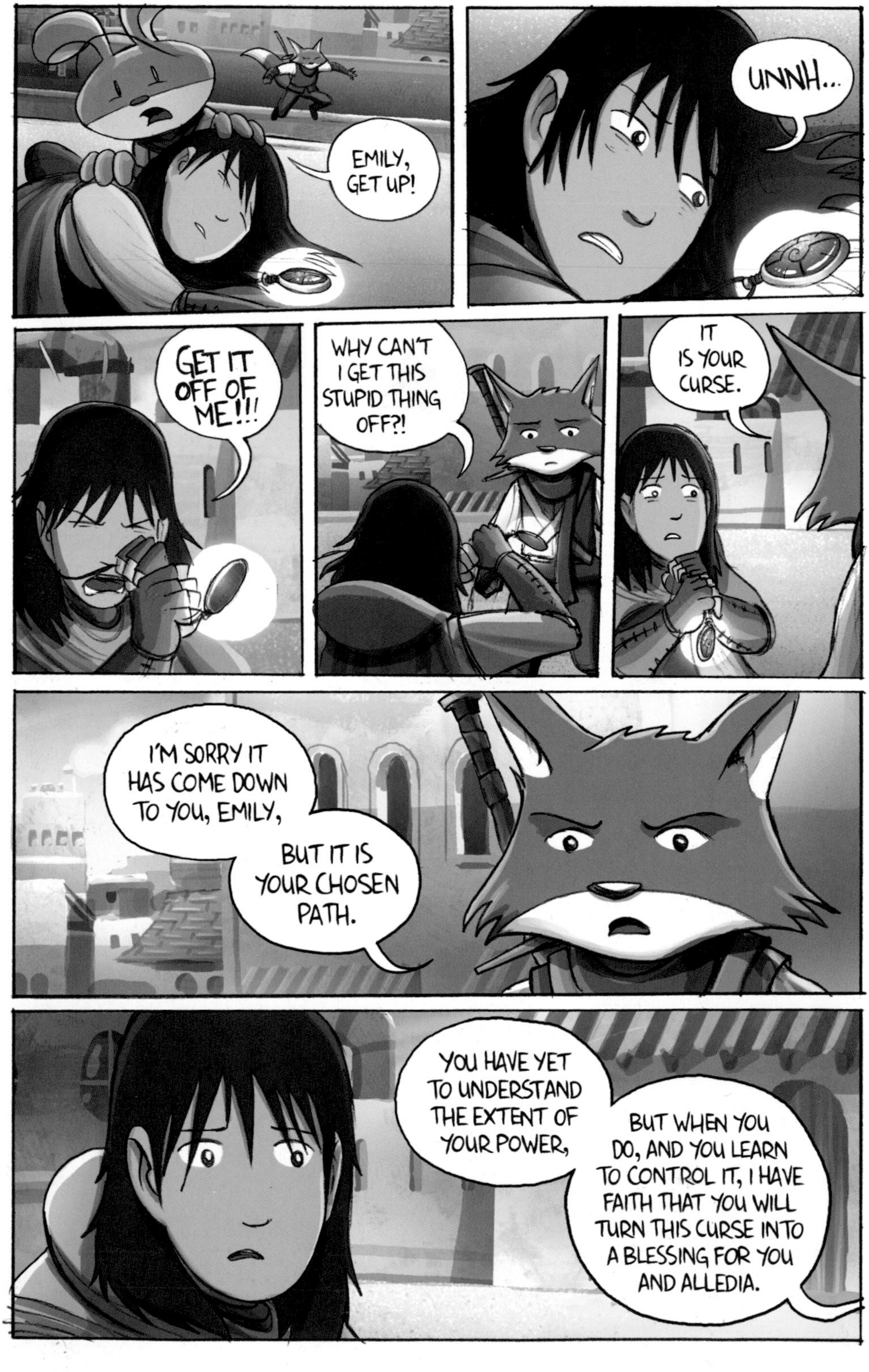
EMILY, GET UP!
UNNH...
GET IT OFF OF ME!!!
WHY CAN'T I GET THIS STUPID THING OFF?!
IT IS YOUR CURSE.
I'M SORRY IT HAS COME DOWN TO YOU, EMILY,
BUT IT IS YOUR CHOSEN PATH.
YOU HAVE YET TO UNDERSTAND THE EXTENT OF YOUR POWER,
BUT WHEN YOU DO, AND YOU LEARN TO CONTROL IT, I HAVE FAITH THAT YOU WILL TURN THIS CURSE INTO A BLESSING FOR YOU AND ALLEDIA.

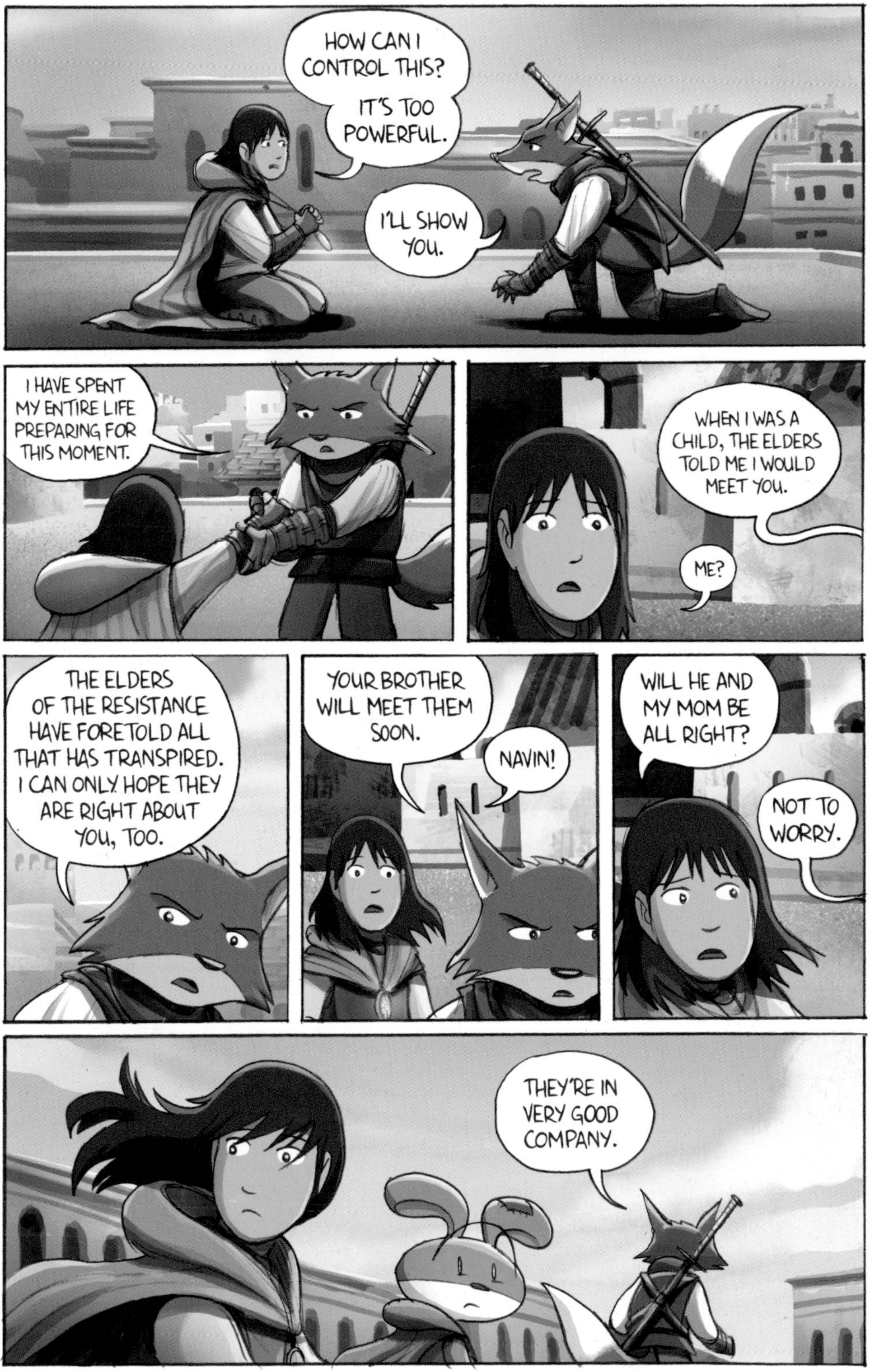
HOW CAN I CONTROL THIS?
IT'S TOO POWERFUL.
I'LL SHOW YOU.
I HAVE SPENT MY ENTIRE LIFE PREPARING FOR THIS MOMENT.
WHEN I WAS A CHILD, THE ELDERS TOLD ME I WOULD MEET YOU.
ME?
THE ELDERS OF THE RESISTANCE HAVE FORETOLD ALL THAT HAS TRANSPIRED. I CAN ONLY HOPE THEY ARE RIGHT ABOUT YOU, TOO.
YOUR BROTHER WILL MEET THEM SOON.
NAVIN!
WILL HE AND MY MOM BE ALL RIGHT?
NOT TO WORRY.
THEY'RE IN VERY GOOD COMPANY.

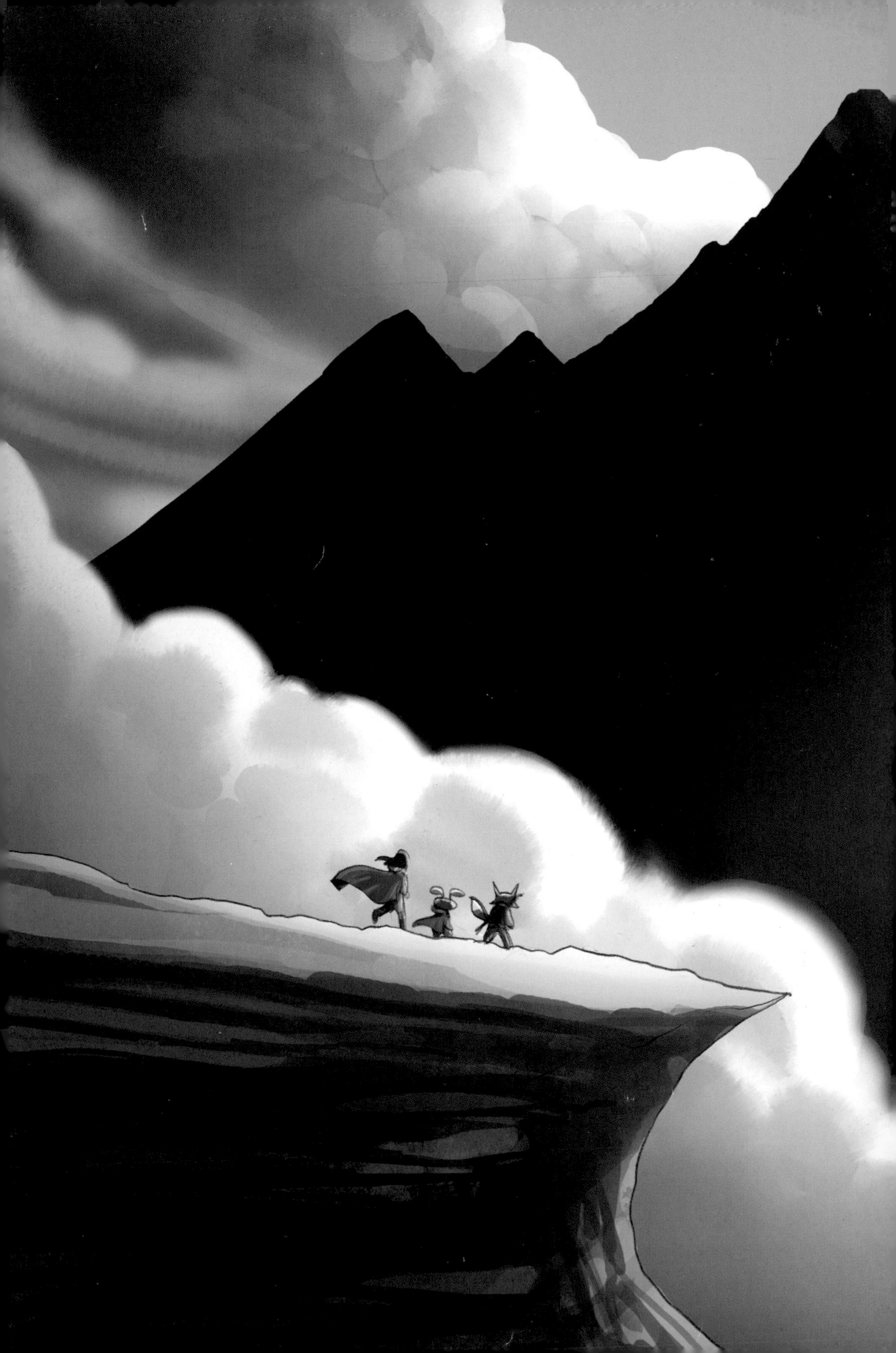

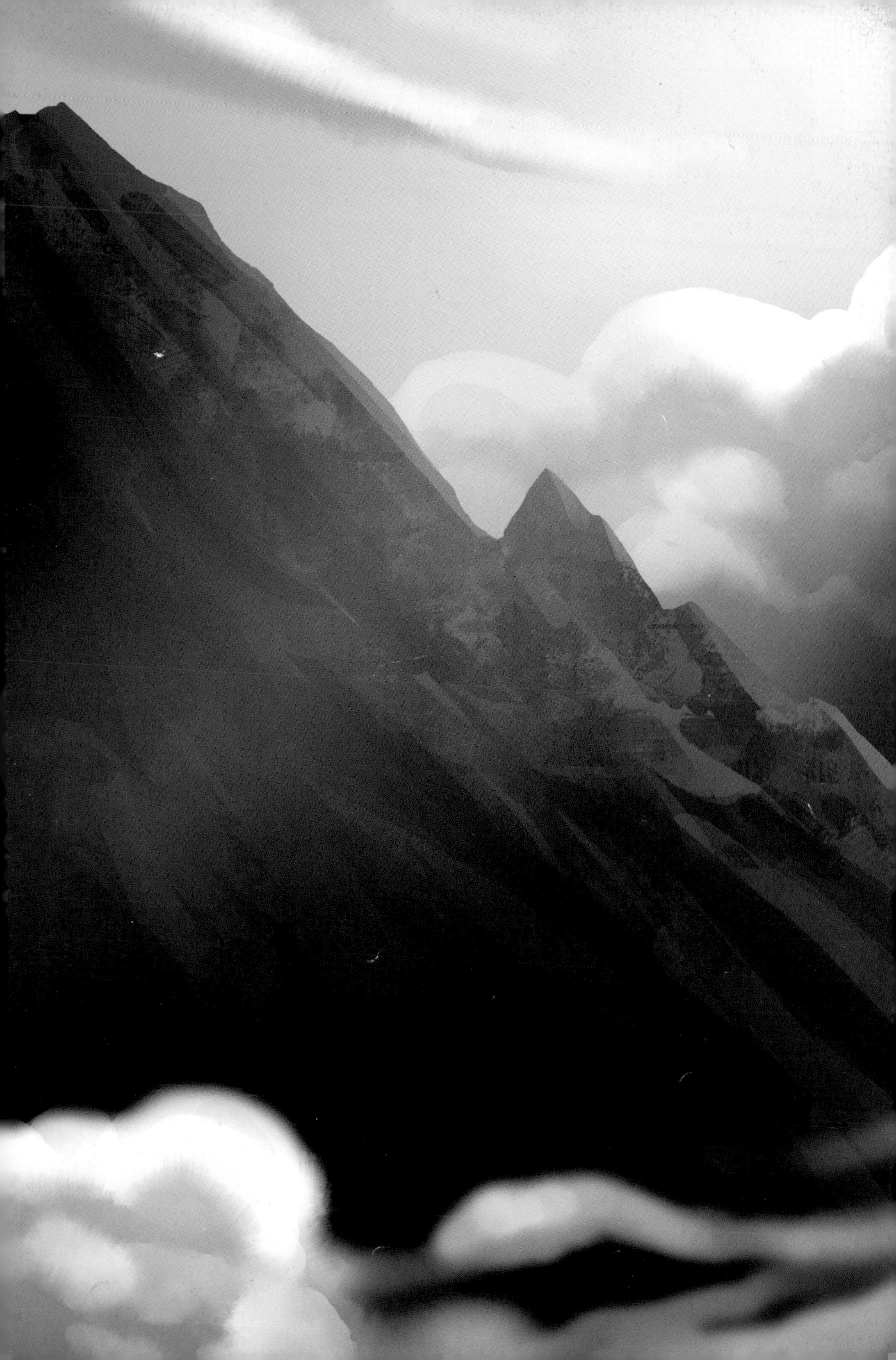

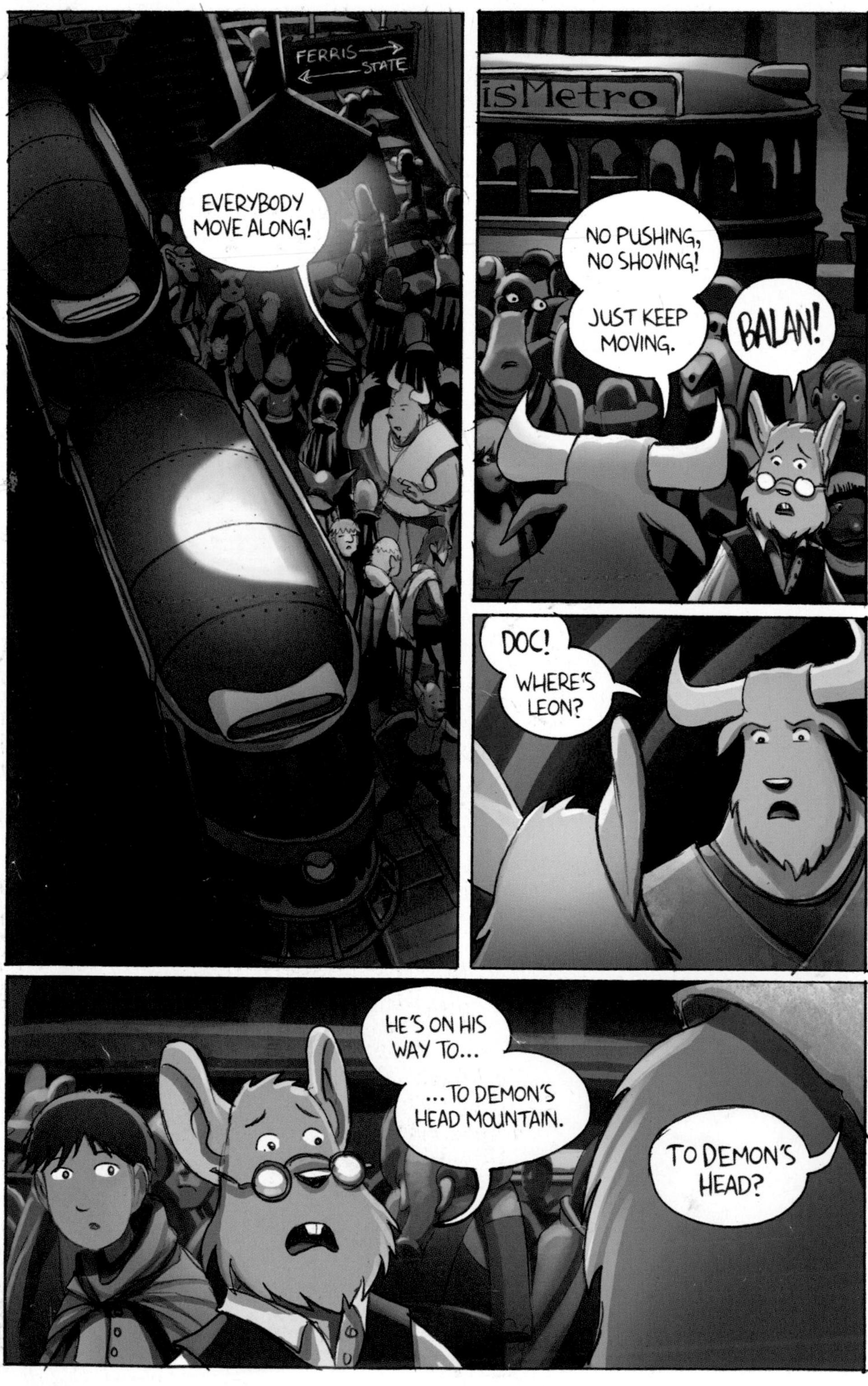
FERRIS
STATE
EVERYBODY MOVE ALONG!
isMetro
NO PUSHING, NO SHOVING!
JUST KEEP MOVING.
BALAN!
DOC!
WHERE'S LEON?
HE'S ON HIS WAY TO...
...TO DEMON'S HEAD MOUNTAIN.
TO DEMON'S HEAD?

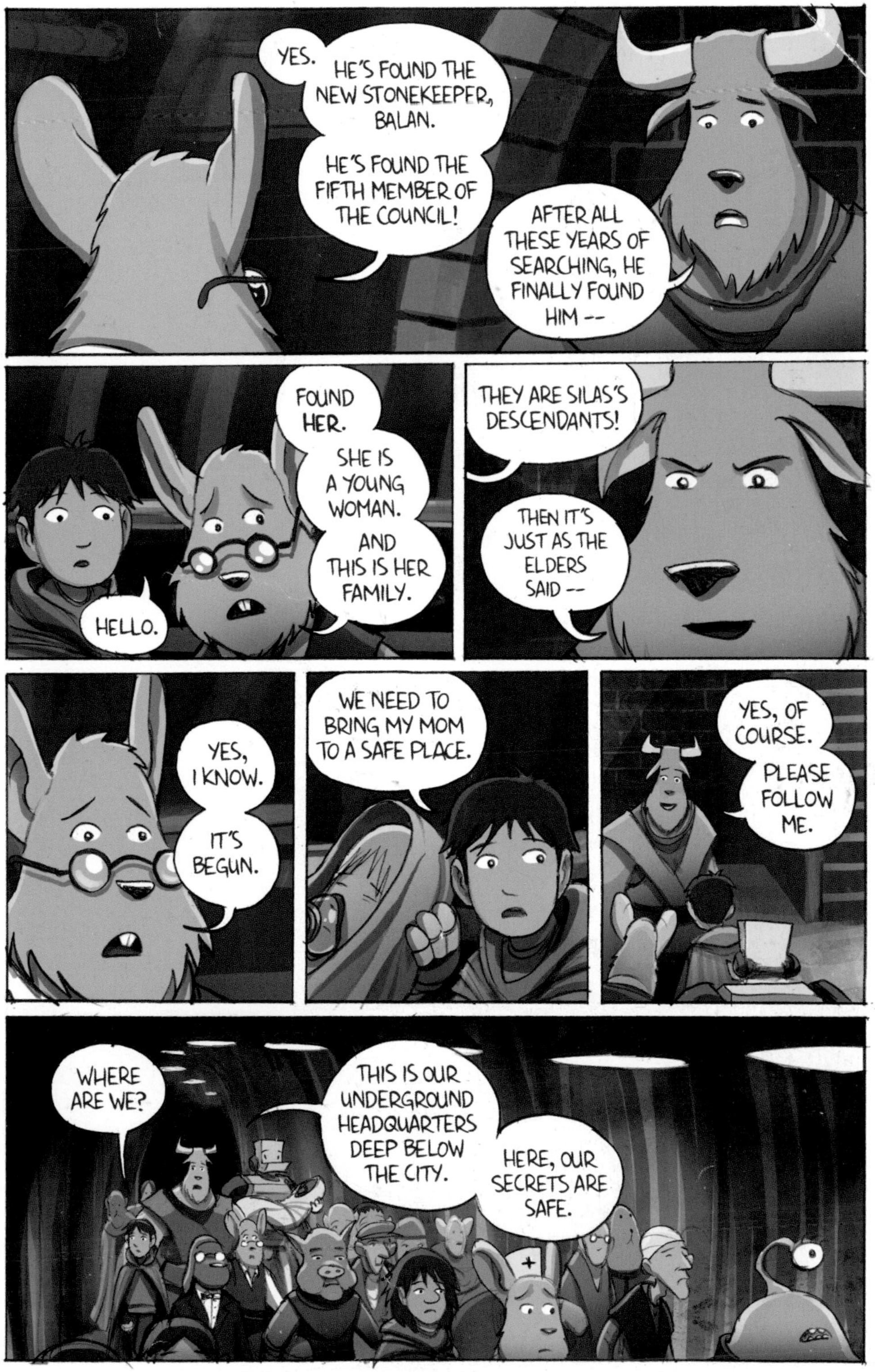
YES.
HE'S FOUND THE NEW STONEKEEPER, BALAN.
HE'S FOUND THE FIFTH MEMBER OF THE COUNCIL!
AFTER ALL THESE YEARS OF SEARCHING, HE FINALLY FOUND HIM --
FOUND HER.
SHE IS A YOUNG WOMAN.
AND THIS IS HER FAMILY.
HELLO.
THEY ARE SILAS'S DESCENDANTS!
THEN IT'S JUST AS THE ELDERS SAID --
YES, I KNOW.
IT'S BEGUN.
WE NEED TO BRING MY MOM TO A SAFE PLACE.
YES, OF COURSE.
PLEASE FOLLOW ME.
WHERE ARE WE?
THIS IS OUR UNDERGROUND HEADQUARTERS DEEP BELOW THE CITY.
HERE, OUR SECRETS ARE SAFE.

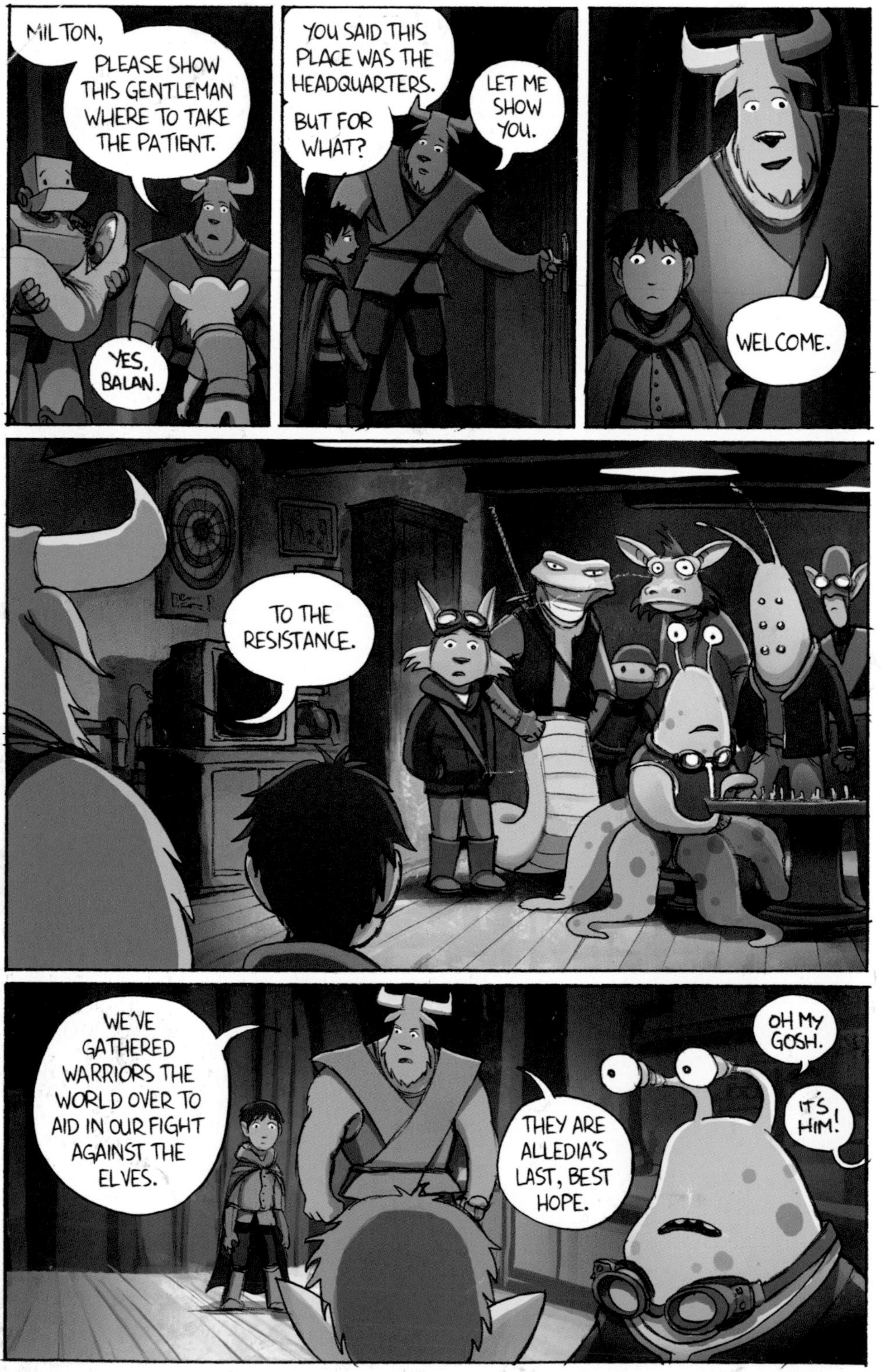
MILTON,
PLEASE SHOW THIS GENTLEMAN WHERE TO TAKE THE PATIENT.
YES, BALAN.
YOU SAID THIS PLACE WAS THE HEADQUARTERS.
BUT FOR WHAT?
LET ME SHOW YOU.
WELCOME.
TO THE RESISTANCE.
WE'VE GATHERED WARRIORS THE WORLD OVER TO AID IN OUR FIGHT AGAINST THE ELVES.
THEY ARE ALLEDIA'S LAST, BEST HOPE.
OH MY GOSH.
IT'S HIM!

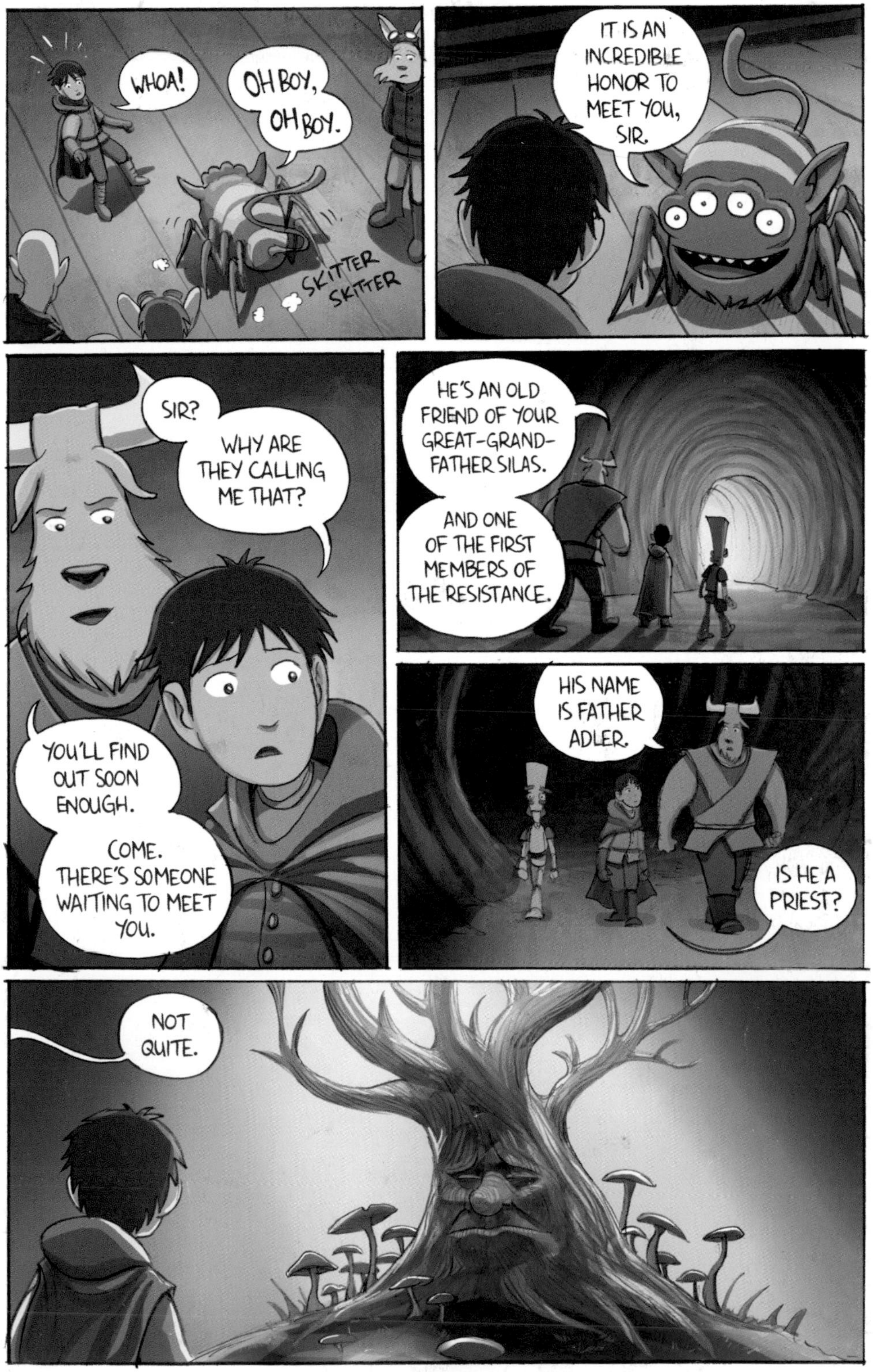
WHOA!
OH BOY, OH BOY.
SKITTER SKITTER
IT IS AN INCREDIBLE HONOR TO MEET YOU, SIR.
SIR?
WHY ARE THEY CALLING ME THAT?
YOU'LL FIND OUT SOON ENOUGH.
COME. THERE'S SOMEONE WAITING TO MEET YOU.
HE'S AN OLD FRIEND OF YOUR GREAT-GRAND-FATHER SILAS.
AND ONE OF THE FIRST MEMBERS OF THE RESISTANCE.
HIS NAME IS FATHER ADLER.
IS HE A PRIEST?
NOT QUITE.

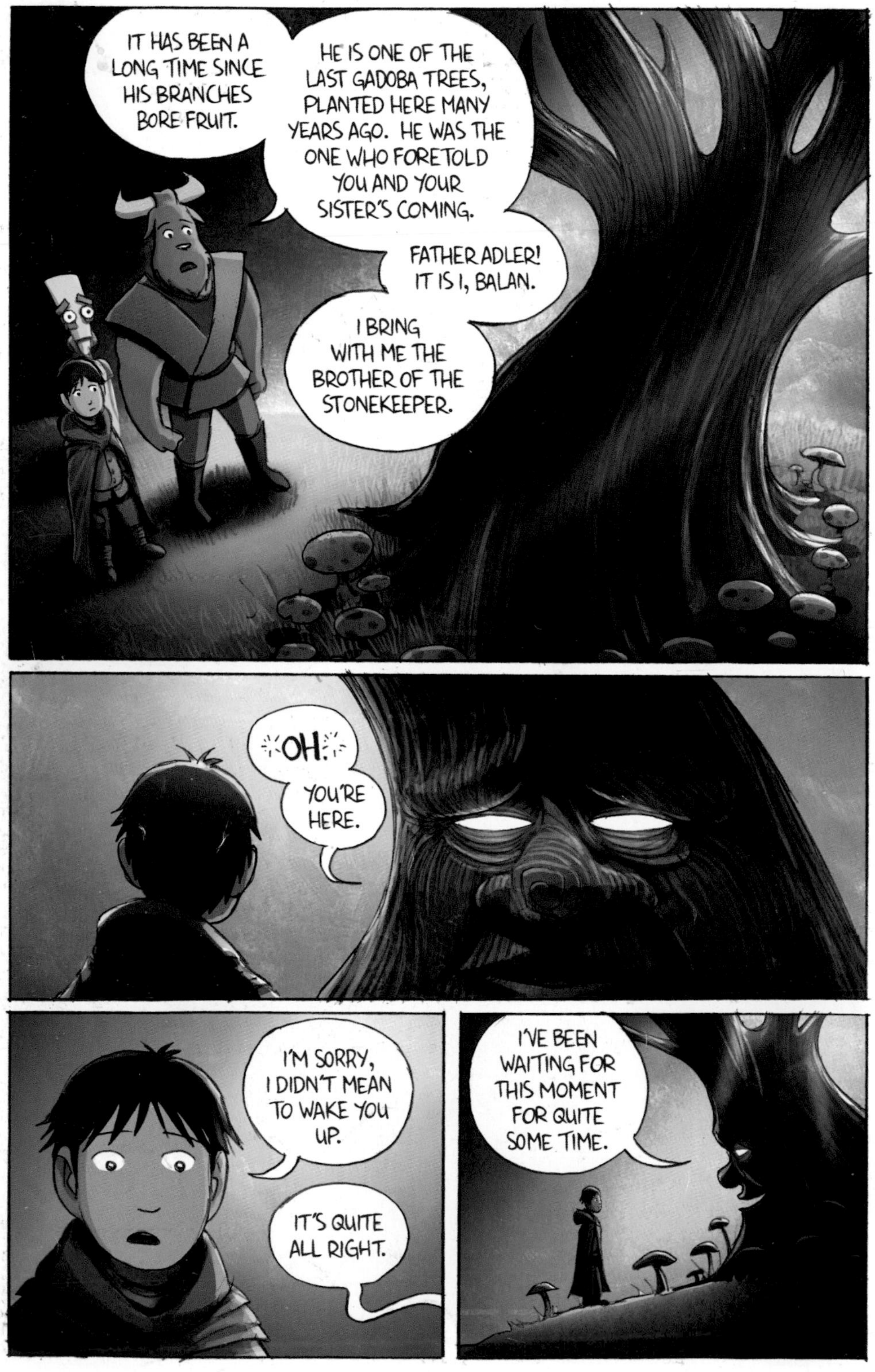
IT HAS BEEN A LONG TIME SINCE HIS BRANCHES BORE FRUIT.
HE IS ONE OF THE LAST GADOBA TREES, PLANTED HERE MANY YEARS AGO. HE WAS THE ONE WHO FORETOLD YOU AND YOUR SISTER'S COMING.
FATHER ADLER! IT IS I, BALAN.
I BRING WITH ME THE BROTHER OF THE STONEKEEPER.
OH.
YOU'RE HERE.
I'M SORRY, I DIDN'T MEAN TO WAKE YOU UP.
IT'S QUITE ALL RIGHT.
I'VE BEEN WAITING FOR THIS MOMENT FOR QUITE SOME TIME.

PLEASE, HAVE A SEAT.

DO YOU KNOW WHY YOU'RE HERE?

WE'RE HERE TO SAVE MY MOM'S LIFE.

OH, BUT YOU WILL DO MUCH MORE THAN THAT.

SO YOU CAN REALLY SEE THE FUTURE?

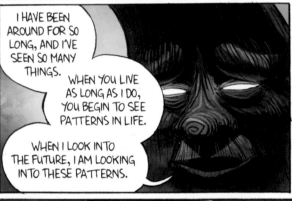

I HAVE BEEN AROUND FOR SO LONG, AND I'VE SEEN SO MANY THINGS.

WHEN YOU LIVE AS LONG AS I DO, YOU BEGIN TO SEE PATTERNS IN LIFE.

WHEN I LOOK INTO THE FUTURE, I AM LOOKING INTO THESE PATTERNS.

YOU CREATURES ARE NOT AS COMPLEX AS YOU MAKE YOURSELVES OUT TO BE.

IF YOU REALLY CAN SEE INTO THE FUTURE, THEN PLEASE TELL ME...

WILL MY SISTER BE OKAY?

IF THERE IS ONLY BAD NEWS TO TELL, DO YOU STILL WISH TO HEAR IT?

IT MIGHT BE BETTER TO SIMPLY HOPE FOR THE BEST.

I NEED TO KNOW THE TRUTH.

WILL SHE BE OKAY?

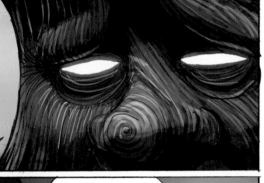

I SEE THE IMAGE OF YOUR SISTER ARRIVING AT THE SUMMIT OF DEMON'S HEAD MOUNTAIN.

THERE SHE WILL MEET MY BROTHERS, AND SHE WILL ATTEMPT TO PICK THE FRUIT THAT WILL CURE YOUR MOTHER.

THE IMAGES THAT FOLLOW ARE MUCH LESS CLEAR.

BUT ONE PICTURE APPEARS VIVIDLY.

IT IS THE IMAGE OF YOUR SISTER FALLING OFF OF A CLIFF.

SHE IS UNCONSCIOUS, AND DEATH AWAITS HER BELOW.

NO.

MORRIE! WE HAVE TO LEAVE!

NOW!

WAIT! YOU'RE SUPPOSED TO HEAR ABOUT YOUR FUTURE!

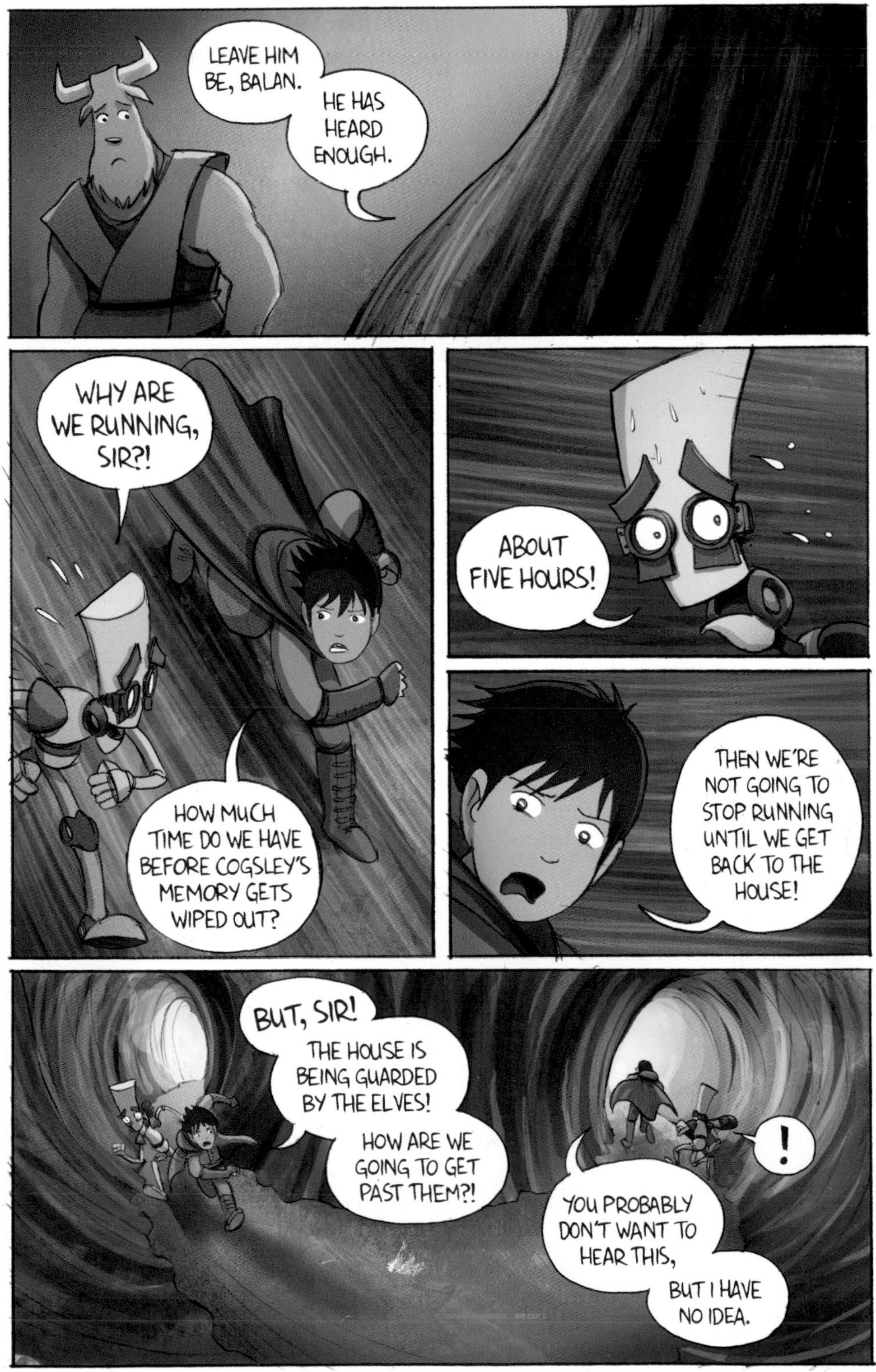

LEAVE HIM BE, BALAN.
HE HAS HEARD ENOUGH.
WHY ARE WE RUNNING, SIR?!
HOW MUCH TIME DO WE HAVE BEFORE COGSLEY'S MEMORY GETS WIPED OUT?
ABOUT FIVE HOURS!
THEN WE'RE NOT GOING TO STOP RUNNING UNTIL WE GET BACK TO THE HOUSE!
BUT, SIR!
THE HOUSE IS BEING GUARDED BY THE ELVES!
HOW ARE WE GOING TO GET PAST THEM?!
!
YOU PROBABLY DON'T WANT TO HEAR THIS,
BUT I HAVE NO IDEA.

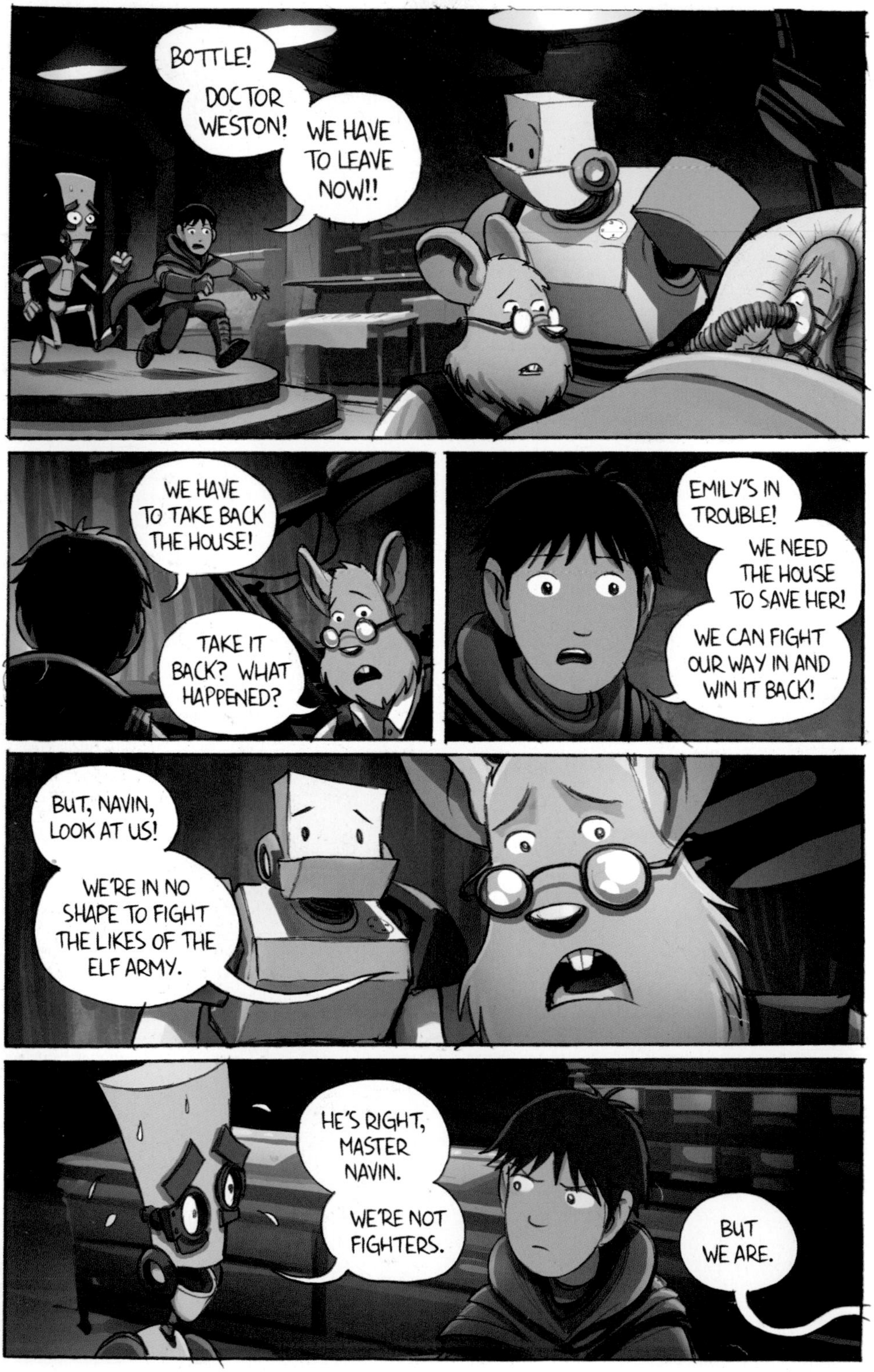
BOTTLE!
DOCTOR WESTON!
WE HAVE TO LEAVE NOW!!
WE HAVE TO TAKE BACK THE HOUSE!
TAKE IT BACK? WHAT HAPPENED?
EMILY'S IN TROUBLE!
WE NEED THE HOUSE TO SAVE HER!
WE CAN FIGHT OUR WAY IN AND WIN IT BACK!
BUT, NAVIN, LOOK AT US!
WE'RE IN NO SHAPE TO FIGHT THE LIKES OF THE ELF ARMY.
HE'S RIGHT, MASTER NAVIN.
WE'RE NOT FIGHTERS.
BUT WE ARE.

PARDON THE INTERRUPTION, SIR, BUT IT SOUNDS LIKE YOU COULD USE AN ARMY.

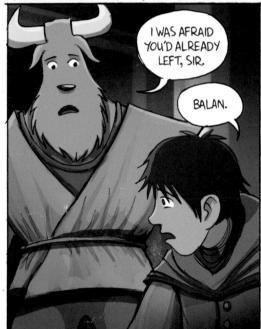

I WAS AFRAID YOU'D ALREADY LEFT, SIR.

BALAN.

NOT YOU, TOO! WHY IS EVERYONE CALLING ME 'SIR'?

BECAUSE YOU ARE THIS ARMY'S COMMANDER.

C-COMMANDER?

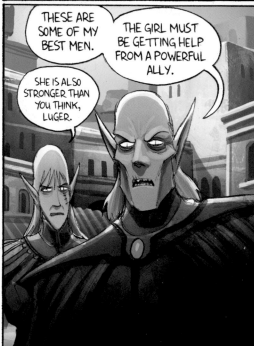

THESE ARE SOME OF MY BEST MEN.

THE GIRL MUST BE GETTING HELP FROM A POWERFUL ALLY.

SHE IS ALSO STRONGER THAN YOU THINK, LUGER.

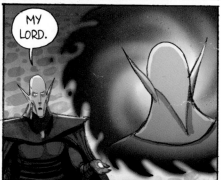

MY LORD.

THE YOUNG STONEKEEPER HAS ESCAPED, AND SHE IS BEING AIDED BY A FORMIDABLE WARRIOR.

YOUR MISSION REMAINS CLEAR.

TRACK THEM DOWN AND KILL THEM BOTH.

YES, MY LORD.

I THOUGHT OUR JOB WAS TO CAPTURE HER.

NOT KILL HER.

MERCY IS FOR THE WEAK, BOY.

IF SHE WILL NOT JOIN US, THEN KILLING HER IS OUR ONLY OPTION.

SHE IS FAR TOO DANGEROUS TO BE LEFT ALONE.

LUGER, I WOULD LIKE TRELLIS TO BE THE ONE TO DELIVER THE FATAL BLOW.

BY KILLING THE GIRL, HE CAN PROVE HIS LOYALTY TO ME.

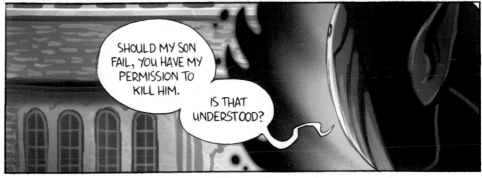

SHOULD MY SON FAIL, YOU HAVE MY PERMISSION TO KILL HIM.

IS THAT UNDERSTOOD?

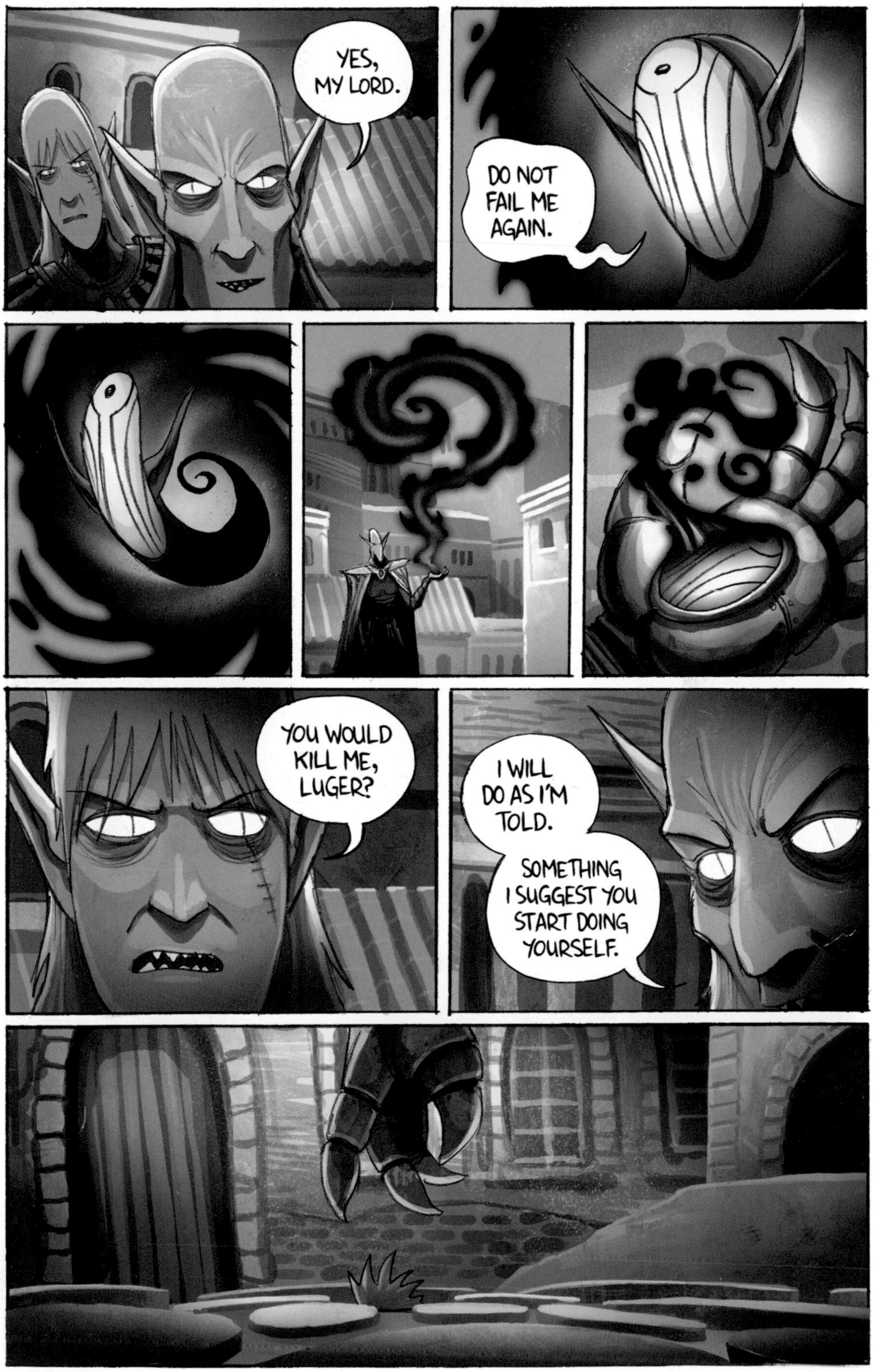
YES, MY LORD.
DO NOT FAIL ME AGAIN.
YOU WOULD KILL ME, LUGER?
I WILL DO AS I'M TOLD.
SOMETHING I SUGGEST YOU START DOING YOURSELF.

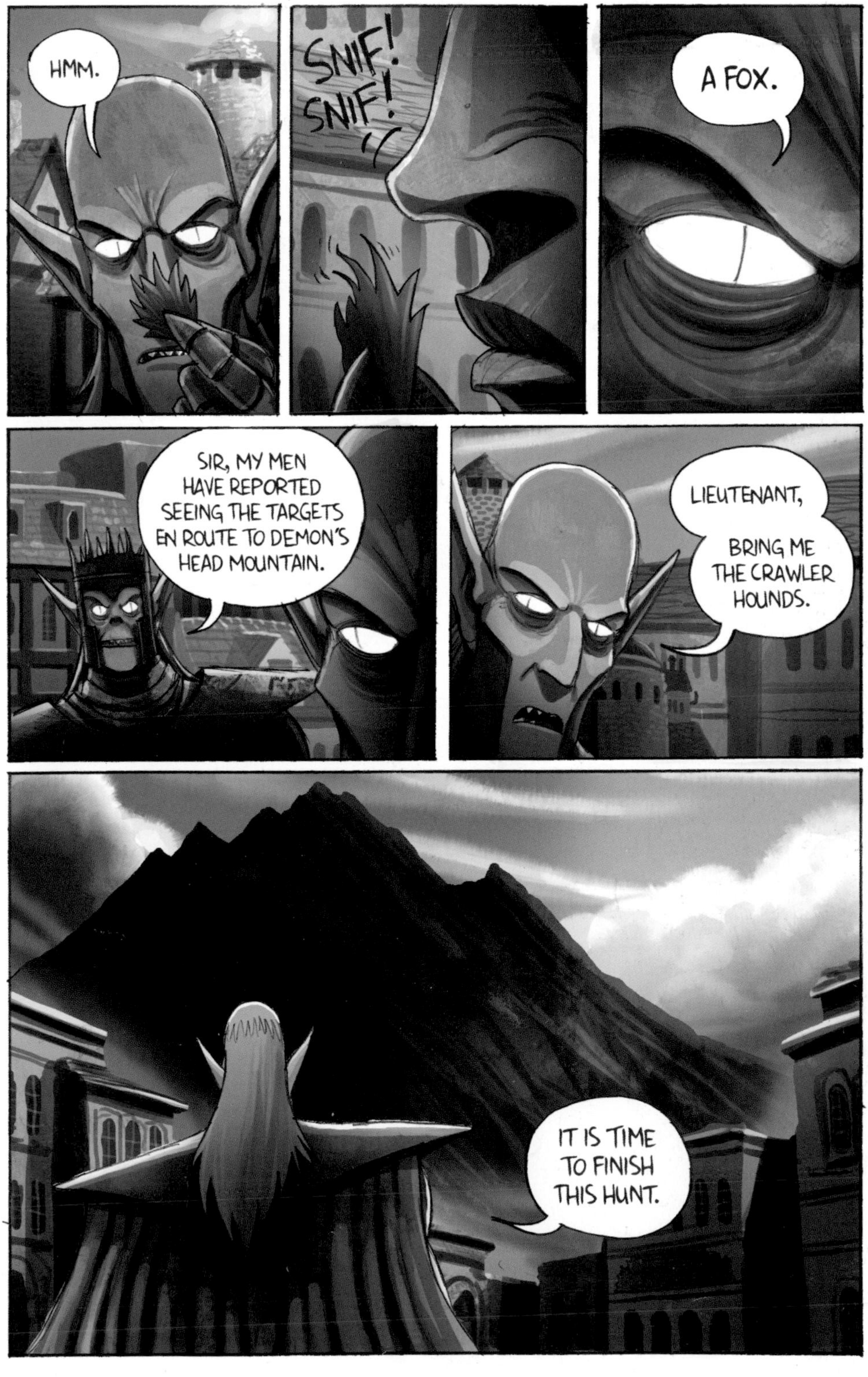
HMM.
SNIF! SNIF!
A FOX.
SIR, MY MEN HAVE REPORTED SEEING THE TARGETS EN ROUTE TO DEMON'S HEAD MOUNTAIN.
LIEUTENANT,
BRING ME THE CRAWLER HOUNDS.
IT IS TIME TO FINISH THIS HUNT.

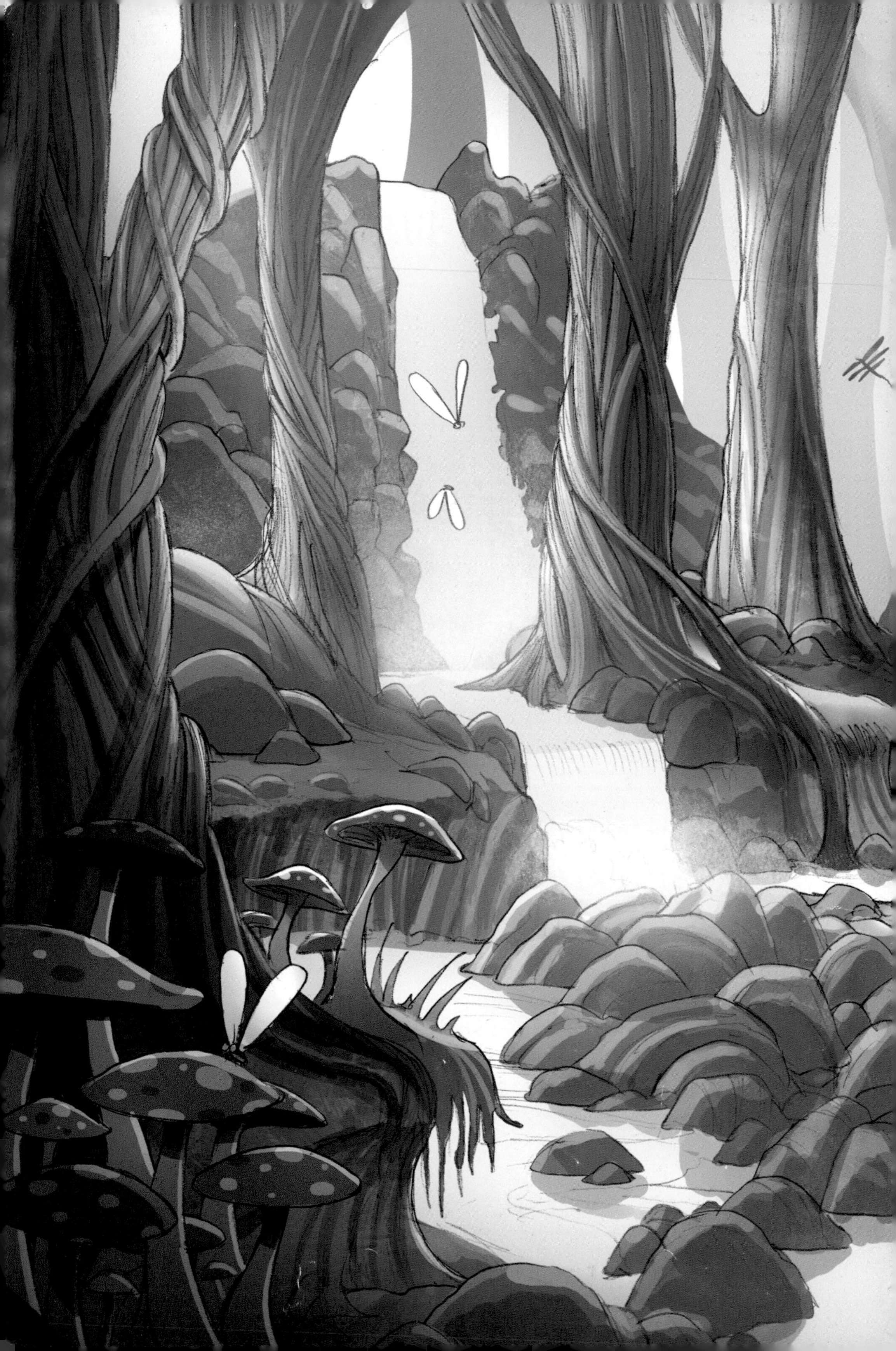

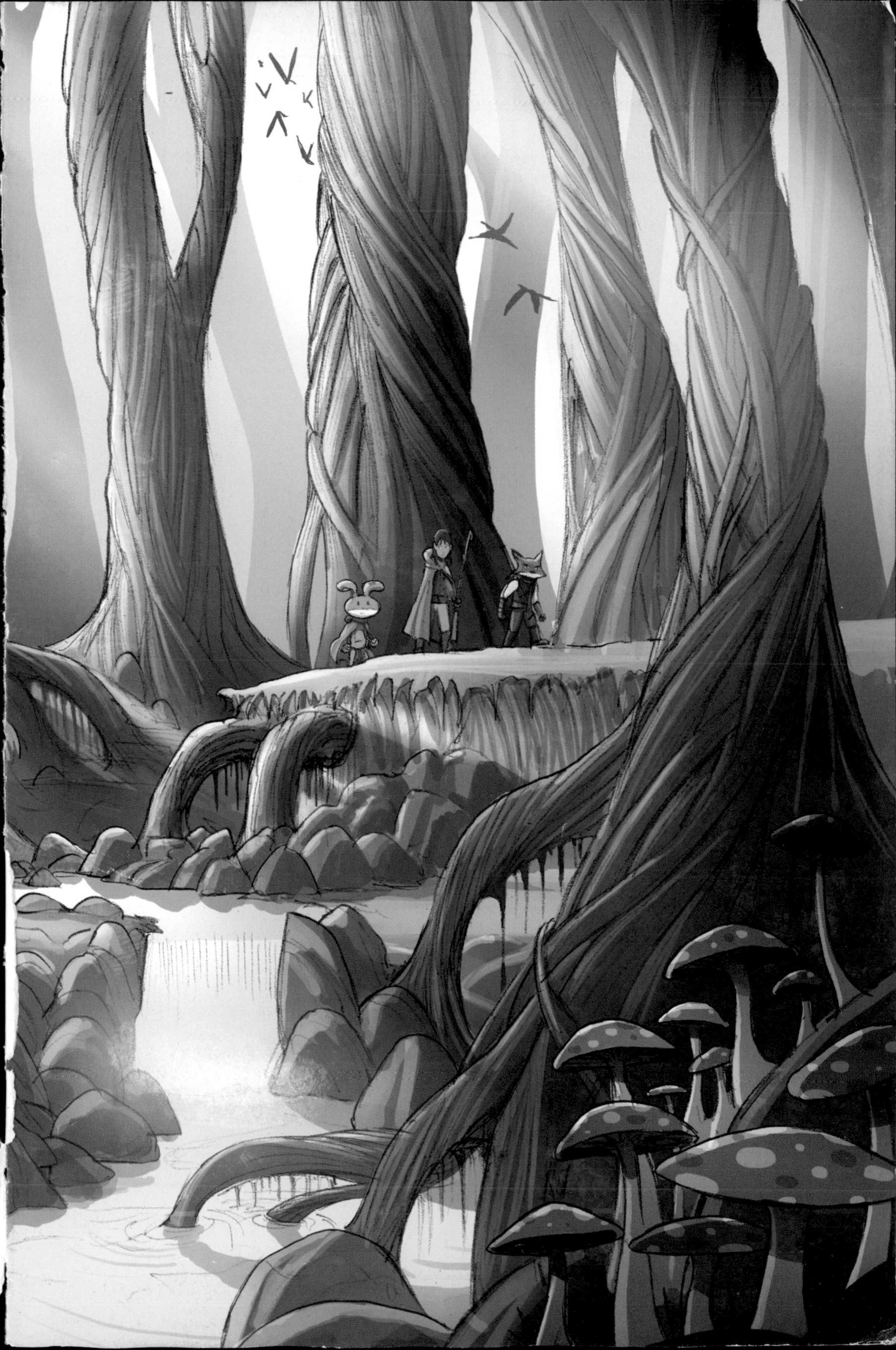

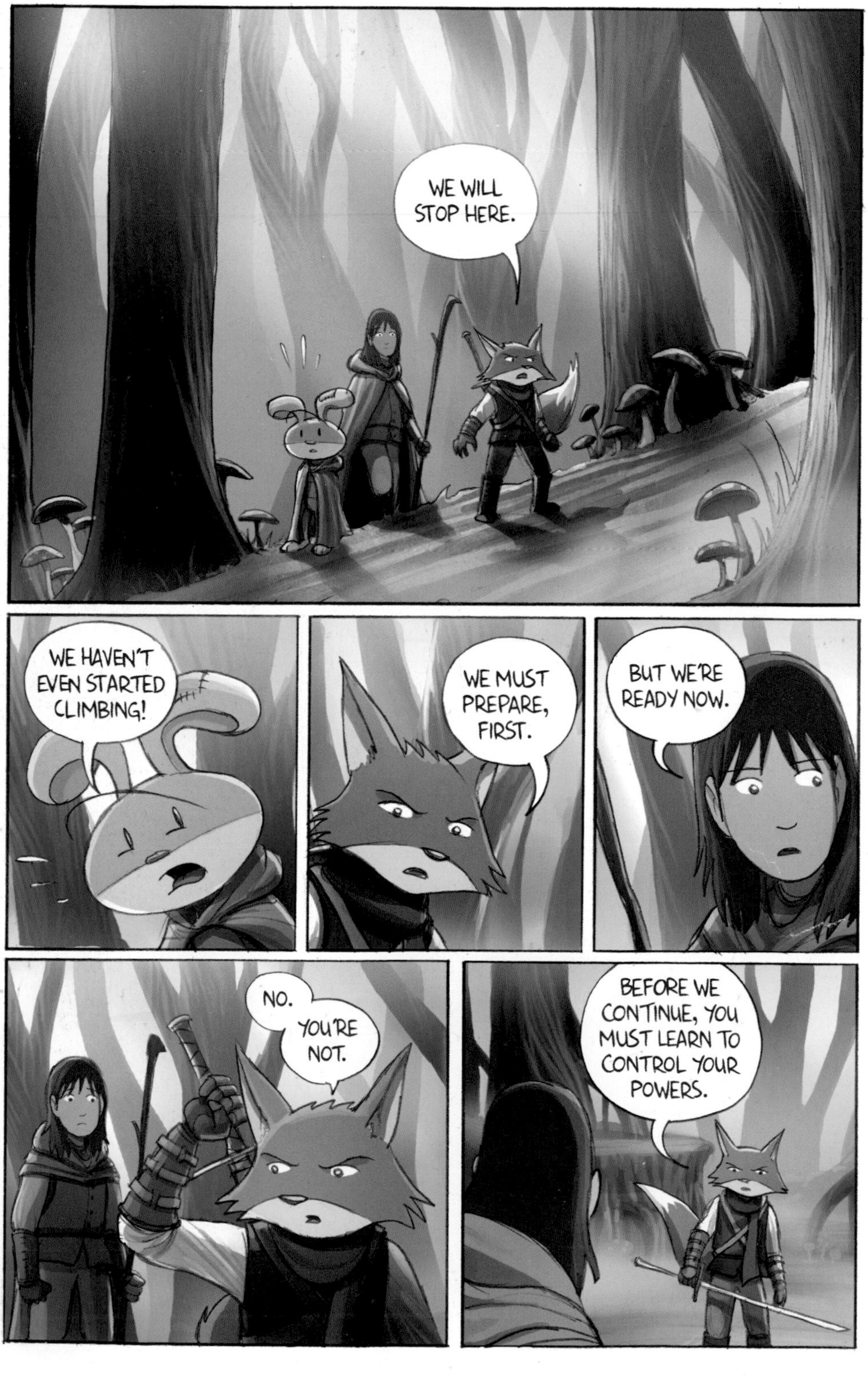
WE WILL STOP HERE.
WE HAVEN'T EVEN STARTED CLIMBING!
WE MUST PREPARE, FIRST.
BUT WE'RE READY NOW.
NO.
YOU'RE NOT.
BEFORE WE CONTINUE, YOU MUST LEARN TO CONTROL YOUR POWERS.

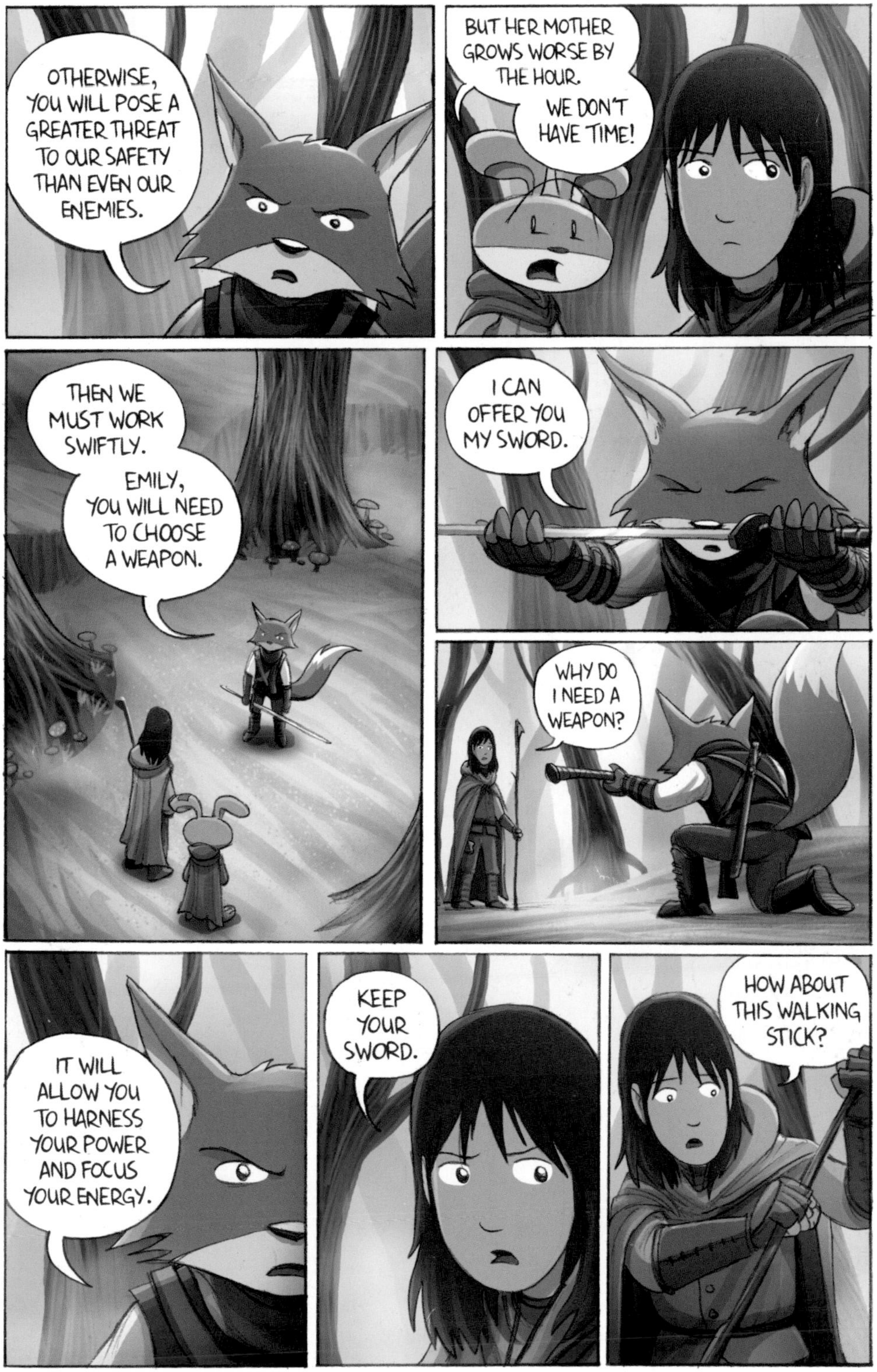
OTHERWISE, YOU WILL POSE A GREATER THREAT TO OUR SAFETY THAN EVEN OUR ENEMIES.
BUT HER MOTHER GROWS WORSE BY THE HOUR.
WE DON'T HAVE TIME!
THEN WE MUST WORK SWIFTLY.
EMILY, YOU WILL NEED TO CHOOSE A WEAPON.
I CAN OFFER YOU MY SWORD.
WHY DO I NEED A WEAPON?
IT WILL ALLOW YOU TO HARNESS YOUR POWER AND FOCUS YOUR ENERGY.
KEEP YOUR SWORD.
HOW ABOUT THIS WALKING STICK?

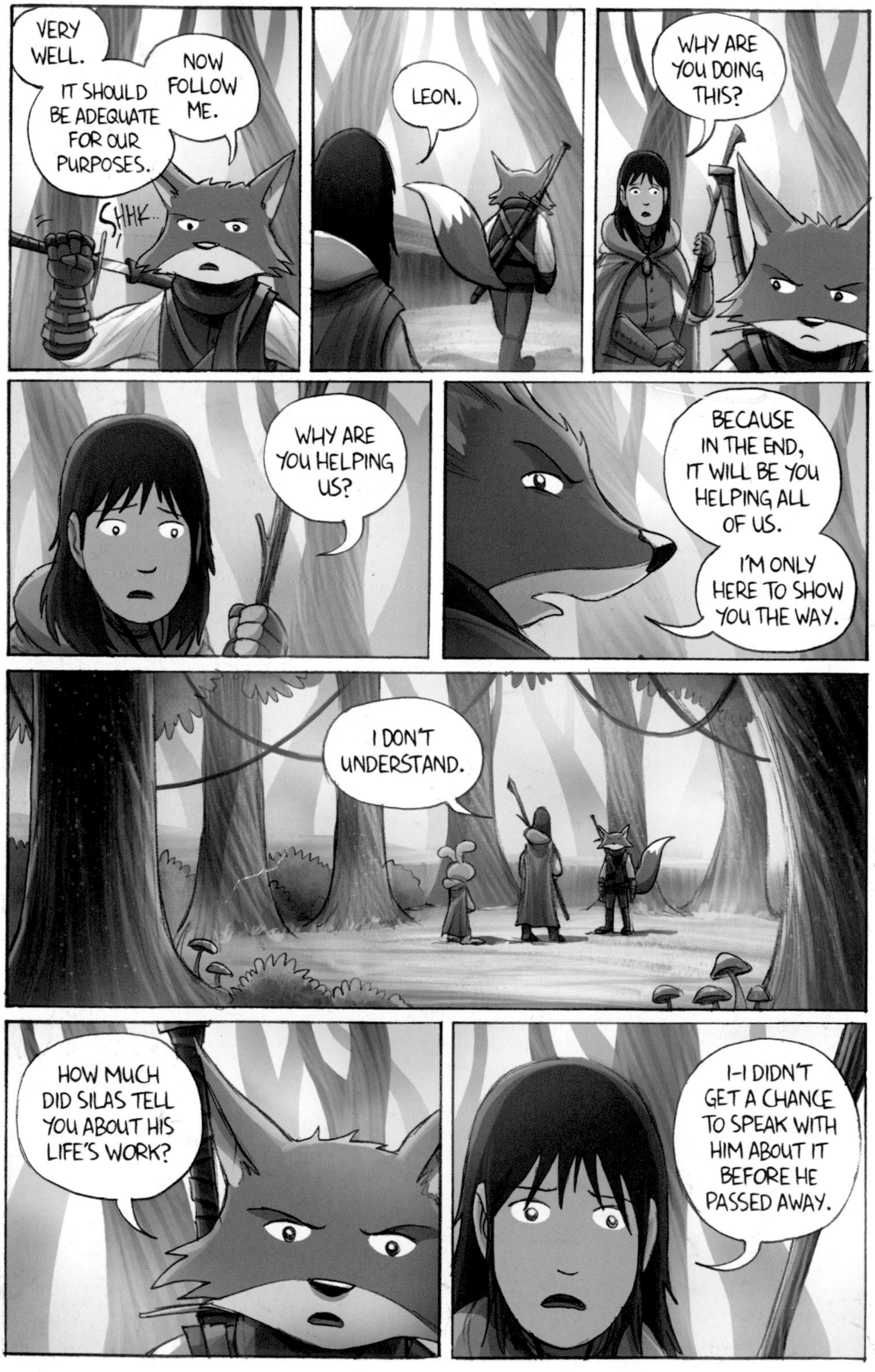
VERY WELL.
IT SHOULD BE ADEQUATE FOR OUR PURPOSES.
NOW FOLLOW ME.
SHHK
LEON.
WHY ARE YOU DOING THIS?
WHY ARE YOU HELPING US?
BECAUSE IN THE END, IT WILL BE YOU HELPING ALL OF US.
I'M ONLY HERE TO SHOW YOU THE WAY.
I DON'T UNDERSTAND.
HOW MUCH DID SILAS TELL YOU ABOUT HIS LIFE'S WORK?
I-I DIDN'T GET A CHANCE TO SPEAK WITH HIM ABOUT IT BEFORE HE PASSED AWAY.

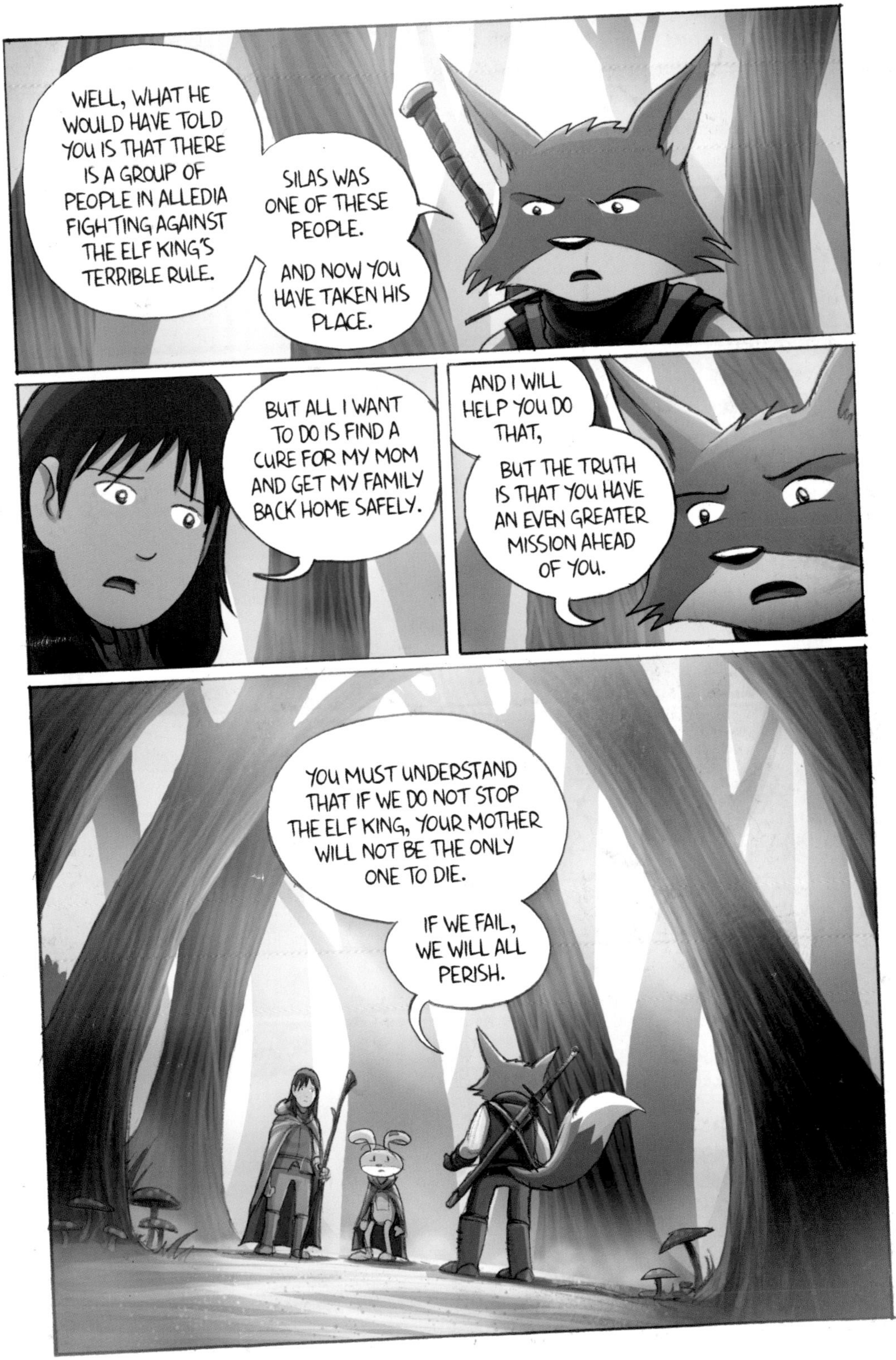

WELL, WHAT HE WOULD HAVE TOLD YOU IS THAT THERE IS A GROUP OF PEOPLE IN ALLEDIA FIGHTING AGAINST THE ELF KING'S TERRIBLE RULE.
SILAS WAS ONE OF THESE PEOPLE.
AND NOW YOU HAVE TAKEN HIS PLACE.
BUT ALL I WANT TO DO IS FIND A CURE FOR MY MOM AND GET MY FAMILY BACK HOME SAFELY.
AND I WILL HELP YOU DO THAT,
BUT THE TRUTH IS THAT YOU HAVE AN EVEN GREATER MISSION AHEAD OF YOU.
YOU MUST UNDERSTAND THAT IF WE DO NOT STOP THE ELF KING, YOUR MOTHER WILL NOT BE THE ONLY ONE TO DIE.
IF WE FAIL, WE WILL ALL PERISH.

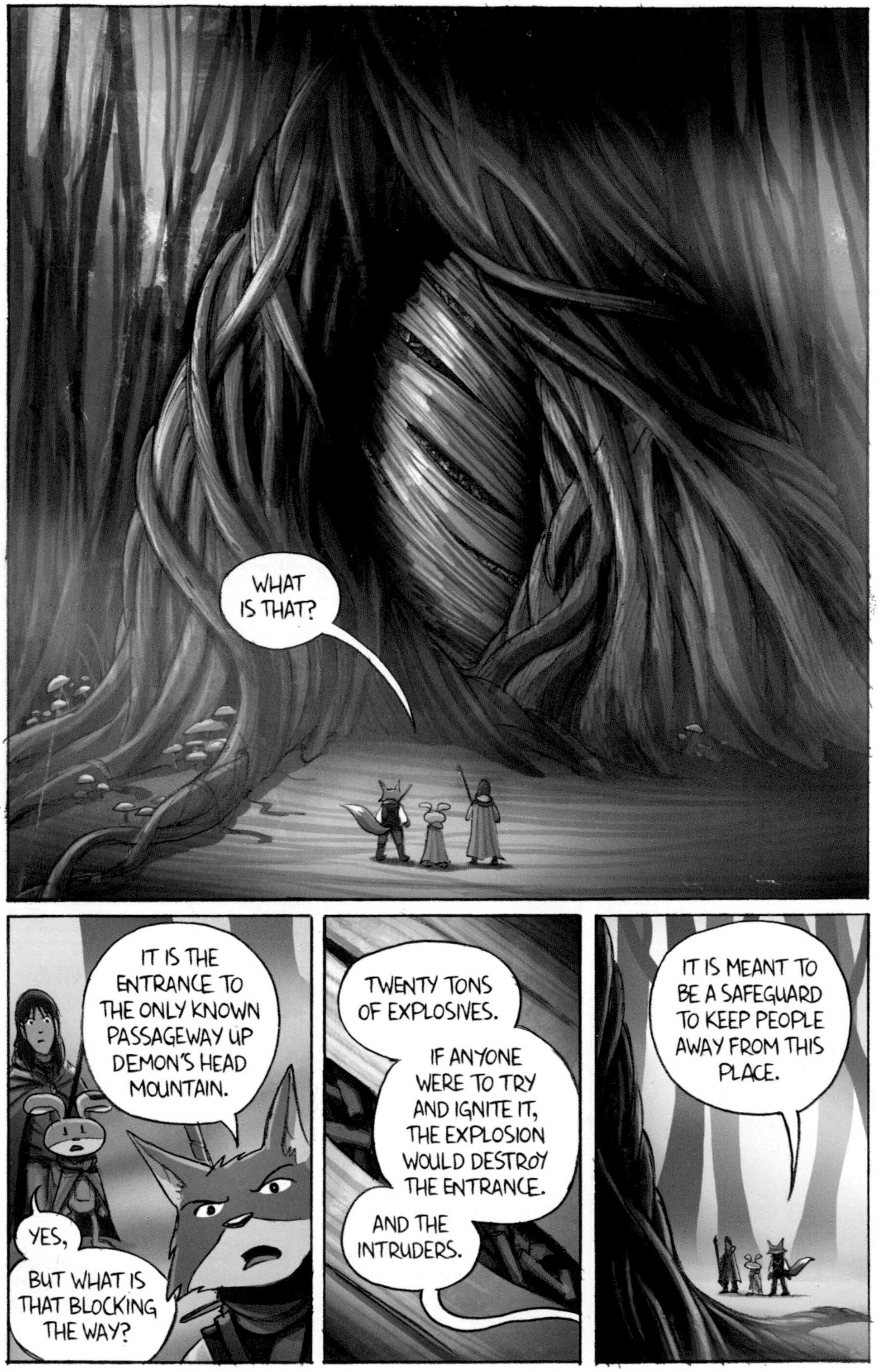
WHAT IS THAT?
IT IS THE ENTRANCE TO THE ONLY KNOWN PASSAGEWAY UP DEMON'S HEAD MOUNTAIN.
YES,
BUT WHAT IS THAT BLOCKING THE WAY?
TWENTY TONS OF EXPLOSIVES.
IF ANYONE WERE TO TRY AND IGNITE IT, THE EXPLOSION WOULD DESTROY THE ENTRANCE.
AND THE INTRUDERS.
IT IS MEANT TO BE A SAFEGUARD TO KEEP PEOPLE AWAY FROM THIS PLACE.

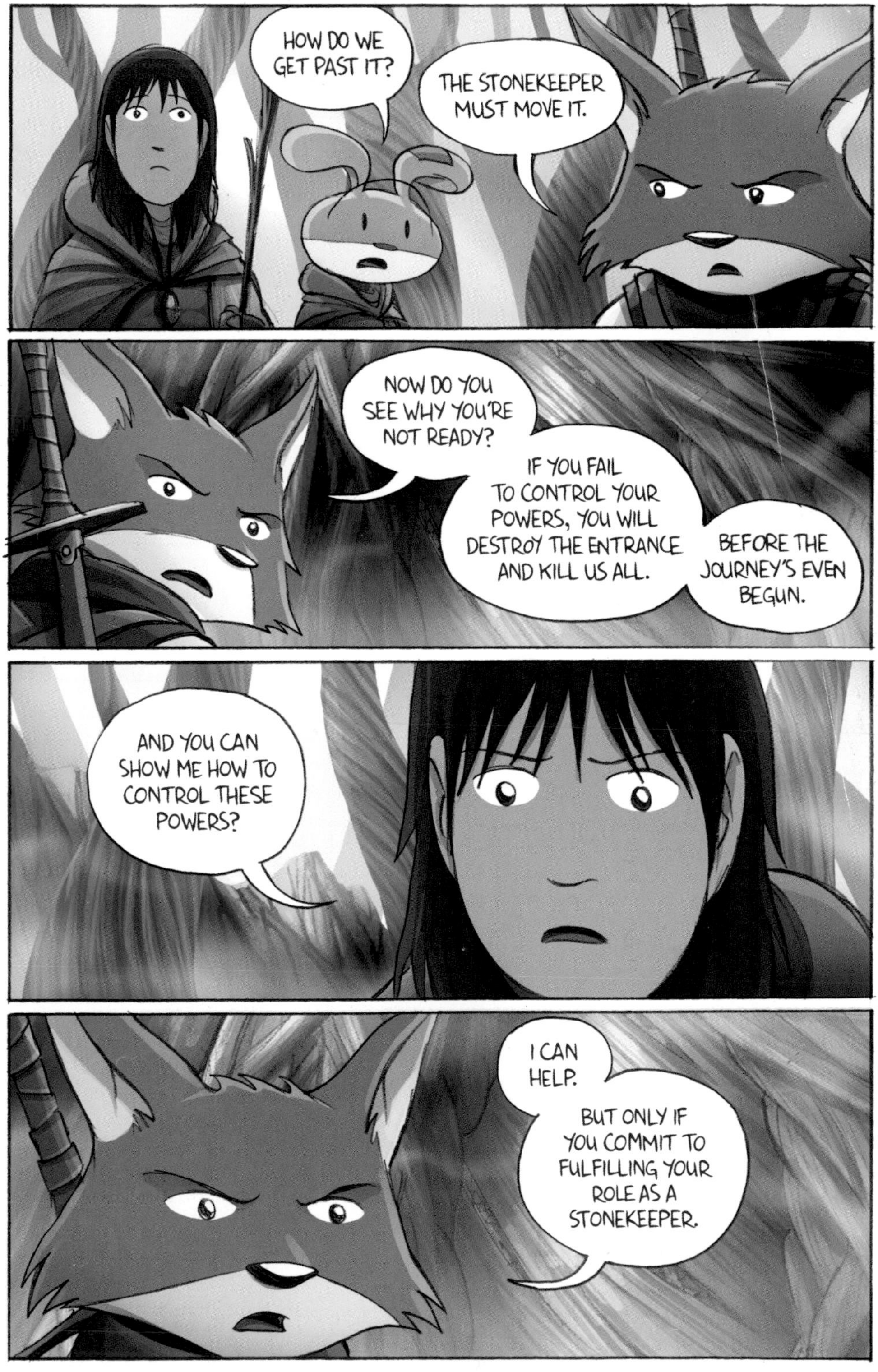
HOW DO WE GET PAST IT?
THE STONEKEEPER MUST MOVE IT.
NOW DO YOU SEE WHY YOU'RE NOT READY?
IF YOU FAIL TO CONTROL YOUR POWERS, YOU WILL DESTROY THE ENTRANCE AND KILL US ALL.
BEFORE THE JOURNEY'S EVEN BEGUN.
AND YOU CAN SHOW ME HOW TO CONTROL THESE POWERS?
I CAN HELP.
BUT ONLY IF YOU COMMIT TO FULFILLING YOUR ROLE AS A STONEKEEPER.

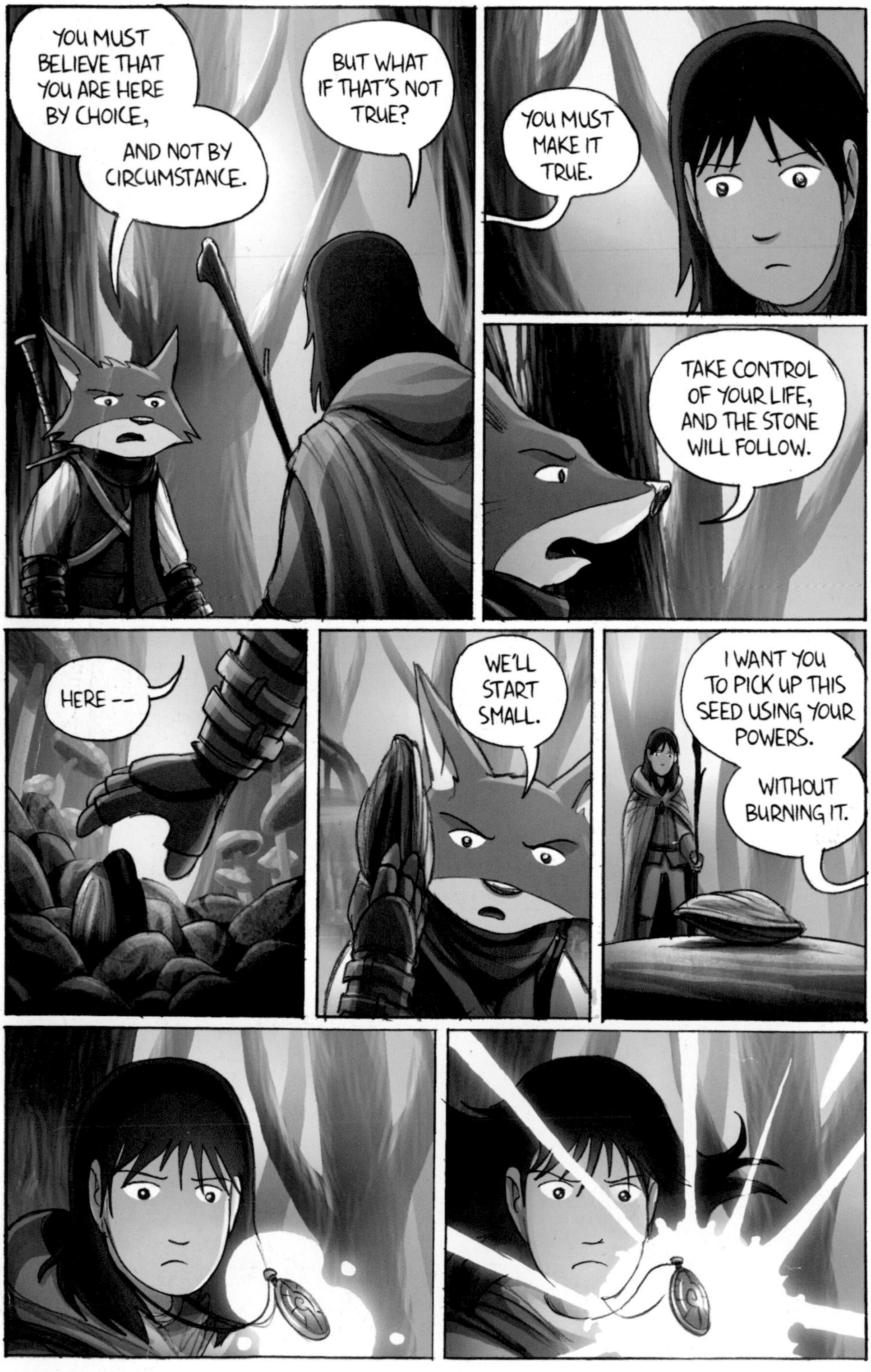
YOU MUST BELIEVE THAT YOU ARE HERE BY CHOICE,
AND NOT BY CIRCUMSTANCE.
BUT WHAT IF THAT'S NOT TRUE?
YOU MUST MAKE IT TRUE.
TAKE CONTROL OF YOUR LIFE, AND THE STONE WILL FOLLOW.
HERE --
WE'LL START SMALL.
I WANT YOU TO PICK UP THIS SEED USING YOUR POWERS.
WITHOUT BURNING IT.

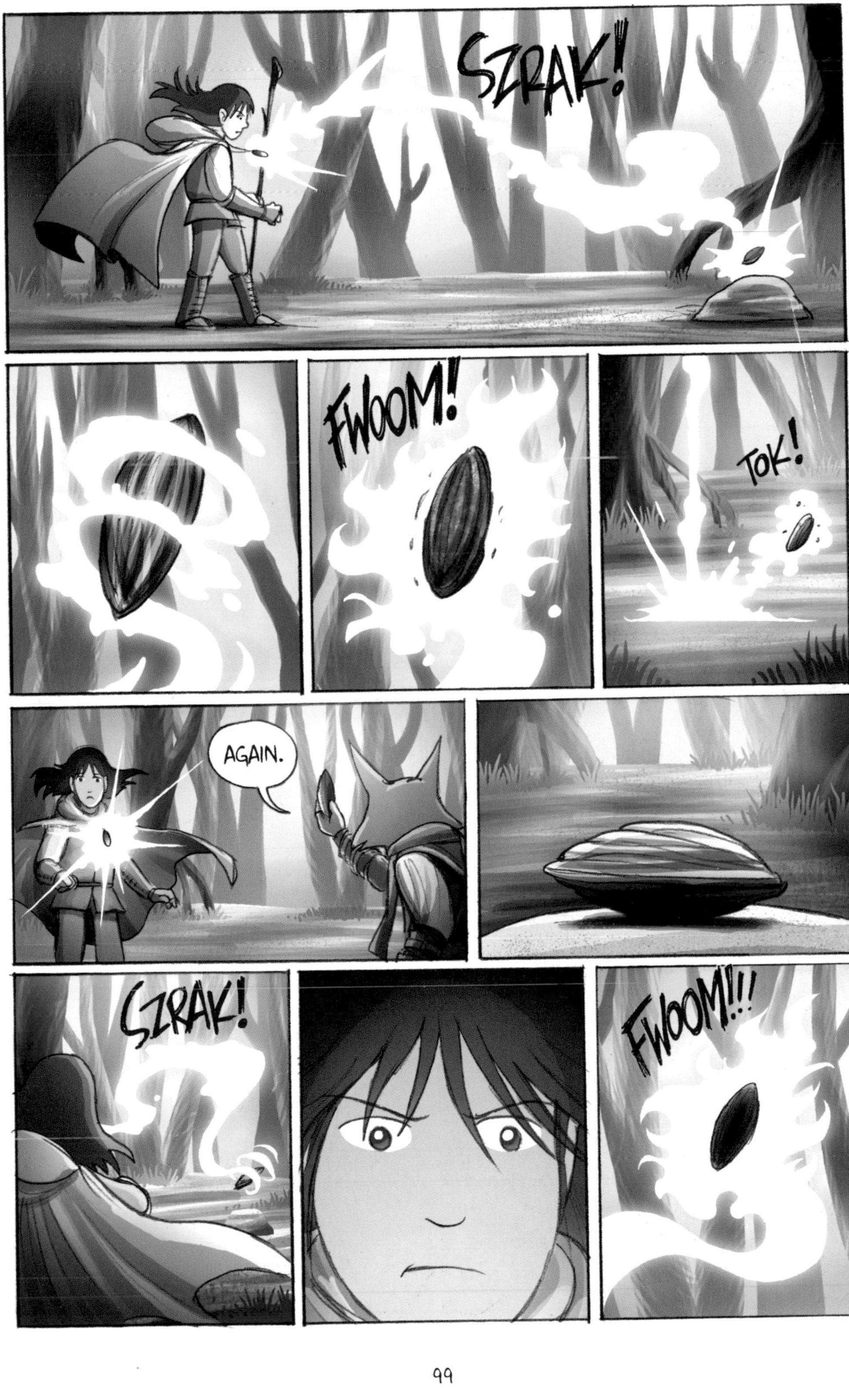
SZRAK!
FWOOM!
TOK!
AGAIN.
SZRAK!
FWOOM!!!

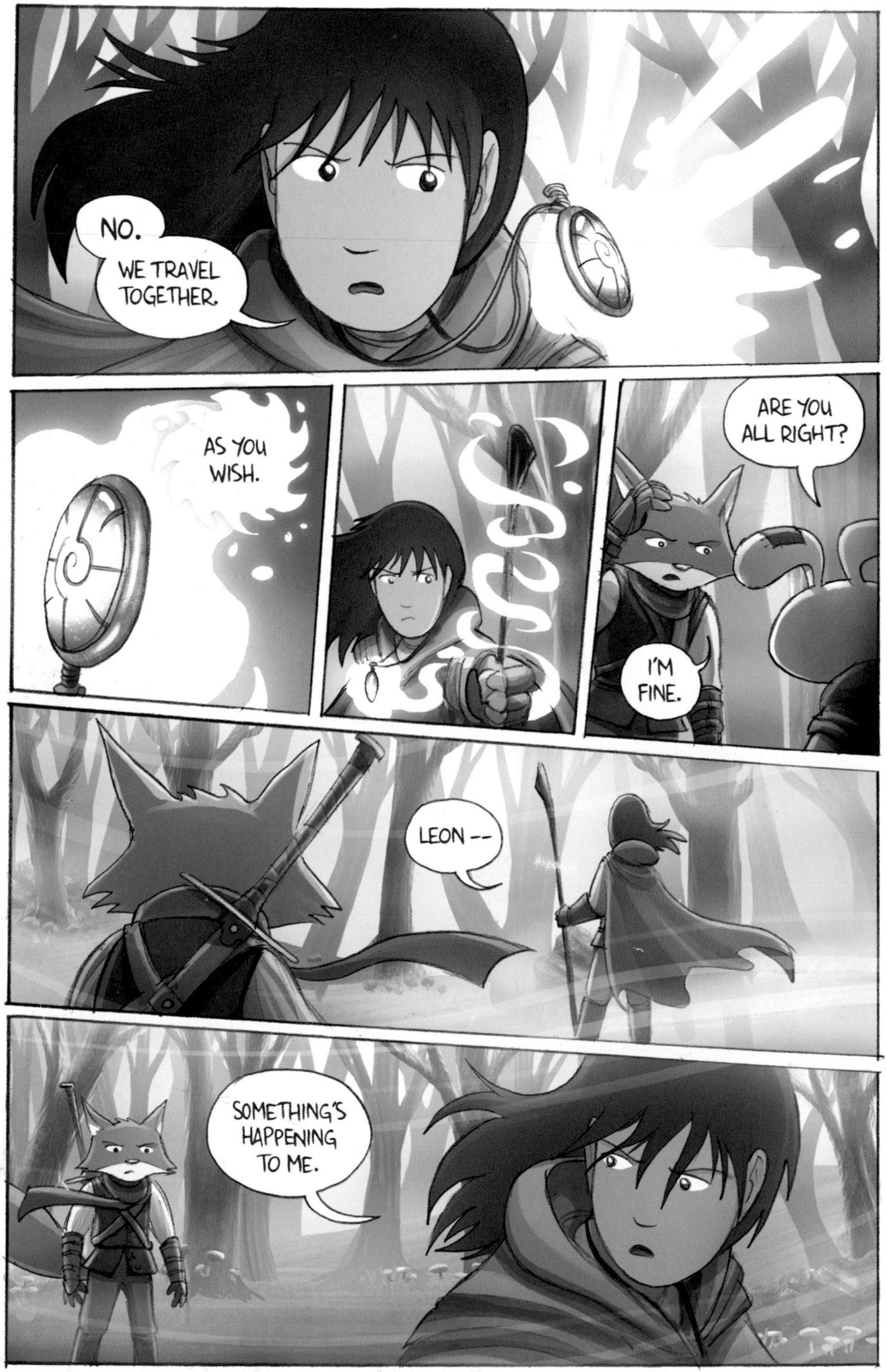

NO.
WE TRAVEL TOGETHER.
AS YOU WISH.
ARE YOU ALL RIGHT?
I'M FINE.
LEON --
SOMETHING'S HAPPENING TO ME.

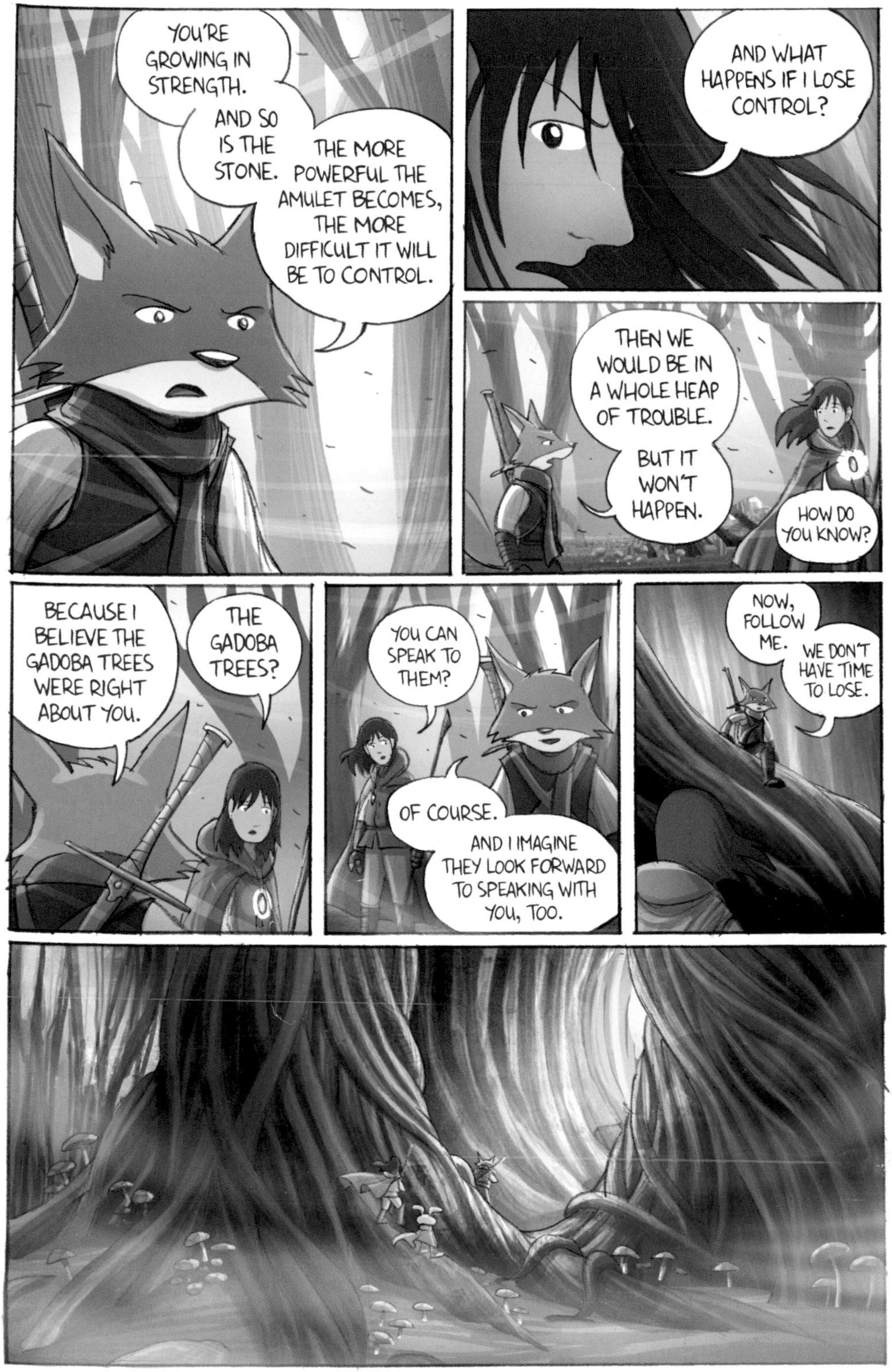
YOU'RE GROWING IN STRENGTH.
AND SO IS THE STONE.
THE MORE POWERFUL THE AMULET BECOMES, THE MORE DIFFICULT IT WILL BE TO CONTROL.
AND WHAT HAPPENS IF I LOSE CONTROL?
THEN WE WOULD BE IN A WHOLE HEAP OF TROUBLE.
BUT IT WON'T HAPPEN.
HOW DO YOU KNOW?
BECAUSE I BELIEVE THE GADOBA TREES WERE RIGHT ABOUT YOU.
THE GADOBA TREES?
YOU CAN SPEAK TO THEM?
OF COURSE.
AND I IMAGINE THEY LOOK FORWARD TO SPEAKING WITH YOU, TOO.
NOW, FOLLOW ME.
WE DON'T HAVE TIME TO LOSE.

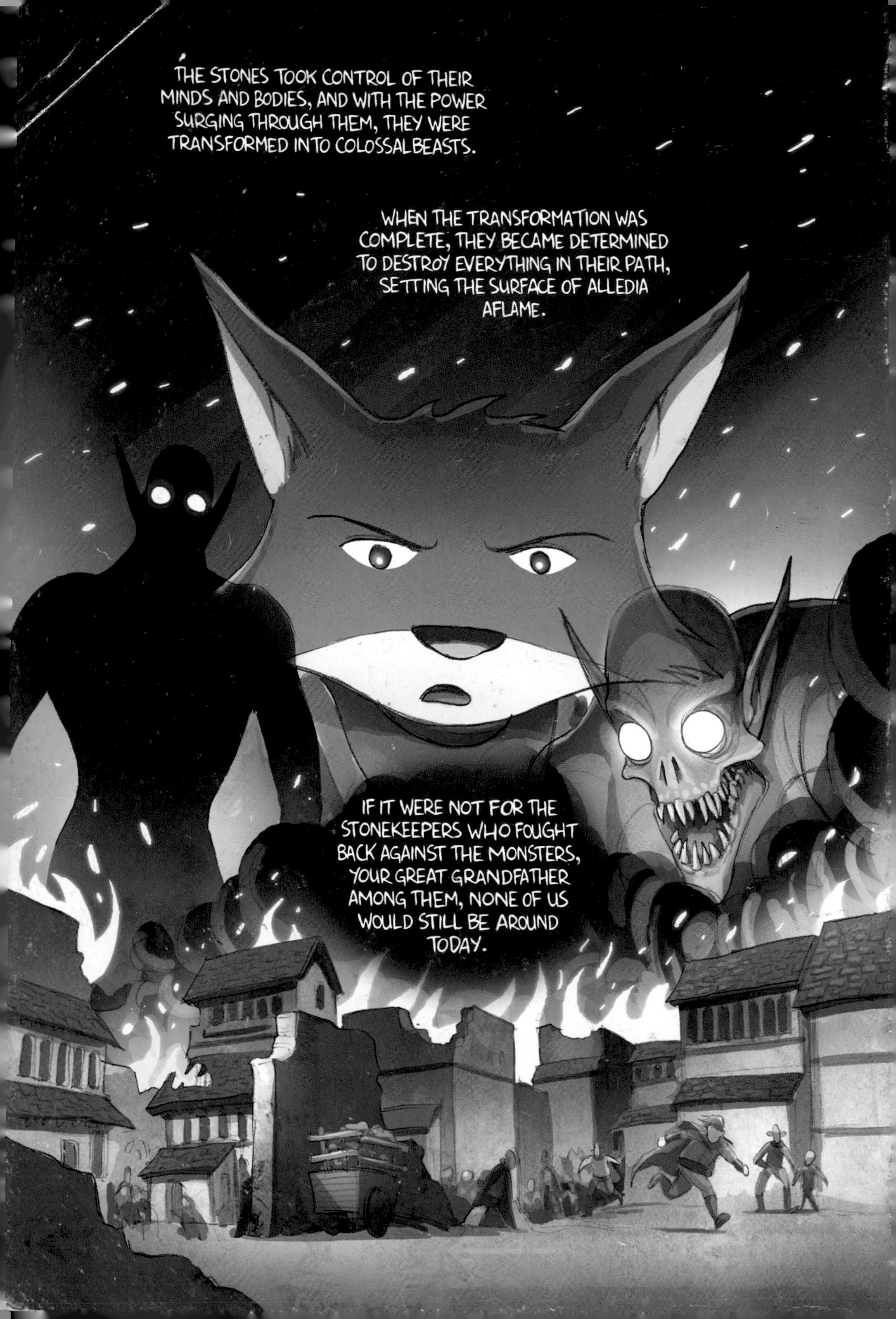
THE STONES TOOK CONTROL OF THEIR MINDS AND BODIES, AND WITH THE POWER SURGING THROUGH THEM, THEY WERE TRANSFORMED INTO COLOSSAL BEASTS.
WHEN THE TRANSFORMATION WAS COMPLETE, THEY BECAME DETERMINED TO DESTROY EVERYTHING IN THEIR PATH, SETTING THE SURFACE OF ALLEDIA AFLAME.
IF IT WERE NOT FOR THE STONEKEEPERS WHO FOUGHT BACK AGAINST THE MONSTERS, YOUR GREAT GRANDFATHER AMONG THEM, NONE OF US WOULD STILL BE AROUND TODAY.

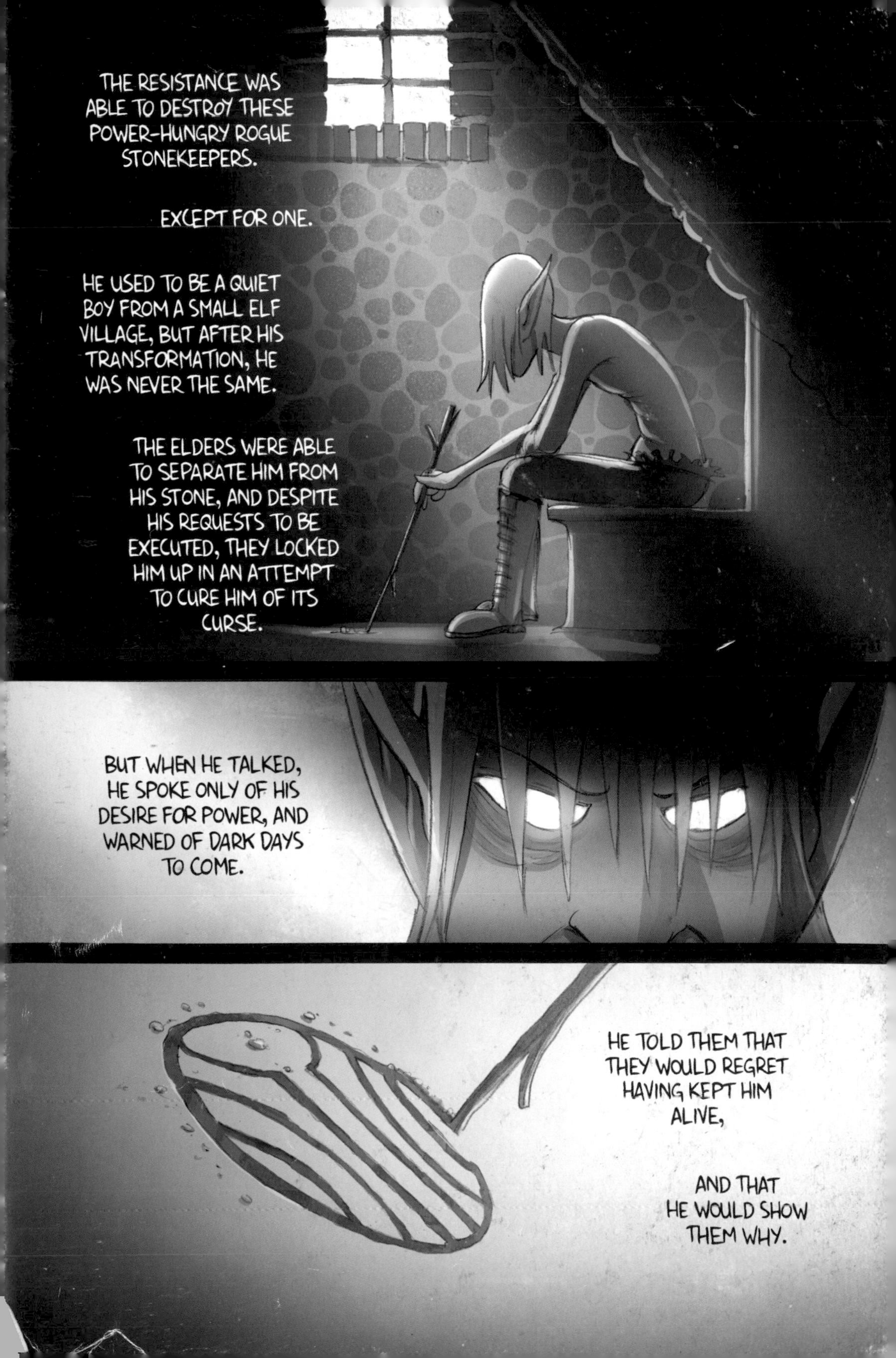
THE RESISTANCE WAS ABLE TO DESTROY THESE POWER-HUNGRY ROGUE STONEKEEPERS.
EXCEPT FOR ONE.
HE USED TO BE A QUIET BOY FROM A SMALL ELF VILLAGE, BUT AFTER HIS TRANSFORMATION, HE WAS NEVER THE SAME.
THE ELDERS WERE ABLE TO SEPARATE HIM FROM HIS STONE, AND DESPITE HIS REQUESTS TO BE EXECUTED, THEY LOCKED HIM UP IN AN ATTEMPT TO CURE HIM OF ITS CURSE.
BUT WHEN HE TALKED, HE SPOKE ONLY OF HIS DESIRE FOR POWER, AND WARNED OF DARK DAYS TO COME.
HE TOLD THEM THAT THEY WOULD REGRET HAVING KEPT HIM ALIVE,
AND THAT HE WOULD SHOW THEM WHY.

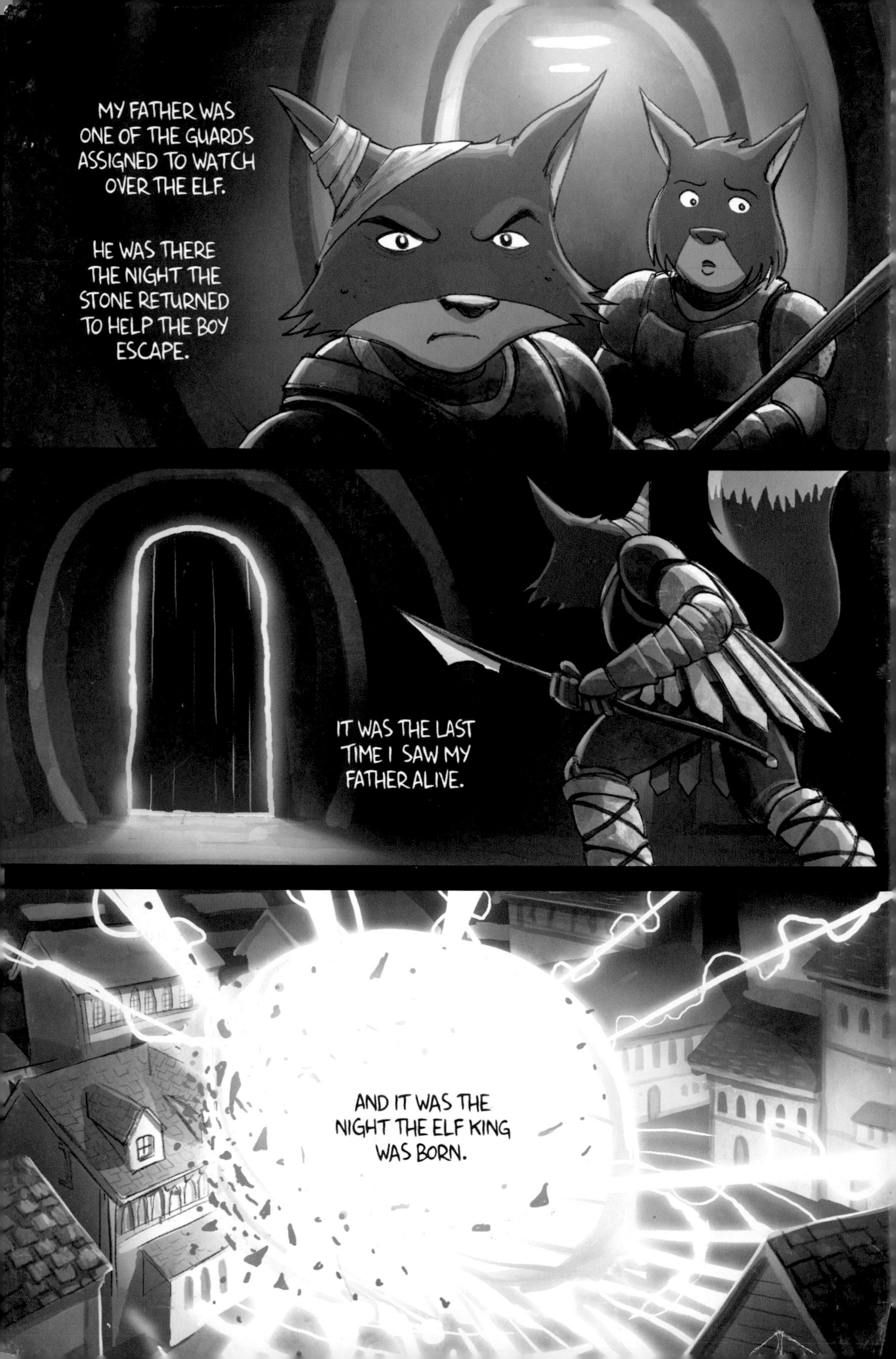
MY FATHER WAS ONE OF THE GUARDS ASSIGNED TO WATCH OVER THE ELF.
HE WAS THERE THE NIGHT THE STONE RETURNED TO HELP THE BOY ESCAPE.
IT WAS THE LAST TIME I SAW MY FATHER ALIVE.
AND IT WAS THE NIGHT THE ELF KING WAS BORN.

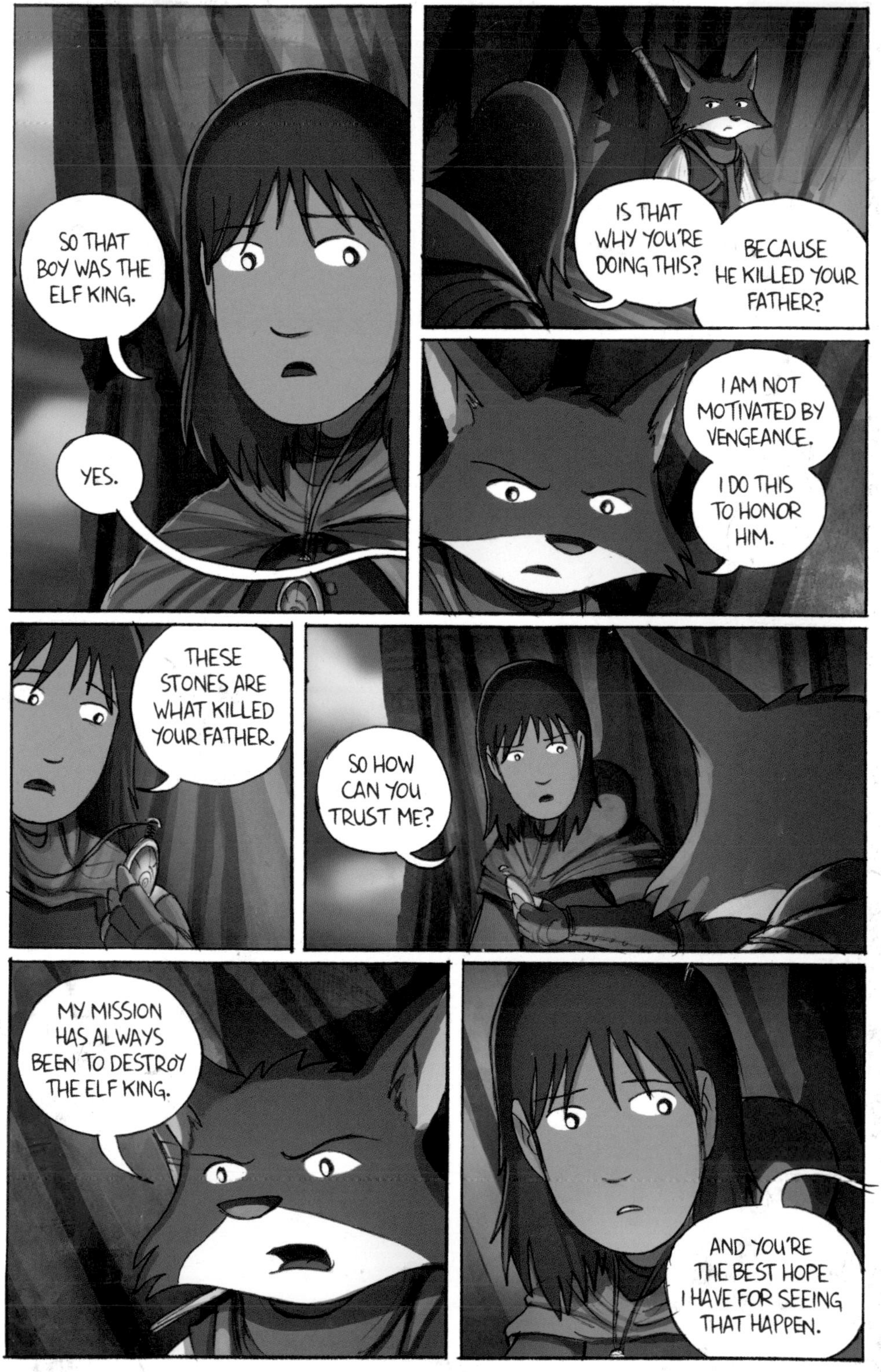
SO THAT BOY WAS THE ELF KING.
YES.
IS THAT WHY YOU'RE DOING THIS?
BECAUSE HE KILLED YOUR FATHER?
I AM NOT MOTIVATED BY VENGEANCE.
I DO THIS TO HONOR HIM.
THESE STONES ARE WHAT KILLED YOUR FATHER.
SO HOW CAN YOU TRUST ME?
MY MISSION HAS ALWAYS BEEN TO DESTROY THE ELF KING.
AND YOU'RE THE BEST HOPE I HAVE FOR SEEING THAT HAPPEN.

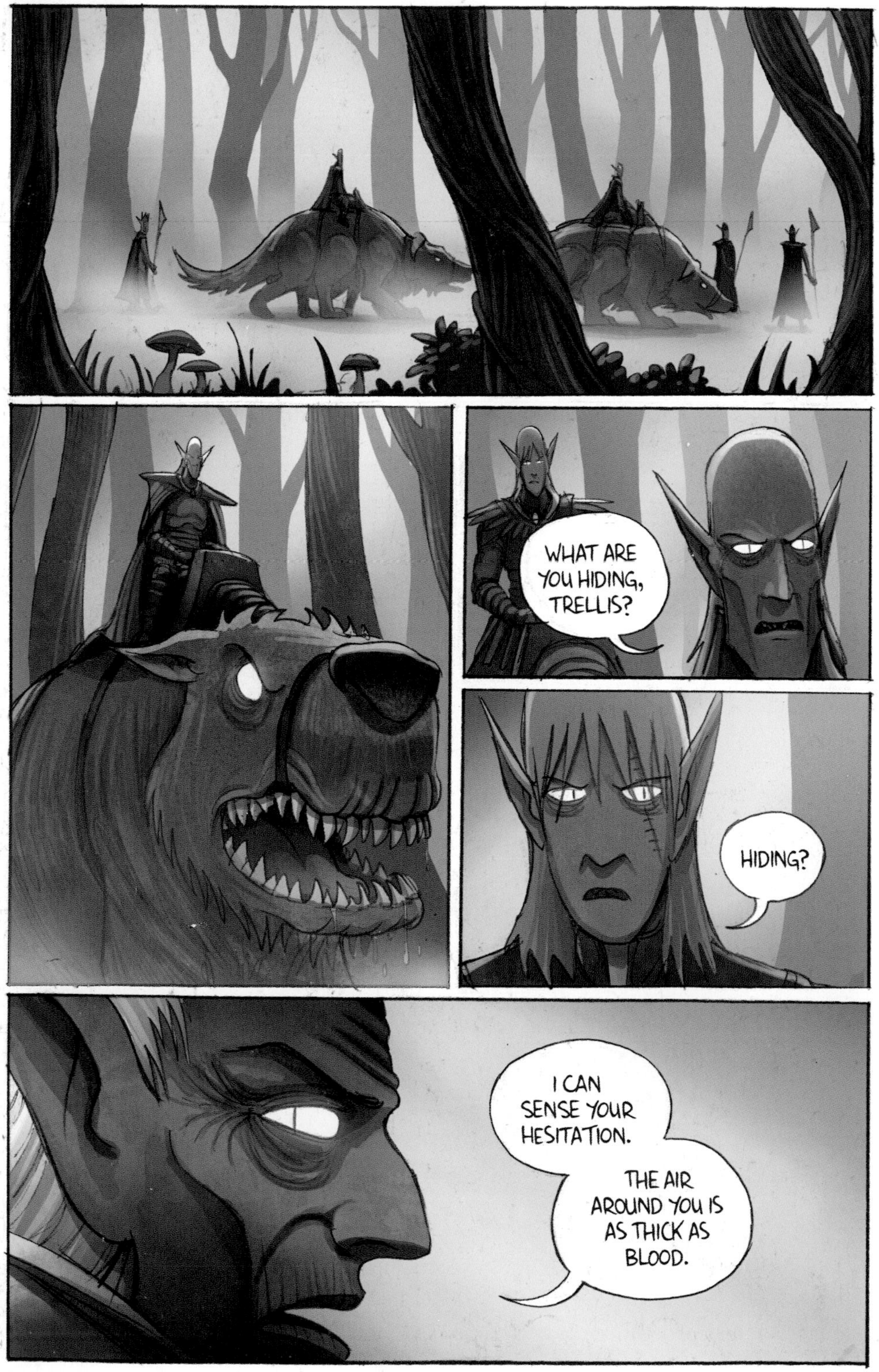
WHAT ARE YOU HIDING, TRELLIS?
HIDING?
I CAN SENSE YOUR HESITATION.
THE AIR AROUND YOU IS AS THICK AS BLOOD.

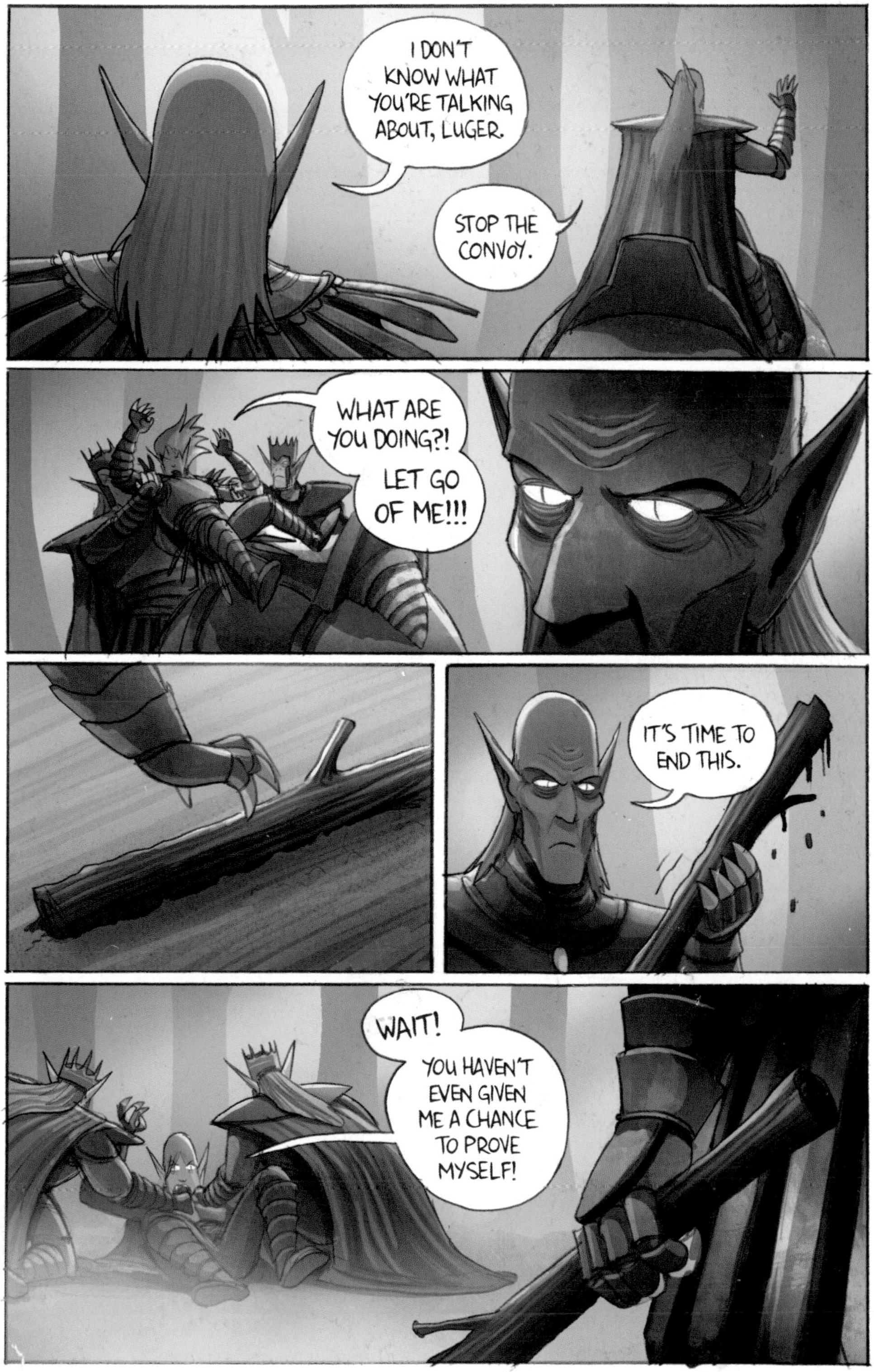
I DON'T KNOW WHAT YOU'RE TALKING ABOUT, LUGER.
STOP THE CONVOY.
WHAT ARE YOU DOING?!
LET GO OF ME!!!
IT'S TIME TO END THIS.
WAIT!
YOU HAVEN'T EVEN GIVEN ME A CHANCE TO PROVE MYSELF!

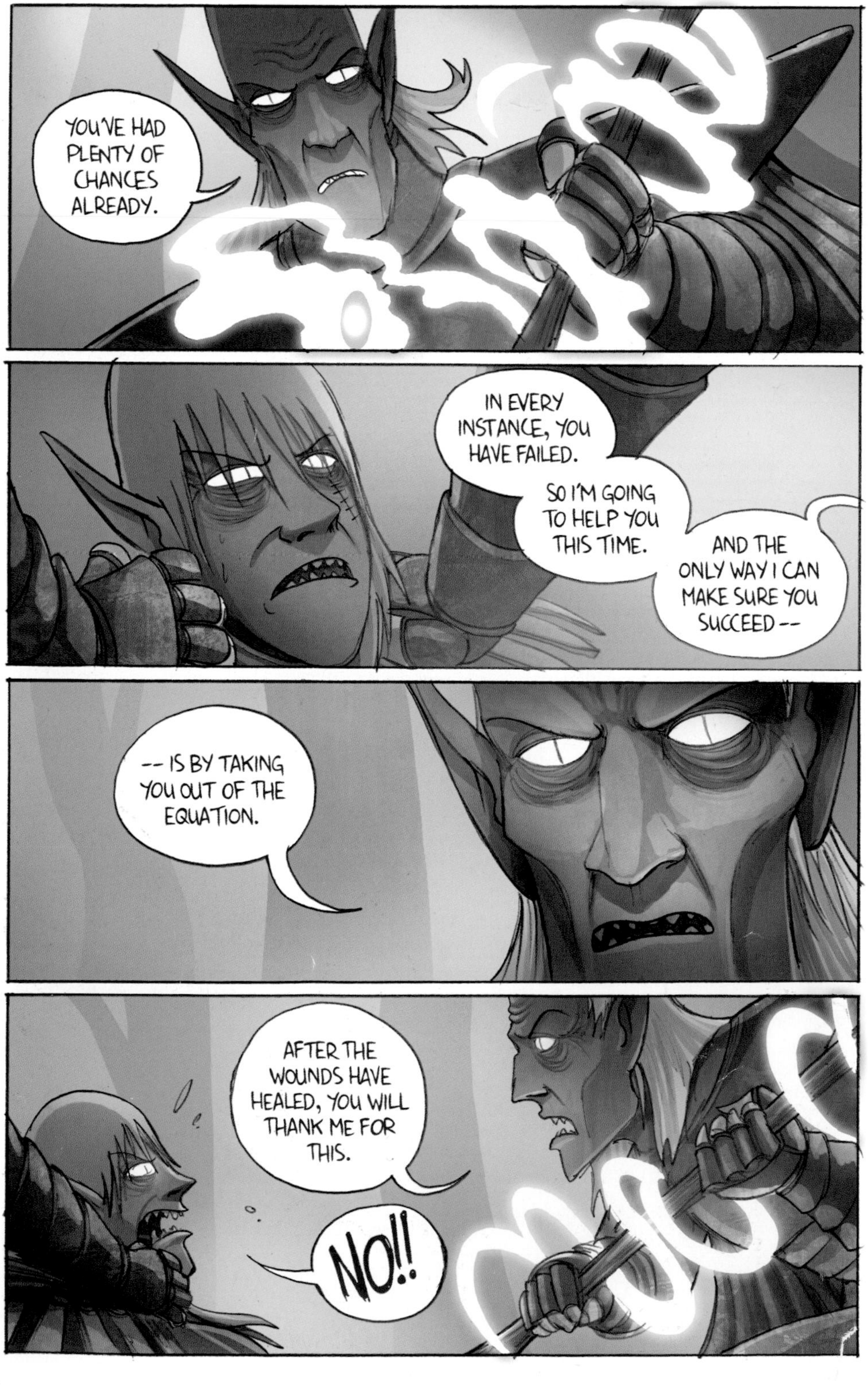
YOU'VE HAD PLENTY OF CHANCES ALREADY.
IN EVERY INSTANCE, YOU HAVE FAILED.
SO I'M GOING TO HELP YOU THIS TIME.
AND THE ONLY WAY I CAN MAKE SURE YOU SUCCEED --
-- IS BY TAKING YOU OUT OF THE EQUATION.
AFTER THE WOUNDS HAVE HEALED, YOU WILL THANK ME FOR THIS.
NO!!

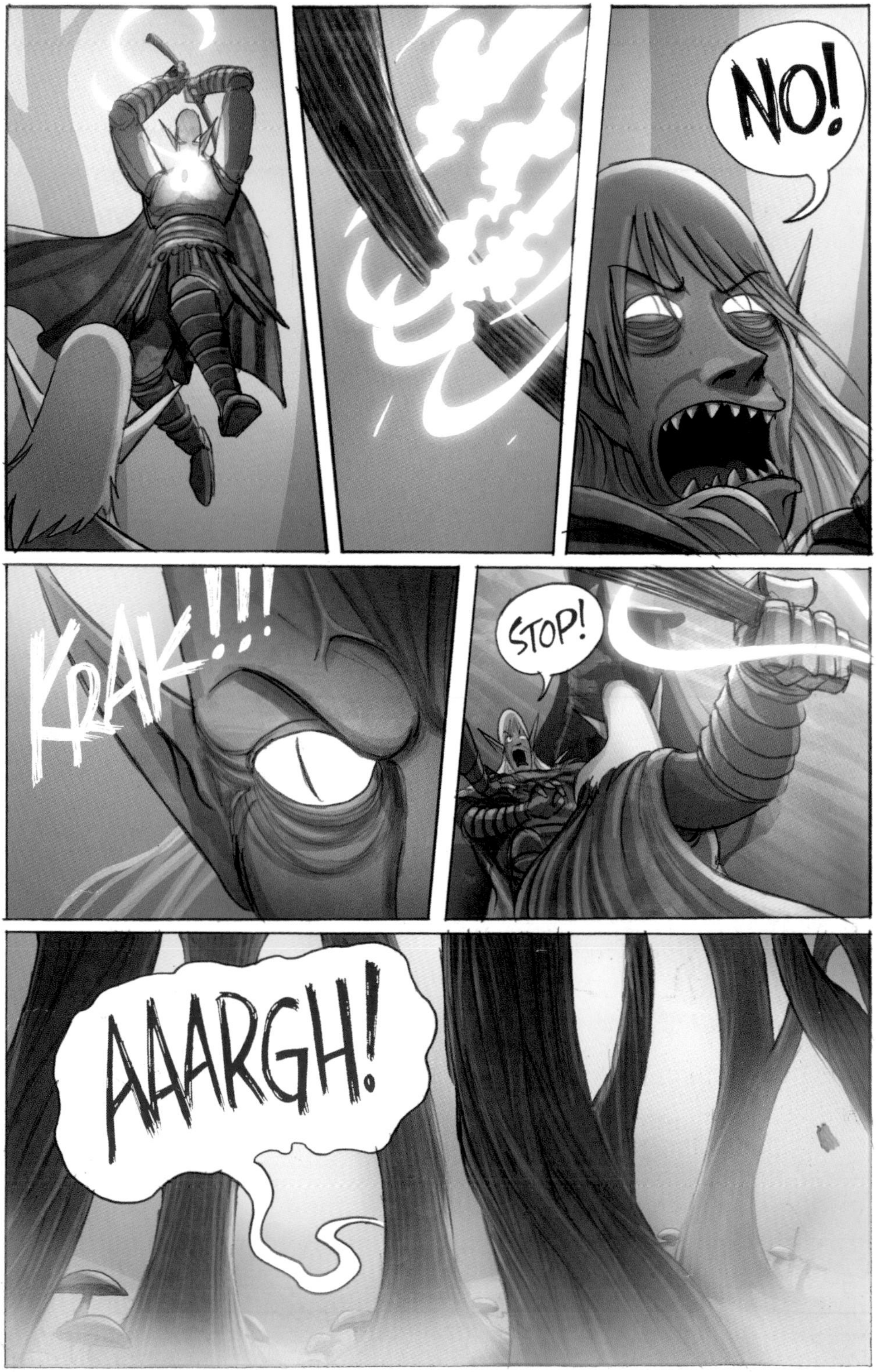
NO!
KRAK!!!
STOP!
AAARGH!

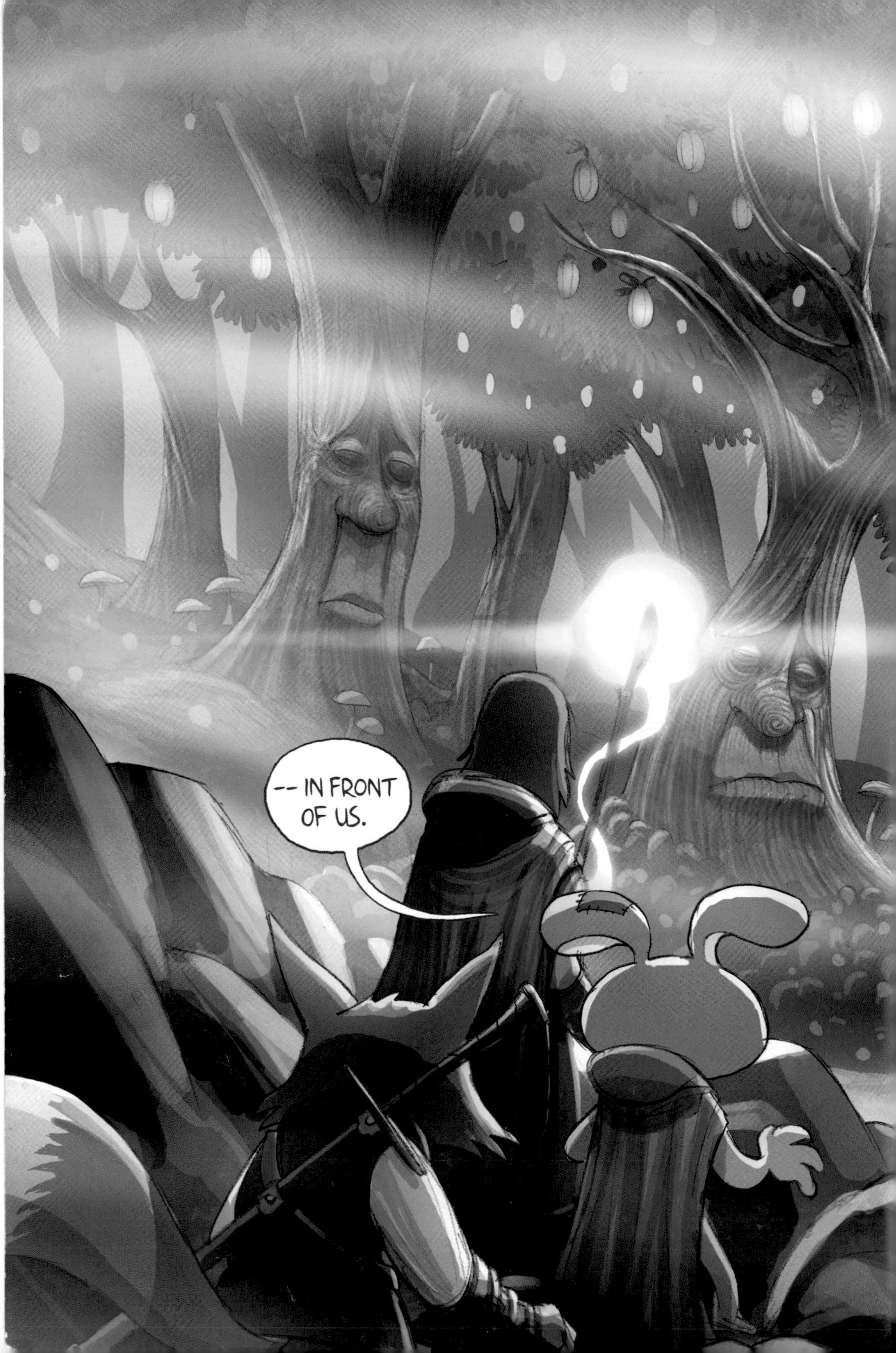
-- IN FRONT OF US.

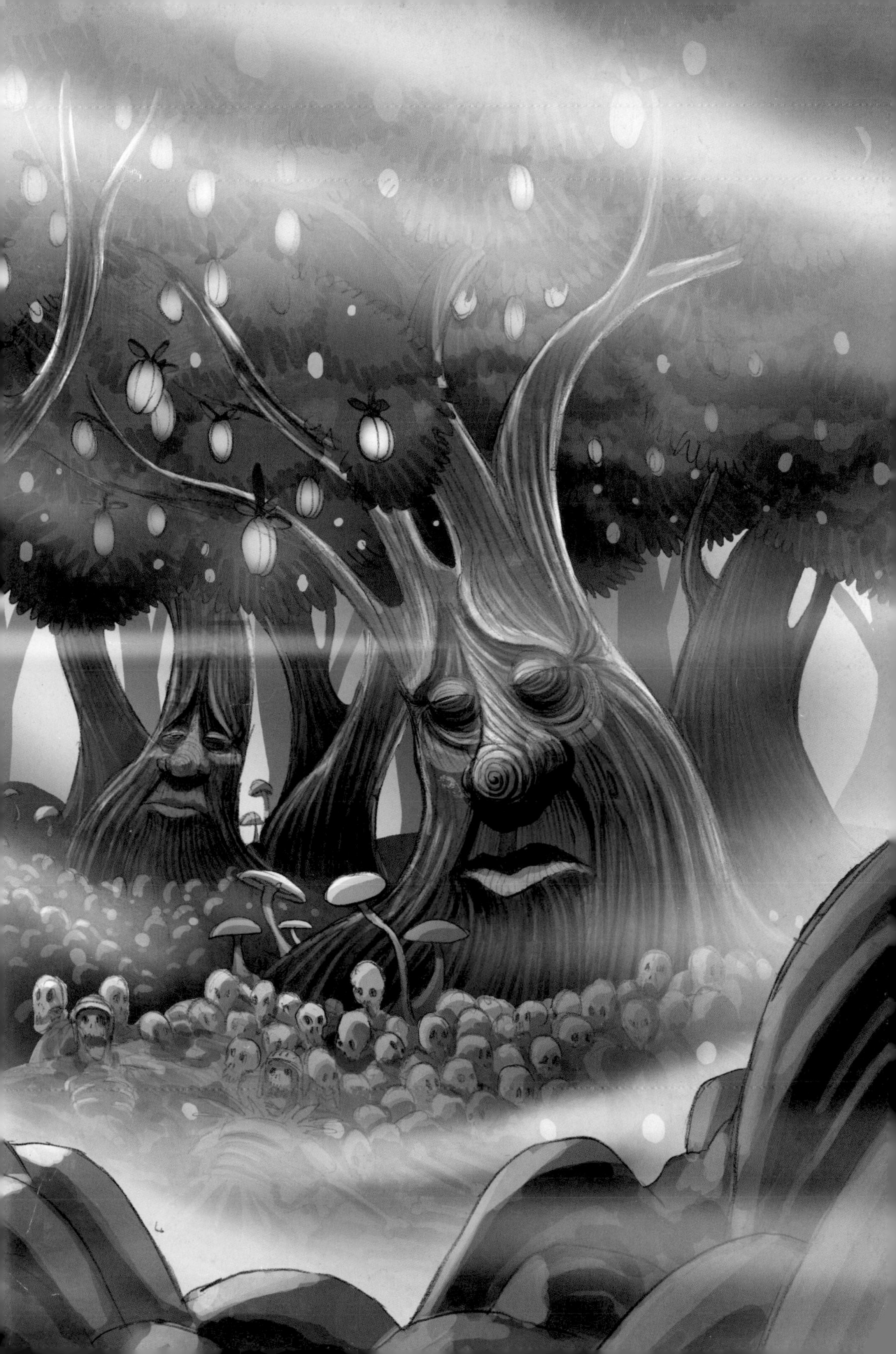

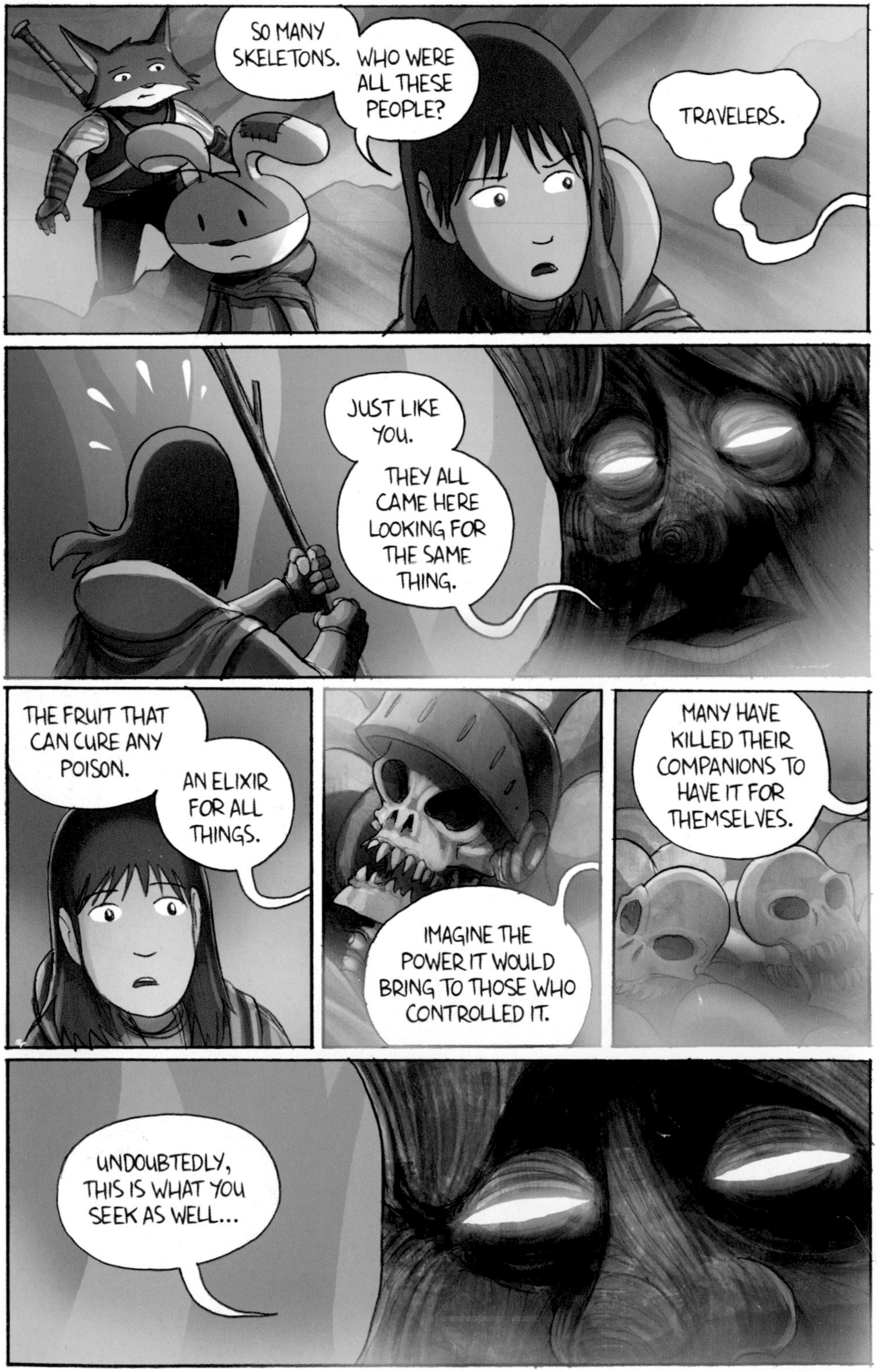
SO MANY SKELETONS.
WHO WERE ALL THESE PEOPLE?
TRAVELERS.
JUST LIKE YOU.
THEY ALL CAME HERE LOOKING FOR THE SAME THING.
THE FRUIT THAT CAN CURE ANY POISON.
AN ELIXIR FOR ALL THINGS.
IMAGINE THE POWER IT WOULD BRING TO THOSE WHO CONTROLLED IT.
MANY HAVE KILLED THEIR COMPANIONS TO HAVE IT FOR THEMSELVES.
UNDOUBTEDLY, THIS IS WHAT YOU SEEK AS WELL...

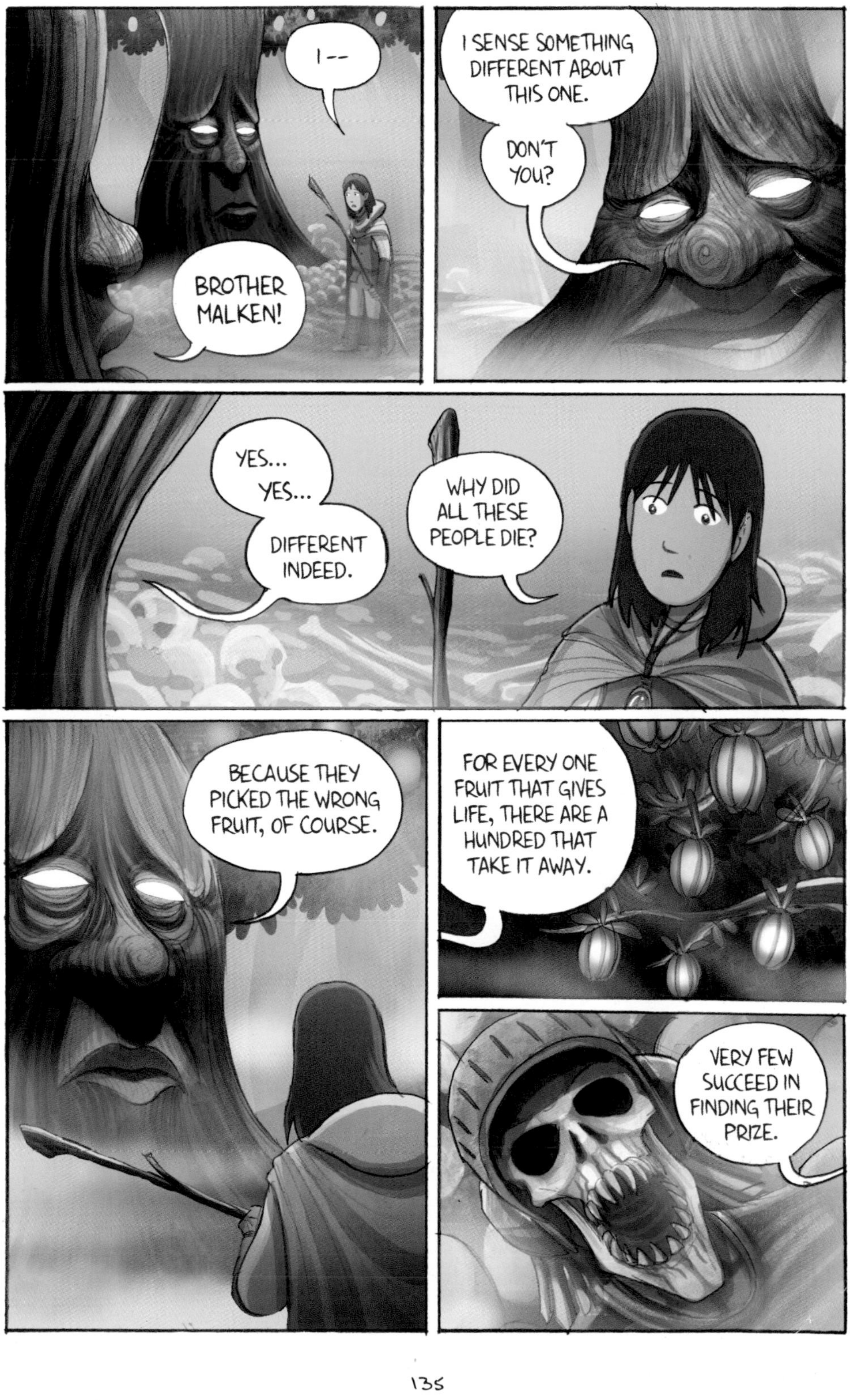
I --
BROTHER MALKEN!
I SENSE SOMETHING DIFFERENT ABOUT THIS ONE.
DON'T YOU?
YES... YES...
DIFFERENT INDEED.
WHY DID ALL THESE PEOPLE DIE?
BECAUSE THEY PICKED THE WRONG FRUIT, OF COURSE.
FOR EVERY ONE FRUIT THAT GIVES LIFE, THERE ARE A HUNDRED THAT TAKE IT AWAY.
VERY FEW SUCCEED IN FINDING THEIR PRIZE.

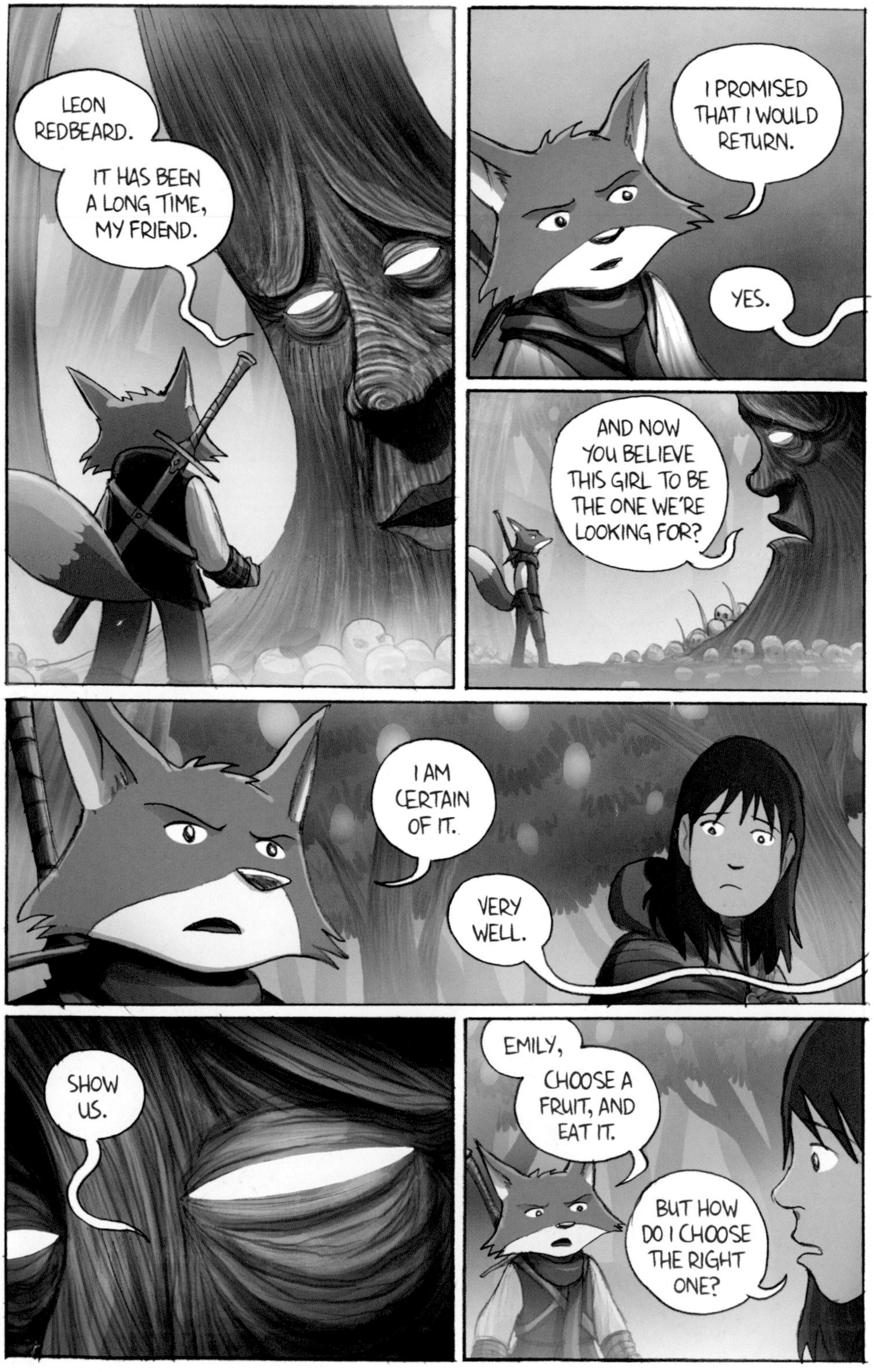
LEON REDBEARD.
IT HAS BEEN A LONG TIME, MY FRIEND.
I PROMISED THAT I WOULD RETURN.
YES.
AND NOW YOU BELIEVE THIS GIRL TO BE THE ONE WE'RE LOOKING FOR?
I AM CERTAIN OF IT.
VERY WELL.
SHOW US.
EMILY,
CHOOSE A FRUIT, AND EAT IT.
BUT HOW DO I CHOOSE THE RIGHT ONE?

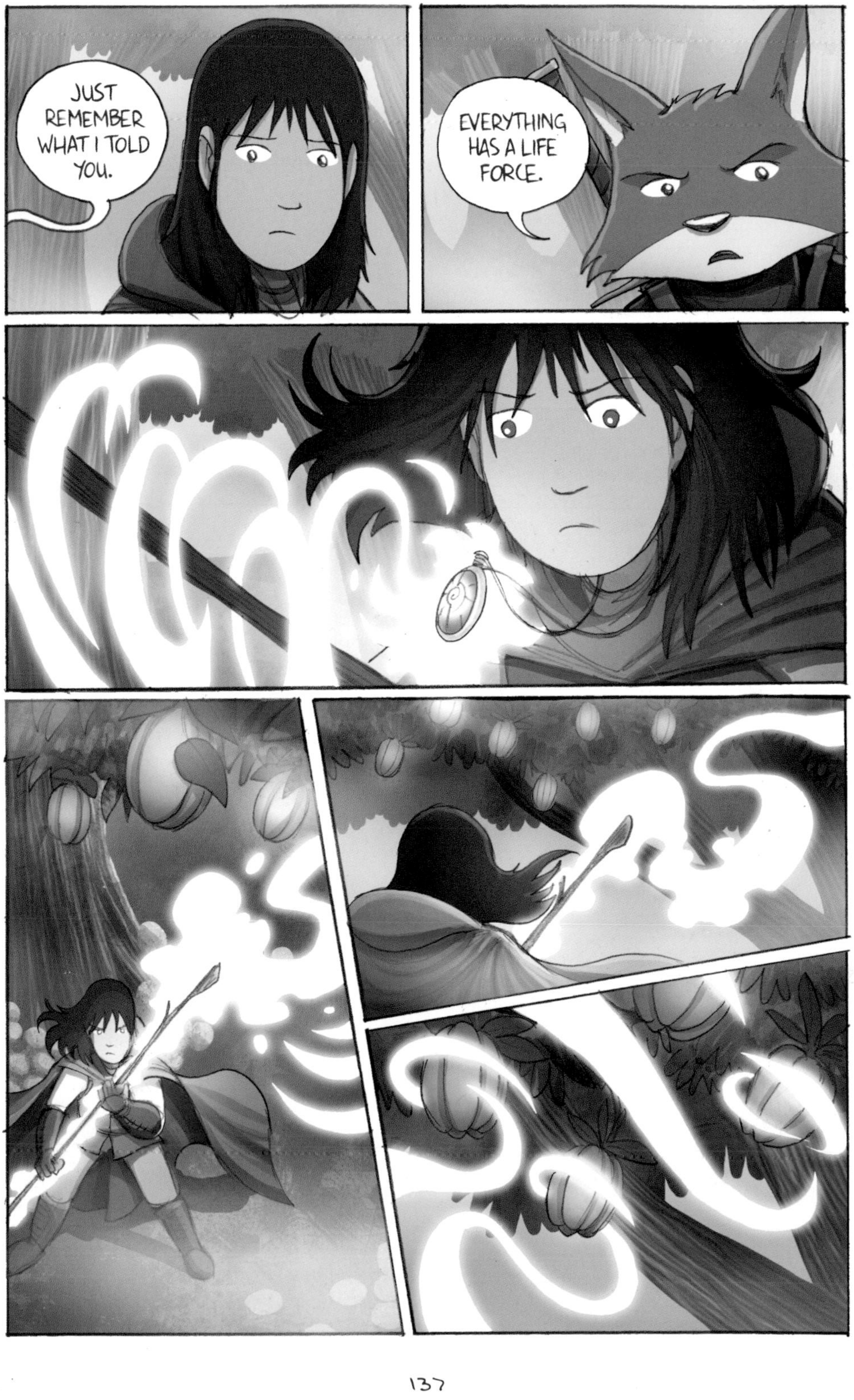
JUST REMEMBER WHAT I TOLD YOU.
EVERYTHING HAS A LIFE FORCE.

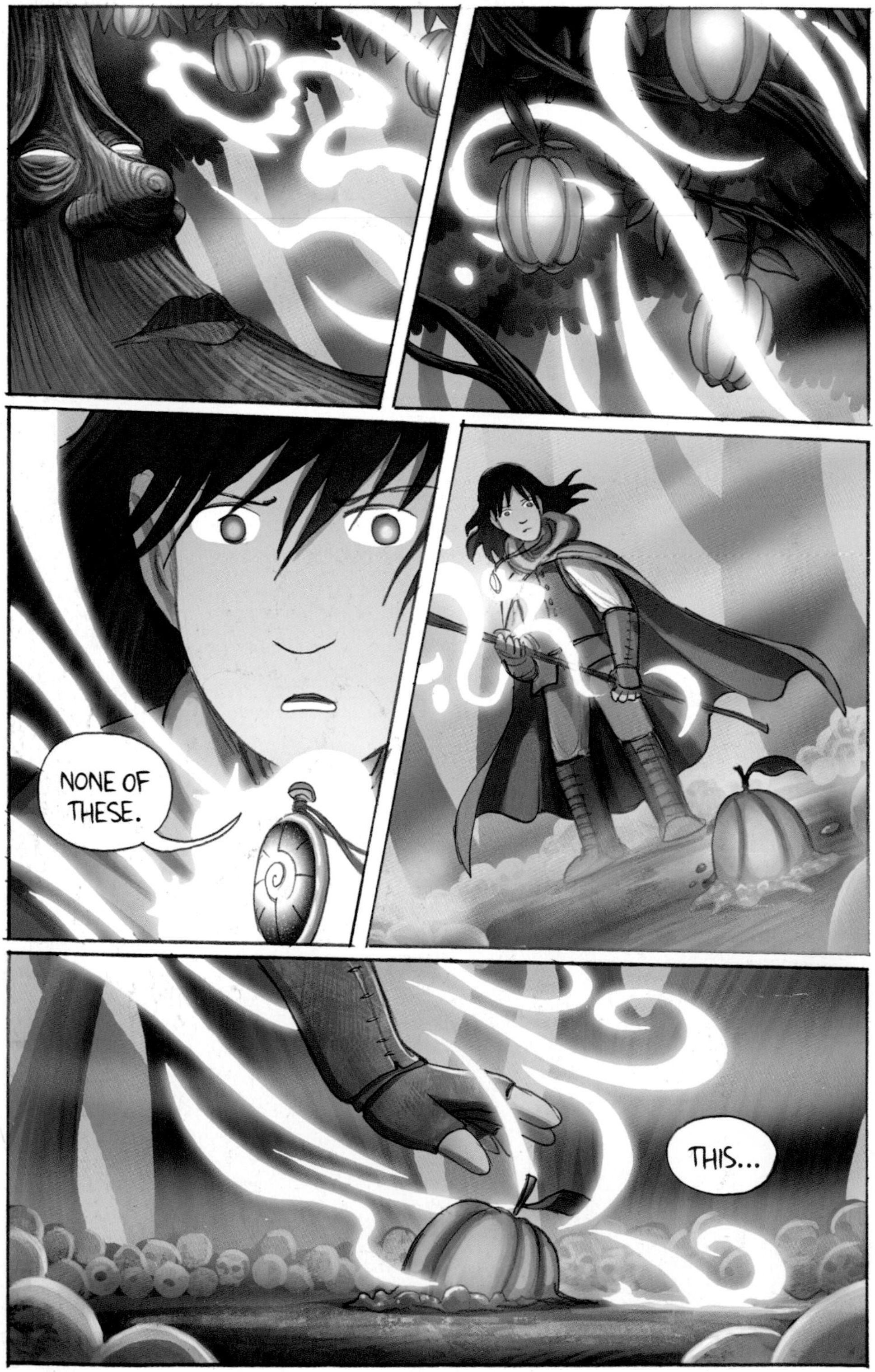
NONE OF THESE.
THIS...

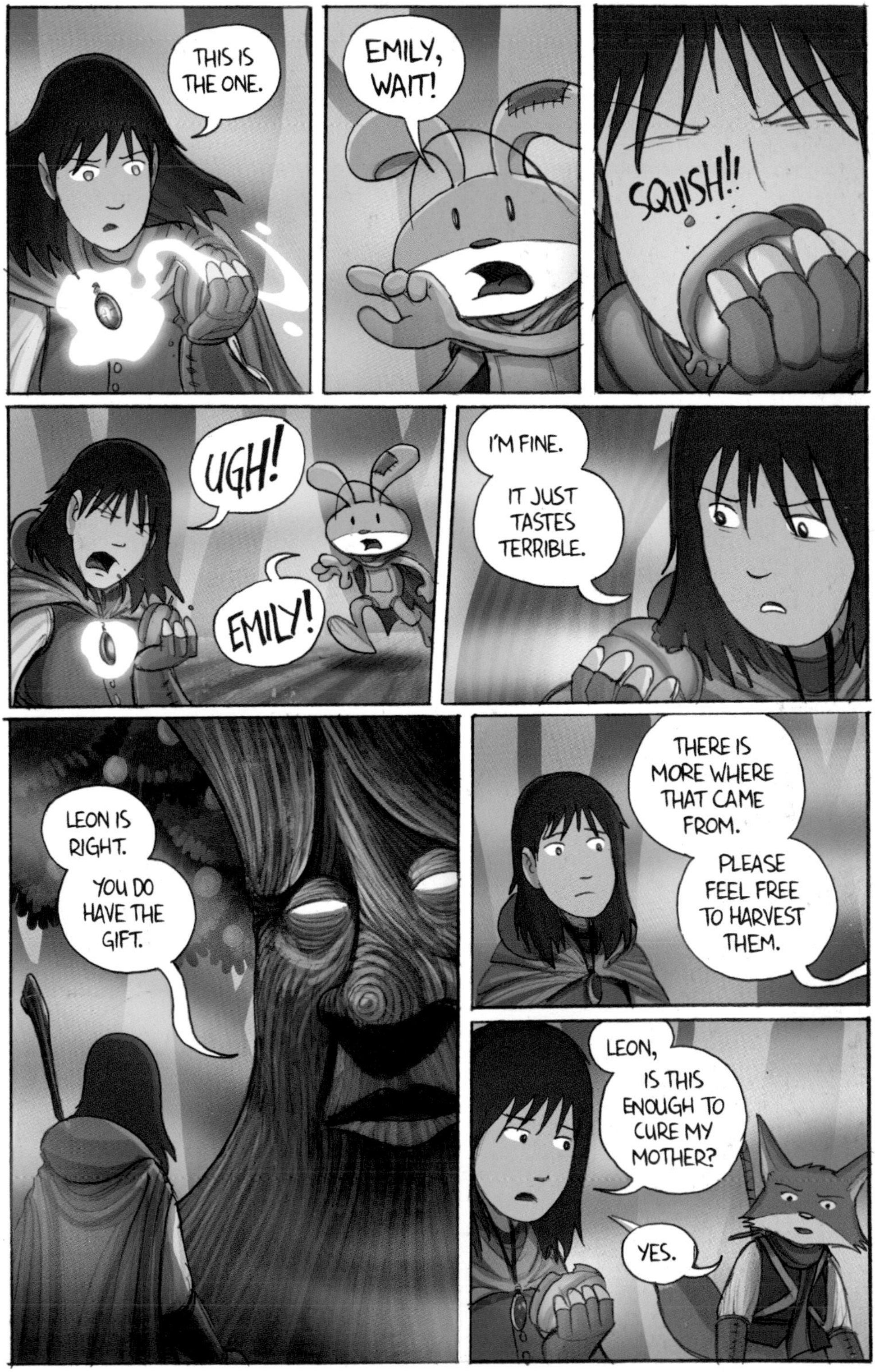
THIS IS THE ONE.
EMILY, WAIT!
SQUISH!!
UGH!
EMILY!
I'M FINE.
IT JUST TASTES TERRIBLE.
LEON IS RIGHT.
YOU DO HAVE THE GIFT.
THERE IS MORE WHERE THAT CAME FROM.
PLEASE FEEL FREE TO HARVEST THEM.
LEON,
IS THIS ENOUGH TO CURE MY MOTHER?
YES.

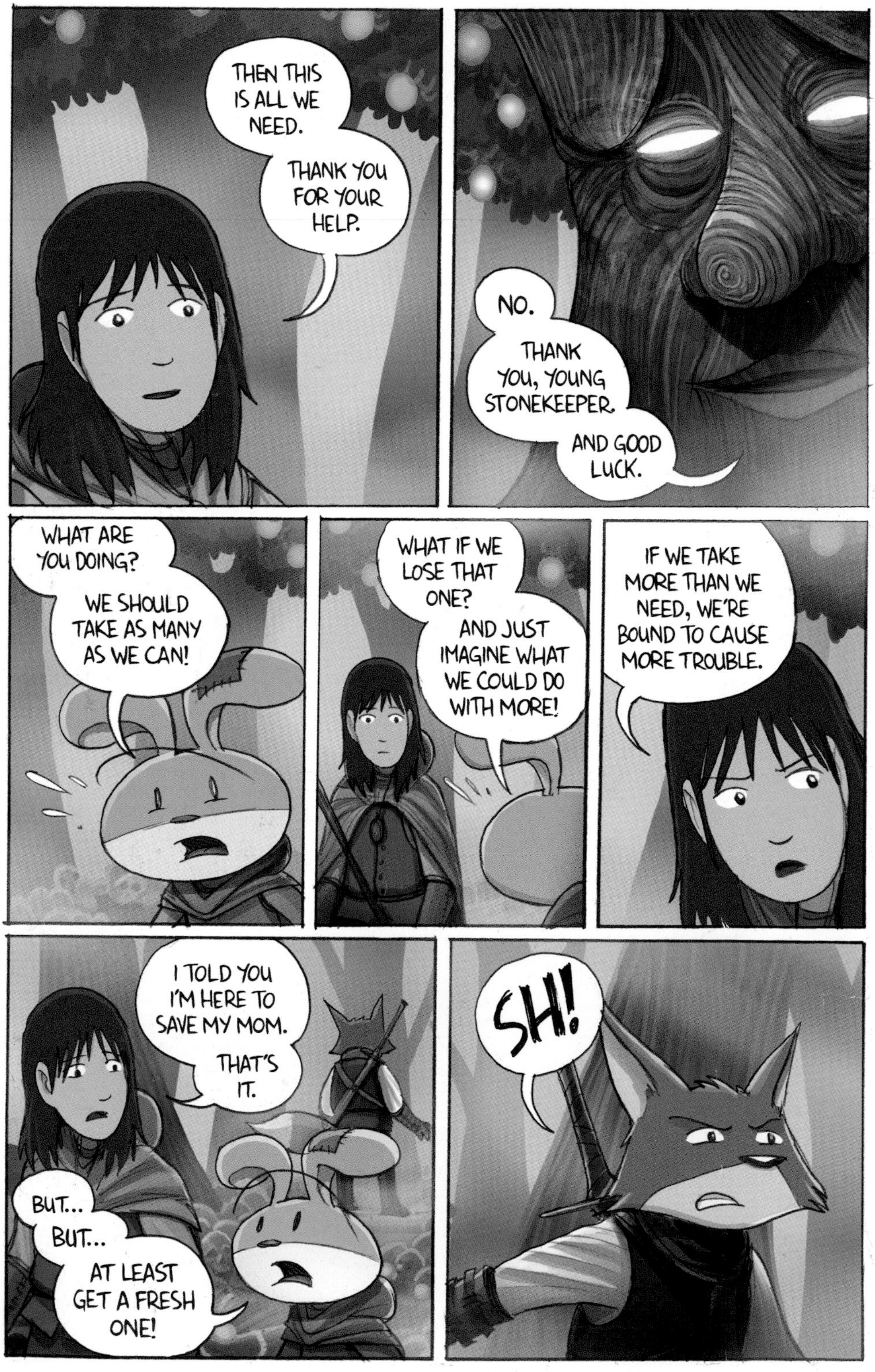
THEN THIS IS ALL WE NEED.
THANK YOU FOR YOUR HELP.
NO.
THANK YOU, YOUNG STONEKEEPER.
AND GOOD LUCK.
WHAT ARE YOU DOING?
WE SHOULD TAKE AS MANY AS WE CAN!
WHAT IF WE LOSE THAT ONE?
AND JUST IMAGINE WHAT WE COULD DO WITH MORE!
IF WE TAKE MORE THAN WE NEED, WE'RE BOUND TO CAUSE MORE TROUBLE.
I TOLD YOU I'M HERE TO SAVE MY MOM.
THAT'S IT.
BUT...
BUT...
AT LEAST GET A FRESH ONE!
SH!

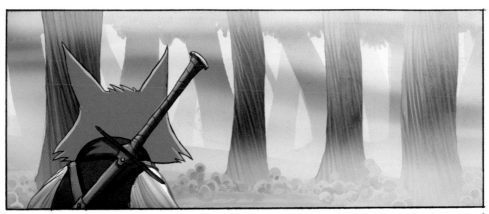

WHAT IS IT?

I SAW SOMETHING MOVING OUT THERE.

WE NEED TO LEAVE NOW.

I'M SORRY, FATHER MALKEN.

IT'S LIKELY THAT ELVES ARE ON OUR TRAIL.

WE WERE CARELESS.

DO NOT WORRY ABOUT US, LEON.

LEAVE QUICKLY AND KEEP THE STONEKEEPER SAFE.

IT WILL BE UP TO YOU TO SEE THAT SHE REACHES HER FULL POTENTIAL.

AND BE CAREFUL --

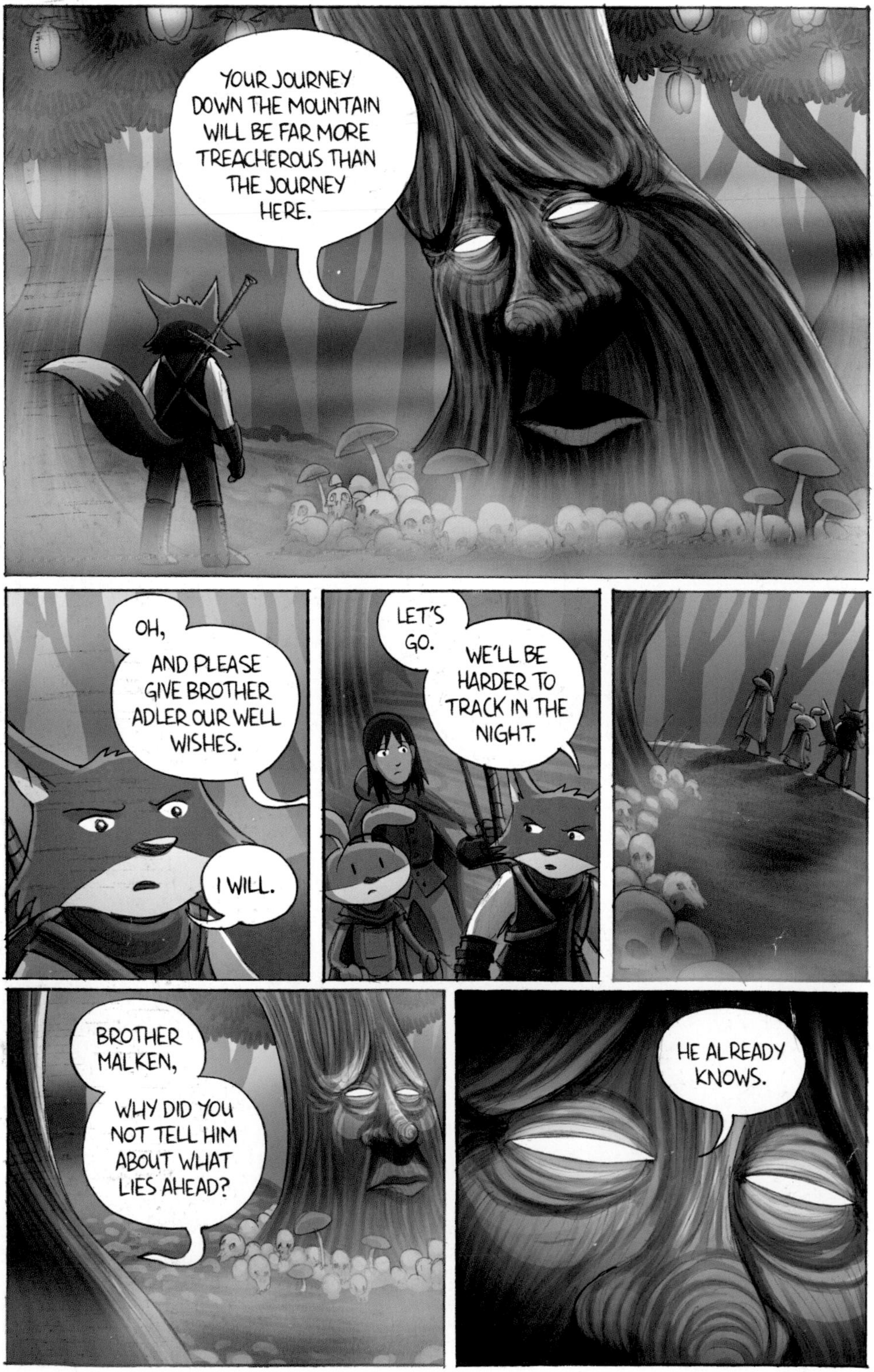
YOUR JOURNEY DOWN THE MOUNTAIN WILL BE FAR MORE TREACHEROUS THAN THE JOURNEY HERE.
OH,
AND PLEASE GIVE BROTHER ADLER OUR WELL WISHES.
I WILL.
LET'S GO.
WE'LL BE HARDER TO TRACK IN THE NIGHT.
BROTHER MALKEN,
WHY DID YOU NOT TELL HIM ABOUT WHAT LIES AHEAD?
HE ALREADY KNOWS.

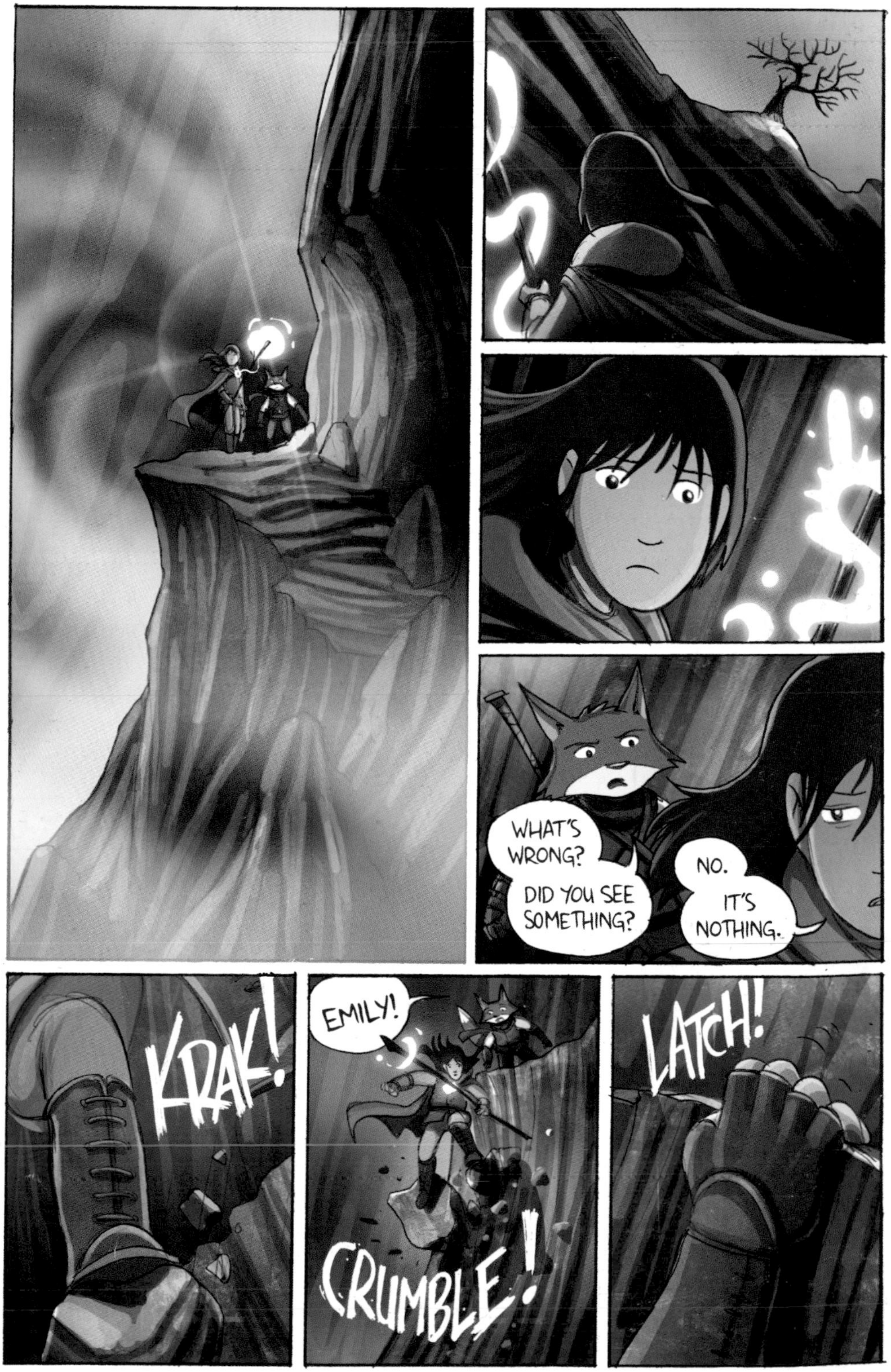
WHAT'S WRONG?
DID YOU SEE SOMETHING?
NO.
IT'S NOTHING.
KRAK!
EMILY!
CRUMBLE!
LATCH!

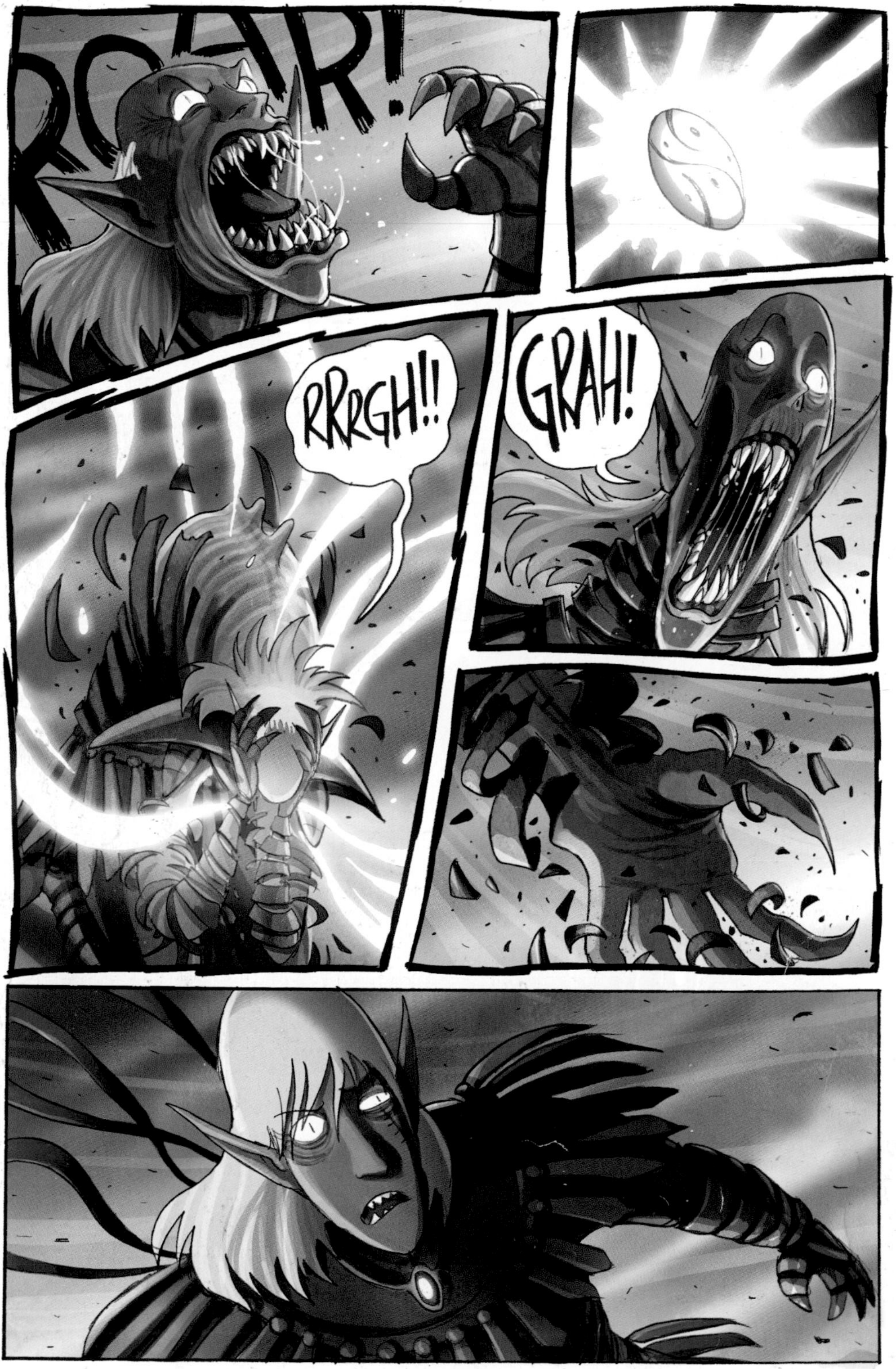
ROAR!
RRRGH!!
GRAH!

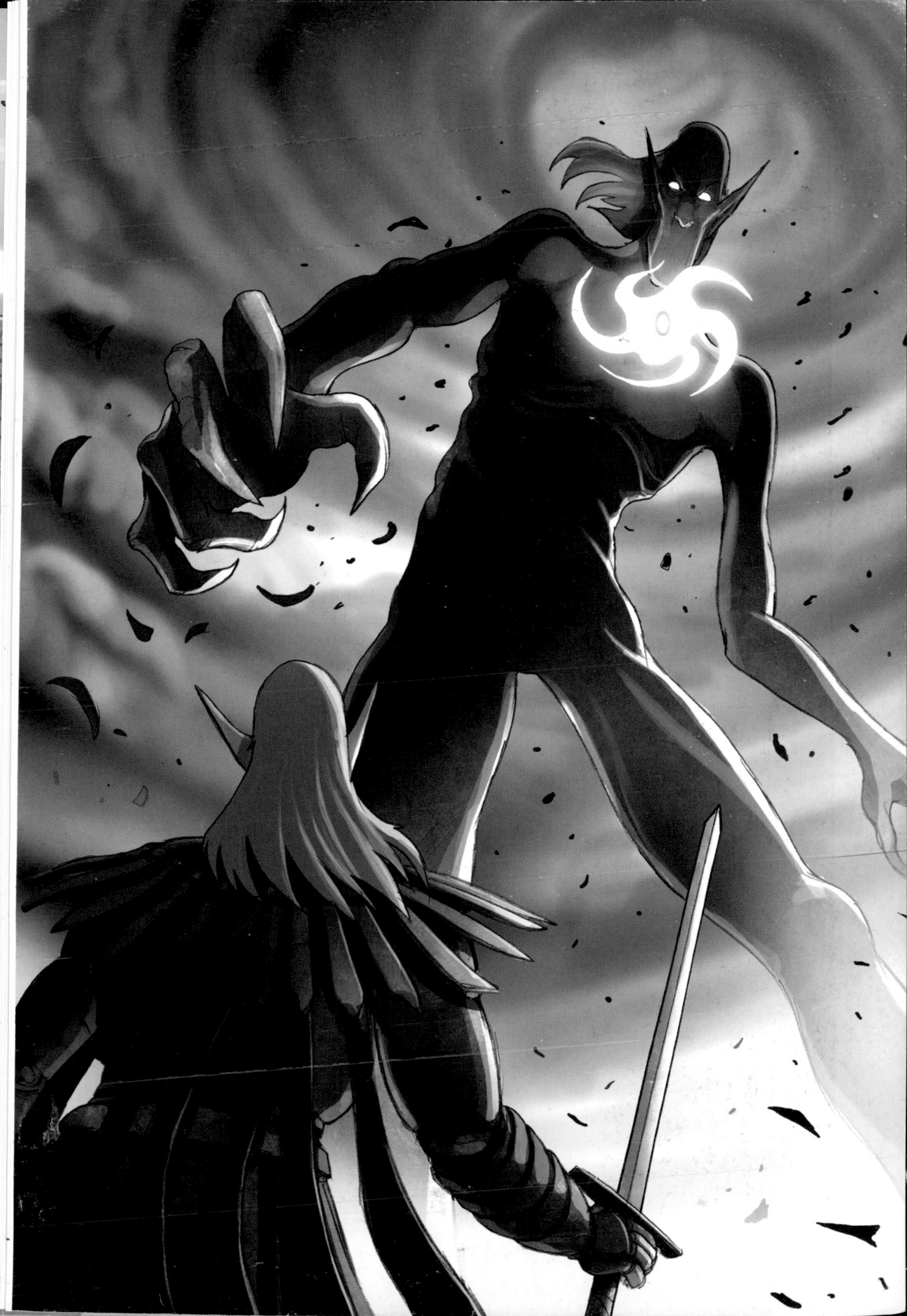

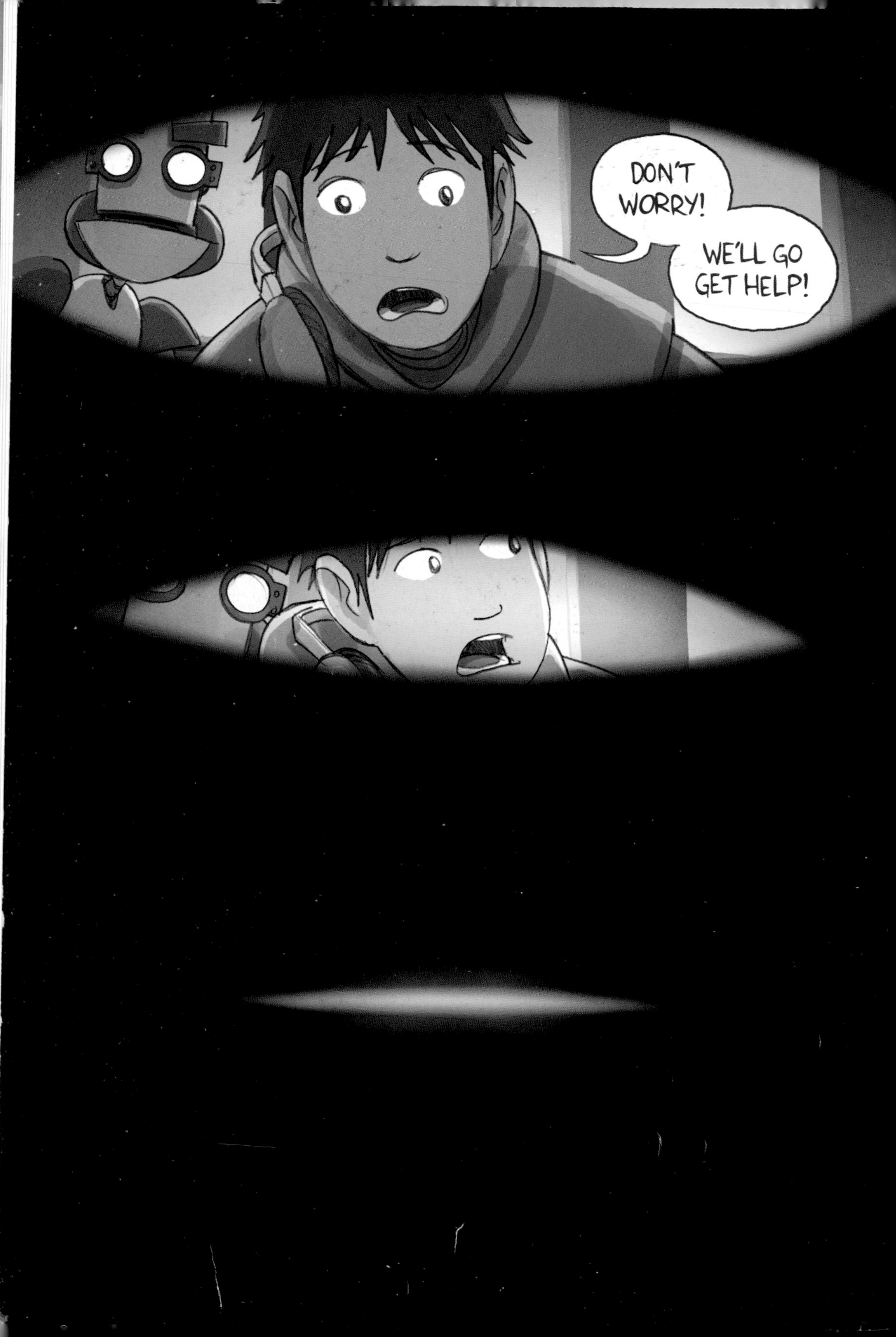
DON'T WORRY!
WE'LL GO GET HELP!

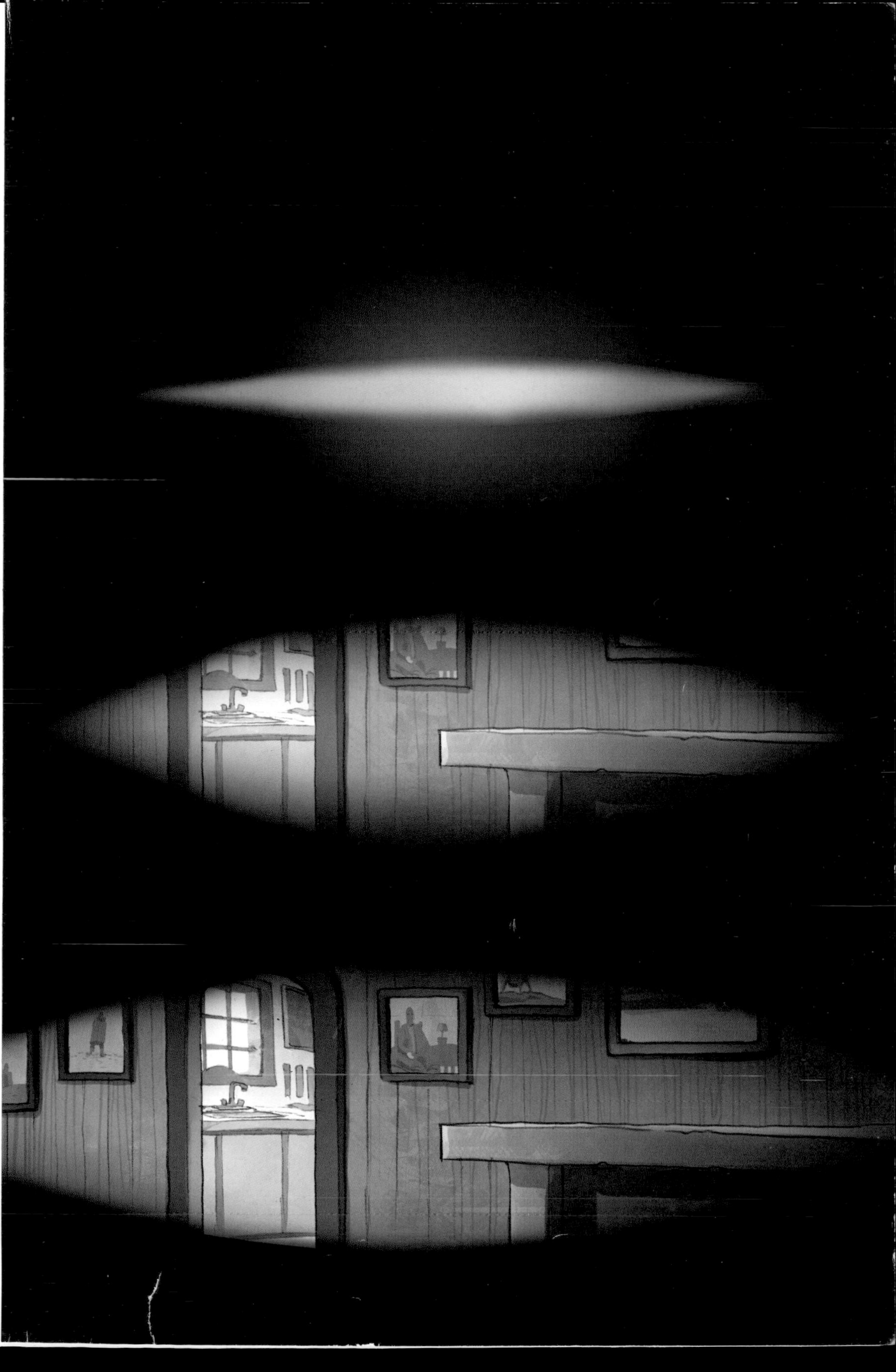

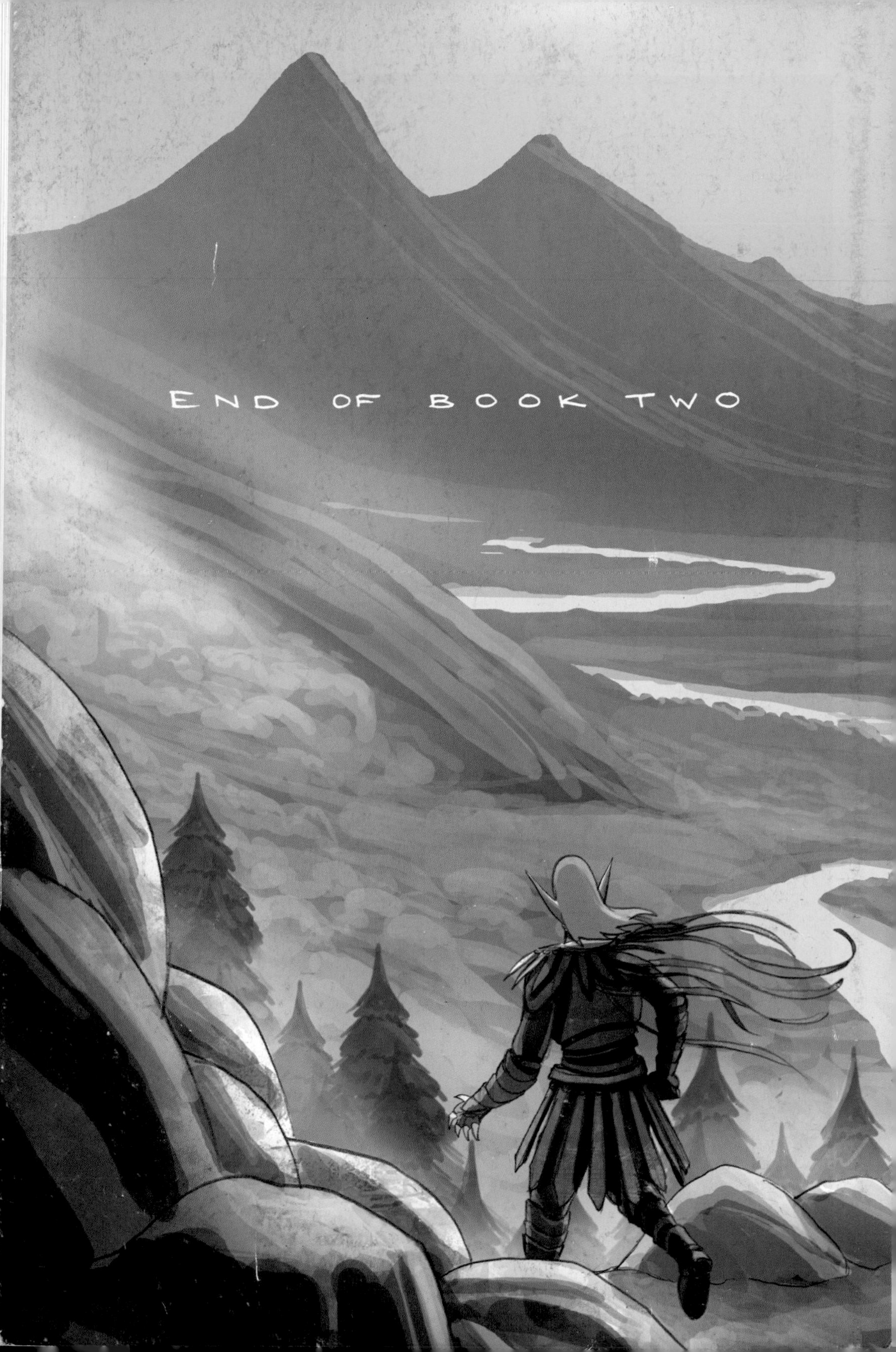
END OF BOOK TWO

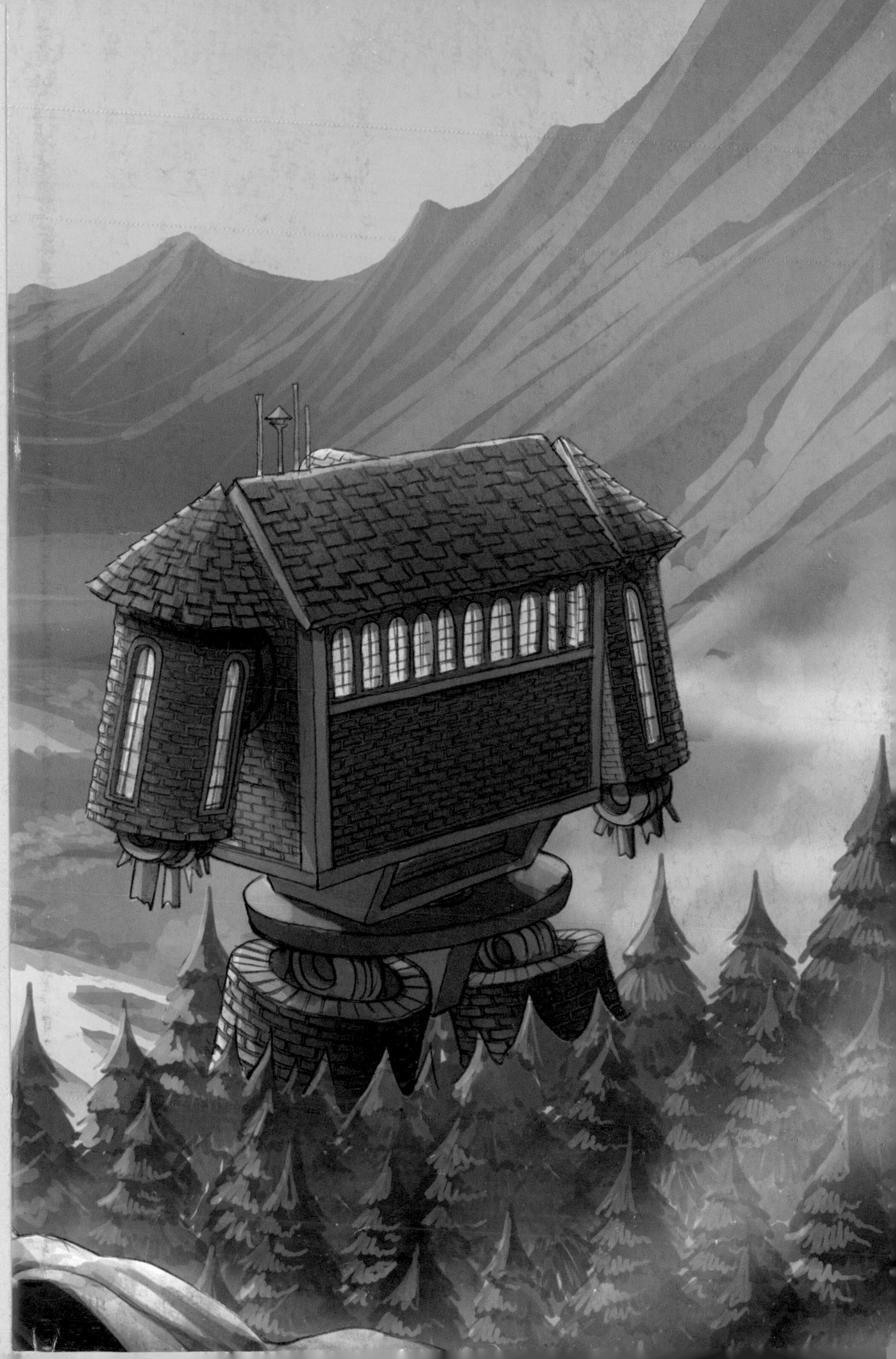